The
Daisy Ducks

The
Daisy Ducks

A Doc Adams Suspense Novel

RICK BOYER

Houghton Mifflin Company

Boston

1986

Library of Congress Cataloging-in-Publication Data

Boyer, Rick.
The Daisy Ducks.

I. Title.
PS3552.O895D3   1986   813'.54   86-3016
ISBN 0-395-35289-4

Printed in the United States of America

s 10 9 8 7 6 5 4 3 2 1

This book is for two important women:
Charlotte Wade, a special friend, and
Betty Hatton Boyer, magna cum laude,
Phi Beta Kappa, and the best mom ever,
who saved time to instill in her children
a love of reading.

There's a race of men that don't fit in,
A race that can't stay still;
So they break the hearts of kith and kin,
And they roam the world at will.

— Robert W. Service,
"The Men Who Don't Fit In"

ACKNOWLEDGMENTS

The author would like to thank John Boyer, Bill Tapply, and Larry Kessenich for their comments and suggestions in preparing the manuscript.

The
Daisy Ducks

SIU LOK'S LOOT

LIATIS ROANTIS is a pit bulldog in human shape.

The stocky Lithuanian fought the Nazis as a teenager. He served with the French Foreign Legion in Indochina at the ill-fated siege of Dien Bien Phu and afterward in the Sudan, French West Africa, and Algeria. In the early sixties he was out of work and joined the U.S. Army. The Cold War had heated up and they needed men with his talents. He took to this line of work naturally.

He returned to Indochina, now called Vietnam, and served three tours. He quit because of America's unwillingness to mount a full-scale military commitment to win the war. He retired and settled in New England to make his living as a martial arts instructor at the Boston YMCU. It was in a beginners' karate course there that I first met him. He is still very good at what he does. He can open your jugular vein with his teeth.

While he was in Southeast Asia, he led a long-range recon team behind enemy lines into Cambodia. They loaded themselves up with supplies and walked far, far into enemy territory. They spied, and reported what they saw by radio. In the dead of night they blew up roads and bridges and supply depots, then vanished, walking softly under that dense canopy in the tropical night.

So much for all that. Except Roantis came to me afterward with an offer: if I could help him find an old army buddy, he'd make me rich.

It'll be a piece of cake, he said.

Right.

1

HOLIDAY TIME! Big party going on at our place.

I was just stopping by the sideboard, pouring myself a big jolt of the Destroyer, when Janice DeGroot oiled past me, cooing. Now there's a pretty lady. All over, I mean.

She looked just terrific, strolling past me in the dark hall. I wanted to grab her and plant one on her. But I had a hunch that that kind of thing would be frowned upon in Concord. Especially by Mary, no slouch herself in the form department. That being the case, you might well ask: why even look at another woman? Because, like the mountain, she's there.

It was almost one, and the gala was in full cry. Guests were swaying on their feet, howling with laughter and good cheer. And, as if a sign from above, Janice stopped right smack underneath the mistletoe. How about that? I snapped a mitt around her waist and drew her over for a chat. She tucked her mouth down into my lower neck. Wet.

"Cut that out," I said.

"Mmmmmm," she sighed. "Kissy-kissy?"

She gave me a quick hard kiss with a lot of suction to it. Very wet. I slid my hand down so it was caressing her flank. She moved her near leg around behind me and inserted her foot in between

3

my shoes, then pressed the inside of her thigh against the inside of mine. It was a brazen and tawdry act. Despicable. It felt like a million bucks.

I sipped my new drink — just what I needed — and eyed the guests. They continued laughing and shouting in small groups. Glancing behind me, I could see the intense gathering that invariably forms in the kitchen. They were discussing the Important Issues like nuclear war, crime, and the Soviet Union. They were deciding what needed to be done about these things that nobody can do anything about. Some of them had even switched to coffee. Saps. Well, it was too late to kick them out.

Nobody noticed the two of us. It was a sign, definitely a sign. I slid my hand down farther until it was resting on the upper portions of her rump. It felt delicious. I walked my fingers down, down, like a tarantula creeping along a branch, until they cupped the shapely ham. Then I felt a bug at my waist. I looked down to see Janice's index finger inside my belt, right near my pelvis. She was wigwagging it. It kind of tickled. She planted another wet one on my neck and let it linger awhile.

"What are you doing after the party?" she purred.

"Stop talking dirty," I said. "You know how I hate it."

"Ohhhh Charlie," she said in a sleepy kitten voice, "you know we've always been close." The finger waggle got more intense. She moved her head and I could smell her hair. Janice seemed to be pulling at me, leading me somewhere. Where indeed? Then I spied the phone closet right underneath the main stairway. Four feet from where we were standing. Dead ahead. She had it all planned out. I, of course, was merely a bystander. But getting fresh with Janice DeGroot in the phone closet seemed like a splendid and sensible idea at the time. Booze will do that.

But then a voice from within cried out. It was the voice of Reason. Of Virtue, and Common Sense. It said: "Watch it, Doc! The game's going too far too fast. Don't be a jerk!"

The voice was heaven-sent, and just in time.

I ignored it.

I disengaged my hand and cranked open the doorknob to the phone booth. All around us was the chuckle and chatter of merrymakers. The house was dim, especially the central hallway where we were standing. Nobody was even glancing in our direc-

4

tion. Janice was busy with my neck again, and I didn't want to keep her waiting.

Inside the phone closet it was dark. I planted a big one on her face. Dee-lish. This was gonna be my night. No question.

. . . gonna be my *night* . . .

The door flew open and the light went on. I blinked in the sudden brightness, like a kid awakened in the dead of night. I turned around and looked at the face staring at me, and my blood went cold. A swarthy Latin face glared in at us. The eyes were intense, and black as obsidian. The general look was piercing and full of death, reminiscent I'm sure of all the hit men who've ever jumped out of shiny black limousines toting violin cases. In southern Italy it's called *il malòcchio.* The Evil Eye. It's how the Godfather looks at you when he kisses your cheek, and you know it's only a matter of days before those big forty-five-caliber slugs will come sailing through your insides. That look can put a crack in the Great Pyramid.

"Hi Mary!" I trilled. "Hiya hon!"

"Ohhhh! Hi Mare!" cooed Janice, wiping her face with her sleeve. "Great party!"

We smiled and gaped at Mary. Janice even managed a little wave: a tiny circular motion with her palm, as if she were polishing a bit of glass. It was cute. We wore the hysterical faces of the condemned. Janice's hand was now placed demurely across my abdomen. Seeing the swift Calabrian eyes dart downward, she removed her hand and placed it on a hip. Mine. Oops.

Mary filled the tiny doorway like the Colossus of Rhodes. She fixed her steely gaze on me.

"I want to talk to you," she said.

"Sure. What about?"

"I think you can guess."

The door slammed and she was gone. Janice stood staring blankly at the door for a few seconds and sighed. Then she squared her shoulders, took a deep breath, and marched out. It was like the final scene from *A Tale of Two Cities.*

I was alone in the closet and didn't want to leave, knowing what awaited me on the other side of the door. I needed help. I glanced down at the phone and considered calling the police. But Concord's police chief, Brian Hannon, was at my party, not twenty feet away at that very moment. Also, another law officer was likewise present: Lieutenant Joseph Brindelli of the Boston State Police. Mary's baby brother. I had a feeling I wouldn't get much help from either quarter. I wanted to stay in the closet, and was contemplating possible barricades and various sleeping positions when the door flew open again. Attila was back.

"Hiya honey. I guess — "

"Don't hiya me!" she hissed. "I saw that vertical foreplay with Janice. And let me tell you — "

"Ah, a momentary lapse, my dear. I assure you that — "

"Shut up!" She looked like Ivan the Terrible on one of his bad days. "You're in trouble, Charlie. Serious trouble. I don't know what's been bugging you lately, but you've been behaving like an adolescent for two months now. I've about had it. I just had a nice talk with Jim and his adorable wife with the nice tail section. You're both going to get it. Jim is looking for you right now — hunting your head. It's doubtful you'll last the night in one piece. Also, your commando friend, Liatis Roantis, just cold-cocked Phil Newcombe in the sunporch."

"He *what?*"

"You heard me. They got into an argument and Phil took a big swing at Liatis."

"That's not a smart thing to do."

"Come on," she said, taking me by the coat sleeve, "and don't think this lets you off the hook."

"About that. Listen, I — "

"Shut up. You'll hear from me later."

Of this, I had no doubt.

Mary marched me around to the sunporch, where Philip T. Newcombe lay stretched out on his back. He twitched a little and moaned. Well, he was alive at least. You can't say that for some people who've tangled with Liatis Roantis. The crowd around the fallen man murmured and stared at Roantis, who was nonchalantly leaning against the doorjamb. He held a glass of ice cubes in his left hand and a newly opened bottle of Dewar's in his right. He filled the glass carefully and set the bottle down on the record cabinet behind him. He looked absently at the fallen man, who was now getting to his knees.

6

"Hi Doc," he said.

"What the hell happened?"

"*I'll* tell you what happened!" cried a shrill voice. It belonged to Marge Newcombe. She advanced toward Roantis, pointing her finger. "This animal attacked my husband and tried to kill him."

"Uh-uh! Not true!" said Jim DeGroot. "Your husband called him a Nazi pig and hit him in the stomach first. Are you forgetting that?"

Marge Newcombe was unimpressed by this tidbit. She went up to Roantis and slapped him hard across the face. It sounded like a rifle shot. Everyone said *ohhhhhhhhh!* He didn't even blink. Undaunted, she grabbed the Dewar's bottle. I grabbed her arm and replaced the bottle on the cabinet.

"Hold it, Marge. That's good booze. Uh . . . maybe the party better end here. I don't know what's happened, but everyone's a little crazy tonight. Must be a full moon or something. Where's Brian?"

"Here," said a gruff voice to my immediate right. Brian Hannon, Concord's finest (mostly according to him), stood next to me. "Possible assault," he said to me under his breath.

"But the other guy hit him first," I said.

"We'll see. Considering your friend's background and training, I'd call it possible aggravated assault. You know, with a deadly weapon."

Nobody heard us talking because the party was breaking up now, people heading upstairs to get their coats. Marge Newcombe helped her husband to his feet. Newcombe was a florid, heavyset man with strong opinions and a loud manner. Nobody in the neighborhood liked him, and Mary and I had invited them only because we'd invited everyone else on Old Stone Mill Road. Newcombe had made it big as a tire distributor, and two drinks were all it took to get him going on what a hot ticket he was. Two more drinks and his prowess and talent increased in proportion to everyone else's weaknesses and failings. Not a nice guy. It gave me secret pleasure to see him stagger to his feet, his eyes still glazed. He'd had it coming a long, long time.

Apparently he'd been badgering Roantis all evening, making

7

fun of his heavy Lithuanian accent and his short stature. Now it's true that Roantis is not tall. But then, neither is a Gaboon viper.

Newcombe now accused Roantis of assault and demanded I call the police. When Chief Hannon informed him that he *was* the police in this particular town, Newcombe demanded that his assailant be taken into custody. Chief Hannon then advised the plaintiff he would have to file a complaint at the department. Then the remnants of the crowd started throwing in their two cents worth. What a nice ending for a party.

"Mistake, Charlie. *Mistake!*" said Mary.

"Huh?"

"Inviting him!"

"Who, Newcombe?"

"Him too. But mainly that trained killer. Look at our guests, Charlie. What kind of ending is *this* for a Christmas party? Oh, why do I ever listen to you!"

Close to tears, she stomped away. I considered the situation. It was a wreck. From across the room Janice stared in my direction with feline eyes. Jim glowered at me. My two sons, Jack and Tony, who'd been promised pocket money for helping to tend bar and clean up, came and went clearing up the glasses, ashtrays, and plates. More and more guests were bidding adieu and donning their winter wraps.

"Hey Doc, I'm asking you a question," boomed a voice.

"Huh?"

"What are we going to do?" asked Brian Hannon. "You're the host. Can you keep this man here until further notice?"

He was motioning toward Roantis, who hadn't moved. He stood like stone against the doorway woodwork.

"If he wants to stay, he's welcome. Personally, I wouldn't try to move him. Mr. Newcombe, are you going ahead with your complaint?"

"Damn right!" he bellowed, buttoning his sport coat. He rubbed the side of his jaw and grimaced as he started for the door.

"I would advise you to reconsider," I said, looking at Roantis. "But we'll stay here until two. If we don't get a call from you before then, Brian, I'll assume he's free to go, okay?"

8

"He doesn't have to stay at all, but we'd appreciate it. Now Mr. Newcombe, I'm going home. I'm going to sleep. If you feel you must register a complaint, you're going to have to drive to the station yourself. Goodnight everyone. Thanks Doc. Where's Mary?"

"Out milking the elk."

"Well, thank her too."

People dribbled out. Some even bothered to say they were sorry that the evening had terminated as it had. I felt a soft touch along my lower back and turned to see Janice and Jim departing. Jim deliberately looked away from me. Janice leaned over and pecked my cheek. She whispered into my ear.

"I'm getting a nasty lecture when I get home. How about you?"

"I *am* home, dummy. And I think I'm due for a lecture too. Actually, I was hoping this fracas would dispel some of the anger. We've got to stop this stuff, you know."

"Nah. We've just got to start doing it right. A cheap motel for a nooner. The whole shot. Right?"

"What're you two talking about?" growled Jim.

"Nothing, love," said Janice, gaily tripping her way down the hall stairs to the front door landing. I saw the last of the guests off. No doubt Janice's little kidding toward the end was meant to cheer me up. It did not. A beefy paw latched onto my shoulder and spun me around. It was Detective Lieutenant Joseph Brindelli.

"You're in trouble."

"Don't I know it. Hey Joe, listen: why don't you stay awhile and have another drink? Maybe you and Mary could — "

"Have a talk? And I could get my sister to forgive you? No way, pal. I grew up with her. When Sis gets mad you can clear the decks. Besides, I've got an early day tomorrow. I'm gonna feel bad enough as it is. Good luck, Doc. Believe me, you're going to need it. *Arrivederla!*"

I started back toward the porch and was intercepted by my second son, Tony, who was hauling a dozen glasses back to the kitchen. He stopped and regarded me as one regards a wounded soldier returning to the front.

9

"You're in trouble, Dad."

"Do tell."

"What did you do?"

"Nothing really. It was a misunderstanding."

"Hell it was," said number one son, Jack, who entered stage left bearing a pile of dirty ashtrays. "You were necking with Mrs. DeGroot in the hall corner. Tacky, Dad. You're in a lot of trouble."

"I know, I know."

I returned to the porch and found Roantis leaning against one of the windows. I thought for a second he was feeling sick. Lord knows, with all the booze he'd drunk — neat, mind you — he should feel woozy. But I noticed he had cupped his hands around his face to block out the room light. He was looking out the window, searching for something.

"You okay, Liatis?"

"Hm? Oh yeah. Fine."

He walked over to the card table and sat down. He shook out a Camel from an almost flat pack, flicked open a shiny Zippo lighter, and lit it. The lighter had a silver and blue crest on it of a winged arm holding a dagger. Underneath were words in French. It was the battle insignia of the French Foreign Legion. Roantis opened a deck of cards and began to shuffle. The cigarette rested between the middle and ring fingers of his left hand, deep in, toward the palm. It stayed there automatically, an appendage. The hands were what palm readers call "earth hands." Straight across the knuckles, straight across the fingertips, with hardly any difference in finger length. Palms squarish. Average size. Earth hands, the palmists say, denote a person with minimum sensitivity and a strongly practical outlook. Such people are supposed to make good middle managers, staff sergeants, and craftsmen. That would fit Roantis, I thought.

The hands didn't look menacing. Only an expert, or one familiar with fighting, would notice the bulbous calcified knobs on the oversized knuckles. Only when shaking hands were you conscious of the horny ridge of callus that ran up the side of the hand from the little finger to the wrist. These were hands that had severed windpipes, broken sternums, mashed jaws,

gouged eyes, torn scrotums, splintered collarbones, and frac-
tured skulls.

Just your little old average pair of mitts . . .

They floated in front of my eyes now, snapping the cards down
on the poker table's green felt top. Roantis said nothing. He took
a drag of his cigarette and a long pull from his tumbler of straight
Scotch, then looked up.

"Wanta play gin?"

"No."

"Wanta drink gin?"

"No. I'll have Scotch."

"Then do it, Doc. I want to talk with you anyway."

"Liatis, are you ever going back to your wife?"

He shrugged his shoulders. They were average size, not a
prizefighter's shoulders. He snapped a card down and grunted.
I poured a finger of Dewar's and lighted a Punch corona. I cut
a second cigar for Roantis and gave it to him. He balanced it
neatly on the lip of the ashtray so it would be ready when he
finished the Camel. The hands and arms were rock steady. He
didn't appear drunk at all. How, I don't know.

"Do you mind staying here until two?"

"Nah. I'll stay as long as the booze holds out. Sorry about that
little scrape, too. The guy asked for it, though. Didn't help the
party, did it?"

"Well, it was about closing time anyway. Listen, I'm in trouble
with Mary — "

"I know. Wanta split for a while?"

"Where?"

"A small country I know. Nice. You'd like it."

"Hmmm. You know, Liatis, something strange is happening.
A year or two ago I wouldn't have given it a thought. Now, I don't
know . . . I just kinda feel like, like busting out of here. I can't
explain — "

"Don't need to. I know the feeling, Doc. Get it alla time. I had
a hunch you're the type who gets that feeling, too. In fact, that's
why I showed up tonight."

I was wondering what he meant by this when I heard low
voices coming from the kitchen. The kangeroo court was in

session. The only thing standing between me and Mary's wrath was Roantis.

"Well, whatever brought you here, I'm glad you're staying. Let's try to keep up a lively conversation. Something she'll like. Then maybe she'll fall asleep. I know that if a certain amount of time elapses, the possibility of violence will ebb. The slow hatred will remain, but not the violence."

He leaned forward and looked me keenly in the eye. Smoke dribbled out of his nostrils. He held my forearm in an iron grip.

"Listen, Doc. I meant what I said just now. I gotta talk to you. It's important."

Mary came in with a mug of coffee and sat down at the card table, glaring at me in silence.

"Sorry," I said. And I was.

"You're not forgiven. And when Liatis leaves the ax will fall. By the way, Liatis, thanks for belting that jerk. I hated him from the start. Now, are you going back to your wife or not?"

"Maybe, Mary. I don't know. How would you like to hear a story?"

"About what?"

"What happened in Cambodia in 1969. If your husband helps me, I think I stand to gain a couple hundred thousand bucks."

"Why do you want Charlie to help?"

"Because he's good at tracking things down. And he doesn't lose his nerve. I like him, Mary. I trust him too. I don't trust hardly anybody, you know. Doc can handle himself, and he's smart at figuring things out. Remember that fishing boat? He — "

"Stop!" cried Mary. "Don't even talk about that!"

"Amen," I said.

Roantis took a pull of whiskey from the tumbler and lit his cigar. He inhaled a deep drag of it, and I winced. It didn't faze him; he let out the pungent smoke through his nose.

"Nice taste," he murmured. "Anyway, Mary, if Doc can help me track down this thing, I'll give him half my share of the loot."

"*Loot?* Liatis," I said, "did you say *loot?* I'm not sure I like the sound of that word. And what is this loot anyway, five pounds of uncut heroin?"

He shrugged his shoulders and returned to the game of solitaire. It seemed the perfect game for him — a symbolic pastime for this battered soldier of fortune.

"Wish I could say it was something else, Doc, but it ain't. It's Siu Lok's loot. That's what it is. And it's mine. Or mine and Vilarde's, fifty-fifty, just like we agreed. Only trouble is, I think Vilarde's dead."

Mary leaned closer during this brief recounting.

"Then there was old Siu Lok. Nice guy. A shame they had to torture him. They took out their belt knives and skinned him alive, right in front of his own wife and children. Took all the skin off his head and chest. The villagers said later you could hear him howl a mile away — and that's through jungle, you know. Sound doesn't carry well through the jungle. And remember: he was an old guy. But you don't want to hear all this."

Mary leaned still closer. She reached over and took a sip from my glass.

"Who says?" she said.

"Huh?"

"Who says we don't?"

Roantis stared at the columns of red and black cards. He swiftly mashed them into a pile, squared the deck, shuffled, and proceeded to repeat the game.

"Stop that game and tell us, dammit!" said Mary. I slipped him a wink. Roantis flipped cards and puffed on the cigar. He could have been on Mars.

"Well?"

"Well what?"

"Well why did they torture him? *Who* tortured him?"

Annoyed, Roantis stifled a yawn of boredom.

"Who did it? Why, the Khmer Rouge of course. They dint mind Siu Lok giving us the loot — hell, they dint even know about the goddamn loot. But I tink they knew he was a river pirate. 'Cause he was. But they were mad he told us about them."

"The loot. What is this loot, Liatis?"

He dug out his wallet. It was a tattered and crusty specimen made from elephant ear. He riffled through its contents: a collection of foreign and domestic bills in all denominations, old

13

photo booth pictures of women (mostly Asians), membership cards of various self-defense and martial arts clubs, and some old and folded color snapshots until he found the item he wanted. It was a crinkled color Polaroid picture. He spun it over the felt table to us. Mary turned it upright and examined it.

"A statue," she said. "A golden statue. Who is it, Buddha?"

Taking the picture, I saw a shiny yellow figure set on a black velvet background. Underneath the statue was an embossed placard that said BARCLAYS BANK, LTD., KOWLOON. It appeared to be an official bank photograph, much like those taken by appraisers and insurance companies. The statue had a Hindu look to it and seemed to be a deity of some kind. It did not have the sagacious and placid expression of the great Buddha, nor his rotund physique. Its face was a fierce demon's, its stance a whirling leap, a frenzied fit of passion, rendered immobile in metal.

"It's a statue of a guy called Siva," said Roantis absently. "It's a Hindu god, and this is his devil form. I guess he comes in a lot of flavors, like Howard Johnson's ice cream. Well, this variety is one of the nasty ones. All I care about is this: the thing is mostly gold. The bank appraiser's estimate was twelve karat. And see those doodads on his head and around his neck? Rubies and sapphires. Not the best grade, or huge. But real."

I looked closely at the picture. Whoever had taken it had placed an upright ruler next to the piece. It was thirteen inches tall. The demon-god, who wore a bow and quiver on his back, held a trident in his hands. Wrapped around his bejeweled neck was a serpent. He was standing on one leg, as if dancing a jig. His foot rested on the fallen body of an enemy, who was also a demon-man. It did not look inviting or pleasant.

"Okay, you've got us going. What's it worth?"

"Guess."

"As one who works with gold, I know what the piece could bring on the current market if it were pure gold, which it isn't, and assuming the piece is solid."

"It's not," said Roantis. "If it was solid it'd weigh a ton."

"And I'm no judge of gems. But they certainly look impressive and well set. Hell, I don't know. Between eighty and a hundred and twenty grand?"

"Close, Doc. Hey, you're good. The appraisal was in sixty-nine, over ten years ago. And they wouldn't certify the appraisal. The piece weighs almost four kilos."

"Let's see, that's uh — "

"Eight point eight pounds," said Roantis.

"Well?"

"The guy said a hundred grand easy. I figure it could be worth double that," said Roantis, dragging on the cigar and sucking the smoke deep. "But we couldn't unload it for anywhere near that then. Now I think we can."

"And you want me to help you find it?"

"Naw. I know where it is."

He reached inside his shirt and caught his stubby finger on a fine silver chain. An instant later he was holding a silver key in his hand. He took the chain from around his neck and flipped the key and chain onto the table. It was a safe deposit box key, deluxe model. It obviously went to a box that was not used for the family burial policy. Long and heavy and made of expensive metal, it had the figure of a Chinese dragon embossed on one side of the crown. On the reverse side were the words BARCLAYS BANK, KOWLOON. Then there was a number: 1001-A.

"The Siva idol is in this bank box in Kowloon, across the harbor from Hong Kong, right where Ramon Vilarde and I put it just about ten years ago."

"Well," said Mary, "you've got the key. What's holding you back?"

"Look at the key closely, Mary. It says one thousand and one — A. There is also key number one thousand and one — B. A is no good without B. You need both keys to open the box. Both keys at the same time, along with a third key belonging to the bank. Guess who's got the other key?"

"This guy Vilarde."

"Yep." Roantis nodded. "So the two of us must be together at the Kowloon bank to get the statue. That's the way we set it up."

Roantis chuckled softly, ironically, to himself, dragging again on the cigar. He let the smoke creep downward out his nostrils like a Chinese dragon.

"That was the only way to set it up. First of all, it was loot. It *is* loot. We had to stash it fast in four days of R and R."

Mary leaned over to Roantis, shaking her head slowly. She said it still wasn't clear. Why had they left it over there in the bank box? Could he start from the beginning? Just what I wanted to hear; he had her going now. I volunteered to make coffee and rose from the table. Roantis said he needed another tumbler of Scotch. Sure he did. But I decided to get him a weak one anyway, since he was getting me off the hook. I walked to the kitchen. The hallway shapes and textures swept by me as if in a dream. The silence sang in my head. I was still a little buzzed. Funny how sometimes you don't notice until after the party. As I was putting the coffee on the phone rang. It was quarter to two. Now who could have the bad manners to call at this hour? I answered it.

"Doc? Brian here. Listen: I'm finally home now and going to bed. I had a cruiser stop Newcombe even before he got to the station. He got belligerent when questioned by the officer. So they took him in and he failed the breath test. Now I made him a little deal — "

"That you'd thought up beforehand?"

"Yeah, well maybe. We drop him off at his house and let him off the hook if he forgets about what happened at your place. Naturally he cooperated. But we entered the DUI anyway, which is serious. I can hold that over him for a while if he gets belligerent again. But the guy's definitely got personality problems. I'm really glad the DUI will carry a jail sentence soon. I'm sick of cleaning dead kids out of cars with a sponge."

"Thanks a million, Brian. I'm sure Roantis will be grateful too."

"Oh yeah. About him. I checked on your friend Liatis Roantis, who bears an uncanny resemblance to a Doberman pinscher. Did you know he wears paper?"

"He what?"

"You know. He's got a sheet. A record. It's not brief either. A whole string of assaults. Two deaths. You know this?"

"Oh sure. It's common knowledge around the club."

"The club? What club is it, for Chrissakes, the *SS*?"

"It's the BYMCU in town. He teaches martial arts there. He's also a director."

"Well watch him — he smells like trouble to me. If I were you, I'd drop him like a red rivet. I mean, look at tonight. Consider it. Things like that happen too often here and the selectmen are on top of me like roofing compound, you know?"

"I know."

"And I heard about the hanky-panky with Janice DeGroot, too. It's the talk of the town, Doc. I heard she was draped around you like the kudzu."

"That's not, uh, entirely true, Brian."

"Izzat so? That's what they all say. I bet Mary's steamed. I don't blame her either. I bet you're in trouble."

I thanked him and took the coffee and booze back to the porch. On the way, I said goodnight to Jack and Tony, who were trundling upstairs. They wished me goodnight, but not with genuine filial warmth. I didn't blame them. I wasn't happy with Dr. Charles Adams this night. I knew I had asked for the trouble I was in. But somehow I wasn't totally sorry. What was this strange restlessness in me?

"You *walked?*" Mary was saying incredulously as I came back into the porch.

"Uh-huh. Oh hiya Doc. You're just in time to hear the story."

And so, declining coffee and taking up his tumblerful of malt whiskey, Liatis Roantis began his tale of war, death, and the golden dancing demon.

17

2

"I GUESS I better give you a little background first," Roantis said, "so you'll understand just why we went into Cambodia in the first place. Cambodia was a neutral country, and therefore safe from American and Vietnamese military action. But see, the enemy used the place to stockpile their arms and ammo that had been shipped down by the Ho Chi Minh Trail. So for years we carried out secret cross-border raids in both Cambodia and Laos. It was done under a secret group called the SOG, Special Operations Group. And it used men from all branches: army, navy, and air force, who worked together. The time I led the Daisy Ducks down past Rang and the Fish Hook was my fourth trip through eastern Cambodia."

"The what?" asked Mary. "The *Daisy Ducks?*"

"Yeah. See, Mary, operations and teams have code names and letter designations. Our designation was Delta-Delta, double-D. So we called ourselves the Daisy Ducks. When we were designated double-M, Mike-Mike, we called our team the Molly Maguires."

"How come you named yourselves after females?" I asked.

He thought for a minute and shrugged, saying he supposed it was tradition. "Why do flyers name their planes girl names?" he asked. "Here she is . . ."

He unfastened his shirtsleeve and drew it up. There was nothing remarkable about the arm. It was not bulging with muscle, although it was heavily lined with blood vessels. I had noticed Roantis's tattoos before, but never paid much attention. The one he pointed to now was remarkable, and still showed the brightly colored ink. The other tattoos were faded purple lines, but this one was clean and crisp and showed a lot of detail. Roantis said it was done in Okinawa, and that Japanese tattoos were the best and most intricate. Both Mary and I laughed when we saw it.

There on Roantis's arm, in full jump gear, was none other than Daisy Duck herself, complete with paratrooper boots, huge eyes and beak, and the big red bow she wore on her head. And she was wearing her red dress too. Except the propwash and her falling had swooshed it up a bit, revealing a pair of lacy panties. Only Daisy wasn't smiling; she was irritated. She wore a snarl as she clutched her chute cords. Behind her, three smaller chutes fell in the distance. On her webbing were three frag grenades and a submachine gun.

Underneath was a furled ribbon with the following inscription: *Long Range Patrol Daisy Ducks — Long Binh, Vietnam — 1969.* And above the entire scene, the crescent AIRBORNE flash. But what caught our eyes was Daisy's quote, underneath the ribbon. She was saying:

"MIND IF WE DROP IN?"

Mary said she thought the tattoo was cute. Roantis stared at her and shook his head slightly.

"Yeah, but thing is, Mary, I don't think you'd wanta meet our Daisy. She was a nasty broad." He paused briefly in reflection, staring at the cards on the table. A hint of regret invaded the eyes. "She was pretty mean was ol' Daisy. Killed a lot of people . . ."

"So what was the mission of the Daisy Ducks in Cambodia?" I asked, not wanting him to stop. I didn't want Roantis morose and introspective. I wanted him talking. He swigged his drink, popped a Camel, and continued.

"Our mission was to sneak up on their supply dumps and blow them up, killing as many enemy as we could. We did it, too. You bet."

"How many men were there with the Daisy Ducks?" I asked.
"Eight."

"*Eight?* You really mean only eight?"

"Only eight. And it was enough. Between us we destroyed thousands of tons of matériel and killed maybe a thousand people. ."

"C'mon Roantis, that's a lot of enemy."

"We were good, Doc. We were very good. But we had a system that made it almost easy as long as we stayed invisible. But the bad part of it was — the bad part of it *is* — that we killed everybody. I said we killed a thousand people, not enemy. I'm sure a lot of them were civilians. Some of them must've been kids, too."

He took a long pull from the tumbler and I realized that he was — finally — drunk. His eyes were glazed and he appeared to wither and shrink before my eyes. He worked his jaws; I could see the muscles on the side of his face bunch and jump as he ground his teeth. He wiped his forehead and wearily ran his fingers through his stringy gray hair. He looked old and tired. He looked like Bogart in the drunk scene of *Casablanca*. Mary, realizing his pain, suggested he stop and that I drive him home. Roantis lived in Jamaica Plain. I told her I was in no shape to drive anywhere, especially all the way to Jamaica Plain and back. She was about to summon the boys, or wake them, when he shooed her off.

"I'm okay, Mary. Stop it. I jus' get a li'l depressed when I think of it sometimes. I'll finish this drink and then get some coffee. Now I need a cigarette too. Or else I need — "

He got up and walked from the porch.

"Where are you going?" I asked.

"Be right back, folks. Don't go away . . ."

We heard him on the stairway, and Mary yelled to him that there was a bathroom on the first floor. He seemed not to hear her.

"Is he going to be sick?"

"Not likely."

During his absence Mary clasped and unclasped her hands and glared icily at me.

"Sorry," I said.

20

"Am I that unattractive?"

"Course not. You're gorgeous. And it was stupid and immature of us. It was the booze making us act out vague, middle-aged fantasies. Do you think if Janice and I really wanted to fool around we'd do it here, during a party? C'mon. And as stupid as it was, I don't think you should make more of it than it deserves. I'll tell you what it is, Mary: I'm bored. And when that happens I do dumb things. And I've been restless lately. I'm not in the mood to be a suburban physician right now. I want to do something a little riskier. Or maybe just different. Now, you see — What's that I smell?"

Roantis had reappeared in the doorway, a glowing joint clenched between his lips.

"Now where the hell did you get *that?*" asked Mary.

"Jack just rolled it for me. Nice kid."

I went to the bottom of the stairway and yelled upward at the darkness, like Ahab.

"I thought I told you guys not to smoke that stuff anymore! I thought we agreed — "

"We're not. Mr. Roantis is!"

"Don't get wiseassed. That stuff screws up your chromosomes!"

"Booze kills your brain cells! You're living proof!"

Well, I was about to go right up there and kick some ass. Yes sir. If I hadn't been so under the weather I would have just gone right up there and done just that. Except those snotnose punks now outweigh me by twenty pounds each and row varsity crew. Oh well, I'd let it pass this time . . .

Roantis was filling the room with pungent smoke when I returned. Mary and I had coffee. I had added a wee drop of Dewar's to mine. I lighted my cigar again and we listened.

Roantis's blue eyes took on a languid softness from the dope.

"The special long-range patrols . . ." he said. Then, as he squinted in recollection, the eyes became focused, sharp, steely gray blue. He hesitated for an instant, fixing the scene in his mind, then continued.

"The special long-range patrols were officially called reconnaissance patrols. We did recon work, sure. But our job was

21

really to search and destroy. This was always behind enemy lines. We carried only small arms and took Russian Kalishnikov rifles so we could use enemy ammo if we had to. We were to radio back the enemy's size and strength. Whenever possible, we were to snatch a man or two and interrogate them to see what they had planned. We would then destroy the staging area and as many of the enemy as possible, moving on to the next target."

"How did you find these targets?" I asked.

"Walked onto 'em. Looked for tire tracks in mud or packed dirt. Fresh oil spots on roads, reflections from windshields . . . you know. But mostly just walked through the countryside until we spotted something . . . or heard some commotion. Oh, they had the stuff hidden from the air. You bet. But not from ground level. They weren't expecting any GIs within eighty miles."

"Then you'd blow up the supplies?"

"Uh-huh."

"But if you packed the stuff in, how'd you carry it all?"

"We dint. We dint carry the explosives. It was all done from the air. All we carried to do our work were dozens of little transmitters no bigger'n a pack of butts. They had metal spikes on their side and bottom: you could stick 'em into the ground or onto trees. Some had li'l magnets so you could stick 'em on a vehicle. Just make sure their li'l red eyes are pointing up, that's all. Then you'd set them so they'd start to transmit all at once at a prearranged time. That beam guides the smart bombs right down on top of them. If you encircled a camp or supply depot with four or five of these, there's no way it could remain on earth — not with those two-thousand-pound bombs coming down on it. So we didn't take anything but small arms and the transmitters. We just didn't need anything else. A B-fifty-two can fly so high it's silent and invisible from the ground. Under the jungle canopy, where the Panvin and VC hid all their stuff and men, there was no way they could know what was coming down on them until it happened. Until it was just too late. That's how the eight Ducks did all that damage. And by the time it happened we were always miles away, walking through the darkness under that canopy. They never knew what hit them."

He paused to snuff out the remains of the joint. When it had cooled sufficiently, he took the roach end and popped it into his mouth, swallowing it with a gulp of Scotch. Then he lit a Camel.

Roantis's body was doomed to a continual barrage of punishment, if not from military foes or crazed karate opponents in white robes, then from his own excesses.

"We'd start these li'l country walks from a secret base in Thailand. Be lifted out either in a chopper or a fixed-wing transport like a Hercules C-one-thirty. If it was by chopper we'd drop into the LZ in the dead of night. If we jumped in — which was rare — we'd do it at dusk so if we hit a hot spot we could evade in cover of darkness. Sometimes the drop zones were picked by other recon teams in the bush. These men, on their way out, would be our reception committee when we hit the zone. The insertion point was usually a two-day walk from the beginning of the staging areas."

Roantis got up from the table and paced around the porch. He stretched and grunted to relieve the tension that had crept into him. He strolled over to the window, peered out quickly, and returned to the table.

"We'd move out right away, putting a few miles between us and the LZ, then go to earth for the night. Then, before dawn next morning, we'd head toward the staging areas near the Vietnamese border. We just walked, single file, sixty feet apart, and as quiet as cats along these jungle and mountain trails. If we had to cross open plains or marshes — and there are a lot of these in Cambodia — then we'd wait and rest under the foliage until dark, then sneak across. We worked as we went. Twice we wasted entire villages because the enemy had commandeered them and were using them as bases. We knew there were women and children in those huts, too. That was one of Charlie's favorite ploys. We never got over it though. It drove Royce nuts later. He never was the same. But in those two villages alone we killed over six hundred enemy soldiers.

"After about eight to ten days of this, we'd head for the border and link up with friendlies. Then, at the first fire support base or special forces camp, we'd lift out to Nha Trang and debrief. After four days of R and R, we'd go back at it again, this time starting from Vietnam. We'd walk into and through Cambodia back toward the remote boonies, where we'd get airlifted out again to Thailand. So there we went, back and forth, back and forth. Just find the enemy and mark him for the kill. No combat. There were lots of these teams operating up and down the border between Tet and late sixty-nine. I tell you, it worked like downtown. And we gave them no peace."

"How long before the Reds caught on?" I asked.

"Hah! Not long, man. They knew right away that there were recon men operating in their midst. How else could we be hitting them square on the noggin each time? I tell you Doc, we made each of those blockbusters count. We hit 'em each and every time — and know what? We scared the shit outa them. Those huge antipersonnel bombs open up a thousand feet above the ground. Each of them spit out twenty canisters of grapeshot. These would fall another five hundred feet, fanning out. Then they'd go off together, taking every leaf off every tree — "

Mary had had enough. She interrupted to say goodnight, and leaned over and kissed Roantis on the side of his haggard face.

"That's for saving my husband's life," she said, then looked at me, "although it turned out not to be worth it. Goodnight everyone. And don't drink any more, Charlie. You're in enough trouble already."

She left us alone. Whether Roantis had actually saved my life or not, he had certainly saved me from a hell of a beating. Four months earlier, two South End bloods jumped me in the parking lot near the BYMCU. One whanged me a good one on the head when I foolishly tried to fight back. I had learned just enough self-defense stuff from Roantis to try it. It was no go. His pal was coming at me with a knife, blade low, edge up, when Roantis blew in on the scene like a dust devil. In less than ten seconds it was all over, though I was on the ground and barely conscious enough to witness it. Roantis was all hands and feet, moving like lightning. Now, as I stared at the weary face of the fifty-five-year-old veteran, it was hard to imagine he'd been so swift and lethal. They led one punk away in bracelets; the other one needed a stretcher.

"Thanks again for saving my skin in the parking lot, Liatis. You knew when you called tonight I couldn't refuse you."

24

He pointed a stubby and stained finger at my chest.

"Now Doc. Maybe you've been wondering why I invited myself here. It wasn't just to mingle with all those fancy people and drink free booze."

"Well I know it wasn't for the fancy people anyway. I assume that your surprise visit, besides enabling you to consume twenty bucks worth of free hooch, has something to do with the statue."

"Uh, right. It's all gotta do with Siu Lok's loot. That's why I brought the pictures."

"But we only saw one picture," said Mary, reentering the porch with a mug of warm milk.

"Decided to hear more of the story?" I asked.

"Uh-huh. Besides, I'm so edgy I couldn't sleep now if I tried. Okay Liatis, I'm all ears again."

"Oh yeah," said Roantis, "the other picture." He produced another folded snapshot. He placed it on the table between us. The picture ran horizontally, with the crease running through the middle from left to right. In the picture were eight men: three standing in back and five kneeling on one knee in front. Rather like a sports team. The white crease lay above the heads of the kneeling men and across the stomachs of those standing. It obscured nobody's face. The men wore camouflage fatigues, but not any fancy insignia or headgear, nor any badges or rank. No weapons were visible. Roantis, looking deeply tanned and quite a bit younger and thinner, was standing proudly in back center, his hands clasped behind him. He was obviously team leader. Two of the men were black, and both wore mustaches. Two seemed to be Hispanic, and one of them wore the trim, lean mustache so favored by many Latinos. One of the kneeling men had a broad, flat Asian face and small tight eyes. Two of the men were very big: one of the blacks and a tall, blond giant with a big gold handlebar mustache.

I saw that three of the men had black X's marked on their chests in pen.

"These guys dead?"

"Yeah. Well, two are dead and the other guy might as well be. Bill Royce, an air force commando, went nuts in seventy-two. He's still in a hospital in the Philippines. This guy here, Larry Jenkins, was an SF trooper who worked with me several times out of Long Binh. He did long-range recon work all over Laos, too. After the Daisy Ducks, he went back to Laos to recruit and train more mercenaries. He was missing in action on the Plain of Jars up there. Larry was the best of the best. This guy here, Ton Youn, was a Korean. ROK special forces. Great soldier. Mean sonofabitch, too. He was our interrogation man. He was hit on the outskirts of Saigon in seventy-one by a sniper."

"So there are five Daisy Ducks left?"

"Right. Mike Summers here was the other black guy besides Jenkins. Ghetto kid from Chicago. Tough as hell, and hands quick as lightning for a big guy. You can see how big he is. Got him from the one-oh-one. Good man. Solid and brave. He's back in Chicago now. South Side. Now this guy, the other spic besides Vilarde, is a Puerto Rican named Jusuelo. Jesus Jusuelo. Now he just might be the best soldier of all the Ducks. He was a navy SEAL. Anyway, Jusuelo's a merc now, just like I used to be, somewhere in Africa I think."

"Do you know where in Africa?" Mary asked.

"Nah. He probably moves around. Hell, there are twenty places right now in Africa where a good merc can find work."

I tapped the man with the big gold mustache.

"This guy looks right out of the SS."

"Hmmmmph! Yeah, could've been, twenty years earlier. Dat's Fred Kaunitz. Big fella from Texas. Heard he can wrestle a bull to the ground. Not a steer or calf, a *bull.* He's slow and deliberate, and very careful. He was a smart kid, Fred, but quiet. Strange maybe. Never talked much. Like I heard that bull story from a friend of his, not from him. He never talked about himself. A loner and a perfectionist. The best shot of all of us. Rifle or shotgun, still target or moving, if it was in front of Fred's muzzle it was *gone.* "

"And where is he now?"

Roantis shrugged his shoulders.

"Don't know. Last I heard, back on the family ranch in Texas. I'll be tracking him down, but I'm sure he doesn't keep in touch with the army guys. It wouldn't be like him, you know? As soon as the job was done, he just went back to Texas. This one's Vilarde. He's the one I want to find. That's why I came here tonight."

"Yeah? Well forget it, Liatis. I know I owe you a big favor. Someday, if you're unlucky in a fight, I'll fix your jaw for free. I'll pull all your family's teeth out — no charge. But I'm not having anything to do with these guys. No way."

"Amen," said Mary.

"Vilarde is as solid as they come. He was second in command in the Ducks. After the Ducks, I quit the army. I knew we weren't going to win over there and I guess I was sick of it. I'd been in one defeat already, up at Dien Bien Phu. I didn't need another one."

Roantis was getting morose again; I persuaded him to put the booze away and switch to coffee.

"Well here's what happened," he continued. "It was on one of our sweeps eastward, from Thailand toward the Vietnamese border. On the fourth day out we came up to a little hillside at dusk and made dry camp. No lights or noise. There was a tiny village down below us in a river valley. We glassed it in the dying daylight just before we turned in. It was only thirteen or fourteen hooches, some of them for three families. It was built along the river, and there were all kinds of boats pulled up on the bank. We planned to get moving before dawn and just bypass it, crossing the river and then following the jungle and mountain trails looking for tire tracks.

"About four in the morning, Jusuelo wakes me up and says there's noise in the bush. It was a platoon of Khmer Rouge moving up and over our little hill. We snuggled down and froze and let them go right over us. If we took them on we'd give away our position and get badly chewed up, too. They went over the hill and down to the village. We used a starlight scope to track 'em and could see clear as day. They surrounded the village, and at first light they stormed in there fast and got all the villagers out of their huts.

"Then they rounded them up in the central clearing and made them sit down. Then they started the usual shit, you know, hitting the wives and kids with rifle butts, cutting a guy's head off — "

"Usual? Usual!" Mary had risen from her chair and was staring balefully at Roantis, whose manner was that of someone recounting the details of a church rummage sale.

"Yeah. See Mary, Asia isn't like Europe or America. It just isn't. Not even in the most modern places. The standard drill for these guerrilla groups is to enter a village and terrorize it. Shows the people who's boss. Shows them they better not screw around. So anyway, they killed two of the strongest men and beat up some other villagers pretty bad. Now we thought of going in right then, but we decided to use the terror to our own advantage."

"So you stood by," said Mary, "and let this happen so when you showed up you'd be the good guys."

"Right."

"You're no better than the Khmer Rouge, Liatis."

"You're wrong, Mary. Know what? We were *worse*. Because if we weren't, we'd be dead. So anyway, they left in midmorning after taking all the rice and dried meat they could lay their hands on. We went in at noon and helped bandage the wounded and bury the two headless corpses. We were the heroes. We talked to the old chief, Siu Lok, for a coupla hours. He was real steamed of course because one of the guys they killed was his son. We told him he was next — him and his whole family — and he had about nine kids. He seemed to know this, and told us the Khmer Rouge would probably return that night to take the young men away for soldiers. So we fixed a plan with Siu Lok. We decided to stay awhile in the village. They gave us food and all the women we wanted."

Mary's lip curled in disgust.

"Remember, Mary: not like Europe or America." He patted his shirt and sides for butts. I offered him a cigar but he declined. Then he vanished again and hiked upstairs. He returned shortly with a cigarette rolling machine and paper. I knew where it came from. He rolled several cigarettes made with my pipe tobacco, lighted one, and returned to his story.

"So, toward late afternoon, the Daisy Ducks fanned out from the village. Summers had a li'l Chinese mortar with him that he'd gleeped off a dead gook, and that was going to be the diversion. At twilight we hunkered down in the bush along the route we thought the enemy would take. Before long we heard that hissing, snapping sound in the jungle that means men approaching.

28

Soon, Kaunitz and I located the point of their patrol. They were walking exactly where we thought, and Summers had his mortar sighted in. We went to earth so they'd go right over us."

"Just a sec," said Mary. "You keep saying you let these guys walk over you. How come they never saw you?"

The Mongol eyes crinkled again in a grin.

"Mary, in dim light I could hide here in this room so you'd never see me . . . until it was way, way too late to save your skin. In a jungle it's a piece of cake. Anyway, when the patrol got past us, heading toward the village, we closed in behind them, and on their flanks, too. Those Khmer Rouge were sure of themselves and moving fast and noisy, never suspecting that we were behind them and on both sides. They don't know they've got bad company. Just before they get to the village — *boom!* Off goes that Chink mortar, and Summers, who's firing it from the riverbank you see, has put the first round right on the money, so that takes out four guys right there. He keeps the bombs coming too, as fast as he can drop them down the tube. Then we'd planted some claymore mines right where they'd entered the clearing before. Sure enough, they come streaking in there again and we triggered four of them by wire, which took care of eight or nine more. By now they're sorry they came back. Then all the Ducks got going with the automatic small arms fire from three sides. That and a few frag grenades finished them. Two guys were still kicking afterward and we interrogated them. Found out a whole battalion wasn't far away and was getting closer, and that they had a big ammo dump and field hospital nine clicks away. So we knew where we'd be headed next.

"But before we took off, Siu Lok and the villagers were so grateful they cooked a pig for us. We feasted and partied, and then Siu Lok appears with a sackful of goodies for us. Most of it was gold pieces and some pearls, but he had ivory too. At first we refused it. But then all of us were thinking about the cash value of this stuff, you know. I mean, you can't help thinking about it. He kept insisting we take it. He knew that the village was doomed and that sooner or later the Reds would take it all anyway. All the Ducks had done was buy him and the villagers a little more time, and we all knew it. So we divvied up the stuff.

Everybody took some except me, and Siu Lok was disappointed.

Then, in the dead of night, Siu Lok himself woke me and led me up the hillside where the cooking wood was stacked to dry. There was a hollow space behind it and a narrow tunnel. We went in — he was leading the way or I would have suspected a trap — and after a ways it opened into a little chamber. As soon as I saw that chamber and what he had stashed in there, I knew Siu Lok was a river pirate. In that li'l cave was his treasure trove. And right inna middle of everything was this golden Siva. When I saw it, I knew it wasn't a Buddhist god but a Hindu god. The Cambodes are Buddhists. So one, I knew the Siva wasn't sacred to him: it was merchandise. Two, I knew he'd stolen it, or got it from another pirate. He really wanted me to have it. So I took it and put it in my pack. Then I thought, what if I get caught with this thing? As defined by the military code, taking anything not needed for military operations is looting. Period. No matter even if the people *want* you to take it. Now everybody knows GIs take a lot of stuff, but it's not big. This is a gold statue. So what if I — the team leader — get caught with it, eh?

"Just as I'm considering this along comes Vilarde — second in command — coming off sentry, and we get to talking. Before long I've taken the Siva out of my pack and we're both looking at it and trying to guess what the market value is. What should I do? Keep it, he says. I won't say anything, he says. I'll even cover for you. Well, I figure the guy's such a straight shooter that I'll split it with him. The odds were pretty good that some of us wouldn't make it back in one piece anyway. So what the hell. It's funny the way you begin to think in combat. In action — especially behind the lines deep in the boonies — a week is a long, long time. I decided to go halves on that statue as easy as giving away a pack of smokes. And I tell you both something, too: I never — until these past few months — regretted it, either."

"And now you regret it," I said.

"Yeah, sure. But not because of Ken. One of the reasons I split it with him is because I knew he hadda wife and kid and they dint have much money. Also, if I was to get hit and the guys'd find the thing in my pack, I'd want them to know I had at least mentioned it to somebody else. And Vilarde, as it turned out,

30

was not only second in command but the only married guy. I thought it made sense. So anyway, we moved out of the village and made our way over to the ammo dump that we'd found out about."

"What happened to those soldiers who were still alive? Did you take them with you or leave them in the village?" asked Mary.

"Oh them. Well, they dint survive Youn's interrogation. Nobody ever did. But what would we have done with them if they had lived? Turned them over to the villagers, of course. Either way, they were dead meat."

I couldn't conceal my revulsion at this, no matter how necessary or expedient it might have been. Mary's similar reaction was written on her face.

"Just before dawn we got to the ammo dump and the main camp of the Khmer Rouge battalion. We placed the bugs and split, walking away in dead silence with the clock ticking. We radioed the secret frequency and the big birds came in overhead, way high up and invisible and silent, and let go their payload. Two days later we were back in Nam, then flown on to Nha Trang for debrief. It was tricky, but we kept that statue out of sight from the brass. We had a leave coming, and we all took off in different directions. Vilarde and I went to Hong Kong with our friend Siva. Our first idea was to sell the thing. But the dealers we tried wouldn't give us squat for it. I think the best offer we got was ten grand. Screw that. Besides, we were going back into combat: what would we do with the money then anyway? We'd just blow it on broads and junk or get ripped off in a cathouse. So we went across the harbor over to Kowloon, where we figured things would be less rushed and more honest. We went to the Barclays Bank and had one of their appraisers look it over. He said it was worth over a hundred grand easy.

"But thing is, Doc, Mary: he wouldn't buy it, or even give us a certificate of appraisal. Same thing was bothering him that bothered everybody else: where'd we get it? Here we are, a coupla army stiffs just off combat. We're not brass. Where'd we get it? Was it stolen? Why would anyone wanta buy a stolen piece? For ten grand maybe, but not for six figures. Too risky.

It was a question of loot again. These merchants and bankers were afraid that the MPs or the British officials were going to come down on them for fencing loot. Vilarde and I went to lunch and thought it over. What was our Siva *really* worth? At that time and place? About ten, maybe twelve grand. We decided the best thing was to keep the statue until our tours were up, then take it to the States and sell it there. That way the thing would increase in value and we wouldn't blow the money in the meantime. We'd each have something when we got out — a nest egg to take care of us, right? We wouldn't tell the other Ducks. They'd gotten their loot and cashed it in. And there was no way to divide that statue eight ways except to cut it into li'l pieces, which would wreck it. The deal between us was this: we each got a key to the box. If one of us got killed, the other guy could claim the statue all for himself if he could show that his partner was dead or if he brought in both keys."

"Couldn't that be faked?" I asked.

"Sure. But it was the best solution we could think of at the time. What should we do? Unload it for a tenth of its value? Naw. It would be damn hard for one guy to get the other's key if he dint wanna let it go. I know it would take at least five or six trained men to get mine — and, if they did, at least two of them wouldn't be alive. Vilarde's the same. But the plan was mainly good because we trust each other. You can't depend on a guy to keep you alive every second of every day for two years and not trust him like a brother."

Roantis paused here to sip coffee and light another homemade cigarette.

"The bank had a deal that if you had a certain amount of money in an account with them, you dint hafta pay box rental. So Ken and I chipped in and opened the account, knowing the statue would be safe there as long as it hadda be. They photographed the piece, locked it up, and away we went. That was over ten years ago. We got back to Saigon and then were flown to the Long Binh special forces camp. Within four days were were back in Cambodia doing the westward sweep toward Thailand again. On the way we happened to be near Siu Lok's village, so we decided to sneak in there and see what was going on. That's when we heard the story of how remnants of the Khmer Rouge battalion fingered him for collaboration with us and skinned him alive. There was almost nothing left of the village, and needless to say the people dint welcome us back. It sort of makes you sad . . . There's no way to win in a situation like that.

"Well, after two more months of this, I was tired and pissed off. When my tour expired I decided to leave. It dint take a genius to see we weren't gonna make it over there, and I dint wanna hang around and watch. Vilarde had almost a year left on his tour, and told me he was going to re-up when it was over. He wanted to be a career man, so I knew he'd stay in Nam as long as America did. So we agreed when he mustered out stateside he'd look me up and we'd fly back to Hong Kong together."

"Weren't you kind of impatient?" I asked.

"Well, yeah and no. I knew Ken wouldn't budge until Vietnam was resolved. Secondly, since he was in constant combat, I knew my odds of getting the whole statue to myself increased the longer we waited."

"Isn't that pretty cold-blooded, Liatis?" Mary asked. She had her chin in her hands and was eyeing the man with a mixture of curiosity and horror.

"Maybe. Or maybe it's just realistic. I think, considering the life I've lived, it's just natural. I knew as long as Ken was soldiering and I was teaching karate in Boston, the odds of my surviving were far greater than his. Therefore, my odds of getting the entire sackful of cash were greater too. But he dint seem to care. Don't forget, he wouldn't even have *known* about the Siva if I hadn't told him. Besides, what choice did I have? I think both of us had the same line of thinking about waiting to claim the statue. Then money got scarce, so I worked awhile in Africa. Ken wired me there in seventy-three to say he was ready, but then I wasn't. In seventy-six I was set to go but he was in the Middle East, in Syria. He didn't reappear until seventy-eight. He was about to do a tour in Afghanistan. But I couldn't go. I was inna li'l scrape with the law just then. Doc, maybe you remember it."

"You mean the kid who almost died after that barfight in the Combat Zone?"

"Naw. Dis was before that. Down in Southie. And a li'l more

serious too, because the guy did die. I was told not to leave the state, so I couldn't leave even if Ken wanted to. So that was that for a year. Finally, last fall, he was back in Washington. We were all set to go just after Thanksgiving. Then he disappeared."

"He was still in the army?"

"No. He left the army after the Afghan thing. Part of it was, I think, he got divorced. He was kinda down on his luck in general. Anyway, he called me from Washington. He said he was going to fly up here and meet me. But he never showed up. I called and called the number he'd left me. I got no answer and later a recording saying the number was no longer in service. I even called Rosie — looked her up where she'd remarried out in LA — and she hadn't heard from Ken in almost a year. So where is he, eh? That's what I need help on."

"Let's see: you and Ken Vilarde put your golden Siva friend in that safe deposit box a long time ago. Over ten years. I can't believe that neither of you has made a move for it."

He placed his palms against the edge of the table and shoved back until he balanced the chair on its rear legs. He seemed to chuckle to himself silently.

"Well, for starters, the round-trip airfare from Boston to Hong Kong is over two grand. Think about that. That's a big stumbling block right there. And remember, we still don't know how much we can get for the Siva. It may not be more than about twenty grand. But . . . I think the odds are that we can get a lot more for it. Another thing is, I'm the kind of guy who lives in the path of least resistance. A bed, a broad, a bottle, and a roof over my head is all I want. Wait: you can skip the roof. Up until now those were my only goals. So I know that if I did get the money back in seventy-two or seventy-six or something, I'd just have blown it. I'd drink and party every night. Buy fast cars, travel, lend money to other broken-down old soldiers. I could promise you — *promise you* — there would be nothing left today. But now there is. And now something's come along that I really want. There's a building for sale down in Quincy that I could make into my own martial arts school."

"And leave the Union club?" asked Mary.

"Yeah. I got a lot of friends there I know, but the pay's lousy.

In my own club I could do what I really like and maybe even make some bucks. Most important of all, maybe I could finally make something of myself besides a broken-down old soldier. Maybe I'd finally want more than just a bed, broad, and bottle, you know? My son's fifteen now. I want him to go to college. I need the money now. I want it. It's mine."

"And Vilarde's."

"Yeah. His too. If he's not dead."

"You think he is?" asked Mary. "And if he is, then why ask Charlie to help find him?"

"I think he's dead because he's *not* here, ready to fly with me to Kowloon to pick up the piece. He wanted that bread as much as I do. So where is he? I've contacted army friends, called his wife . . . I've reached a dead end. I don't know where to go next. Now, I've seen the way Doc can track down things, Mary. He's good. And if you help me, Doc, half my share's yours, whatever the piece brings. If it turns out he's dead and I get the whole thing, then you get half the total."

I stared down at my coffee cup. Tan-white swirls of cream spiraled in its center, like a miniature galaxy.

"No," I said. "If you want, maybe I can get some of my policemen friends to do some digging for Ken Vilarde. But as for me going snooping around a bunch of paratroopers and mercenaries, helping you find your partner, no way. I'm sorry, Liatis. But I've used up all the survival luck I have during that last caper."

"Listen Doc: that's why I want *you*. You got guts and brains. You got what it takes."

"Not anymore I don't. There's nothing like getting beat up and shot at and almost killed to make you have no more guts left. Now are you going to call Suzanne and tell her you'll be spending the night?"

Mary shot me a glance that both questioned and accused. But soon she was convinced of the wisdom — the necessity — of not having Liatis attempting to drive all the way to Jamaica Plain — or around the block, for that matter. We offered him the guest room but he declined, saying it was too much trouble. He flumped down on the porch sofa, explaining that he had enough antifreeze in him to forgo the blanket Mary brought him. She left it by his side anyway. He nestled down into the pillow and asked if he could borrow my Browning nine-millimeter auto pistol for the night.

"Get serious. There won't be any intruders here. This is Concord, not Jamaica Plain or Roxbury."

"I'll just sleep better with it. Habit I guess. If I don't have it in my hand or near me I'll keep waking up."

So I trudged upstairs and took the piece from its hiding place in the bedroom, removed the loaded magazine and flicked out all thirteen rounds, checked the breech, replaced the clip, decocked the hammer, and took it downstairs. I saw Roantis standing in the dark, looking out the window again. I handed the pistol to him. I knew he would know instantly if the magazine weren't in place, but I wasn't counting on the fact that he could tell by simply hefting the gun that it wasn't loaded.

"Don't trust me, eh?" he said, his eyes crinkled up in a mischievous grin. "Sure, I can tell by the weight. I can tell by the weight if half the rounds are gone. Now when you go get them I can go to sleep, okay?"

"This is dumb, Liatis."

"Please Doc. Force of habit. I do it every night. You can ask Suzanne."

When the piece had been loaded Roantis placed it on the coffee table inches from his face, closed his weary and bloodshot eyes, and began to breathe deeply. He made no noise as he slept. He did not snore heavily like so many people — myself included — who have been partying. He was silent and motionless, his left arm bent and hand near his head, ready to reach out and snatch the pistol in an instant. Was this grotesque bedtime ritual a habit, a preference, or the indelible hallmark of the long-range boonie stalker?

I went up and joined Mary in the sack. She was already asleep. I nudged her, then put my arm around her and began nuzzling her neck. But she drew away, turning her head. Unusual. Was she still angry, or was it something deeper? I felt a cold shudder go through me. I suddenly felt a gap widening between us, cold and desolate. I hadn't felt it before, ever, and it scared me.

This would not make sleep easier. Nor would the fact that

36

Liatis Roantis was asleep on the lower floor. Asleep and no doubt dreaming of pleasantries like laser-guided bombs, victims flayed alive, and a golden dancing god guarded by thick steel doors and inscrutable Chinese.

And the rest of the Daisy Ducks . . . Where was that glorious gaggle now?

Perhaps I'd breathed too much smoke from Roantis's funny cigarettes, but I had an unforgettable dream that night. It was filled with vivid sound and laced with bright color. I was in a lifeboat in the North Atlantic, watching the sinking of the *Titanic.*

In my dream, for some reason, the ship was our home. Mary and I had lived aboard her for twenty years together. The lights on the ship were still twinkling as she dove slowly down into the icy blackness in a roar of rushing water. The moon was out, and icebergs were floating by. Mary was on one of them, talking to friends. She did not seem concerned and was enjoying herself. I yelled at her and waved my arms, but she never turned her head. Bright colored lights shot up on the horizon. The northern lights. Mary watched them, laughing and smiling with her friends on the ice floe. I beat my hands against the cold as the ship went down. I was crying. Mary was laughing. Whales leapt and snorted in the dark. The moon was bright. I called and called, but Mary and her friends drifted farther and farther away. Then the tears were frozen on my face.

3

WHEN I AWOKE, the world was looking razor blades at me. It was not going to be a nice day.

Fuzzy-tongued and with ringing head, I rolled over to look at Mary, who stared at me with big brown eyes.

"How do you feel, Don Juan?"

"Okay."

"Bullshit. Close your eyes before you bleed to death."

"Mmmmm."

"Now we must get rid of your hunter-killer friend downstairs, then finish cleaning up, then — "

"Stop. Not so fast. I've got to slide into this day obliquely — if I hit it head-on it'll kill me. Now we'll just quietly amble downstairs with our fuzzy bathrobes on. Put on soft music. Soft. Then sip a bloody mary and some coffee. Then we'll take a long sauna bath followed by a cool shower. Then we'll do it again. Next, we'll have our deli brunch of lox, bialys, cream cheese and tomatoes. Then I'll run four miles. Slowly. Can't do six today, but four in this cold air will help. Then it'll be time for the opera broadcast. Today it's *Tannhäuser*. Finally the playoffs at four-thirty — "

"Wrong. We're going down and cleaning up the kitchen.

You're doing the floor. Then you've got to clean the gutters. Remember, you were going to do it last week?"

Her words struck me like ringing swords. I huddled down under the covers again and wished it weren't so.

"Seriously, how do you feel?"

"I feel like I'm inside a painting by Hieronymus Bosch."

"Oh dear. You mean those weird pictures that show people being pecked apart by giant birds? And imps hatching out of giant eggs? And people with flowers stuck up their butts?"

"Uh-huh. That guy. And I don't like it one bit."

"Well it serves you right. You go around fondling Janice's ass again and you won't have one of your own to stick a flower up. Understand? Now *get up.*"

We dressed and went downstairs to find a note from Jack and Tony saying they'd gone into Boston and wouldn't return till nightfall. That simplified the day somewhat, except it meant I had no young co-workers to help me with the chores. The thought of hanging on to a steep slate roof three stories high working on gutters did not appeal. I ambled into the sunporch, expecting to see Roantis supine on the couch. He wasn't. He was standing at the windows peering intently out, sweeping his keen predator gaze to and fro like a leopard on a limb.

"See anything you like?" I asked.

He spun around fast, then smiled.

"Naw. Morning Doc. Hey, you look like I feel."

We walked into the kitchen and he snagged a St. Pauli Girl from the refrigerator, downed it, and poured coffee. He chased that with a slug of neat malt. Roantis never missed a beat. He winked at us and kept pouring, then retired with his breakfast to the card table, where he proceeded to roll more cigarettes with my pipe tobacco. When he'd lighted up he took the deck of cards, shuffled it, and began to play solitaire. It was as if we'd never gone to bed. It was surrealistic, like a movie by Antonioni. It stunk.

We had the sauna bath and deli breakfast. When we'd finished the pot of coffee, Roantis put on his fleece-lined leather flight jacket, wadded up a huge pair of leather mittens and stuffed them into the inside breast pocket, thanked us for the hospitality, and apologized for the rough stuff the previous night. He mentioned his offer of the hundred grand again, quite forcefully. If I could help him locate Ken Vilarde and get the piece, a big share of the loot was mine.

"Think about it, Doc. No hurry. I'll wait even a week. Bye Mary. You sure been great to this old man."

He kissed her on the cheek and she hugged him.

I said I'd walk him to his car. We went out into the cold December morning. It was gray and gusty, with newly formed ice on the paths. We walked carefully along the brick path that runs by the side of the house to the front. From there you can look down the hill in any direction, to the gardens and orchards in back, or Old Stone Mill Road and the big orchard and woods in front. It's a pretty view, even in winter. We danced nimbly along the front walk, avoiding the slickest ice patches. A stone wall runs along the bottom of the yard, with a gate in the middle. We walked through this and out onto the road. There is no sidewalk. Roantis's car was a good forty yards away, parked against the wall. He had arrived late at the party. It was an old maroon Dodge with big splayed tailfins. It seemed odd and unfair that a man who'd continually risked his life for America over a twenty-year period should have to drive such a wreck. Then again, most of his personal and financial problems had been brought on by the lifestyle he'd chosen. I looked again at the old car: a bent coat hanger for a radio antenna. Two crumpled fenders. Trunk lid ajar and wired down. Rocker panels rusted clear through. Yeah, Roantis needed dough all right.

Still, looking at the crumpled, rusty wreck, I couldn't help feeling a little envious of this broke and battered soldier of fortune. Sure, I had a nice family, big house, beach cottage, nice practice, community respect — all the things one is supposed to want and to work hard for. But possessions are chains, and I envied Roantis's free-wheeling life. Who else could take off to a small country for a month on a moment's notice? Who else of my acquaintances went through life doing what he damn well pleased, answering to nobody? Only Liatis Roantis.

And once again in my responsible, suburban life, I wanted part of that action. Call it male menopause, midlife crisis, whatever you want . . . I wanted a little dirt and danger for a change.

But I kept these thoughts to myself as we walked along. Twice I slipped and almost fell. There was only spotty snow cover, but it was cold and slick underfoot.

I was looking down Old Stone Mill Road, white-gray with snow and ice, and at the low stone fence alongside it, when Roantis did his big back flip. It was a beaut — right out of the Keystone Kops. As I leaned down to help him up, the world seemed strangely silent. Then, extending my hand to the man lying on the frozen road, I realized why. There was a great noise just dying away. An explosion. A fast-fading echo of a giant wallop.

Just off my left ear came a crack: flat, dry, electric. A ferocious sucking of high-speed wind. A snapping crack like a muleskinner's whip. Bullet. Then the endless cavernous echo.

I dropped down. Roantis had not moved. A geyser of rock and ice erupted a yard from my head. The pieces flying from it stung my face. Another one. Closer. Somebody was telling me to get off the road. I jumped up and sprang over the wall. I don't remember landing on the other side, but then there I was, in the bushes, scared as hell.

I stumbled along the wall in a crouch. I was in a dream; the cracks and crevices and mossy gray loaves of stone that swept by my face were all the stuff that dreams are made on. I stopped and poked my head up over the wall for a second. I saw a man in a tan parka leaning against a great gray beech. His hood was up and he wore a balaclava helmet and dark aviator glasses. His face was totally hidden. He held a jet black rifle to his cheek. When he spied me, he swung the muzzle fast and shot. He was so fast that I saw the spark of flame before I moved. The slug whined off the top of the wall not two feet away, spewing up a little gray shower of shattered stone. I ducked down again and scampered toward the house as fast as I could. Roantis had not moved, not even a little.

Twenty yards from the house, I stood up and sprinted for the side door. I crossed the lawn and yanked at the brass handle. When it gave, I turned and looked back down the hill. The man in the tan parka was kneeling over Roantis. He had a knife in his

41

right fist. A black knife. He looked up. The huge, shiny black lenses stared up at me like the eyes of a gigantic praying mantis. In an instant the rifle was up and sparking. A slug tore into the doorframe above my head.

I yanked the door full open and skipped inside, stopping just long enough to slam the bolt shut behind me, then rushed into the kitchen to tell Mary to phone the police. But she'd obviously heard the shots and looked out the window. She had the phone to her ear, her face pale with shock. She drummed on the receiver button and clenched and unclenched her fist.

"Nothing, Charlie! The line's dead!"

"Figures. He sneaked up here early and cut the wire. Lock the front door, then lie down on the floor and don't move!"

I was about to go upstairs when I remembered Roantis's strange request of the night before. At least it had seemed strange then. I dashed into the porch and grabbed the Browning from the coffee table. When I drew the slide back, a cartridge flew out. So Liatis had primed it. I ran back to the side door. Cautiously, I leaned around and peered out the window. There was nobody in sight, but I couldn't see over the stone fence to the road. I marched through the entire downstairs, looking out all the windows. The man in the parka didn't seem to be anywhere around. I opened the door and went out. As I left, I heard Mary scream at me. It almost made me change my mind. I knew the pistol was no match for a rifle, especially in the hands of an expert like the fellow in the parka. But Roantis was in trouble.

I crept to the big oak that stands in our front yard and edged my face around it. I still could not see far enough down the road. I ran back to the house and told Mary to run through the orchard to the Burkes' and use their phone. She didn't like the idea, but when she heard Roantis had been hit she threw on her parka and skedaddled out the back. I crept back to the oak, then went on down to the stone fence. I saw Mr. Parka jog-trotting down the road. I stood, ready to go over the wall and help Roantis. I looked at the prone form. Hell, Liatis Roantis was dead.

Just then I saw a flicker of motion from the corner of my eye. Old insect eyes had turned to cover his retreat. He now saw me and swung the rifle low, shooting from the hip. There was a great popping and crashing among the stones of the wall, and I found myself down on the ground again, eating dirt for safety. An automatic rifle. I lost my temper then. Within two seconds I was hidden in a holly bush that was right behind the wall, the automatic held up in both hands. Aiming low, I pumped off two quick shots at the departing figure. As he turned again I pumped off two more, and saw him grab his thigh. He spun around like a ballerina and began a spastic hopping and jumping up the hill. I squeezed a careful one, aiming low, and took a big divot of turf just in front of his feet. He was hopping around like crazy now, plenty scared. Leave it to a bully to panic once the tables are turned. He finally disappeared into the woods, and I knew it would be stupid to follow.

I went to Roantis. He raised his right arm, then dropped it. He moaned once, then again. He wasn't dead . . . yet. Within a minute I heard sirens. Two police cruisers swung around the curve, lights flashing. They were followed by an ambulance. The ambulance attendants and I knelt over Roantis as the two cruisers sped away to search for the rifleman. Although I had no doubt slowed his departure, I had a feeling he was long gone.

Mary came down in time to see them place Roantis on the litter and carry it toward the ambulance. Her face was all puckered up and her eyes were wet. She clutched the down coat around her throat; her hair was blowing all around her head. Just then Roantis reached out and grabbed her sleeve. He squinted his half-open eyes at Mary.

"Daisy!" he whispered. *"Daisy!"*

4

I LISTENED to Mozart's "Little G-Minor" symphony as I drove home the syringe plunger, injecting a full cc of lidocaine into Arnold Lutzak's lower jaw. He was listening to the music too, through earphones. I've found that the earphones distract my patients. This is helpful, particularly during any procedure that results in what we physicians euphemistically call "discomfort."

Although my patient received two hefty jolts of the local, I wanted the distraction of the music as well. My psychiatrist friend Moe Abramson — who is crazy — likes to lull his patients with music too. And if that isn't enough, he has a tank full of hideous fish to ensure distraction.

It had been almost two weeks since Roantis had taken the rifle slug in his chest, and he was still alive. Not only that, he was recovering nicely. Why? God only knows. Considering the life he's led and the fact that he's still hanging around this planet, he must have a guardian angel somewhere up there. Or maybe *down* there. But there was another reason: he was wearing a leather jacket when he was shot, and he had stuffed a pair of thick leather mittens in the inside breast pocket. All that leather and fleece lining had helped to slow the slug. But mainly, I guess, Roantis survived because he's as tough as old hunting boots.

After the lidocaine took hold, I tapped the floor switch with my foot and summoned my assistant, Susan Petri. She appeared, complete with surgical mask and smock, and stood at my side holding the suction tube ready. I took the elevator and tweaked Arnold's third molar, then fastened the Hu-Friedy "Cowhorn" forceps around it and rocked it right out of its cradle. Blood flowed from Lutzak's mandible like the Hoover Dam had burst.

I had almost finished suturing when Susan popped her head around the corner to inform me that Chief Brian Hannon was on the phone. I finished the suture and inserted the gauze packing. Susan handed me the phone.

"Hey Doc, I'm here outside the Emerson Hospital OR. Doctor Nesbit — you know him? — who just finished working on Roantis, just gave me the slug they finally dug out of his rib cage. He says it's a good thing they waited; it was lodged right up against his spine. Our ballistics man says it's a three-o-eight slug. That's the same as the seven-point-six-millimeter round. It's the NATO round."

"Makes sense, Brian. It was an automatic rifle, and it looked like military issue to me, even from the fleeting glance I got of it."

"Oh yeah? Well, I don't know too much about rifle ammunition except the old stuff. Your friend's come around now and he wants to talk to you. Can you stop over when you're finished?"

"Uh-huh. I'll be there within the hour."

I stopped in to see Moe before I left the Concord Professional Building; his office is two doors down the hall from mine. I found him reclining in one of his Eames chairs. Two grand a crack. He was swiveling back and forth, back and forth, like the inertia wheel on one of those air clocks, humming Haydn to himself. His last patient had just departed.

He stared at me, head bowed slightly forward so he could see me over his half glasses. His face was covered with a close-cropped dark beard streaked with white. He had a high forehead that was straight and made more prominent by the thinning hair. Lots of gray matter in there. A bit warped, but plentiful. I was amazed that he made his living unwarping other people's heads.

"Yeah well?" he said.

45

"Just thought I'd pop in. My move?"

He swiveled ponderously in the great chair, pointing it in the direction of the chessboard like the gun turret of a battleship.

"Your move," he answered. "You lose in six."

"Bullshit. You're cooked, Moe, and you know it."

I examined the board closely for several minutes. I had been very cautious in this game because I was sick to death of losing to him. This time it was not going to happen. After several more minutes I advanced my knight. There. A nice cautious move. Offensive, but not bold. My pieces controlled the center and protected each other. I was in good shape. I grabbed the big beach stone with the arrow painted on it and turned it to face his side of the board. Moe leaned over and moved his bishop without studying the board. Then he turned the rock around.

"You lose in four," he said.

"Hmmmmmmmm," I said. It was the only comeback I could think of. "What makes you so sure?"

"Simple. Bishop to king four. You counter with pawn to king four. Knight to bishop six, *check.* King to bishop two. Bishop to knight six, check and *mate.*"

During this quick discourse, his thin fingers raced nimbly across the crowded board, picking up pieces and rearranging them like lightning. He laid out several scenarios in a twinkling, then took the game back to its present position. He had memorized it all, of course, just the way he had memorized all the previous twenty-some moves. He made me sick. All the scenarios he demonstrated looked very bleak for yours truly.

"So I lose in four, eh?"

" 'Fraid so. You should've kept that bishop's pawn back a rank earlier. That's where you blew it."

I kicked his desk, shaking all the pieces on the board, and cussed. Then I cussed because my foot hurt. Then I cussed him, saying I wasn't going to play anymore. So there.

"Now c'mon Doc. No need to be immature about it."

"Who's being immature?" I shouted. Then I told him if he called me immature one more time, I was going to hold my breath.

"Where are you going gin such a huff?"

46

"I'm going *gah,*" I said, "to see my friend Liatis Roantis, who's recovering from a bullet wound in his chest."

"Oh yeah. *Him.* Heinrich Himmler's nephew. You hang around wit' some weird guys, Doc."

"Uh-huh. Like the present company."

"Hmmmmph! You should be so lucky." He sniffed with his nose elevated. He rose and went over to the enormous tropical fish tank. He dropped in a pinch of Tetramin food and the tank boiled to life with scores of darting fish. They winked and glowed in the light and spun around the tank quicker than the eye could follow, grabbing the food flakes off the surface and diving back down among the plants and rocks. The plants and rocks held some loathsome sea creatures. I looked in warily.

"Now where the hell's that ugly thing? That bottom-feeder sea snake. Where?"

"You mean Ruth? My loach?"

"That's the one. Jeez Moe, even the name's repulsive. *Loach.* Sounds like a cross between leech and roach. Ugliest damn thing I ever — "

"Ruth died," he said plaintively.

"Well, hot damn. First good news I've had in weeks."

"I got a replacement. Of course he'll never take her place ..."

"What's he look like?"

"Uh, interesting."

I rose to leave.

"Wait Doc. Here he comes now. See, behind dat coral fan? Here he comes. C'mon Charlie ... C'mon boy ... He's shy."

"Why do you call him Charlie?"

"Named him after you, Doc. Who knows? Maybe I'll teach him to play chess. C'mon. Atta boy — "

A horrid, flat-headed creature oozed out from behind the coral. It was purplish gray and blotched. Its wide head had two popeyes. Its sucking mouth sprouted whiskers: long, pointy tendrils of pink flesh that waved and flipped about obscenely. Suddenly it snapped upward, wriggling snakelike through the water, then slammed itself against the side of the aquarium, affixing its mouth and flat belly to the smooth glass. In the center of this pink-gray nightmare of flattened tissue, a raspy radula pulsed. On its back, just behind each glaring eye, a foul hole snapped open and shut, open and shut, with its breathing.

I wanted to puke.

"Whaddayuh think, Doc?"

"What do I think? I *can't* think. I'm too nauseated. I'm leaving. Moe, you need professional help."

"But I *am* professional help."

I left the lost chess game, my cuckoo-genius friend, and my repulsive namesake and hotfooted it over to the hospital. I timed my arrival perfectly; Brian Hannon had just finished speaking with Roantis and was talking with the surgeon, Bill Nesbit. They said I could go on up to see my battered soldier friend.

Roantis was sitting up in bed watching a TV game show. It was some kind of association game. "Ready?" said the host. "Okay: *banana.*" As soon as he said the word, a big clock started ticking with chimes. The young housewife clenched her fists and jumped up and down, her eyes shut tight in concentration. "Uh . . . uh . . . *ape!*" she screamed. But the clock kept going.

"Ohhh! . . . Uh . . . uh . . . *Chiquita!*" Nope. Still incorrect. *AWWWWWNK!* came the buzzer, and the poor housewife went limp. "Awwwwww!" said the audience. "I'm sorry, Mrs. Kemp," said the host, "the correct word was *split.*" The crowd murmured in sympathy. "But," he retorted, "before you go away mad, look what you've *won!*" Bugles sounded. A big curtain swept up to reveal a trash compactor. The crowd said, "Oooooooooooooo!"

I flipped the set off.

"Hey Doc — Why'd you turn off my show?"

"You weren't really watching that trash, were you?"

"Why not? It's kinda cute. See, each player tries to think of a word. Then they — "

"I don't want to hear it. I see you've been making excellent progress. Hard to believe that two weeks ago I would've sworn you were dead. They were smart not to remove the slug until your strength was back. When do you go home?"

He frowned and sank lower into the covers.

"Not for ten more days. Maybe more."

"Well that's not too bad. You could use a rest anyway. And

some time off the booze. They say your liver looks as big as a beachball."

"Ahhhh screw 'em!" he said, waving his hand impatiently. "That's not what I'm worried about. Listen: I got no health insurance. You know what the bill's gonna be for this? About ten grand."

"Sounds about right."

"Yeah. And I got no savings either. How am I gonna pay? Doc, I gotta get that statue now. *Gotta!*"

"We'll talk about that later."

"We'll talk now. Look!" He pulled the front of his hospital johnny down, revealing his bare neck. "He took my key. That's why the guy shot me, Doc. To get my key. Christ, he's probably been there and gone by now. With my gold Siva!"

I thought back to that morning on the frozen road, to the man in the tan parka with the black knife in his hand hunkered down over Roantis. That was what the knife was for: to cut the thin chain from his neck and take the safe deposit key.

"The gunman knows you, Liatis. He knew about the key and he knows you. Who is he?"

"I don't know, I never saw him."

"You spent a lot of time looking out our porch windows, remember? And you asked for my automatic before you went to sleep. You knew something was up. What?"

"I don't know exactly. Just something. It's an instinct I've developed, I guess. I knew something had happened to Ken and I suspected it had to do with the loot. I still think that. That's why I came to you in the first place. Thing is, before it was just something I wanted for myself and my son. Now it's something I need."

He reached out to grab the water pitcher on the table but couldn't do it. Wincing, he returned his arm to its resting place across his chest. Nesbit had done his cutting from the back, but any arm movement on Roantis's part picked up painful signals from the severed tissue. It must have hurt; I saw a shiny film of sweat along his brow and chin — and Liatis Roantis knew pain as most of us know our shadows.

I picked up the water pitcher and poured him a glass, but he told me it was the paper underneath the glass that I was to take. I picked it up and saw a list of names and addresses: Jusuelo, Kaunitz, Royce, Summers, and Vilarde. The Daisy Ducks. After each name was an address and a phone number.

"Did some checking up while lying here on my back. Those are the last known addresses. Can't say for sure on any of them except Royce. I'm pretty sure he's still at the VA hospital in Manila. They've got him in a padded cell and he's never getting out."

"He violent?"

Roantis shrugged and yawned. "Who knows? Maybe. He's wacko though. Summers is probably still in Chicago if he's not dead yet. But Vilarde's da guy I want."

"Liatis, which of these guys shot you?"

He shook his head slowly back and forth on the pillow.

"Doc, it wasn't any of 'em. Trust me. The only one of them who knows about the Siva is Ken, and it couldn't be him. I'm giving you the list because these guys are good leads to finding him."

"You're sure."

"I'm positive. What I'm not positive of, I'm not positive he dint tell any of the others. I don't think he'd do that, but you never know. A lot of time has passed and we were all pretty close."

"If you were all so close, then why not sell the statue and split the cash eight ways instead of two?"

"It was hard enough trying to split it two ways. Can you imagine eight guys — scattered all over the globe, God knows where — each waiting for his hunk of the loot? The way it was, I took none of the first loot Siu Lok dished out, those gold pieces and gems. I gave them to the guys. Old Siu Lok took *me* to that cache in the dead of night. Me alone."

"So who was the rifleman? Who knows you well enough to have tracked you down to my place? Somebody must have been tailing you for days, Liatis. Who was it? If not one of the Ducks, then who?"

He gave me the weary headshake again.

"It was a three-o-eight slug," I continued. "That's the same as the NATO round."

50

"I can tell you right now what the rifle looked like, okay, Doc? Can you remember it in your mind? It was jet black, with a black plastic forepiece with three vent holes in the side. Barrel projecting from the lower part of the forestock, and a carrying handle above the receiver."

"I can't remember it clearly. I saw it mostly from the muzzle end."

"It was a Belgian FAL rifle. Take my word for it. I know. It's the mercenary's rifle, worldwide. But that still leaves it open. I know quite a few mercs, and some of them don't like me."

"All right. But he took the key. He knew you were wearing it and snipped it off you. You looked dead enough, so he didn't finish you with his black knife."

"A black knife. You sure it was black?"

"As coal."

Roantis stroked his stubbled chin in thought. He pointed at the paper I held in my hands.

"Find Vilarde. If I saved your life you can help me find Vilarde. Besides, you're getting paid, too."

The phone on the bedside table rang and I picked it up. It was Roantis's wife, Suzanne. I handed the receiver to him and he grunted into it. He grunted again, and again, and his face grew agitated. Then he swore, sighed, and seemed to collapse into the pillow. His eyes were closed. I thought he'd passed out, but then the eyes opened again.

"Read it to me again," he said.

There was a pause, then another sigh.

"Yeah, okay. I figured as much. What was the date again? Yeah. No, nothing we can do. But I've got some good help, so don't worry. Huh? His name is Charles Adams, you remember him. He's standing right here."

I was not heartened by this monologue. I went over to the guest chair and sank down into it. I smelled the bouquet sent to Roantis by the Boston Tai Kwon Do Club. It didn't smell nice. Nothing would have. Roantis hung up and glared at me.

"We just got a fancy receipt from Barclays Bank in Kowloon. Guess what it says?"

"That the golden statue has danced right out of his hiding place."

"Right. According to their records, Ken and I took possession of the contents of Box 1001 at ten-thirty on the morning of December thirty-first. The last day of the year. That's two days after I was shot."

"And you're still positive Ken Vilarde didn't shoot you?"

"Just find him, Doc. Or find out what's happened to him." He sank back into the pillow and closed his eyes. I left the room.

As I descended the stairs, I turned on the landing and found myself looking into a pair of shiny black eyes that were level with mine. The eyes were surrounded by flawless olive skin. A small delicate nose. Full lips that pouted a little. Jet black hair that glowed. The eyes were almond-shaped, the cheekbones wide and high. It was an Asian face that was staring at me. The straight black hair was gathered in a bun behind the woman's head, and fine tendrils of it drifted around her beautiful face. The eyes and face bore a look of sublime seriousness.

She was a six-footer — unheard of in Asian females. I quickly looked down at her feet. Was she wearing high-heeled boots? No, moccasins. Was she Mongolian? The North Chinese are huge. But her face wasn't Mongolian. The skin was too dark and the face too rounded. She looked Vietnamese. A gorgeous Vietnamese giant. How long did I stand gaping at her? Six months?

"Excuse me," I murmured, too bewitched to move.

She didn't reply. I was dying to hear her voice, but she slipped by me, silent as a wraith. Just as our faces met she smiled quickly. Beautiful. The last I saw of her was from behind, her lithe form dressed in white jeans and a ski parka, rounding the turn on the landing to continue up the stairway. Then she was gone.

5

I WENT HOME after that and made a pot of steaming keemun, which I drank in the living room while holding the list in front of me. Certainly Roantis needed help; he was dead broke and soon would be over his head in debt. And I owed him a big favor.

Big, but not huge.

The five-by-seven list in my hand looked huge. It had the presence of the Magna Carta or the Declaration of Independence. I picked up the phone and dialed the overseas operator. Manila was on the opposite side of the globe from Boston. I told the operator I wanted to place a call to the U.S. military hospital there at ten P.M., which would be midmorning over there. Next I called the number after Vilarde's name. Out of service. So much for that. I called Rosie Vilarde in LA. No answer. I called the Flying K Ranch in Leander, Texas, and asked to speak to Fred Kaunitz. A nice lady with a heavy Mexican accent said that Señor Kaunitz was "no en casa" at the moment. I left a message for him to call me back collect, saying I was a close friend of a mutual friend, Liatis Roantis. I wasn't certain she got the message entirely correct, but it was clear enough. Back to Rosie Vilarde, still not home. On to Mike Summers. Last known address was 5472 South Woodlawn, in the Hyde Park section of the

53

South Side of Chicago. As a sometime visitor to the University of Chicago, I was acquainted with the area. Parts of Hyde Park are very nice. Other sections are very mean. The address indicated that Summers lived north of the Midway Plaisance, which meant it was probably decent. South of the Midway, you might need an armored personnel carrier to get around safely. There was no number. I called Information and was told there were eight or nine Michael Summerses in Hyde Park. None lived at 5472 South Woodlawn. I finally boiled it down to three likely prospects, and struck out on all of them. Next I tried the Summerses under women's names. I finally found it under Ella C. Summers, 9605 South Blackstone. Ella herself answered, saying she was Mikey's mamma. Mikey worked for a security company, night shift. She didn't know where he was now. Probably down at the Blue Flame Lounge around the corner.

It didn't sound as if Michael Summers, formerly of the Daisy Ducks, had found himself a comfy and lucrative niche in the civilian world. I asked Ella Summers to have Mike call me collect when he returned. I did not expect him to take me up on my offer, but I'd keep trying anyway.

I went out to the florist's and bought Mary a dried flower arrangement as a token of peace. Then I went to the wool shop and bought her some new tartan cloth that had just arrived from the Outer Hebrides. She could sew herself a kilt from it. A couple of silver Scottish thistle pins completed the package. These I gift-wrapped and placed on the hall table. I was not trying to buy her off; one does not buy off a woman like Mary. I was just trying to smooth the way a little. She had remained pleasant, but distant, during the past two weeks.

Mary got home at four-thirty. She loved the gifts. That was a real smile on her face. But somehow, the feeling that usually came out at me through her eyes didn't. It wasn't there.

Dinner would cheer her up. I had been marinating lamb shanks in olive oil, lemon juice, garlic, wine, and crushed herbs and mint leaves. These I browned in oil, then baked in a covered pan with some of the marinade still in the pan, which was, in effect, braising them. I served them on a bed of rice pilaf with a Greek salad and a carafe of red. We sat in the kitchen nook, watching the news as we ate.

"What are you thinking?" I asked.

"I don't know," she said absently. "I guess I feel rather unfulfilled lately. Did I tell you I'm going to visit my mother next month?"

"No. First I've heard of it. Want me to come along?"

"Won't you be busy?"

"Actually, the office is being redone. Remember? I think I'll have about a week."

"Oh, I don't know . . ."

I suddenly felt she was a million miles away. I felt all alone: the boys were back at school, not to return again until semester break. We cleaned up and Mary went into her pottery workshop while I returned to the study. I sat at my desk and looked at the rows of books in their shelves . . . out the window at the bare apple trees. Mary, I thought, I'm smothering in your distance. Drowning in your coldness. If it's just a game, please don't play it anymore. It hurts.

Fred Kaunitz called me at seven o'clock, six Texas time. I keep thinking that Texas is way out West. Not so; it's way down South, at least the eastern half, and in the Central Time Zone. His voice was deep and confident, with a relaxed drawl reminiscent of Don Meredith.

"So you know Roantis. Is he still in trouble?"

"Uh-huh. With practically everyone."

There was a dry chuckle at the other end.

"Figures. He was a hell of a good team leader though. I'll never forget Liatis, though I'd like to forget those days entirely. Still have some bad dreams about 'em. He tell you what we did over there?"

"Yes. He's anxious to find Ramon Vilarde. I guess you called him Ken."

"Yeah. Well, I don't know where he is, Dr. Adams. You know, those guys in the Ducks were a strange breed. They could be anywhere, doing anything. We were like coati bears over there. Roaming around getting into all kinds of trouble, living off the land . . . destroying as we went."

"Fred, do you have the faintest hunch where Vilarde might be?"

"No. I'd think Liatis would know better than anyone since they were close. I think Ken was also close to Jesus Jusuelo. Last I heard, he was going to be a lifer."

"Right. But then he got divorced, and quit the army, too. He was last living in DC. About two months ago he called Roantis to say he was flying up to meet him. Then he disappeared."

"Maybe he just changed his mind. Who knows? Maybe an overseas job came up. Does Roantis think something bad happened to him?"

"Frankly, yes. Do you know anyone, in the Ducks or otherwise, who had it in for Ken?"

"Nope. But that sure doesn't mean there weren't any. Not in that line of work."

I finished the conversation by asking Fred Kaunitz three questions. The first was whether or not he had any desire to see his old team commander again. He answered sure, but he wouldn't go far out of his way to see Roantis, saying he wished to put as much of that part of his life behind him as possible. The second question dealt with Siu Lok's loot. Did Fred get any of it? What did he do with it? He took his share of the gold and silver and emeralds and cashed it in at a Tokyo shop. He spent the money on books, artwork, and three Japanese swords. The third question was whether he would be willing to meet with me for a few hours in early March, when I'd be in Texas for the annual convention of the College of Oral Surgery. He said fine, and that ended it.

I lighted a pipe and sat at my desk looking at the list of Daisy Ducks. Jesus Jusuelo. What sort of fellow was he? Roantis had said the best of the best as far as soldiering was concerned: a Navy SEAL. But I'd heard amazing things about the SEALs. Scary things. Apparently their training included some sort of dehumanizing process that was much more pronounced than the ordinary military variety. Some people said the SEALs were the closest things to killing robots ever produced. I hoped that one of the Ducks knew his whereabouts. Certainly knowing only that he was on the continent of Africa wouldn't do us any good. But even if I could find out where he was, I wasn't sure I ever wanted to get within five miles of him.

Just before ten the overseas operator rang up, saying I could place my call to Manila. I talked briefly to the staff at the VA hospital. Information on patients was strictly confidential. I said I understood, but could they tell me if Bill Royce was currently a patient there? They said they'd check, and they did. Bill Royce was no longer a patient. He had been discharged in late June. Where had he gone? They didn't know or wouldn't say.

I brooded over this interesting piece of news, thinking how timely it was that Royce was sprung just a few months before Vilarde disappeared. Probably just coincidence.

Afterward, I read magazines until midnight. Actually, I looked at the pages and pictures and thought about Mary and me, and what the hell was happening. What *was* happening? Then I trudged upstairs. Mary had been asleep for an hour. At one-thirty the phone rang. In a panic, I grabbed it. It was either a crank call or an emergency. Like any parent with children away from home, I dreaded the late phone call.

"Chief? Hey chief!"

The voice was heavy and slurred. The man sounded black. I brusquely told the caller he had the wrong number and hung up. But just before I returned to sleep a thought slipped into my head, and before I fully considered it, the phone rang again.

"Hey chief! That you?"

"Is this Mike Summers?"

"Yeah, tha's right. Who's this?"

Summers was apparently calling from the Blue Flame Lounge. A saxophone squeaked and honked in the background. There was the loud murmur of a crowded night spot.

"This is Charles Adams. I'm a friend of Liatis Roantis, who's just recovering from a gunshot wound. Can you talk for a minute?"

Mary had turned on the light. She sat up in bed, squinting and frowning.

"Yeah I can talk. On your nickel. I'm about busted, man. Where's Roantis?"

"In the hospital. It's a long story. Can I call you back tomorrow morning?"

"Yeah, lemme give you a number."

"Who is it, Charlie? What time is it?" asked Mary.

"It's late. It's one of the Daisy Ducks: Summers."

But Mary was unimpressed. She was even annoyed, and

57

flumped back down and turned over, growling. I copied down the number Summers gave me and went to sleep.

"And so that's it. Royce is out, but God knows where. Maybe he isn't exactly sure where he is. That leaves Jusuelo and Vilarde not pinned down. Your guess is still as good as mine."

Roantis squinted at me over the rim of his glass. It was a novel experience seeing him drink water. He sank back on his pillow and stared at the ceiling.

"How did Summers sound to you?" he asked.

"Wasted. He was drunk when he first called me and shaky as hell next morning. It seems the security firm just fired him too. He doesn't know how long he can keep his tiny apartment in the ghetto, and his mother is moving to her sister's in St. Louis. I think when she splits he'll go down the chute real fast."

"Shit," murmured Roantis under his breath. He shook his head slowly back and forth on the pillow, then lighted a Camel. I don't know how he got the cigarettes; the doctors had nixed them. "I tell ya Doc, this soldiering sucks the heart right out of you. Then it takes the center of your soul and rots it away. Summers had a lot of potential. A shame."

"I'm going out to Texas to see Kaunitz in March."

"Yeah? Good. Freddie's a good kid. Kid? Hell, he's pushing forty by now. He speaks good Spanish, you know."

"So?"

"Just crossed my mind. I remember him talking to Ken and Jesus in Spanish a lot of the time. I guess a lot of people in Texas speak Spanish."

"On the way back from Texas, I've got a two-hour layover in Chicago between flights. I've talked Summers into taking the train out to the airport and meeting me there for an hour."

Roantis smiled up at me, remarking that it was nice I'd decided to accept his offer. I replied that I had not accepted the offer. I was merely gathering a little preliminary information for him. No way had I accepted the offer.

But he kept smiling at me. Why was he smiling?

"Where's Bill Royce gone?" I asked, changing the subject.

He shrugged his shoulders in thought.

"He's from North Carolina someplace. A little town up in the mountains near Tennessee. Show me a map, I could remember the name. A lot of the recon men were from the Smokies. Good in the wilderness, you know? Anyway, maybe he's gone home. I don't know. And maybe he's fine now. He was a nice guy when he was with us. Then he cracked. He was real unstable then, and dangerous."

"How did he get along with Vilarde?"

"Fine. I tell you, Doc, I don't think he had anything to do with Ken's disappearance or with shooting me. A lot of people don't like me, you know."

"I can understand that. But Bill Royce should be checked out. How many days and nights did it take you to get back after you took the statue?"

"Two days and two nights."

"And during that time, could any of the other Ducks have discovered the Siva in your pack while you slept?"

"Uh-huh. Sure."

"And what would they have thought if word got out that you had it?"

"Hard to say. Anything could happen. But it would be unlike them to go through my stuff."

"Yeah. But were the packs private? I mean, didn't each of you carry stuff for the whole team? What if they were just looking for something and didn't want to wake you up?"

"Could happen. Could happen easy."

"Is Suzanne picking you up this afternoon?"

"She was. But the car's busted again. Guess I'll take the bus."

"No you won't. I'll drive you home. I'll come back at three when they discharge you."

I was out the door before I remembered the beautiful woman I had seen on the stairs.

"Hey Liatis, you don't happen to know a gorgeous Asian girl about six feet tall, do you? Wears a white ski parka and her hair up in a bun?"

"No, why?"

I explained the chance meeting, and he cussed me out, saying I should have sent her to his room. I left him lying in bed, watching *All My Children.*

59

6

I PICKED ROANTIS UP at the hospital at three, as promised. But I had decided not to take him back to his apartment in Jamaica Plain. How could I be sure that whoever took a shot at him wasn't going to try again? Brian Hannon's detectives could find no trace of the lone gunman around Concord. Was he still in the vicinity? It seemed he was only interested in the key, and that he'd gotten what he was after. But who knew? Maybe he wanted Roantis dead.

So I'd called Suzanne and convinced her to pack clothes for both of them. She didn't need much persuading, and one quick look at her small apartment told me why. Suzanne Murzicki Roantis was a pretty, petite, brown-haired woman ten years younger than her husband. She had a nice pair of big blue eyes. But years of living with a professional soldier–karate champ had taken their toll: the eyes were dulled, the face around them lined with worry wrinkles. Poor kid; she needed a break — probably even more than Roantis. Suzanne was with me when I waited at the desk for them to wheel out the ex-mercenary. He was momentarily taken aback and confused when he saw us together, then gave his wife a dutiful hug and kiss from his wheelchair and stared blankly ahead while I wheeled him out into the parking lot. We got him settled comfortably in the Audi's front seat and headed for the Adams household.

"What's going on?" he asked finally as I helped him into an overstuffed chair in the living room. "And how about a drink, Doc?"

"Nix on the booze. You remember what the doctors told you. If you can stay off the stuff for another month or so, you'll be in good shape. Now, later tonight Mary and I are going to drive you and Suzanne down to Cape Cod. We're going to put you up at our cottage, where you can recover in peace and safety. Nobody else knows where you're going. In six or eight weeks, you should be almost as good as new."

Surprisingly, he didn't fight it. The bullet had apparently sapped a bit of his cussedness. I wheeled him into the kitchen to help prepare dinner. I knew that a lot of protein would help him heal, so Mary and I had put a huge standing rib in the oven. Roantis made the mashed potatoes while Suzanne helped me make dressing for the salad. When Mary and I make blue cheese dressing we add onions, capers, seasoned black pepper, and a dash of white vinegar to the cheese and oil, and blend these in the food processor before adding the mayonnaise and additional crumbled blue cheese. It gives the dressing more bite, makes it less heavy and cloying. We poured this liberally over big lettuce wedges. With the meat, potatoes, and buttered broccoli, it was quite a feed. We ate in the kitchen nook, and when Roantis sat down, he stared at the sprig of prickly ash that Mary had set in a vase in the middle of the table.

"Where'd you get that?" he asked, not taking his eyes off it.

"At Lexington Gardens, especially for you, Liatis," said Mary.

Roantis broke off a sprig and sniffed it. He placed it in his breast pocket so he could smell the aromatic oil. The prickly ash is a member of the rue family. To all Lithuanians, the rue plants are special, almost sacred. No Lithuanian household, either in the old country or America, is complete without them. Rue plants are to the Balts what the shamrock is to the Irish, the thistle is to the Scots. "Thank you, Mary," was all he said. But his eyes said it all. Then he dug into the grub like there was no tomorrow.

61

After dinner, we returned to the living room with coffee. Roantis was quieter and more subdued than I had ever seen him. He looked positively elderly.

"We're not going to start until around midnight," I told him. "Mary's brother, Joe, advised this. He says that any tails will be easy to spot then. As additional insurance, we'll have Joe with us in an unmarked state car. Liatis, we've notified the BYMCU that you'll be on leave for at least six weeks. All we want you to do is lie low, relax, and eat well. If you behave, nature will do the rest."

He nodded, placid as a sheep. Roantis was a changed man.

At ten minutes after midnight we swept out of the driveway, followed by Joe in his unmarked car. We arrived at the Adams cottage, the Breakers, at two-thirty. The cottage sits on a bluff off Sunken Meadow Road in the town of North Eastham. It overlooks Cape Cod Bay. We trundled down the sandy footpath in the dark to the gray, cedar-shingled house, painted with white and navy blue trim. All was dark and quiet. There had been no sign of a tail along the way. After a mug of coffee, Joe climbed back into his cruiser and left. He'd just given up five hours of his off-duty time to see Roantis safely stowed. Typical.

Next morning after breakfast, Mary and I went into Wellfleet and bought several weeks' worth of groceries for Liatis and Suzanne. We didn't skimp on the grub, laying in lots of steaks and lamb chops. We stocked the freezer and refrigerator, and I left Suzanne with $200, despite her protests, to tide them over until our next visit. Roantis sat in front of the stone fireplace, soaking up the heat and looking out over Cape Cod Bay. In midafternoon, he discovered the stereo system and the collection of classical tapes. He played them continually and scarcely moved until suppertime. Suzanne told me she'd never seen him so relaxed.

"It's not relaxation, Suzanne," said Mary, who was throwing leaves of romaine into a huge teak bowl, "it's resignation. It's his sense of survival talking to him. Finally, after years of self-destructive behavior, common sense is getting the floor. Charlie, do you think it's a good idea for Liatis to see Moe a few times?"

"A very good idea, if Moe's willing."

"But Moe loves helping people. I'm sure he wouldn't even charge anything."

"I know. But I don't know how keen Moe would be on trying to reform a professional soldier. The fire on the grill is almost ready. Where's that meat?"

Mary handed me a fat beef tenderloin, which I rubbed with peanut oil, took outside to the deck, and placed in the covered smoker-grill. Soon delicious aromas emerged from the contraption's top in the form of light blue smoke, which swarmed around the cottage walls in the sea breeze. I threw on a down vest and sat on a beach chair to watch the sun go down over the bay. It was warm for midwinter and, if you managed to avoid the direct breeze and sit in the sun, almost balmy. Roantis came out and joined me.

Suzanne appeared at his side and handed him a mug of hot chocolate, which he sipped. I heard a faint whine and growl off to my left and turned to see a coastal trawler inching along the horizon toward Wellfleet. Ahead of it was a low, dusky patch of darkness on the water. Billingsgate Shoal. I thought back to the close calls I'd had in connection with that sunken island and felt a big adrenaline rush. There was fear there, too — but the surge of excitement muted it and won out. I remembered my adventure, how I'd prevailed against substantial odds, and the rush grew. Sad to say, we live in a world in which risk is minimized or nonexistent. Most things are taken care of for us. And life, while comfortable and safe, has lost its challenge. We slip through our days in tired, pathetic routines, as if smeared with petroleum jelly. And then comes old age and death and we look back and ask ourselves, what have we done with our lives except follow the dots and mark time? Adventure is absent from twentieth-century life, and it's a damn shame. I had to admit that Roantis's predicament sounded more and more attractive to me. I couldn't help it. I turned back to the scarred and gnarled man who sat next to me, sipping from the steaming mug.

"Tell me a little bit about professional soldiering, Liatis. Who are these guys, and where do they hang out? And why were you so sure about the kind of rifle that was used to shoot you?"

"Hmmmmn," he said. "Mercking is dying out, I think. The

63

world won't stand for it much longer. Not that it's not needed sometimes. Sometimes it's the only way out. But I guess in twenty years or so there won't be any more mercs. Where do they hang out? The big European cities, especially Paris, Marseilles, and the ones in Switzerland. Then there are the better cities of the Far East, like Kyoto, Hong Kong, and Bangkok. A lot of 'em can be found in Manila and Sydney, too. South America's full of them: Rio, Buenos Aires, Caracas . . ."

"How about here?"

"In America, the best single city is probably Miami. Why? Because it's a wide-open town, for one thing. Shit — with all the drug dealing and Mob hits going down, a merc doesn't stand out, you know? Good place to lie low and look for action. Also, Miami's close to Mexico, the Caribbean, and South America. They're all just a short hop away. DC's another place. You'd be surprised how many contacts you can make there. More than half the American mercs I know have worked for the Agency at one time or another. There's always some dirty little job they want done. And they pay like crazy, too."

"C'mon Liatis, I have trouble believing that."

"Suit yourself."

"How many mercs are there in Boston?"

"Ha! Boston? Probably none except me. But there're some in rural New England . . . You can bet on it. See Doc, there are basically two kinds of men who go into this line of work, this life. First, there's your sicko killer types. These guys are a little off in the head, you know? They like to kill people. Period. If they can do it legally and get paid too, so much the better. These guys usually have military or law enforcement backgrounds, but they're not really soldiers. They're misfits. They'll take any job that comes their way, any excuse to pull that trigger. They'll work for any government, even a ruthless dictatorship. These guys you'll generally find in the big cities, bumming around in bars and cathouses. They're scum. I've never worked with them and never will."

"And the second type?" said Mary, who had come out on the deck with Suzanne. She snuggled down into her parka, drawing the collar tight around her neck. "How is the second type any better?"

64

"Well, the other type is a true professional soldier. Generally he's spent ten to twenty years in a major military service and has a good track record in elite forces. He doesn't like to kill people, but is good at it when he must. This man is guided by strong opinions and political ideals. He will take on only those contracts which he feels will benefit the world as well as his wallet. He's a professional soldier because it's what he knows and does well. Almost always, this man has another source of income besides soldiering, since he's picky about his merc contracts."

"And what's this other source of income?" I asked.

"Could be just about anything. With me, it's teaching martial arts. I know several mercs who are couriers and bodyguards. Two guys I know own bars. One is a heavy hauler. A lot of them are ranchers or construction workers. Quite a few are in the security equipment or firearms business. Some are bush pilots. It all depends. But this second-type guy, chances are he won't hang around the big cities trying to make a contact. He's good enough so people find *him*. Also, he's a loner. You won't find him working for somebody else, certainly not at a desk job. Chances are, he'll be out in the country where he can hunt, fish, screw off, and do what he damn well pleases."

"And that's why you said there are mercs in rural New England?"

"Yeah. Especially upcountry in Vermont, New Hampshire, and Maine. But even more down in the southern mountains . . . around the Smokies and the Blue Ridge. I can't think how many great trackers and recon men came from there. Been doin' it since they were toddlers, practically. So don't look for these guys in the city dives. You'll find them out in the boonies, but only if they want to be found. Otherwise, forget it."

"And you're the second type, of course," said Mary.

"Of course. See Mary, I was forced into soldiering by the Germans. I killed a man when I was a teenager. I shot the soldier who killed my best friend. Then I had to leave Lithuania with some of my buddies because the Nazis were hunting us. We wound up in England, where we joined the Polish Resistance under Sossobowski. I fought in Operation Market Garden as a paratrooper at sixteen. I guess I don't know anything *but* soldiering."

65

We took the meat off the grill and hustled it inside, where I sliced it into juicy fillets. Roantis tucked into the steak like a lion on the Serengeti. Afterward, when Mary and Suzanne were talking over coffee in the kitchen, he and I sat in the study corner of the living room and talked about military small arms.

"How come you're so sure about the appearance of the rifle that shot you?" I asked.

"Because I know the kinds of rifles mercs use, that's why. The modern military small arm is called the assault rifle. It's an automatic rifle that can be fired as a semi-auto single-shot."

"I know."

"Right. Now the U.S. military has adopted the Colt M-Sixteen as our standard military arm. Too bad. That two-twenty-three cartridge just can't hack it. Although it's a good rifle for women and Asians, who are small. They like the li'l two-twenty-three Armalite because it's lightweight and doesn't kick. Now, on the wrong side of the iron curtain is the Kalishnikov, the AK-Forty-seven. Nice rifle. Practically foolproof . . . and fires a hefty round, too. Remember Doc, we used the Kalishnikovs in the Daisy Ducks. We carried very little spare ammo with us — we dint need it."

"And the others?"

"Well, Germany, Switzerland, and Italy all make very nice combat rifles. Israel and Finland both make nice ones too, based on the Russian design. But the best is the Fusile Automatique Légère, the FAL, made by Fabrique Nationale in Belgium. It's used by most of the NATO forces and has been the standard British rifle for a long time. It's top of the line. Accurate, dependable, and fires a hefty three-o-eight round. They sell for two grand — and that's military issue, with no fancy custom work."

I whistled. "And so that's what was used on you?"

"I'm willing to stake heavy bucks on it. What I keep saying is: the guy was a pro. Don't you go after him, Doc. I know you're good and smart, but leave this guy alone. You're in enough trouble with him already, shooting him in the leg. He's probably still pissed at you. And these guys, they don't go to court. They go for your throat."

"So you don't want me to help?"

"I do want you to help. I want you to find Vilarde. Just lay off the other trails. Don't try to find the marksman. Hell, he's out of the country now anyway. Let him be. I'll go for him later. How long am I supposed to stay here?"

"About a month. Maybe longer."

"And how much will I owe you?"

"Nothing. It's all been taken care of."

"Bullshit. How much?"

"Nothing. Anyway, your being here sure isn't costing me anything except a couple of bucks for food. Just relax and rest up. If I get a solid lead on Vilarde, I'll want you healthy enough to go looking for him — because I'm not going."

"Look Doc, we both know I can't pay you back now. But remember, we get the Siva, you get your part of the cut and all the expenses too, okay?"

"Yeah. Don't worry about it. Don't worry about a thing except healing. See how little you can drink and how much you can eat and sleep."

Mary and I pulled out of there the next morning after coffee. We turned out of the drive and headed into Wellfleet to our market, instructing the owner to put every and all purchases made by Mrs. Roantis on our tab — no arguments.

An hour from home, Mary asked me if Roantis and I had discussed the cost of his little respite on the Cape.

"No. In fact, I told him it wasn't costing me anything. I said that so he wouldn't feel bad."

"Jeez Charlie, it's cost us over five grand already. You didn't tell him you'd paid Bill Nesbit's fee, plus a portion — a hefty portion — of the hospital charges?"

"No. Not yet anyway."

"And what are the odds, do you think, of Roantis's ever paying you back?"

"Slim. As slim as spider's silk. But the odds of my being here now in one piece would be nonexistent if he hadn't saved my skin in the parking lot."

"I know. I think we're doing the right thing. Maybe you shouldn't even tell him."

"I'm not going to tell him unless we recover the golden statue. Then I'll hand him the tab."

She sat in thought for a minute, then asked me what the odds were of actually recovering the gold Siva.

"Uh . . . slim. As slim — "

" — as spider's silk. I thought so."

7

MOE TURNED the small aluminum crank and the windowpanes squeaked and squealed their way open, letting in the breeze that was colder by the minute. He bent his tall wiry frame over to peer out the tiny aft window of his ancient Airstream trailer.

"Gonna snow, Doc. Feel it?"

"Uh-huh. Haven't you eaten yet? Maybe I'm here too early."

"Dinner's almost ready. Want to join me?"

He took four plastic bags out of his breadbox, along with a black loaf of Russian rye bread. He put a big hunk of bread and some cream cheese on a plate and from the bags took out dried apricots, apple slices, soybeans, and cracked wheat. To top it off, he placed a patty of tofu on the plate and covered it with two scoops of steaming bulgur.

"You're not really going to eat that, are you?" I asked.

"Yes, and so should you," he replied, taking the plate and a glass of skim milk into the living room, which was built onto the aluminum trailer. He dug in, washing it down with sips of the bluish-gray milk.

"Gee, you really know how to live it up. Do you have any cold cuts?"

He held up his hands as if to fend off evil spirits and moaned

69

and grunted as he chewed. He made the same gestures of repulsion when I inquired after other foods I liked. I could see myself starving to death if I had to stay in Moe's trailer home for more than a week. As it was, I was merely stopping over for a quiet game of chess and some nice conversation. I watched Moe eat and sipped my beer. Outside, the two Nubian goats bawled. The wood stove tinked and purred, making the air above it dance.

"Where's the picture?" he asked.

I flipped the photo over to him. He stared at it and shook his gray head.

"Dis isn't good, Doc. Not good at all. Siva is the evil form of the Hindu god — a dancing demon devil. Not good."

"It's a goddamn statue, Moe. Period."

He shook his head again and looked me in the eye.

"I'm concerned about you, Doc. So is Mary. I know because we've had a little talk about you. I heard all that happened at your party a few weeks ago, including the fondling of Janice DeGroot. Now that's not the first time that's happened. You seem to be looking for any kind of trouble you can find. Why?"

"I don't know why. It's just that life seems, well, a little stale lately. It seems to have lost its spark."

"Well if you're not careful, *you're* going to lose your spark. You are fast becoming an adult delinquent."

I pondered these words. As usual, Moe was correct. It was time to quit moping about the imponderables and to make sure I held on to what I had, which was considerable. I heard a faint whisper against the windowpanes. The snow had begun. In much of literature, I had read somewhere, snow symbolizes death. Is that what it meant then? The death of a relationship? Were Mary and I simply having a difficult time, or was this the beginning of the end? I thought it could never happen to me, but most people probably think that. Half the marriages end in divorce now. And divorce is not confined to brief marriages, either. I bowed my head and ran my hands through my hair. I think I must have sighed, because Moe looked up at me, a worried wrinkle on his high, shiny forehead.

"Things not going too well lately?"

"No. I just feel — I don't know — like I want to go off by myself for a while. I think maybe Mary feels the same way."

"You seeing ganybody else? Huh?"

"No. Course not, Moe. I still love Mary. It's just that I feel . . . confined. I need a break."

"You think she's seeing ganyone?"

I looked up, shocked.

"Hell no! At least I hope not."

He shrugged his shoulders in a noncommittal way.

"You never know, Doc. You got a lot to lose. Both of you. But you know what? I agree with you. I think you two should get away from each other for a week or two. Have fun on your own, get into your own identities and interests. Then, when you come back, you can make a fresh start. It usually works."

Moe walked over to the patio-style sliding doors of his living room addition, flipped a switch, and a floodlight came on, illuminating his little goat corral. The goats stood huddled in the cold, the snow on their backs and their breath coming in great steamy clouds. Moe's little residence, smack in the middle of Walden Breezes trailer park, across the road from the famous pond, was cozy indeed. He threw another chunk of red oak into the stove, and we played chess.

After he won two games, I rose to leave. "Have you finished *The Kingdom of God Is Within You?*" I asked.

"Yes. But you may not have it until I get my own copy. It's the best thing Tolstoi ever wrote."

"But you've been saying you're going to get your own copy for two years now."

"Don't rush me. And give me five dollars for leaving, and five for the chess lesson."

I took out a ten-dollar bill and Moe stuffed it into the oatmeal carton with the slot cut in the lid. His Charity of the Month. At the door he handed me back the picture of the dancing gold statue.

"Steer clear of this, Doc. This thing and your Nazi friends in fatigues. I have a bad feeling about all of it."

I said I'd think about it and went out to the car. I looked back at the shiny trailer with its attached room and small corral. Above the scene, the floodlight glowed like a star, and its bright light reflected off the trailer and fresh snow with startling luminescence. The goats were lying next to each other now, puffing their steamy breath. It looked like a real live manger scene.

As I started the car, however, the idyllic mood was broken by a clap of thunder. Yes, in New England — and only there, as far as I know — we sometimes get thunder in snowstorms. This was a giant clap of thunder, and it was thunder on the left.

Ten minutes later I sat at the breakfast nook in the kitchen and watched while Mary placed the skewered shrimp on the electric grill and doused them with a little hot-and-sour sauce.

"What do you mean, 'thunder on the left'?" she asked me as she poured two Asahi beers for us. "What's that mean?"

"Some superstition about bad luck. If thunder is heard on your left, it bodes no good. I think it's a British sailor's superstition."

"Well, God knows in this case it's probably true. Couple that with the devil statue and Liatis's being shot, and everything else, and you see what I mean. Face it pal, this caper is just too deep for you. Leave it to those other guys who like killing and being killed. Stick to your job — your work makes people look better and feel better. It's important and beneficial, and you're very good at it. In short, Charlie Adams, stop being a jerk."

"You're right," I said, rising and kissing her. I held her for several minutes. Neither of us spoke. Was she thinking what I was thinking? I rubbed her shoulders and she sighed.

"I understand why you've got to go to San Antonio next month. But for heaven's sake, don't contact that Kaunitz guy. Leave it alone. Only a jerk would follow it up. I mean, I know you'll eventually use your own good judgment and do what's best. After all, the meeting is over a month away and you've got plenty of time to make the right decision."

"Right, Mary."

"And I just know you'll decide not to see Fred Kaunitz. After all, only an idiot would. And we both know you're a little wacky, but not an idiot."

"Of course. Uh, Mary? Mind if I ask a personal question?"

"What?"

"Are you having an affair with anyone?"

She leaned back in my arms and stared at me with wide eyes and a frown.

"What!"

"Well . . . ?" I could feel my heart skip a beat.

"No, Charlie."

I hugged her again, heaving a silent sigh of relief.

"But of course if I were, I wouldn't tell you."

I didn't say anything for a minute, then held her out at arm's length, dead serious.

"Honey, you're a million miles away right now," I said.

She bit her lip. Her eyes came unfocused.

"So are you," she said.

8

SIX WEEKS LATER, in San Antonio, Fred Kaunitz rang the bell to my hotel room in the Del Rio Hilton.

I was sipping coffee after having run five miles up and down the Paseo del Rio, the riverway that snakes through the old part of the city. Twenty years ago, the canal-like stream was a favorite place to dump dead bodies. And the town was so rough that there seemed to be an ample supply each night. But it's been cleaned up, and the riverway is now the city's main attraction. I had walked out onto the balcony and was looking down at the live oaks that lined the stream. Big grackle-like birds screamed and whistled in the trees, thrashing their long tails back and forth. They sounded like mynah birds. I liked them. It was March first, but crisp and sunny out. In fact, the day would be downright warm by midafternoon. I didn't miss New England one bit. I whistled an imitation of the blackbirds' song, and they answered me.

I had showered and dressed by the time the bell rang. I opened the door and there stood Fred Kaunitz. I had to look up when talking to him. He was dressed in blue jeans, a faded cotton shirt, and rough-out western boots. He did not wear a cowboy hat with a crown of feather plumes and silver in front.

He did not wear a big elaborate belt buckle with a silly saying or a beer or firearm company on it. He did not wear a string tie with a turquoise thunderbird or arrowhead on it. He didn't have a can of Skoal or Copenhagen with an engraved silver lid. He didn't seem to need these things. At a glance and a handshake, I knew that Fred Kaunitz was the real thing, the genuine item: a cowboy.

He sat opposite me in a plush chair, placed his tan Stetson hat on the end table, and poured himself a cup of coffee. He was lean, with a flat stomach and wide shoulders that sloped down like a gambrel roof. The hair was blondish and short. The big handlebar mustache was now trimmed short and flecked with gray. His eyes were very blue and piercing, and from the tan lines on his face you could tell he often wore aviator sunglasses. The eyes were interesting in another way. They had a keenness to them that was predatory. They could have belonged to a falcon or eagle. They were piercing but impenetrable; behind their burning intensity, I could detect no signs of feeling or emotion. The man was an incarnation of his native state: big, strong, rich, and rough around the edges.

He looked at his watch and then at me.

"Dr. Adams, I've got to move seven hundred head of cattle this afternoon, so I can't stay long. I hope you understand."

"Certainly. In fact, I was surprised you offered to fly down here. I was perfectly willing to drive up and — "

"Naw. I like to get away from the ranch every so often. In fact, one of the reasons I flew down is because I have to see some financial people here. Are you tied up all day?"

"I'm chairing a panel at ten and have a seminar at one that I have to attend. That's over at three and I'm done for the day."

"When's your first engagement tomorrow?"

"Eleven."

"Fine. Then we'll talk in the plane on the way up to Flying K. Tell you what: I'll meet you here at lunchtime and take you to a great little Mexican restaurant in the heart of the old city. We can talk a little then, and you can think of other questions you want to discuss during the flight."

"Great. I've got two questions I want to ask you now. One: do

75

you know of anyone in particular who would want to kill Roantis?"

His eyes crinkled around the edges and he smiled, shaking his head.

"Nobody in particular, but a lot of people in general."

"Anyone in the Daisy Ducks?"

"Naw. Of course, he got along with some of us better than others. But hell, it was a pretty intense group. I mean, you get eight guys on a long patrol who are that highly trained and motivated — there's bound to be friction. The one common quality in everyone who does this kind of work is fierce independence. We all wanted to be generals, even though Roantis was the group leader. Now, he and Bill Royce never got along. Bill and I were both air force — we did a stint together before the Daisy Ducks thing. He was my friend, a good fighter and smart. But he was also high strung. I guess you heard he went over the edge. In a hospital now somewhere."

"He was released."

"Yeah? Well, whaddayuh know. Well, Roantis and Summers had some trouble too. Summers claimed he was a racist. Maybe he is, a little. But Summers had a chip on his shoulder too. Roantis seemed to like me, Vilarde, and Larry Jenkins best. And Jenkins was black. Jesus, what a great soldier and great guy Larry Jenkins was. What a shame we lost him."

"He was MIA?"

"Yeah. Laos, in seventy-one, I think."

"And you lost the Korean, too."

"Uh-huh. Ton Youn was killed right outside Saigon by a sniper. But he wasn't MIA like Larry — they took his body back to Seoul."

"How did Roantis get along with Jusuelo?"

"*Hmph!* He's the mystery man. He and Vilarde were close: Vilarde was Mexican and Jusuelo Puerto Rican. They used to speak Spanish a lot. Sometimes I think they forgot I also speak it."

"Ah. Any interesting comments you overheard?"

"Not really. Except that twice Jusuelo commented under his breath that Roantis was incompetent. Over the hill. You know,

76

too cautious some of the time and too reckless other times."

"And were these comments justified?"

"Maybe. Roantis made some decisions I wasn't happy about. But we never lost a man on the long walks. That's amazing when you consider the frightful losses we inflicted on Charlie. You've also got to remember that in unconventional warfare you throw away the rulebook — you make life-and-death decisions minute by minute and think by the seat of your pants and by your hunter-killer instincts. It's kind of weird."

"Okay. Question two: do you know where Ken Vilarde is?"

"No. Your guess is as good as mine on that."

"Did Ken stay in touch with the other Ducks? Would he contact you now and then?"

"Not me. Maybe the others. But probably less and less as the years went on. You know how that is. But I think he would have kept in touch with Jusuelo and Roantis. He and Roantis were close, and Ken was second in command. And I told you already about Jusuelo."

"Where is Jesus Jusuelo now?"

"Who knows for sure? I was up in Denver busting a bottle with some old Vietnam buddies a while back, and they said Jusuelo was mercking in Africa. That was last year."

"Can you give me a name or two to contact?"

"Rather not. If I did, they wouldn't talk to you anyway. We're a pretty closed group. But I can get in touch with them myself if you want and ask what they've heard lately about Vilarde and Jusuelo."

"That'd be great, Fred. Both Roantis and I would be in your debt."

"Where do you come in, if I can ask? Why are you so interested?"

"Liatis has helped me out more than once. He asked me to do some digging around while he recovers. I figured as long as I'm in Texas, why not see you?"

"Fair enough. And I still think enough of Roantis to help in any way I can."

Suddenly his eyes narrowed, and he peered intently into my face, as if measuring me.

77

"Well, well, Dr. Adams, welcome aboard. Having you up to the ranch might be more fun than I thought."

"Thanks," I said, shaking his hand. "Call me Doc."

At noon I walked into the Hilton lobby to find Fred waiting for me. We took a cab to a little Mexican restaurant in a rather rundown neighborhood. It was decorated with garish statues and Christmas tree lights. I suppose I had severe doubts about the place . . . until I tasted the food, that is. When Fred ordered for us, I got a sample of his fluent Spanish. I don't speak it, but to me his pronunciation seemed perfect; he sounded like a native Mexican. I announced that the seminar I was scheduled to attend had been canceled. He seemed pleased, and said we could fly up to the ranch as soon as we finished eating.

"What is it, some kind of shuttle flight? I assume I can get my ticket at the gate."

"The flight is anytime I decide to go, Doc. I flew my own plane down here."

We finished our chile relleños and returned to the Hilton, where I packed my small carry-on bag with overnight gear. Just before two o'clock, our taxi dropped us off at Martindale Army Airfield, at the edge of town. Already the day was hot enough so that the horizon wiggled wet and seemed to come unglued, jiggling and dancing with the rising air currents.

Flying K's plane was a Mooney, made in Texas. I know nothing of planes, but it appeared to be a top-of-the-line model. The tail looked as if it had been put on the fuselage backward, so that it leaned slightly forward. We lifted off at two-twenty, made a wide circle, and headed north-northeast over the hot Texas plains, dotted with live oaks and the tiny, dark, moving specks that were cattle. The cattle seemed to cluster like sardines near the water holes and river gullies, which were shiny brown blotches against the buff-colored range grass. Kaunitz flew the plane with a calmness and detachment that showed his self-confidence and skill. Certainly, to a guy who'd been in the scrapes he had, flying a plane was child's play. In less than half an hour we were over Austin and approaching the Kaunitz ranch.

During the flight he related to me the events that occurred

during the march of the Daisy Ducks through the village of Siu Lok. It was the story Roantis had told me back home in Concord, all right. But it differed in a few important ways.

"And you say that Roantis and Vilarde sought the old chief out?"

"Yes. They corralled him after the dinner feast and took him off into the bush somewhere."

I said nothing. But why did Kaunitz's version of the story differ from the one Roantis had told us at the card table? Was it memory lapse over time, or hadn't Roantis totally leveled with me?

Then Kaunitz stood the airplane on its port wing, throwing us into a steep turn. Below us was a magnificent set of buildings laid out in perfect geometric symmetry, with adobe walls and red Spanish tile roofs. Kaunitz pointed down straight at it as we circled.

"The Flying K Ranch," he said, drawing off his sunglasses. His eyes flashed with eagle-like intensity. "All fifty-three hundred acres of it. Been in the family for five generations. Hang on, we'll be on the ground shortly."

9

FRED KAUNITZ set the four-passenger Mooney onto his black-top runway as smoothly as a falling snowflake. Since we had been bucking some strong thermals as we made our approach, it was clear that he was a master aviator. We taxied to the hangar complex and tied down the plane. A stripped-down jeep was waiting, apparently where Fred had left it earlier in the day. I noticed a raised pedestal seat in back, complete with a safety harness. The jeep also had a roll bar and twin spotlights. A gunrack was welded to the rear part of the chassis, and in it were an old twelve-gauge pump and a semi-auto carbine. I put my gear in back and hopped in. The jeep had been sitting in the sun, and it was as hot as a laundry iron. We headed along a gravel road toward the main house. Gee, it took a long time. Fred gave no indication that he wanted to impress me with the size and grandeur of Flying K, but impressive it was. The terrain was gently rolling hills covered with rough range grass and dotted with live and scrub oak: short, roundish trees with gnarled limbs that resemble those in California and Spain.

Rolling to a stop beside a corral with a steel fence, we got out of the jeep and walked over to the fence, climbed it, and sat on the top rail. Inside was the biggest bull I have ever seen. It must have been ten feet long and almost six feet at the withers. It had long pendant ears, a huge flappy dewlap under its neck, and a hump on its back.

"What the hell's that? A Brahma bull?"

"Sort of, Doc. A Brahma crossbred with an Angus. Called a Brangus. Three-year-old. Greatest producer we've got. A hundred twenty thousand and worth every cent. Name's Rasputin."

"How's his disposition?"

"On a good day, just awful."

"Hey, you ever do any rodeo riding? I thought I heard Roantis mention it."

Kaunitz made a laughing grunt in reply. "Yeah. Now and then, when things get slow, I do a little bull riding. Wrecked my leg a bit last fall."

"Is that why you're limping a little?"

"Yeah. And ranch work aggravates it. Well, let's head on in. You like to shoot?"

"Yes. Very much."

"Well, we can go out to the range after breakfast tomorrow. If you like to fish we've got a nicely stocked reservoir too. Some nice fat largemouth . . . In the creek there's some big catfish."

"Gee Fred, a guy could hang out here forever."

"He sure could," said Kaunitz as he started the jeep, "but it gets boring too. The heat, the work, the same people. I like to get out and around once in a while."

The ranch house was a U-shaped single-story building. The open side of the U was not open; it was an adobe wall that enclosed the Spanish-style patio and formal garden. In the garden were live oaks, Russian olive trees, cacti, and all kinds of creeping vines and flowering shrubs. It was both intimate and spectacular. I knew that Mary, with her fondness for Latin courtyards, would love it. The middle wing of the building housed the kitchen, dining areas, living room, and sleeping quarters for three generations of Kaunitzes. One wing was mostly workrooms and living quarters for the household staff and a family room. I was to stay in the wing opposite, which consisted of two guest suites, the living quarters for the senior ranch help, and the gunroom. In addition to the main ranch house, there was a separate bunkhouse for the general ranch help, a workshop, a horse barn and tackroom, and all the other outbuildings one usually finds on big ranches, including, in this case, a separate office to manage the day-to-day business of a five-thousand-acre ranch and breeding farm.

Almost before we coasted to a stop outside the building, two men came running up to the jeep, awaiting Fred's instructions. They were accompanied by a huge black and tan German shepherd, whose name, I found out later, was Lothar. Fred spoke to the men in brisk Spanish and they disappeared. He asked me to follow one of the men to my rooms. I did, and walking through the enormous gunroom, I got a quick glimpse of the trophy-lined walls, the big pool table, and many old photographs of the ranch and the elder Kaunitzes who built it.

"How tall you, señor?" my guide asked.

"Six feet, even."

"How you weigh, señor?"

"One seventy-four."

"How big you belt, señor?"

"Uh, thirty-two inches."

"Tang you, señor."

The man disappeared on the gallop, and I had a minute to examine my luxurious accommodations before he reappeared, flinging blue jeans and a western shirt down on the bed.

"You be ready pronto, hokay? Señor Kaunitz say for you: don forget we has to move seven hundred head cattle. You wan help?"

"Certainly. Pleased to."

"Hokay. How big your foot, señor?"

I told him, and a few seconds later he came with a pair of rough-out boots with walking heels. Standard issue to guests, I gathered. I dressed in less than two minutes and rushed out to the jeep. Fred was waiting with the engine running, and what followed was one of the most brutal and enjoyable afternoons of my life. We drove for twenty minutes through high grass and dust to where the big herd was. They were mostly Herefords, but quite a number of Brangus and other crossbreeds dotted the herd as well. In the next three hours I spent an hour on horseback, an hour at the wheel of the jeep, and the final hour at the corral chutes sorting yearlings and young calves. Sometimes the animals were panic stricken or stubborn, and required some hauling, kicking in the butt, and sometimes even carrying.

It was after six o'clock when we finally finished. I could scarcely move. Not having ridden a horse in two years, I was on fire everywhere between my waist and my knees — front, back, and in between. It's amazing what happens to certain muscle sets when you don't use them. Likewise, my upper body glowed with that special hurt of exertion that feels so good. My feet hurt from the western boots, and I was drenched with sweat from working in the heat. My throat, nose, and eyes were full of red range dust.

But I felt great. And then I knew what it was that kept people like Fred Kaunitz down on the farm. It was the elemental joy of being physical, of overseeing your own piece of turf, and of not having any twentieth-century fallbacks to bail you out when the going got rough. It was just the land, the cows, and us. Period. And I was loving it.

It was at the day's end, just as work was finishing, that it happened. It scares me even now to think back on it. We were getting ready to load a small batch of steers onto a truck from a holding pen at the edge of the corral complex. From the pen, a cattle chute sloped up and out, terminating at a gate the height of the truckbed. I approached the chute to slide the gate open for Fred's helper, Jimmy, as he backed the truck up to it. There were seven or eight animals on the chute, scared as hell, each one weighing maybe nine hundred pounds. I was to pull the sliding gate aside as the truck came up, allowing the animals to hop inside it. But somebody hadn't fastened the gate properly, and it had crept open a few inches, sliding along its roller track. Just then Fred came storming up the sloping boards of the chute from the pen, yelling and whistling to get the animals moving. Move they did, and the lead one, a Hereford with fear-bugged eyes, slipped his big head through the crack and pried that gate right open. The truck had not quite arrived, and four of the steers came spilling out the top of the chute — and onto me. I felt a hoof strike my chest and a horn brush my head as I went down. Just before I passed out, I saw the two sets of double truck tires spinning my way and managed to roll between them and underneath the axle.

I came to less than a minute later, stunned and shaking. There was a bruise as big as a saucer on my chest, but my ribs were intact. I had a nice egg on my noggin, too. Fred was steaming, and he cussed out all the help in Spanish. But if memory served me right, he had been the last man at the gate. I walked off the injury, deciding to let the whole thing drop. It had been a close call, and I mainly felt lucky to be alive.

When everyone was sure I'd be all right, Fred and I walked back to the jeep. He apologized for the mishap, and seemed shaken, too. I told him to forget the whole thing. He seemed relieved, and we sped back toward the ranch house in the soft early evening light. The sun was low in the sky, with pink and purple clouds around it. The rolling hills were full of light and shadow. Suddenly Fred turned and accelerated. I saw a vague shape jump and flicker ahead of us and to our left. It was an animal, bounding over the plains at an unbelievable speed. Was it Lothar, the German shepherd? No; Fred had told me he stayed on the ranch house grounds. Fred braked to a halt.

"Drive, Doc. Follow that coyote. Better belt yourself in good first. Go!"

He was already on the high pedestal seat in back, the carbine across his knees. Soon I had the jeep in high gear, chugging and bouncing along at about forty, which felt just great on my bruised and aching body. We gained on the coyote. Fred shot once and I saw a puff of dust ahead of the animal. The second shot connected and sent the little wolf into a double somersault before it crumpled into a heap of fur and lanky bones. We got out and looked. The animal's eyes were open, and its dog face wore an ironic, toothy grin. I wasn't too pleased. I know that coyotes are varmints that kill livestock, but I still felt like an accessory to murder. The feeling was intensified by the coyote's doglike appearance. It just looked too much like a pet to me. The whole thing seemed to have happened before I knew it; I never even expected Fred to connect. The shot was nearly impossible, considering the speed of the chase, the motion of the coyote and the bouncing vehicle, and the low light. But then I remembered

Roantis recounting Kaunitz's incredible skill with firearms. He had remarked that whatever got in Fred's line of sight was dead. It was true. Fred put the animal in the back of the jeep, and we drove on until we came to a high spot overlooking a dried-out creekbed. Fred got out and gutted the animal, leaving its entrails for the buzzards, and replaced the little wolf in the rear of the jeep. I walked toward the front seats on the passenger side of the vehicle.

Spang!

Two feet from me, the side mirror exploded in bright pieces. My hands and wrists stung with flying fragments of glass. I heard a nasty buzzing over my head and Fred's swearing as he leapt for the carbine at the rear of the jeep.

"Get down, Doc! Hit the dirt!"

Spang!

The spotlight casing blew apart. I saw a sputtering electric spark inside it in the dusky light. I was down, eating some of that good old red Texas dirt. Not again, I thought. I'm really getting sick of this.

"Let's go!" I shouted to Fred as he rolled to my side of the jeep and came up on the balls of his feet, carbine to his cheek. He crouched forward, keeping low, his eyes scanning the dry creekbed in the distance. The tiny canyon, or arroyo, as it's called, was choked with thickets. Here and there dwarf, bent willows hung over the gully. A tiny brown trickle of a stream ran through it. What it was was a perfect place to hide, and both of us knew it.

"We're not going, Doc. Not just yet. Listen: roll under the jeep and stay there a minute. I'm gonna crawl up to that rim and wait to see a spark. Shooting at their muzzle flash is the only way we can connect. They're well hidden, and it's almost dark."

"Who the hell are they?"

"Wish I knew. We've had trouble with some labor agitators, though. Want all our guys to swear allegiance to Chavez. Well, the Flying K isn't giving in, and our guys don't want it either. But they're mean and pushy. They've taken some pot shots at the help in the past coupla months, but never at me. If I get them in my sights on my land, they're gone."

He belly-crawled up the sandy slope and hunkered down under the rim, motionless and waiting. We stayed this way for fifteen minutes. Not a peep. From underneath the jeep I gazed at the thicket-clogged arroyo in the dying light. Hell, you could hide a platoon in there; it would be suicide to approach it.

"Doc, listen: don't do anything you don't want to do, but it'd be mighty helpful if you could crawl up to the driver's side and cut the lights. Just stay down and reach up to the knob?"

"No problem," I said. I squirmed forward, raised my arm, and hit the black knob on the dashboard, shoving it in. We were now in the dark, and almost immediately I heard the *keeeyeew-ahhh! keeeyeew-ahhh!* echo of rifle shots. This was followed by a steady drumming of Fred's carbine, spitting out slugs as fast as he could pull the trigger. With the carbine empty now, he skidded back down the slope, jumped into the jeep, and raced the engine.

"Jump in now, Doc, and hold on!"

I did, and we flew out of there, bouncing and jouncing. We went the first several hundred yards without lights, then Fred switched them on. Shortly, we hit the gravel road again and headed back to the ranch house.

As we walked through an archway of adobe and timber into the walled garden, I could feel my knees and legs tremble slightly from fatigue and stress. I eased myself down onto a stone bench and groaned. It had been quite a day. The big dog came up and sat staring at me. I petted it. Fred hopped inside and reappeared with two cans of Lone Star, which we cracked open and drank sitting on the bench next to the Spanish fountain. The sky in the west was still red, and the warm light reflected down into the garden, where the trees sighed softly in the evening breeze. Swallows and grackles called. The breeze was cool now. I stretched out my feet and grunted. I would be sore and stiff all over in the morning. A nighthawk sailed overhead and cried a high, nasal *breeent! . . . breee-oop!*

"You sure you're okay?" he asked.

"Yeah. I hurt a little, but it's nothing serious."

"Good. Well, it's been a day full of surprises. I don't know if I winged that dry-gulcher or not, Doc. One thing: the firing sure stopped quick after I gave him a dose. I just hope you're not too shook up, is all."

"No. I'm a little shaky now, but it'll pass. You don't think they'd sneak up to the house, do you?"

"Naw. They're chicken shit. Anybody who sneak-shoots from cover is a chicken shit. Besides, if anybody strange approaches this place, Lothar will let us know. Maybe that dusting I gave them will end it. If not, I'm taking some of the boys and ride 'em down. Listen Doc, I hate to leave a guest, but I've got to have a word with my dad about ranch business. I thought you'd want to clean up a bit, then if I'm not back here when you're through, you can just wait here or in the gunroom, okay?"

We both left the garden and I went to my room and took a long cool shower, changed clothes, and returned to the garden, which was now chilly. I did two circuits of the garden and was heading back to the cloister way that led to the gunroom when I heard voices arguing. I did another round of the garden. The voices were softer, but still raised. They were coming from a far corner of the compound, away from the garden side. I ambled along the white adobe wall, left the garden through another archway, and began a circuit of the main residence. Soon I was standing directly underneath a high double window.

". . . so a lot of those finishing expenses will depend on the sorghum crop," I heard Fred say. "If it's as good as it should be, we'll use it in the main feeder lot. That will pretty much take care of that column."

"And that leaves how many notes on capital improvements?" said a gruff voice.

"Four. And I've got two more lined up in San Antone."

"Let's hope to God the weather holds. Any word on the plane?"

"Still got a guy interested up in Waco."

"Well Fred, if it doesn't move in a month we've got to put it on the block. Hate to do it — I know how much it means to you — "

"Let's hope something turns up," snapped Fred.

"Well it probably won't. Just be prepared for it."

I completed my walk around the house, returned through the same archway that Fred and I had gone through before, and went into the gunroom. I racked up the balls on the pool table, scanning the trophies that hung high on the wall over the gun cabinets.

I fired the cue ball at the racked triangle of balls and watched it explode with a loud whack. I gave a low whistle of amazement at the frozen menagerie that stared down at me. The trophies certainly were impressive. The Kaunitz family had taken all the North American big game: all three deer species, moose, elk, caribou, antelope, cougar, and a grand slam in sheep: Desert, Stone, Rocky Mountain, and Dall. They had one each of the three big American bears: grizzly, brown, and polar. If this weren't enough, they'd managed to bag two jaguars, a leopard, most of the major African antelopes, and a cape buffalo. I couldn't imagine what these hunting expeditions had cost. It also boggled the mind to think of taking all those endangered species from the planet. I walked over and looked closely at the mounted heads. Then I knew. They were old trophies. Very old. Well preserved, but the dullness of the fur and horns revealed their age. They looked as if they'd been taken about thirty or forty years earlier, perhaps before Fred was even born.

From the sound of the pieces of conversation I'd eaves-dropped on, the financial situation at Flying K wasn't altogether rosy. What had happened? Several bad droughts? Soft beef market? Labor problems? Water rights? Poor planning and decision making? Whatever it was, it was clear that Flying K and its inhabitants were not now enjoying the gentrified life that they had in the past.

Next, I looked closely at the guns in their stained oak cabinets. I knew the rifle I was looking for: Belgian FN-FAL assault rifle, black plastic foregrip and stock, carrying handle . . . three vent holes in the fore end.

I didn't find it.

And then Fred and his dad walked in.

The elder Kaunitz, Walter, was almost as big as his son. Although age had shrunk the massive chest and arms somewhat, the giant frame was still in evidence. His face was heavily lined with deep creases and fixed with what seemed to be a permanent tan. He took my hand with a gorilla grip and proceeded over to the bar to pour himself a hefty gin and tonic. Fred and I did likewise, and then we all sat in low chairs, upholstered in Navajo cloth, in front of the empty fieldstone fireplace. It was almost cold in the room due to the air conditioning. It felt good after the hot afternoon's work, but I could feel my sore muscles beginning to lock.

"I hope you're enjoying your stay with us at Flying K," said Walter Kaunitz as he lighted a Camel, "even though you got more of the Old West than you bargained for, eh? Fred told me about that sniper. I think it's time to take off the gloves with those bastards. Nobody's doing that to Flying K, let me tell you."

"Well, it's been an adventure. You gonna go to the law, or what?"

"Yeah. We'll meet with the sheriff and the highway patrol. But I'd like to catch 'em myself, red-handed. Sure Fred feels the same way. Appreciate it, though, if you didn't mention it at supper, Dr. Adams. The women worry, you know. Hey, Fred also tells me you're quite a ranch hand. Well, enjoy it all while it's still here. The medium-sized ranches, like this one, are fast disappearing. They're selling out, either to the huge outfits or to the real estate developers. Damn shame. Part of the reason is that crow bait who bushwhacked you. Look over your shoulder. See that bearded gentleman and his family? That was my great-grandfather, Franz Josef Kaunitz. Behind him is the sod house he built on this site back in 1868. That's when the ranch was started."

"Is there any reason to think that this ranch will disappear soon, Mr. Kaunitz? I sure hope not. I haven't had such a good time in years."

"Naw. We'll hang on to this speck of land for a while anyway, won't we, Fred?"

"For sure, Dad."

"I'd hardly call five thousand acres a speck of land," I said.

"Well, you come from where? Massachusetts? Well hell, no wonder. That state's only as big as a postage stamp. Out here, though, we're a speck."

"Did you take all these?" I asked, waving my arm around the room.

"'Bout half of them. The others my father took in the twenties. Freddie here took two of the bears and that Greater Kudu. Did he tell you what he did in Vietnam? Now that's really the most challenging hunting, right, Fred?"

His son grunted a reply. I had the feeling Fred wasn't anxious to discuss his career with the Daisy Ducks. A boy of twelve skipped in. It was little Freddie Kaunitz, who announced that dinner would soon be served. We followed the boy back through the garden and into the kitchen-dining building, where I met the wives. Beth and Margaret Kaunitz were attractive, reserved women. Margaret, Fred's mother, wore her salt-and-pepper hair back in a bun. She was very tall, which helped account for Fred's height. Beth was about thirty-five, with dark eyes and hair. I thought she might have some Latin blood in her. She was as dark as Mary, and that's dark. The dinner was beef Bourguignon with vintage French red, which was a pleasant surprise. I was, of course, expecting chili, barbecue, or giant steaks. Every attempt I made to bring the ladies into the conversation fell flat. They answered my questions politely, but were careful not to offer their own opinions. After dessert, I was beginning to wonder if they even had their own opinions. I also discovered that the women never ventured into the gunroom. I was surprised at all of this, but figured it might be common in rural Texas to have this kind of domestic relationship. In any case, it was apparent that the women of Flying K, while enjoying every material comfort, did not participate in the daily ranch decision making. Nor were they friends or companions to their husbands.

We returned to the gunroom, where Walter opened a beer, lighted a Jamaican cigar, and switched on the television. Fred and I walked out into the garden and sat near the fountain again. My body was now so sore that I'd had difficulty rising from the dinner table. I told this to Fred and he laughed, saying it was natural and that I was obviously in far better shape than most of his guests. I decided then and there to come right out with the question I most wanted answered.

"Fred, who shot Roantis?"

"Not me, if that's what you're asking. You still think it was one of the Ducks?"

"I don't know."

He shook his head slowly and drank from his can of Lone Star, then grunted a soft beer belch, the kind that stings the inside of your nose. He shook his head again.

"I don't think it was any of the guys on the Daisy Ducks patrol.

Period. Why do I think that? Because the kind of person who is a double volunteer in an elite armed services branch is not a thief. A thief by nature looks for a short cut, an easy way out. Just like that chicken-shit bastard who shot at us tonight. A bum. Nothing but a fucking bum. And if I catch him, I'll kill him. Now, the kind of guy who does what we did — tromping through the jungles and mountains for weeks at a time, with no outside help and in constant danger, isn't the kind to take short cuts. Sure, maybe some of us have fallen on hard times since then. I guess Roantis especially. But still, I just don't see how it could be any of the Ducks. You know Roantis's recent lifestyle better than any of us. You know the kinds of people he's been hanging around with. I think they're far better bets as suspects in the shooting than any of his army buddies. What do you think?"

"Well, there's no doubt he's been known to associate with some pretty rough customers."

"Then I'd look there, not in the Ducks."

He said this last statement with finality and force, and I realized that I had perhaps insulted him and his comrades in arms by suggesting that one of them might be responsible. But I knew that nobody outside the Ducks knew about the statue. I said nothing, and when we finished our beers we each retired to our sleeping quarters.

My room, done in adobe and oak, had a small balcony attached to the outside wall. When you walked out, you saw you were one story up on that side, since the ranch house was built on a slope. The windows and door on the courtyard side were at ground level. I opened the Spanish-style door, walked out onto the balcony, and listened to the night sounds. There was the chirping and buzzing of insects and the distant hoot of an owl on the wing. A breeze cooled my face and washed over my tired body. It smelled of grass, cattle, blossoms, mesquite and cedar trees. I went back inside and tried to do my daily fifty pushups with my feet up on the bed and my hands on the floor. No go. I tried the standard version. No go. I managed twenty sit-ups before my butt and stomach hollered in pain. I hauled my sore body into the sack and dropped into sleep's deep, dark well slightly faster than the speed of sound.

But I woke up twice during the night. The first time I simply sat up in bed wondering where the hell I was. Strange sounds. Strange room. The second time was more interesting, because what had awakened me was the sound of my doorknob turning. I sat up again and leaned forward, toward the door. I could hear the latch turning slowly, back and forth. Very slowly, so as to keep silence. Just before I could spring out of bed and fling open the door to catch the nighttime visitor by surprise, the noise stopped and I heard very soft footsteps outside. Then a tall human figure appeared at the window on the courtyard side, silhouetted against the thin curtains. It leaned close, then was gone. Who was it? The dry-gulcher, perhaps, returning to try again? Was it one of the household staff, checking to see if I was safe? Did someone think the room was vacant and wish to use it for a tryst? Was somebody trying to rob me? Kill me? Who was it? I got out of bed, double-checked the lock, and went back to sleep.

Next morning I awoke at six and couldn't return to sleep. The nighttime visitor had me going. But I decided not to say anything about it, not to anyone. Whatever his intentions, they obviously weren't aboveboard or he wouldn't have come calling in the dead of night. But I was unharmed, and Fred was upset enough over recent events on his ranch. So I was going to keep mum.

I staggered out of the sack and into the shower, letting the hot water work on my sore, stiff body. My head felt better, but the bruise from the kicking steer still ached. I got dressed and eased out onto my little balcony to watch the sun come up over the hills.

I saw a lone figure in the distance, a man running among the scrub oaks that dotted the horizon. I kept watching the figure, and soon it was obvious that the strides weren't regular; there was a lopsided loping to them. It was Fred Kaunitz, running on his bum leg. The man kept himself in A-1 shape, that was for sure.

We had breakfast at seven-thirty and then went to the rifle range. My score surprised Fred, and he said so. At pistol silhouettes I surprised him even more. Then we shot skeet, using autoloading shotguns in twenty-gauge. I got about three quarters of the clay targets, which is as good as I ever do. Fred got all of them. We returned to the pistol range and shot nine-millimeter and forty-fives. In slow fire I equaled him in the nine-millimeter and finished slightly behind with the forty-five. Then we did a few targets in rapid fire, in which each shooter must empty his magazine in twenty seconds. I fell slightly behind in this event, but not much.

"You do a lot of pistol shooting," he said.

"Yes. But mostly slow fire. Fifty-yard paper targets and some steel silhouettes."

"Ever do any combat events?"

"Never. Just some rapid fire."

"Well, let's walk over to the combat course we've got laid out here. I'll put you through your paces. We don't have time for more than a couple of walk-throughs, but you'll get the idea."

Near the skeet range, and connected to its power source, was an automated combat simulation course. It was a series of moving and pop-up targets that you walked through, pistol holstered. When the target popped, you were to draw and fire from a crouch. Sometimes two targets came up at the same time and you were to make the best decision as to which to go for first. At the end of the course there was the plate event, in which each contestant was to see how many rounds of a full clip he could put into a circular steel plate at twenty yards. We walked through the course. Fred was phenomenal in his speed and accuracy. The big forty-five was up and in his paw instantly. The shots came so fast they sounded like a single long explosion. He hit the center mark on all the pop-up targets and filled the plate with all seven rounds each time. I stunk at it.

Fred kept himself razor-sharp in those combat skills. Why? Was it pride in his past military service? Was it necessity, brought about by the labor agitators or whoever they were in the bush? Was it, like my target shooting, pure pleasure? Or was it . . . What was it? We spent the remainder of the morning on a long tour of the ranch. Fred never mentioned anything about the finances, but it was obvious that he loved every square inch of the huge family estate and that something was bothering him. We returned to the house and I packed my gear, then we drove out to the airstrip.

The flight back to San Antonio seemed very short. Almost before I knew it, I was stepping out on the wing of the little Mooney and waving good-bye to the handsome pilot who'd been such a fine host and straight shooter. And the man who, of course, couldn't have had anything to do with the shooting of Liatis Roantis up in Concord.

But there were a few things bothering me.

I considered the events at Flying K Ranch as I watched the little aircraft taxi back down the blacktop. The first thing was my near miss at the loading chute. It looked ninety percent like an accident. But ninety isn't a hundred. Then the two bullets that came within inches of my chest as I got into the jeep after Fred had nailed the coyote. Certainly Kaunitz had nothing to do with firing the shots. But was it just coincidence that we stopped within range of the hidden gunman? Then there was the midnight visitor to my room. It's a Southern tradition not to lock doors. I'm not a Southerner, and I had locked mine with a throw-bolt. The figure who peered into the room was tall. None of the Mexican ranch hands were tall. There were only three tall people I'd seen at Flying K: Fred, and his mom and dad. Now the nighttime stalker could have been the dry-gulcher or another outsider, but I doubted it. I doubted it because Lothar, the big watchdog, slept in the courtyard, and there hadn't been a peep from him. So the odds were overwhelming that Fred Kaunitz was the person at the window. Why was he there, in the dead of night, softly turning my doorknob?

And then there was something I'd inadvertently seen after breakfast, when we were shooting at the range. I'd gone into the range shack to retrieve another box of cartridges. But instead of looking in the left storage locker, I'd absent-mindedly swung open the one on the right. There were no cartridges, just targets and hunting jackets. Still unaware that I had opened the wrong locker, I searched through the dark closet, even reaching around the corner past two hunting jackets that were hanging on hooks.

It was behind the jackets, leaning upright against the locker wall. Black plastic fore end, three vent holes, folding carrying handle over the receiver. Exactly as Roantis had described it. The FN-FAL assault rifle. I closed the locker door and, after a second's delay, found the cartridges in the opposite locker. I took them to Kaunitz without a word.

Finally, Fred's bum right leg, injured in the same location that my lucky bullet struck just after Roantis was hit. Like Fred, that gunman could shoot like crazy. And Fred needed the money. And he had the means of transportation too . . .

Wait a minute, sport. No hasty conclusions. It's all circumstantial, held together with half-baked theories and bubble gum.

But, as I headed back to the Del Rio Hilton in the taxi, I looked down at the scrap of paper in my hands. It was the registration number of Freddie Kaunitz's Mooney airplane. Call it a hunch, but some inner voice had told me to make a note of it.

10

"AND YOU never *listen!*" Mary said.

Actually, "said" isn't the right word; "shouted" is better.

"That's the pisser, Charlie. I thought we agreed that you wouldn't see this guy Kaunitz. So what do you do? You go to his goddamn ranch and get *shot at* and *trampled!* Sweet Jesus!"

I held the receiver a few inches away from my ear to cut down on the decibels, and also to let some of the steam escape. I guess I shouldn't have mentioned the little incidents. But if I couldn't talk freely to her, how could I level with her? And if I couldn't level with her, who could I level with?

"Now Mare, you're making too much of — "

"No I'm not. I've about had it with your little adventures, pal. You keep it up and you'll have all the freedom you want . . . and more!"

After she hung up, I eased back into the tweedy chair of the private airline club. Just outside the rosewood door, thousands of frantic travelers rushed to and fro along the miles of O'Hare International Airport's corridors. What a madhouse. I had just arrived from San Antonio and had a two-hour layover until the Boston flight departed. I looked at my watch. One-thirty. Would Michael Summers, former member of the 101st Airborne Brigade and the Daisy Ducks, show? I thought not. He

96

hadn't sounded that together when we'd talked earlier.

But I was wrong. At quarter to two, I was just beginning to doze in my easy chair when the receptionist tapped me on the shoulder.

"Dr. Adams? The man you've been waiting for has arrived. This way, Mr. Summers."

The man who sat down opposite me looked big and mean. His thick, dark face wore a scowl; his huge body seemed to dwarf the big easy chair he'd lowered himself into. He resembled the late Sonny Liston, the heavyweight slugger Muhammad Ali called "The Bear." I rose, leaned over, and shook his hand. It was a beefy paw that encircled my hand, hiding it. The handshake was firm but not brutal. Mike Summers was confident enough in his own strength and toughness not to have to parade it. I sat back again and looked at him closely. In an instant, my medical training told me that underneath the great size and strength, Mike Summers was in trouble. The whites of his eyes had a yellowish hue, and there were rust-colored patches there, too. The face and hands were puffy. Too much booze and a bad diet.

"How you doing?" I asked.

"Been better. I want a drink. Okay?"

"Sure. What'll it be?"

"Double Scotch on the rocks and a bottle of Miller's."

That was three drinks, not one. But I didn't feel like pushing the point. I went up to the bar and got his order and a bottle of Heineken's for myself. On the way I stopped by the front desk and asked the receptionist if she could get me a blood pressure cuff. She balked at first, but I assured her the airlines or the airport clinic had one somewhere on the premises. I returned to our chairs and placed the drinks on the table between us. Soon the barkeeper brought us a plate of cheese and pretzels. Summers picked up the whiskey and tossed it off as if it were a shot glass. Then he sipped his beer, let out a slow, deep growl of relief, and lighted a Lucky Strike.

"Well, Mike, I've just spent two days with Fred Kaunitz, who sends you his best."

"Hooweee, man. Well, I think even his best ain't gonna help me much now. Got throwed out of my place today." He nodded in the direction of the coatroom in the front of the club. "Everything I own is in that GI duffel bag up front. Everything."

"Where are you going? What will you do?"

He shrugged his massive shoulders and let out a slow breath of smoke. "Can't go back to the South Side, that's for sure. I'll be on the street for keeps in a month."

I pushed the cheese tray at him but he declined, saying he'd appreciate it if I bought him another round. This I did, and after another jolt of hooch he managed to attack the cheese and pretzels. It wasn't an ideal diet, but it was solid food anyway, which was more than he'd probably had in a few days. Mike Summers, war hero, was another of the walking wounded. The Daisy Ducks had had their wings clipped but good. The receptionist came up with a leather pouch and placed it on the table.

"What's that?" asked Summers.

"A blood pressure cuff. Do you mind?"

"Hell yes I mind!"

Then he leaned forward in his chair and placed his big dark face inches from mine. He seemed to loom over me like an ancient monolith. He spoke in a soft, menacing whisper.

"You a nosy motherfucker — you know that?"

"Suit yourself then," I replied as nonchalantly as possible.

He eased back in the chair, staring at me. Then his eyes softened a tiny bit; the frown wrinkles relaxed just a tad.

"All right then," he said, unbuttoning his sleeve. "Then will you stop messing with me?"

I checked the readings twice: one eighty-two over one thirty-one. Mike Summers was probably days, maybe only hours, away from a massive stroke. I hated to think what his systolic pressure had been twenty minutes earlier, before he'd had the drinks. I explained frankly what the readings meant. At first he scoffed, saying he was fine. I just sat back and waited, and soon he admitted he'd felt pretty rotten for months.

"What have you been eating mostly?" I asked.

"You know, bar food. Peanuts, salted pork rinds, chips — stuff like that."

"Why don't you let me buy you a square meal?"

"Yeah. Maybe later."

I looked at my watch. In twenty minutes I had to proceed to

the gate. I looked at Summers, slouched in the chair, then back at my watch. Then I realized I had already made the decision. That's what I get for hanging around with Moe Abramson.

"Wait here a minute," I said.

"Is there another seat available on my flight?" I asked the receptionist. She tapped some keys on her computer terminal and said there was. I snapped my credit card down on the desk and asked her to reserve it for Mr. Summers. In less than a minute we had adjoining seats in the smoking section of first class.

Then I called home to touch base with Mary. Nobody answered; she was out somewhere. Maybe it was just as well.

It took a third round of drinks to get Summers to even listen. But then he stared down at his big, puffy brown hands and considered his options. He had none. And so at the appointed time we left the airline club and walked toward the gate, only half a mile distant. We already had our boarding passes — another benefit of the club — so there was no waiting at the gate. In the airliner, Mike Summers eased back in the seat and directed the overhead stream of cold air on his face. The stewardess poured him another champagne.

"Don't you want another one?" she asked me.

"No thanks, I already gave him mine. What's for dinner?"

"Chicken Kiev or beef Bourguignon."

After liftoff, Summers smoked a cigarette and had two more Scotches. These did the trick. He seemed to shrink back into the cloth of the seat. His hands ceased their endless drumming and trembling, and his breathing became deep and regular. In a jiffy he was out cold. I woke him up for chow. At first he dabbled at his chicken. Then he ate two genuine mouthfuls. Then he inhaled the remainder in less than a minute. I snagged the stewardess and said that if at all possible, my friend who'd just gotten back from the wars would really appreciate a second meal. Did they by chance have one left over? Soon it was placed in front of him and he inhaled that one, too. After a cup of coffee he crashed again.

He slept like a baby all the way to Boston.

* * *

99

I never realize how much I love Boston, or how homesick for her I've really been, until the plane breaks below the cloud cover (that's there ninety percent of the time I fly in) and begins its steeply banked descent over the bay. From a plane's height, the water of the bay and harbor have the wrinkled appearance of avocado skin when the waves are up, except the color is bluish gray. I look down at the fishing boats trailing their comet-like white wakes across it. Then I see Boston Light, or even Minot's Ledge if I'm lucky, and Spectacle Island and old Fort Warren, and the old warehouses that seem to be sliding right into the water, and I'm glad to be back in Beantown.

Mike Summers awoke when the passengers were filing out. We walked up the ramp into the gate area and headed for the baggage claim. The bags came snaking around on the conveyor belt. I grabbed my big suitcase and we waited, and waited, for Summers's big duffel. It didn't appear.

"Sheeee-it!" he growled under his breath. "I know what went down, man. I checked the bag late, you know? It didn't make the flight, is what went down."

But just then two men with wide shoulders, mustaches, and bulky sport coats came up to us and flashed their badges. The bigger of the two looked at Summers.

"You Michael Summers?" he asked. Mike nodded, and the man asked both of us to accompany him. It then flashed through my mind that perhaps Summers, in his recent life, had had a brush with the law. Chicago's South Side being what it is, anything's possible, especially to a guy down on his luck. If this were so, then I, Dr. Charles Adams, was guilty of aiding and abetting a fugitive from justice.

Swell.

The men led us into a baggage locker, a room with wooden tiers on which rested all kinds of suitcases, overnighters, steamer trunks, and cartons. Smack in the middle on a table sat Summers's army duffel. He grinned with relief and made a beeline for it. But before he'd gone two steps the tall security guard grabbed him by the arm. I saw a gleam of metal in the guard's hand. Not a gun. Handcuffs. Summers looked momentarily confused. Then the look of surprise was transformed into a bearlike glower.

And then all hell broke loose.

With speed that was unbelievable in such a big man, Summers grabbed the guard's outstretched arm with his left hand and jerked him forward violently. At the same instant he threw a short, straight right at his jaw. The poor guy was snapped right into the punch, and the effect was devastating. Still holding the guard's arm, Summers pulled him down and across his outstretched leg, tripping him. Before the guard could rise, he chopped him hard on the nape of the neck. The guard oozed down onto the floor and didn't even twitch. But during this brief encounter his buddy had been circling behind Summers. Now he reached up, wrapped his arms around Summers, and tried to put a bear hug on him. Dumb. Even I know enough never to do that. Almost faster than the eye could follow, Mike swung back his left foot and hooked his toe around his attacker's left ankle, locking it. Then he threw his fullback weight backward and slightly to the left. The official landed with a thud that shook the floor, and the poor security guard — make that former security guard — happened to be underneath. The guard's face knotted in pain. His breath hissed between clenched teeth, like a steam engine. An electronic paging device on his belt began to beep.

"Time to fade," Summers said, grabbing his duffel bag. I stayed put. As far as I could tell, Mike Summers was infinitely more dangerous than the two goons he'd cold-cocked. I'd just have to explain myself to the authorities and take my chances. But Summers was scarcely out the door when he rushed back in again. He didn't even look in my direction — just dropped his duffel, flung open the zipper, and began to rummage through it as fast as he could. Three more men came through the door, men with real, honest-to-goodness Boston Police uniforms on. All the men had their revolvers drawn. I felt like sinking right into the floor.

"You won't find the gun in there, Mr. Summers," said the man in front. "We discovered it in your luggage, that's why you're being held." The man stopped to stare down at the two fallen plainclothesmen. His mouth opened in disbelief and fear. I saw Summers looking at the first fallen man, whose sport coat had flipped up to reveal a small holstered revolver.

"Mr. Summers, you're being held in violation of the handgun law of the Commonwealth of Massachusetts — "

But he didn't get a chance to finish his little speech because Summers dove for the gun in the fallen man's belt, and I discovered, not particularly to my surprise, that I was also in midair, diving for that same gun so that Summers would not get it. I knew, in the millisecond I was airborne in my horizontal dive, that Mike and I would collide. I also was aware that when we did — the laws of physics being what they are — I would emerge the loser. That is, *if* I emerged. It did not surprise me that I was doing this fool thing. I seem to have a knack for stepping into a big pile of you-know-what every chance I get. I'm gifted that way.

Well, I arrived at the gunbelt just ahead of Summers and in enough time to grab the small revolver from the holster and spin it along the floor to a far corner. Meantime, the fuzz had all jumped on Summers at once. One bluecoat smacked him on the side of the jaw with a big, flat sap. It went *poimf!* against the side of his open mouth, and Mike was going down. They manacled him then, and sat him on the edge of a table.

One of the cops helped me to my feet. I was dizzy from the collision with the big man and from the combined weight of three other men on top of us. I was a wreck.

"Mr. Summers, you are being held in violation of the handgun law of the Commonwealth of Massachusetts," began the cop again. But Summers told him to go fuck himself, and they hauled us both off to the pokey.

Twenty minutes later I was sitting across from my traveling companion in the interrogation room at the Hanover Street branch of the Boston PD. We'd gotten there in the back seat of a squad car. A lieutenant came into the room and placed a forty-five automatic on the table. The action was back and the magazine was out.

"Don't go for it, Summers — it's empty."

"So's your head."

"It's a fluke the baggage handler discovered it, I'll admit. Many airports have metal detectors that scan checked baggage, but what tipped him off was feeling this piece through the canvas of the duffel. You put it in there so you could get to it quickly. Why?"

"Habit I picked up in the service."

"We checked your service record. Very good. Perhaps you should have stayed in."

"I get one phone call," I said. "And so does Mr. Summers."

Mike called Roantis, who had returned to his job the previous week, at the BYMCU number I'd given him. I didn't think this was a hot idea, but I said nothing.

They handed me a phone. Luckily, Joe was in his office at State Police Headquarters. I explained the situation. As I feared, he was not overly sympathetic.

"Doc, for Chrissakes, how many times do you expect me to bail you out? Violation of the Fox-Bartley gun law is serious. It's a year in the can. No ifs, ands, or buts."

"Okay. *One:* Mike didn't know about the gun law. I know it's what everybody says, but I hauled him out here at a moment's notice. *Two:* he wasn't packing the piece for any special reason. He just had all of his worldly belongings in his duffel, including the gun. And they rode in the cargo hold, not the cabin."

"And you say this guy's a friend of Roantis?"

"Uh-huh."

"That's all we need. Listen, I've got good friends at the Hanover Street station. I'll come over and see if we can straighten it out."

Well, he got us off the hook, but I think Summers's military career helped as much as anything. Cops like soldiers, especially good ones. Fortunately, the two meanies Mike assaulted weren't policemen. They were airline employees. Summers was instructed to stay put until charges, if any, were filed. I told the Boston Police that, for the time being, anyway, he was staying with me in Concord.

We got into Joe's cruiser and he drove us back through the Callahan Tunnel to East Boston so I could retrieve the car at the airport. Right in the middle of the tunnel, amid all the roaring and rushing, honking, and deadly CO fumes, he dropped a bombshell on me.

"Who's your lady friend, Doc? Sure was a knockout."

"What are you talking about?"

"Don't play dumb with me. I know you're not telling because I'm your wife's brother. Who in hell is she and where did you run into her? San Antone?"

"Huh?"

"Okay, clam up. I'll find out eventually. And so will Mary. You can't keep it secret forever, you know. After all, this Mystery Lady is the one who sprung you and your friend."

I stretched my feet out to relieve the numbness and cramping brought on by the plane ride, the scuffle in the baggage room, and sitting under the hot light at the BPD. I let out a weary sigh. The recent events had all the earmarks of a Kafka novel. I wasn't having much fun.

"Joe, what the hell are you talking about? You know there's no woman in my life except Mary."

"And that blonde you were glomping on to at your party the other night."

"No, not even her. Now, who's this other lady?"

"I don't know, that's why I'm asking you. She looked Mexican a little bit, so I guessed maybe you met her in San Antonio. But actually, I thought she looked more Japanese or Chinese. But she was too tall for any of them."

I stared ahead and saw light at the end of the tunnel. I remembered the tall, gorgeous, sandalwood-scented woman in the ski parka who had glided by me on the hospital stairs. But it couldn't be.

"Did she, uh, have her hair back in a bun?"

"Naw. In a single thick braid down one side of her head. God, those eyes! So where did you meet her?"

"I've never met her. But I have seen her. Once. And that's a face I'll never forget."

"Haw-haw-haw!" roared Summers from the back seat. I turned and looked at him. He wore a big grin, and the laugh was genuine. It was the first time I'd seen him even smile. I turned around again and stared at the tunnel exit. Summers seemed to know something I didn't.

"Well, this woman, whoever she is, showed up at the station ten minutes after I got there. She waltzed in there and snagged Captain Catardi. They were in the next room for maybe twenty minutes. Then Catardi comes back in alone and says let them go. He wouldn't tell me doodily-squat. So who the hell is she, Doc?"

"I wish I knew, Joe. I wish I knew . . ."

11

FOR SOME STRANGE REASON, Mary was not overjoyed that I had brought Mike Summers home with me.

"You've got to be *kidding,* Charlie!" was all she managed to say as Mike clomped around above us in the guest room, a double Scotch in his huge mitt, unpacking his duffel.

"I tried to call from Chicago and tell you my plans. By the way, where were you this afternoon?"

"Since when do I have to report to you?" she snapped as she stormed off. Ten minutes later, after a brief phone call to Janice DeGroot, she left to go shopping. I wanted to ask her when she planned to return, but I didn't push it. It was a hell of a way to treat a war hero like Mike Summers. But I could see her point. One doesn't exactly expect one's spouse, who's blown a sizable wad of the family savings on rehabilitating an ex-mercenary, to bring another one home. I knew that Mike couldn't stay at the Adams homestead longer than a day or two without disastrous consequences. I sat down in my study and thought for a few minutes. Why had I volunteered to bring Mike Summers home with me? What had gotten into me that I would take this man, one step away from the gutter — or jail — and whom I'd met only minutes before, under my wing? Why?

Because he needed help, that's why. And he had nowhere else to turn. And I knew who was really behind it: Morris Abramson. Dammit! I'd been hanging around Moe too much; I was becoming a bleeding heart sap, just like him. Moe Abramson, the sucker who'd let a grizzly take his leg off and then stop to lecture the critter because eating meat was bad for its health.

There was only one course of action at this point: I was going to take Mike up the road to Carlisle and put him in Glendale Hospital, a posh detox clinic. Lord only knew what Mary was going to say when she heard this plan; the cost was astronomical. But I solved that problem: I decided I wasn't going to tell her.

But another difficulty loomed. What if he didn't want to go? A man of Mike's background and disposition wouldn't want to be confined or restricted, even if it was for his own good. And if he didn't, how could I persuade him? It'd be like telling King Kong to get off that building right this instant — *or else.*

There were only two men I knew who would even have a chance at handling Mike Summers. One was Roantis, of course. But although he'd returned to work, he was still disabled. The other was the giant affable Irishman, Tommy Desmond. But I liked Tommy too much to send him on a suicide mission. There was only one answer: I had to persuade him myself.

I went upstairs and knocked on the guest room door. No answer. I opened it; Summers was asleep on the bed. The clock-radio was playing loud soul music. I turned it off, drew down the blinds, and tiptoed out. He slept through the night. After Mary got back from shopping, at nine, I promised her Mike would not stay long. We had a late snack together and watched part of an old movie before she said she was tired and went up to go to sleep. I followed, and we snuggled for a bit. I thought I was going to get lucky and have a chance to put all the disagreements in the past. But then she rolled over to her side of the sack and froze there in a fetal position. I reached over and stroked her flank.

"Don't, Charlie. I'm tired and . . . and confused. I want to sleep now."

"Sorry about Mike Summers being here. He's leaving tomorrow."

"Charlie, I need to get out of this place for a while. I need to get away."

"We'll talk about it later," I said.

"It won't change," she said.

The next morning, Mary was up and out of the house early for hospital duty. As a relief RN, she works two or three days a week. I wasn't hungry, but I ate a small breakfast and called Glendale Hospital. The director, Mr. Clarence Featherstone, answered.

"Now let me get this straight, Dr. Adams, you say the patient is from out of state, has no health insurance plan or means of payment, and you want to have him admitted at Glendale?"

"That's correct. I am prepared to pay the full week's charges in cash, in advance." This changed his attitude considerably.

"This, uh, man is a relative, then?"

"No."

"He is then a — *harrrumph!* — a friend, I presume?"

"No, not exactly. I just met him."

He cleared his throat again a couple of times and made sucking mouth noises.

"Are you trying to ask me why I'm bringing him in?"

"Uhhh. Yes."

"Because I can't let him die. Does that sound reasonable?"

"Oh, of course, Dr. Adams. Do you have him on medication now?"

"No. But he should be on something for hypertension, and soon. I assume your attending physician will probably prescribe it."

"Of course, doctor. Now, when can we expect you both?"

"That's a good question. Whenever we get there."

I hung up and heard a heavy tread on the front stairs. I met Mike in the dining room. I thought I might as well get it over with, even if it meant a knee drop to my kidney and a broken spine.

"Mike, I'm taking you to a hospital, a private clinic, for you to rest and recover for a week. After you're sprung, you can do whatever you want. But for the next seven days you're going to rest in bed, eat good food, take the right medicine, and get sober."

He raised his head and stared at me.

"It's a nice place," I continued. "It's just up the road, in the country, and peaceful. You won't have to pay anything."

"What's the gig, Doc? Why you doin' this?"

"Somebody's got to. It might as well be me."

"This gotta be some kinda bullshit."

"The only thing bullshit is the way you've been treating yourself. Roantis says you've got great potential. You're not living up to it."

"Where the hell I gonna use my potential on the South Side?"

"You're in New England now, the Home of Potential."

"Hmmmph! Who said that?"

"I just did. You think the governor's office will go for it?"

"*Dayum!* I want a Scotch."

"The last thing you need. Okay, Mike, you can have a Scotch. I hope you enjoy it. It'll be the last one you'll have for a while."

I said this half expecting a left hook to the jaw. But Mike said nothing, and thanked me softly when I handed him the drink and told him to pack what he'd need for the next week or so in the small grip I gave him. He could leave the rest of his gear in the guest room.

We arrived at Glendale at ten-thirty. Poor Clarence Featherstone almost slumped through the floor when he saw Summers. He waited until Mike was being escorted to his room before he spoke to me, making nervous throat noises and wringing his hands.

"You — uh, *harrumph!* — didn't say he was black."

"I assumed you'd figure it out sooner or later."

I signed a check for four figures. The man stood twitching before me. Cheap hairpiece, pale skin, watery eyes, yellow polyester necktie. Definitely not my type.

"This, uh, certainly is a first for us. *Harrumph!* We've never had a, uh, black person stay here before."

"Life is full of surprises. Just remember: Dr. King would be proud of you."

"Oh, yes indeed. Yes indeed. He, uh, *will* behave himself, won't he? I mean, he seems awfully big . . ."

"Yes and no, Mr. Featherstone. Yes, he is awfully big. But not as big as he is mean. And no, he will *not* behave himself, not if he feels slighted. Do you follow me?"

He stiffened at this.

"It is Glendale's right to refuse admittance to anyone who might threaten —"

"I see. Why don't you walk down the corridor and tell that to Mr. Summers? Now do you want this check?"

He took it, handed me a receipt, and returned to his office. No doubt he wished he'd never gotten out of bed. I walked down the hallway to say good-bye to Mike. They'd put him at the end of the wing, in a corner room with two exposures. Outside, the ground was covered with patches of snow. It was sunny and cold, and Mike could look out his windows and see groves of birch trees. Cardinals and goldfinches perched in the trees and called to each other. Summers was in bed. He looked tired and peaceful.

"I'll be back this evening with a tape player and some jazz and blues, okay?"

He nodded. He hadn't said ten words to me all morning. Finally he rolled up on one elbow and seemed to stare at me.

"Thanks Doc," he said softly, and fell back onto the pillow. His eyes were shiny. I crept out of the room. For some strange reason, I felt happier than I had in weeks. Moe was right after all. Hell, I would've signed a five-figure check.

I arrived at the Concord Professional Building in time for my first patient. While I was waiting for the local to take hold, I had Susan get Brian Hannon on the phone. I explained to him I had an idea for determining who shot Roantis. Could the department get in touch with all the nearby airports catering to small private aircraft and find out which planes had arrived and departed in the four-day period two days before and after the shooting?

"That's a lot of work, Doc. I also kind of doubt they'd cooperate. Can you narrow it a bit further?"

"Then ask for info on all small planes arriving from and returning to points west of the Mississippi. That'll eliminate three fourths of the aircraft at least."

"Well, maybe. But don't expect this as a regular thing."

"Course not, Brian. I know how busy you are. What are you working on now? Eight down, or three across?"

"That's not funny."

* * *

"Gin," said Mike Summers, and laid down his hand. "Haw! Caught you with a boodle, didn't I?"

He raked up the cards and began to shuffle them. I poured him another hot cocoa out of my steel thermos. We were sitting in his tiny room at Glendale Hospital listening to vintage Duke Ellington on the portable recorder.

"So you say it wasn't a week after the first visit to the village, but only four days later that you returned there?"

"Right. Roantis could speak their lingo pretty good. He also can speak French real good too. A lot of the Vietnamese still spoke French, you know. He could always talk to them. I don't know how he learned Khmer, or whatever it was. I knew Larry Jenkins could speak it. He was the best of all of us."

"That's what everybody says, Mike. So Roantis was the only one to speak to old Siu Lok?"

"Uh-huh. Don't know all of what they said, either. But the old chief did give us a big share of the community loot."

"And what was that loot?"

"Gold and jewels. I guess the official term is 'precious stones.' They wadn't all shined up yet. They were rough, you know, like plain rocks. But anyway, they was precious all right: I cashed in my share for almost eight hundred bucks in Saigon."

"Did you ever see what Roantis carried in his pack afterward?"

Summers's face clouded over in confusion. He shook his head back and forth slowly.

"You never saw an interesting . . . art object?"

"Naw. Nothin' like that. Hell, we went into his ruck coupla times for some shit we needed. He had the same stuff as us. Sides, I wouldn't want no art object anyhow. Just the loot."

"And Ken Vilarde? What did he carry away from the village?"

Summers shrugged his big shoulders and began to shuffle the cards again. I let the whole thing drop. But a suspicion was beginning to grow in my mind.

"Do you have any idea where Ken Vilarde might be now?"

"No idea. No idea at all. We weren't that close. His big buddy, besides Roantis, was Jusuelo. Jusuelo was Puerto Rican. From the city of Mayaguez. I remember the name of the place because I was still in the service when that cargo ship, the *Mayaguez*, got captured. That's how I remembered the name of the town. You might try Jusuelo if you want Vilarde."

"Can't get a line on either one of them."

"Discard, Doc."

I did, and was about to discard the entire line of investigation too, except for one more question.

"Would any of the Ducks turn against Roantis and try to kill him?"

He looked up and stared into my eyes, wearing a little frown.

"No. The Daisy Ducks was a mean outfit. Highly trained and deadly. But we was loyal to each other. Hundret percent. We had to be. Any other way and we all woulda died out there in the boonies."

"What do you know about Bill Royce?"

"Mystery man. A puzzle. He what you call a . . . can't think of the word. Somebody who always want things to be right."

"Perfectionist?"

"Naw. Idealist. That's what Royce was. He was good, and careful. I don't think he liked to fight as much as some of the guys — as much as I used to. But he was real smart. Knew what he was doin'. But I know what we was doin' in Cambodia really bothered him. Got to him. See Doc, Daisy Duck's a mean ol' bitch. Like, she on the rag alla time, you know? Well, a lotta what we done, we just destroyed right and left. A lot of villagers and civilians got it too."

"I know. And Royce began to feel guilty about it and eventually had a breakdown."

"Yeah. I felt pretty close to coming unglued over there more than once . . . and I'm a pretty mean dude, if you hadn'ta noticed. He kinda went off the deep end. I think he in some military nuthouse, what I heard."

"He's out. He got sprung last summer."

"Hmmph! So you think it musta been one of the Ducks? Is that it? Why not somebody else?"

"It has something to do with Siu Lok's loot. But there are some things I can't tell you yet. I promised Roantis. If we assume for a minute that one of the Ducks is gunning for Roantis, would Royce be a better bet than the others?"

He glared at me from over his fanned-out hand of cards.

"Am I a suspect too?"

"No. At least I'm pretty sure you're not. I got in touch with you and Fred Kaunitz for help."

"You don't think Freddie coulda done it?"

I was silent for a second or two.

"Do you?"

His eyes swept over the cards in his hand and he rearranged them, closed the hand, and fanned it out again.

"Ain't no tellin', is there? Just no tellin'."

"Why did you lay down that seven, Mike? You know I'm saving sevens," I said, picking up his discard and sliding it into my hand.

He grinned at me.

"I hear Royce is back down in North Carolina somewhere. Up in the mountains, I think. Should I go track him down?"

"Why not? But your best bet would be finding Vilarde."

"I'm beginning to get the feeling Ken Vilarde isn't around anymore," I said.

"Could be, Doc. Could be. *Gin.*"

Twenty minutes later, I rose to go. The nurse had just given Mike a hefty bolus of chloral hydrate and he was fading fast. I waited at the doorway until he was almost under. Now would be the time to catch him, I thought. I opened the door and turned back, as if the question were only an afterthought.

"By the way, Mike, who's Daisy?"

"Haw-haw! Why she's — "

He caught himself, turned to me, and tried to sit up in bed. The pill wouldn't let him.

"Like you say, Doc. Some things I can't tell you yet. Now just rewind that tape to 'Mood Indigo' and lemme cop some Zs. Catch you later."

12

A WEEK TO THE DAY after he was committed to Glendale, I went up the road to Carlisle and sprang Mike Summers. He had lost twelve and a half pounds, mostly of intercellular fluid, and his blood pressure had dropped considerably. Most important, he no longer had to live with a drink in his hand, and he had eaten huge quantities of nutritious food during his stay. In short, he was a new man, and although the bill had been hefty, I considered it one of the best investments I had ever made.

"I'm restless now, Doc. I feel good, you know? I wanta run around a little — "

"That's just where we're going," I said. We stopped at the house only long enough for a big lunch, which Mary and Mike ate. I don't eat lunch anymore; three squares a day in modern America will turn you into a blimp in no time. I just had coffee and a small dish of yogurt. We packed the rest of Mike's things and took off for Somerville. There was a vacancy in the YMCA staff there, and they had agreed, based on a strong recommendation from Roantis, to hire Summers as a temporary staff member in exchange for a room at the Y and a small salary. It was perfect. We had him settled into the room in less than an hour. I loaned him my cassette player and a large selection of tapes. The room had a television, so he was pretty well set.

Then I showed him the gym and workout rooms. I had run on the suspended running track above the gym before. It was nice and springy — twenty-nine laps to the mile. I left Mike circling it at a shuffle that was gradually speeding up to a slow lope. I reminded him I'd pick him up the next evening for dinner at our place, and I left.

Driving back to Concord along Route 2, I kept thinking of Fred Kaunitz at the controls of his airplane. With the skill and savvy he had, honed by years in the air force, there seemed to be no place he couldn't go. I turned off on a side road and went over to Route 2A, then took the exit for Hanscom Field. Hanscom is primarily a military airfield and houses a lot of air force people and their dependents. But part of it, I knew, was reserved for private civilian aircraft and a few commercial charter flights. I entered the base and followed the signs to the civilian field.

As I entered the civilian gate, I noticed the guard booth at the entrance to the military field. The guard wore a blue beret. I took special notice of him now, since both Kaunitz and Royce had been air force commandos. Kaunitz and Royce. Hmmmmm. Both American WASPs, the only two out of the original eight Daisy Ducks. All the rest were black, Hispanic, and/or foreign-born. I was trying to think of the sociological significance of this. Also, both were nice country boys. Southerners. Well raised. Well educated. Outdoorsy types. They had a lot in common, yet Kaunitz never seemed to indicate they were close. At least, he never told me. And now Bill Royce was out and around . . .

I parked and went into the main building, where I found seven people, one of whom, James McGrevan, was eager to help.

"You want to know if we keep a record of all planes that use this field? The answer is no," he said almost apologetically. "A lot of them just come in to refuel or check a misfiring engine cylinder, then take off again. You can understand that if you're in the air and your engine starts sounding a little funny, you don't waste time checking it out."

"Right," I said. "But how about a plane that spends the night here? Don't they sign in?"

"Oh sure, for a tie-down. They pay for a tie-down in advance. The rate varies according to the size of the aircraft. They leave us a local number where we can reach them. Then we have these . . . "

He slid a slip of yellow paper over to me on the counter. It had a Shell Oil logo on top and a list of instructions underneath, much like a service repair order from a mechanic's garage.

"This is an aircraft service order. Almost always, when a pilot ties down, he'll want some things done. Maybe some fuel, an oil check, maybe have his tires looked at, things like that. Well, we fill this out, he looks it over and signs it. When we're through, he keeps a copy and so do we."

"Ahh. And how far back do you keep the copies?"

"A month. If we don't lose them in the meantime."

"Oh. So you would have no idea what planes came and went back in late December?"

"Oh no. No way."

"Well, don't these planes, wherever they're going, don't they have to chart a course or something so they don't collide with other aircraft? I mean, we've got a crowded sky around here."

He then explained briefly some of the numerous air navigation laws, which were complex and strict indeed, as well they should be.

"But see, these are all procedures. The only thing officially written down is a flight plan, which tells the tower, that's us, where the plane is headed, and along what course, at what altitude, what time of day, estimated time of arrival, and so on."

"That sounds helpful. How far back do you keep those?"

"We don't keep them. By law, they must be canceled within thirty minutes after the pilot reaches his destination. If not, we send out planes looking for the downed aircraft. Needless to say, if we have to send out a search party for a guy who simply forgot to cancel his flight plan, we're not happy about it." I inhaled and exhaled deeply a few times, summing up all the various and sundry information in my noggin.

"So, what the whole thing boils down to," I said wearily, "is that these small planes can go anywhere they want and leave no tracks."

James McGrevan thought for a few seconds before replying.

"Uh-huh," he said, rubbing his chin, "I guess that's about right."

115

"What about during landing and takeoff? Aren't they in radio contact?"

"Certainly. They must get tower clearance for both."

"What about just flying near an airfield? Don't they have to say they're flying in the airspace of a certain town or airfield?"

"There are lots of regulations about that. One thing: most planes now — even the smallest ones — have a transponder. This device emits a powerful radio signal which is picked up by the nearest airport tower. The tower can therefore track the aircraft accurately and warn the pilot if he's not where he should be."

"Is the pilot required to turn on the transponder whenever he's near a town or airfield?"

"No. It's for his safety as much as anyone's. Most pilots have their transponders on all the time."

"Mr. McGrevan, if a pilot were willing to take the risk of flying without instruments, perhaps even without running lights, and fly low, who could find him?"

"Nobody. But flying by the seat of your pants can get you killed."

"I'm sure it could."

"Unless you know how to do it," he added. I looked up and saw him grinning.

"Do you?"

"Oh yeah. I flew FACs in Nam. Those little two-seaters. FAC stands for forward air controller. We flew those little Cessnas and Beechcrafts to direct artillery fire and do nighttime reconnaissance work. We had some of them modified for circling over a target for eighteen hours or more. Others were modified to run silently, with no engine noise, so you could skim the treetops at night without alerting the enemy. That way, Charlie didn't know we were watching him."

"How far can a small plane go without refueling? What's the range?"

"Standard for a little two-seater is about three hundred miles, or three hours flying time at a little over a hundred per. A four-seater goes between four and five hours at a slightly higher speed, so figure about five hundred miles range. Course, a four-seater retractable — hell, you can go seven, eight hundred, maybe more. But if you wanted, you could easily take out some of the rear seating, or use the extra cargo space to install an auxiliary fuel tank. If you did that, hell, you could fly from here to Paris. Remember, that's just what Lindbergh did fifty years ago."

I thanked him and left, having learned one reason private planes are so popular: you can go anywhere fast, return, and leave no trail.

Back home, Mary and I went over her trip to Schenectady to visit her mother.

"You're sure you don't want to come?" she asked.

"No, I can't. Remember what Moe said, Mary, and our talk. I think we both need a little space right now. A week or so should do it fine. And since we're redoing the office building, I'd like to oversee it, at least at the beginning. Then I thought I'd go down to the Breakers for a week and fix the screens."

She sat on the edge of the bed and looked at her nails, the way people do when they're preoccupied.

"Charlie, remember when you asked me if I was having an affair?"

The words went through my gut like an artillery shell. My heart skipped two beats. Steady, Adams.

"Uh-huh. Want to tell me?"

"No, dummy. I want to *ask* you. Are you?"

"No. No way."

"You and Janice aren't — "

"No. Absolutely not."

"Then what's wrong?" She was biting her nails now, and there was wet on them.

"We know and we don't know, Mary. It's simple and complicated. I could explain it to you in a few seconds, and you could to me. And we could never explain it or understand it in a thousand years. We need a break . . . and then a coming together again."

"I guess I agree. I've felt so . . . so annoyed with you lately, Charlie. And so far away, too."

"And you've had reason to be. I think I've got to get a little of this wanderlust out of my system."

"Listen: watch out for Roantis and Summers. Those two will

117

get you into trouble, Charlie. They won't mean to, but they will. Trouble seems to follow them wherever they go."

"Maybe it doesn't follow them, Mary — maybe they tote it with them."

A week later, I drove Mary down to Framingham to catch the train to Albany. I took her luggage into her compartment and put it on the overhead rack. I sat down on the facing seat and looked at her. A true knockout. Her nylons hissed as she crossed her legs. I like that sound. Leaned over and kissed her. Her dark eyes bored into mine.

"You going to behave while I'm away?" she asked.

"Of course. What a silly — "

"You're not going to fool around with Janice, are you?"

"Certainly not. The very idea makes my stomach churn."

"Anything else churning?"

"C'mon Mare . . ."

"Well, I just wonder sometimes . . ."

"Listen, as soon as I get back, I'm going to stop by the office and watch the beginning of the renovations. Then I'm going to pack and head down to the Breakers. Then . . ."

"Then *what?*"

"I, uh, don't know what. Maybe I'll stay down on the Cape for some fishing."

"It's too cold for fishing, Charlie."

"Well, there's just not that much to do in mid-March. Tell you what: when you get back, let's fly down South somewhere. Florida, Nassau, maybe St. Thomas, okay?"

"Deal. But you behave, hear? I just know Janice will be waiting for you at the house."

"Oh, the hell she will. And you must know that I would never commit any act that would require premeditation."

"Just impulsive acts."

I didn't answer. She was painting me into a corner. I kissed her good-bye and waved when the train pulled out. I missed her even before I got back to Concord.

When I walked into the Concord Professional Building, the odor of paint, joint compound, and carpet cement hit me full force. I heard shouting at my end of the hall. "Watch dat tank!" screamed Moe at the workmen. In my heart, I wished they'd drop the tank, destroying it and the entire host of loathsome sea creatures within.

"It's not gonna work," said Moe ruefully. He tugged at his short beard and ran his fingers through what was left of his hair. He stomped around in the hall and fumed. "It's no use. I can't get anything done around here, not wid dis cockamamy — "

I surveyed the situation and was forced to agree with him; even remaining on the premises was a waste of time. Moe and Susan Petri and I went to the main lobby and got cups of machine coffee. Moe tasted it and gasped.

"Susan, I want you to take the week off," I said. "If you don't go out of town, you might want to stop in every few days for half an hour and play the answering machine tape and set up appointments. Moe, are you going to come in at all?"

"Of course, dummy. To feed my fish."

"Then," I said, getting up, "I am leaving, knowing that everything here is in good hands."

"Where are you going?" asked Susan, who was pursing her luscious lips at the edge of the paper cup and blowing softly on the hot coffee. "What will you be doing?"

"I'm so glad you asked," I said, pausing at the door, "because I haven't the faintest idea."

13

I SAT ALONE on the rough teak deck of the teahouse, wrapped in a Japanese robe. I held a steaming cup of keemun tea in both hands and watched the water ripple in the tiny pond. The pond was bordered by rocks and bamboo staves. Dwarf bonsai trees grew from the rock crevices and in big pots that Mary had made. Except for the whisper of the miniature waterfall and the faint sound of the wind chime, it was still. Two big goggle-eyed goldfish ghosted into view from the depths of the water, then flashed away, their bronze sides winking faintly. I rose, walked through the small house, and peered out its rear doorway to the driveway and the back of the house.

The motorcycle, bright metallic red, was where I had left it earlier. It represented everything that I, a middle-aged suburban professional and married father, should not do. It was everything forbidden. It was the embodiment of rebellion, danger, and freedom.

I loved it.

Two days earlier, I had returned from the Concord Professional Building — and my little visit with Moe and Susan Petri — to find a car in the driveway. Its door opened and a pair of stunning legs snaked out, tipped in tennis shoes.

"Oh hi there!" Janice had squealed as she advanced. "Is Mary around?"

I replied that she was not; she was out of town. Janice's face bore not the slightest hint of surprise at this tidbit. For good reason: she knew Mary was away. And standing there in the driveway looking at her in the tennis outfit, I knew it would only be a matter of time before I would give in to temptation. Don't get me wrong; I didn't want or plan to. But, like Mae West, I never give in to temptation . . . unless it overwhelms me. Sooner or later it would. So I made small talk with Janice for almost twenty minutes. I did not ask her to come inside. After a while, she left.

But she would be back.

That's when I first thought about leaving town. I went down to the cottage and did a day's work, then drove back to Boston. That evening I treated Liatis and Suzanne to dinner at Legal Sea Foods with Mike Summers, who had continued to lose weight and build muscle, revealing a physique that was mythically hewn. All during dinner, from the raw oysters through the lobster and scrod to the dessert and coffee, Roantis kept prodding me about the Daisy Ducks and the loot that was rightfully his. He'd obviously told Summers all about the golden statue and the pact with Vilarde, too. Far from being angry at having been excluded from the original deal, Mike seemed anxious to get involved in the search for a chunk of the action.

The next day at the BYMCU, Mike went through his paces in the ring with Tommy Desmond. The force of their sparring punches seemed to shake the old building's floor. I did my five miles, worked out on the Universal gym machine, and returned to Concord where, filled with boredom and dissatisfaction, I soon found myself looking idly through a road atlas. I had a week, perhaps ten days, to be off on my own. Since Mary and I were in what's popularly called "a bad place" in our relationship (which I hoped to God was temporary) and considering Moe's advice, I was further induced to leave Concord — and New England as well. Should I fly down to Tarpon Springs for a week of deep sea fishing? No. I had promised Mary that that would be her vacation, too.

My eyes had wandered over the map. Texas had been nice. Perhaps there was another area, closer to home, where spring came early. My eyes settled on North Carolina and the Smoky Mountains. I began to think about Bill Royce. Roantis had remembered Bill's hometown, a place called Robbinsville. I found it on the map. I realized I could even call down there and ask around for Bill's whereabouts. The more I thought of this approach, the more I realized it wouldn't get me anywhere — except maybe in trouble.

Then I had gone into the garage and started the bike. I was out on it, touring the back roads and country lanes that were temporarily free of ice and snow, for two hours. I purred along at forty, leaning into the gentle curves and accelerating on the straights. It had been a feeling of total freedom.

And now I sat at the lacquered tea table and stared out at the bike, silent and still on its stand, yet with the aura of a crouched cat, ready to spring forward with exhilarating speed and power. Even parked, a motorcycle is not boring. It's adventure on wheels. A rolling death wish. I walked out of the little garden and along the driveway toward the garage. I had a list in my head; it was time to pack.

I unlocked the Krauser hardshell bags from each side of the bike and took them inside. They looked a bit like Samsonite suitcases and weren't much smaller. I filled one of them entirely with clothes; in the other I packed clothes and other things I might need, like my binoculars, a camera with two lenses, a steel thermos, and my Browning Hi-Power pistol with spare magazines.

I called Western Union and sent a Mailgram to Mary at her mother's. She would receive it the following day, by which time I planned to be well inside Pennsylvania. Then I returned to the bike, locked the bags onto the frame and locked them shut, took a sauna bath, made a drink, thawed out some spaghetti sauce in the microwave, cooked dinner, and ate. I called my neighbor, Jim Burke, and asked him to feed and look after the dogs. After that, I gathered all the material I had on the Daisy Ducks and sat down with it. I went over everything: notes I had made on the phone calls, notes on visiting Kaunitz, snatches of information Roantis and Summers had given me, and the information on the remaining Ducks — or the *presumed* remaining Ducks.

Just before I went to bed I called Roantis and told him I was going off on a motor trip to the Southern Highlands.

"*Tomorrow?* Early? Jeeez Doc, you dint give us much notice — "

"*Us?* Who's us?"

"Uh . . . me and Mike."

"Why do you care? You're not coming."

"If you turn up something we will. Bet your ass! Look, how long will it take you? When do you expect to get out to Robbins-ville?"

"Day after tomorrow, in the evening I think. But that could change."

"Listen Doc, stay in close touch. Me and Mike want to know where you are at all times, okay?"

I promised him I would, and said I hoped both of them would live clean and not misbehave. Then I went to sleep.

Next morning I awoke before dawn. I was too wound up to return to sleep. Outside it was dark and cold. Ordinarily, hydraulic levers couldn't have pulled me from under the covers. But today was different, and I was up and dressed in many warm layers before five o'clock. At five-o-three I inserted the ignition key into the control nacelle of the big BMW and felt the two wide, transverse cylinders hum and vibrate. I rolled out of town, out Route 2 West, south on 495, out 290 through Worcester before that city had even begun to blink awake, down to 90 West and then onto 86, which would take me southwest into Hartford.

I cleared Hartford before seven-thirty, and with the growing light felt I could push the bike a little faster. I discovered I could go close to seventy with nobody seeming to care. On to Interstate 84 West all the way to Danbury, where I stopped for coffee and a twenty-minute breather. Then across the line into New York, where I ate, finally. I hummed across the bottom pointed end of that state and entered Pennsylvania shortly after eleven. Then came Scranton; I picked up my long road there: Interstate 81 South. This road would shoot me right down the pipeline — the long series of valleys of the Appalachian chain.

The road was almost deserted, and I made the bike sing. At seventy, the moving air around a motorcycle is chilling, even in the summertime. In early March in New England, it'll freeze your flesh dead in no time. But I had the touring fairing on the front of the bike, and I sat comfortably behind it in the relatively still air. The twin cylinders, which on a BMW stick straight out to the sides, were right in front of my feet, and the slipstream around them was warm. I had on winter longies, flannel-lined jeans, and insulated boots. Up on top I wore two sweaters and a fleece-lined leather jacket. The jacket was not to look tough; it was to keep the wind off and, in the event of a spill, to keep at least a little bit of my skin on. I had a thick wool scarf and my full-face helmet over a watch cap. Then, of course, I had my huge, gauntleted riding gloves to prevent frostbite.

Many people wonder why anyone would choose to ride a motorcycle when they could drive a car. Certainly a motorcycle is much more dangerous and uncomfortable. But the difference between even the hottest sports car and a good bike is the difference between that sports car and a station wagon — times two. On a bike you can lean into corners, matching the degree of lean with your speed and the sharpness of the curve. After you've spent, say, three thousand miles on a bike you get the feel of it, and soon you can make even the sharpest curves all but disappear.

But the real reason people ride bikes is the feeling of total freedom they give the rider. On a bike, even a trip to the drugstore is an adventure. With the pavement slipping underneath you in a blur, the ground surging up to kiss you on either ear as you lean over in the turns, you are conscious only of speed, power, and a sense of flight. Because after a while on a cross-country ride, something strange and wonderful happens: the bike disappears. And then it's just you, suspended three feet over the road, flying. The closest thing to it is downhill skiing.

So I flew on and on down the interstate, with Tinkerbell's magic dust on me. I stopped every two hours, then every hour as the afternoon wore on. Riding a bike is strenuous; your attention cannot wander, even for an instant. The noise, motion, and vibration all contribute to the fatigue. My pace slackened sharply after three o'clock. Toward four-thirty, I realized I was all biked out for the day, and I rolled into the Holiday Inn at Winchester, Virginia, where I took a room and soaked for almost an hour in a steaming tub.

I dressed and shaved and thought about calling the Boss. Mary had received my Mailgram by this time. The more I thought about it, the less attractive it seemed. What was I going to tell her? I thought up a little white lie to make things go smoothly. I sprawled out on the bed and dozed for an hour, then went into the dining room and ate. Roast beef, au jus. It wasn't too bad, considering it had been frozen and was thawed in a microwave. I ate lots and lots and returned to the room, where I poured myself a Johnnie Walker and water and called Mary.

"Hello?"

"Hi Mary. Guess what?"

"I know what. You're nuts. I got the telegram this morning."

"I'm in Virginia."

There was a sigh of resignation. Or was it exasperation?

"Charlie. What the hell's going on? Are you trying to see how much our marriage can stand before it snaps? I was finally understanding why you didn't come with me to Schenectady and you said you wanted to oversee the office renovations and now *this*. It's too much — "

"I know, but listen. Brady Coyne called me after you left. He's at this private fishing reserve in the Smoky Mountains where they fish for brownies all year round. He asked if I wanted to join him and, well, I just couldn't say no. It's been so long since I've really been fishing — "

"What's this lodge called?"

"The uh, uh — oh hell, I forgot. But I have a number to call him there when I get close. Listen, I'll call you again when I get there tomorrow night, okay?"

"All right, Charlie. But behave yourself, and be careful. Which car did you take, the Scout or the Audi?"

"The, uh, German vehicle."

"Oh. Well, take good care of it. And you be sure to call me tomorrow night, okay?"

"Yes."

"Who else knows where you are? Did you tell the kids?"

"No. You're the only one who knows. Susan knows I'm not coming in until the redecorating's finished."

"Wait a minute, Charlie. Something's fishy. You didn't tell Moe. Why not? You tell Moe everything."

"Uh, he, uh, was out somewhere. I couldn't reach him. I packed and left early this morning."

I was getting increasingly nervous. Calling Mary hadn't been such a good idea. Why didn't I listen to my instincts? All I knew was that Brady was a safe bet; I happened to know that he was down in Bimini, fishing the bonefish flats. Lucky stiff. It was only a white lie. I just didn't want her to worry unnecessarily.

"Charlie."

"Yes?"

"Charrr-lie?"

"What is it, love? I don't think we should talk much longer. I need my sleep."

"Give me the number of the fishing lodge where you and Brady are staying, okay?"

"Uh, I can't. It's out in the bike."

"Oh, well as soon as you — Did you say out in the *bike?*"

"Huh? Course not. Why would I say that?" *Dammit!*

"Yes you did. You said, 'Out in the bike.' I heard you."

"Naw. Bad connection. I said it wasn't where I *like.* "

"Bullshit. You said bike."

"Uh-uh. Like."

"Bike."

So we went on with that for a while, then said a civil good-bye and hung up. I could tell she suspected. The one thing about Mary is this: she always finds out. Always.

I drew up the covers and studied the map. I was a day and a half away from Robbinsville, North Carolina, reputed home of one William L. Royce, former USAF commando. The phone rang.

"Charlie."

"Hiya hon. What's new?"

"Cut the crap, Charlie. You lied to me. I called Brady Coyne's office and guess what?"

126

"It was closed, that's what."

"Uh-huh. But his tape machine was working just fine. His message said he was in *Bimini.*"

"Oh."

"Yeah. And guess what? I called the Burkes, too. I knew you'd ask Jim to feed the dogs while you were gone."

"Yep. I didn't want them to starve."

"I asked him to take a stroll over to our house and look in the garage."

A chill went up my spine.

"He reported to me that both the Scout and the Audi are in the garage. Your motorcycle's gone. So you *did* say bike."

"I am a responsible adult, Mary. I can do as I please."

"Hah! You're a six-year-old — ask any of our friends. And how can you expect me to be happy, or respect you, when you lie to me and carry on and — "

"Mary — "

"No! Now I *order* you to turn right around tomorrow and head straight back to our house before you get yourself killed. I know where you're headed, pal: you're headed for that little town in the mountains where that wacko mercenary lives, aren't you?"

"Can't we just discuss — "

"No!" She was crying now. "You come right back . . . before I . . . before — "

Then she broke down and hung up. Damn.

I tried to call her back, but the line was busy. Then the phone rang again. I picked it up.

"Listen Mary, I just — "

"This isn't Mary," said a gruff voice. "Is this Bird-Brain Adams?"

"Speaking," I said. "Listen, Brian, why don't you just — "

"No. Why don't you just listen. You're in trouble again, bub-blehead. Mary just called me. After hearing your latest shenani-gans, I'm not surprised she's upset."

"There are no shenanigans. I have a week or so to spare and am taking a motor trip. I don't see that it's any business of yours or the Concord Police Department."

"Hell it isn't. It may interest you to know that I have many friends on various police forces around the country. I know a lot of powerful people in the Carolinas, too. If you don't turn around pronto, I'm going to unleash my influence down there: you won't know a moment's peace. They'll follow you wherever you go, day and ni——"

"Yeah, well I'm not going to hold my breath, chief. Mary put you up to this. I think you'd just better let it be."

He replied that this would not happen. He said that he and his agents were going to follow me like yesterday. He hung up. I was almost asleep when the phone rang a third time. It was Dr. Morris Abramson, my former friend. He informed me that after hearing Mary's description of what I was up to, he was convinced I had lost my reason. Accordingly, for my own good, he had no choice but to notify the appropriate people and have me confined to a lunatic asylum.

"Oh is that so?"

"Absolutely. And when they get you in harness, fella, *dat's it.* They'll put you in a little tiny room wit' padding. It won't even have a window. Just a lightbulb high up, so you can't strangle yourself wit' the cord, and a li'l tiny slot to peek in at you once a week."

I pictured the scene in my mind. It was grim. But I thought of the bright side.

"Heck Moe, at least the weekends won't seem to fly by like they do now."

"Remember Doc, you've been warned."

Then he hung up. Ominous, especially for Moe, who can barely bring himself to swat a fly. I was down; I fell back on the pillow and sighed. My own best friend turned against me. But just before I fell asleep the phone rang yet another time. It was Moe again, calling to apologize. I should have known. The world's biggest sap.

"It was to scare you," he admitted. "Mary thought it might make you turn around and come back."

"Tell Mary I *shall* turn around and come back. In just a few days. She cannot control my entire life. Okay? Now I'm not going to do anything stupid. And, if you'll recall, a major reason for this journey is the advice you gave me."

He wished me luck. God bless Moe. As soon as the lump in my throat subsided a bit, I slept. But just before my mind started the lazy, crazy-quilt mosaic of unrelated thoughts and images that marks the drifting off, I knew I had not been altogether truthful with him. The main reason for my solo journey south was simple: I wanted the adventure of it.

In the predawn darkness I awoke with the traveling fit still upon me. I was out of bed and dressed before five and on the road soon afterward. When I stopped for coffee at seven I was past Staunton. I ate breakfast in Roanoke, took a break, and pushed on. I entered North Carolina before noon, going south on Interstate 77. By one I was on I-40, headed west for the mountains. But where were they? The land all around me was flatter than any I had been traveling through. Were they a myth? I passed through Hickory and Morganton with no sign of the fabled Southern Highlands.

And then, at the little town of Old Fort, it happened. I could see — far ahead, and to the left and right as well — an awesome purple swelling in the distance that seemed to reach halfway up the sky. The road tilted upward into a hill. The hill went on, without dipping even slightly, for five miles. I downshifted the bike into fourth, then finally into third gear, with the throttle well opened up. The high-torque, low-revving engine pulled me up that huge incline making a noise like a Singer sewing machine. The hill wouldn't stop. I passed semitrailers slowed to a crawl, their diesels roaring with a deep brassy whine as they struggled up the mountain. My ears popped, then popped again. The air took on a rarefied quality, with the aroma of pines and spruces. The sun was getting low in the sky now and sent undulating shadows along the sides of the mountain ranges. Far off on any horizon, the mountain ranges were set one behind the other in layers, like gigantic frozen ocean waves. The colors of the ranges varied with the distance. Close ones were bright green. The farther ones were turquoise, and the ones farthest away purplish blue or even bluish gray with the distance. The sky was blue and gold. My, it was pretty.

At the top of the big hill the highway leveled out a bit into a series of sweeping curves that wove through mountain peaks.

Then there was the little town of Black Mountain. Pulling off the interstate to gas up, I swept into a Shell station that sat on a tiny plateau surrounded by wide valleys and high, greenish-blue mountain walls. I kept looking and looking to make sure it was real. Real, all right, and gorgeous. The attendant was waiting for me with the nozzle. He was experienced; he knew how much motorcyclists appreciate not having to get off their bikes and lower the kickstand unless they're ready. I filled the tank, handed back the hose, and swept around to the side of the station, where I parked. I pulled a Mountain Dew from the soft drink machine — it seemed appropriate — and guzzled. Two more bikes pulled in, a big Yamaha cruiser and a Honda Goldwing Aspencade. The Honda had full fairing, twin tufted bucket seats, a stereo system, a cabled intercom system, bags and trunk, and two sets of extra running lights. It looked like a Chris Craft. The riders parked their machines and came over to where I sat on the station apron. They had taken off their helmets and stowed them in the trunks; they wore billed caps. Both tipped their hats at me before sitting down. I liked that.

"See you got one a them Kraut bikes," drawled Honda, lighting a Winston. "Them's good bikes I hear. But expensive."

"Uh-huh. And slower than some, too. But they do last a long time. Where are you from?"

"We're from Sylva. Little bitty place between Asheville and the Smokies. I'm Pete and this is my ridin' partner, Jimmy."

We shook hands all around, and they began to talk about riding in the mountains. How they could talk. I enjoyed every minute of it. Pete must have offered me cigarettes a dozen times. We bought coffee, and they asked if I wanted to ride with them "for a spell." I said sure.

We finished the coffee, hit the head, and mounted up. We rode off into a sunset that was drowning itself in a magnificent gap in the far mountains, a huge V of red and gold. My God, it was lovely. Beethoven's Fifth in color. Our engines hummed and thrummed under us, and we made wide, leaning sweeps through the curves, heading for it.

I was tingling with excitement, glad I'd come along.

14

WE RODE ALONG I-40 WEST together until we got to Asheville forty minutes later. Asheville sits on a high plateau between two mountain ranges. It was getting dark and the temperature was falling. We parked our bikes and sat in what was left of the sun in a parking lot that belonged to the phone company. From where we sat, I could see the far ring of mountains all around. My new friends pointed out the sights. There were fine old buildings below us, a big, neoclassical courthouse right next to an art deco building that they said was the town hall. Pete took out a can of Skoal and shoved a pinch down behind his lower lip. Then he lighted a Winston. He gestured at my bike.

"Massachusetts, eh? You a long way from home, seems like."

"Uh-huh. I'm taking a week off for a private vacation. How far is a town called Robbinsville?"

"Robbinsville? Two hours. Pretty ride, too. Real doggone pretty, eh Jimmy?"

"Yep. She's right on the Tennessee line, you know. They hunt boar and bear there a lot."

"I especially want to find someone who lives there. A friend of a friend of mine. Ever hear of a family named Royce?"

They shook their heads, and a long silence followed. Jimmy

worked his lips around, savoring the sting and buzz of the wet snuff oozing nicotine into the tiny blood vessels of his mouth. I decided not to tell him about my several encounters with the effects of wet snuff on the mucous membranes of the nose and mouth. I did know, having tried leaf tobacco a few times on fishing trips, of the tremendous wallop it gives the user — more powerful than two big Jamaican cigars.

"What you want to find them Royces for anyhow?" Jimmy asked finally. The tone of his voice was friendly, but I sensed the faint beginnings of distrust and suspicion. I stretched out my legs, appearing as nonchalant as possible, and said that a friend of mine in trouble was seeking help from an old army buddy. He was too injured to travel, so I was helping him out.

"Well, that's good. A Christian thing to do. But don't you move too fast on 'em. We mountain folks, we're nice as pie most of the time. But outsiders should be careful, too, especially if they're from up north a good ways. We don't rile easy. But when we do, we're like a nest of copperheads. What'd you say your name was again?"

"Charles Adams. Call me Doc."

"Are you a doctor?"

"Yes, a surgeon. I operate on people's jaws and teeth."

"Well I never! A biker-doctor. But like I was sayin', Doc, if you want to get along, just be easy."

Jimmy settled back against a young locust tree and chuckled softly to himself. Meanwhile, Pete went over to his bike and took a steel thermos of coffee from his saddlecase. We passed around the cup and talked. Pete looked at his watch.

"We're a hour from home, Doc. I like to get home before five on a Sunday. The missus likes that. Even we tough road hogs got to foller the rules."

He winked at Jimmy, who chuckled again. I debated whether to push on or spend the night in Asheville. It was the biggest city in the western part of the state and seemed pretty and pleasant. But then they asked me to ride along with them as far as Sylva and have supper, so off we went, down through town and back onto the highway. We purred into Sylva as night was settling down over the place like an old down comforter. It was brisk out, but not cold. I heard the far-off murmur of waterfalls and the whisper of wind in the trees. We wound up a road that was really a wide path in the mountains until we stopped in front of a clapboard house dug into the cliffside. It was faded white, with a gingerbread porch on two sides, facing down a valley. Pete led us up onto the porch and pointed across the valley at a mobile home set on cinder blocks. Lights twinkled around it; vines grew around the carport and the tiny attached porch.

"That's Jimmy's place yonder. He lives alone since his wife died, but spends a lot of time over here. Let's set out here a spell."

We sat while Pete left and reappeared with a plastic gallon milk jug half full of water. His wife, Liz, followed and welcomed me warmly, without hesitation or surprise. In the near-darkness I could see her glasses and brown hair done up in a bun. She said we would have roast pork, potatoes, and leather breeches for supper, with biscuits and cold buttermilk afterward. She went into the house. I asked what leather breeches were, and was told I would find out. Pete poured the water into three jelly glasses. It was water, all right: firewater. I added some branch water to mine to smooth it out a bit. It wasn't bad. It wasn't good particularly, but it wasn't bad. And it packed enough of a punch to warm me up after the ride. We drank and talked and watched the last bluish light disappear from the valley. Pete pointed up the valley to where it seemed to end in a solid green mountain wall.

"See that, Doc? This here's called a cove. Lots of coves hereabouts. A cove is a valley that's sealed up at one end by a mountain. What it is, really, is a big gully carved by a mountain stream, you see. Where the stream begins, up in the mountain yonder, that's where the cove ends. Open only at this end. Coves is right private places. Only one road in, one road out. Families own their own coves, mostly. This here is called Sluder's Cove, named after us. Only way in here is the little road we was just on. Everbody else stays *out.* Yep, coves is private."

After forty minutes or so of chitchat and illicit whiskey, we went inside and sat down around a table covered with blue gingham-patterned oilcloth. Pete said grace, being sure to thank the Almighty for each and every thing we were about to eat . . . and all the people involved, too, including me. It took a while. I liked it. And I was beginning to like these people a whole lot, too. Everything was terrific, except perhaps the leather breeches, which were dried beans in their pods, soaked up and boiled in pork broth. Must be an acquired taste. After supper we sat and drank coffee. I lighted a pipe and asked if there was a motel nearby. But Pete and Liz Sluder wouldn't hear of it. They showed me a cot in the sleeping porch. The screens were covered with plastic, which cut the chill a bit. I brought my bags inside and settled in. Liz knocked at the door and waltzed in with two enormous quilts — comforters, really. The quilt designs on them were beautiful. She caught me looking at them.

"You like these, Doc? This here's called the Double Irish Chain. Idn't it pretty? And this one's what we call a story quilt. That scene in the middle. Took me three months to finish."

I looked more closely. The central picture was of a young blond man under a fallen tree. A double-bitted ax lay nearby.

"That's Bill. My only nephew. We never had any young 'uns of our own. Bill was kilt by a falling tree out in the Snowbird Mountains when he was logging there fifteen years ago."

"I'm really sorry."

"No need, Doc. He's in heaven now. A right pleasin' young man. I made this story quilt so we'd always remember him. Goodnight now."

She left the room. I turned out the light and climbed into bed. The mattress was too soft, but the covers weighed a ton and the night was really cold now. The plastic wrap on the windows sucked in and out and flapped against the screens. Outside was the sighing and hissing of the strong wind through the pines. I heard the distant rush of falling water and the hooting of nightbirds down the valley. I could have been ten thousand miles from Concord, Mass. And perhaps sixty years away, too. I snuggled down in the comforters and was gone.

I was up before dawn again. What was wrong with me? I slipped out of bed, dressed, and carried my saddlecases out to the bike and attached them. I wanted to leave behind a gift of some kind, but I didn't have anything. I wanted to slip away without inconveniencing the Sluders further, although I wanted to say good-bye as well.

"Where you think you're goin'?" said a gruff voice behind me. I turned to see Pete Sluder on the porch.

"I thought I'd just mosey on without bothering you any further."

"Well, not before you eat you ain't. Lizzie's gettin' a big breakfast going."

So I stayed for that, too. Sausage, eggs, biscuits, country ham, and grits with red-eye gravy. Red-eye gravy may not sound appetizing, but served over hot grits it was the finest surprise I got in the South. With all this we were served cider and percolator coffee that was prescription strength. I rolled out of there at sunup. As I purred down the gravel lane, Pete caught up with me.

"There's several Royces in Robbinsville. I think the one you want is north of town. There's a widder lady there with a son living with her."

"When did you find this out? I thought you didn't know about the Royces."

"Oh, we knew a little bit. We just didn't want to say nothing until we figured you was all right. Good-bye, Doc. Stop back here on your way back home and we'll do some ridin'. Good luck. Be careful out there. Look sharp."

We shook hands. I yelled good-bye to Liz and was off.

The scenery along the road to Robbinsville put everything else I'd seen in the shade. Sometimes the valleys were so narrow and steep that I had a sense of claustrophobia, which was understandable perhaps for someone raised in the flat cornbelt. But in these narrow valleys the high rocky walls of the nearby mountains were so close and steep that they seemed to loom up around you, almost blocking the sun. The valleys were very sparsely settled; those with people living in them had only one or two shacks hanging from the cliffsides. How their residents got their pickups up there and down again sure had me puzzled. In rugged mountains like these a neighbor who lived half a mile distant might be an hour's trek by steep footpaths. This was the reason for the legendary clannishness of the mountain people, and perhaps, too, for their violent reaction to much of the outside world. The land had imposed a Dark Ages isolation on the hillfolk. They were, for all practical purposes, a thousand miles distant, a hundred years behind the times.

I rolled into Robbinsville a little after eight and had the whole day to find Bill Royce, or his homestead. Robbinsville was not a wealthy town, but it was getting by in a frontier sort of way. I cruised around town first, giving it the once-over. There was a huge furniture factory on one side of town, with a never-ending lumberyard and log depot attached. It reminded me of the lumber and paper mills in interior Maine. From this, and from reading the bulletin boards and the local paper, I assumed that lumber and hunting were the two primary revenue getters. There were a lot of advertisements for bear and boar outfitters. I ordered coffee at a diner and looked through the phone book. Six Royces. I wrote down all the address and phone numbers. Most of the Royces were on Royce Cove Road. I knew what that meant: they were all snuggled up together in one of those box canyons with only one way in, one way out.

I found the dime store and bought a town map. It was really a hunting map prepared by the North Carolina Fish and Game Department, showing hunters where to find big game in the mountains. The map was bordered by photos of trophy black bear and Russian boar. The specimens were huge and nasty, even in death. Wild country, no doubt about it. Royce Cove Road was indeed north of town, and it wound around the mountains for a goodly distance. It paralleled a small branch stream on the map with the unlikely — not to say ominous — name of Hanging Dog Creek. I tucked the map into my breast pocket and cruised out of town until I picked up the road. It was a single-lane dirt path, and I wound my way up the foothills slowly, keeping an eye on the mailboxes. I passed four boxes with Royce painted on them and went all the way to the end of the road, which terminated in a steep path up the side of the mountain. The path was dark; I couldn't see up it farther than about twenty feet. In the distance I heard the plashing of a waterfall. I turned the bike around on the narrow road. I would work my way back down the cove and out. So I stopped at the first mailbox, the one farthest in. The lady who answered the door was friendly and said she was the widow Royce. Her son, Edward, was an electrician who was working on a big job at a nearby sawmill. When I asked her about Bill Royce, she fell silent for a few seconds and asked who I was and what I wanted. I explained I was a friend of a friend and wanted to see him. Squinting at me, she finally asked if I knew what had happened to him overseas.

"Yes. I was sorry to hear that he's been . . . not well. I hope he's better now."

"Well," she answered, massaging her lower lip with a thin gray hand, "it's just hard to say right yet how he'll turn out. He seems a'mighty glad to be home here in the mountains. I think that helps a body more than anything else . . . being home, that is."

"Do you think he'd mind if I stopped by?"

She kept rubbing her lower lip and staring off down the cove with a worried expression. She seemed to be deciding something and asked me to have a seat on one of the metal porch chairs. I had seen these on almost all the porches in the South: metal armchairs painted green or gray, with a back like a giant scallop shell. I sat down. Through the curtained window I could see her talking on the phone. Five minutes later she was back on the porch.

"You can go on down there. Second house on this side of the road. Her name is Sairy."

I thanked the widow and left. At the second house I parked the bike and walked up to the porch. This house was in fine repair. It had shutters that were painted canary yellow. The porch railings and screen spindles were gothic gingerbread, freshly painted. Sairy Royce — I assumed her name was really Sarah — came to the door and opened it halfway. She seemed torn between welcoming me with open arms and kicking me off the porch.

"Mrs. Royce? I'm Dr. Charles Adams. Your son Bill and I have a mutual friend, a man Bill was with in the army."

"Bill was in the air force, mister. And why are you here?"

"Another friend of Bill's is missing, and I was hoping to ask your son when he last saw him."

She looked me up and down.

"Your name is Adams?"

"Yes ma'am."

She opened the door and asked me inside.

"I know some of your kinfolk, Mr. Adams. They's a whole bunch of Adamses over to Shooting Creek. Nice folks. You sit down and I'll fetch you some tea."

So she did. Perhaps she thought I was going to call on my kinfolk as well, since I was in the neighborhood. She brought the tea and some cookies, sat down in a straight-back chair with a woven seat, and looked at me keenly. Sairy Royce was pretty, with bright blue eyes under iron gray hair. Her teeth were perfect. Too perfect.

"You're not from the war, Mr. Adams? Billy hasn't never met you?"

"No ma'am, he hasn't. But I've been in touch with several of the men he knew in the war. Is he here now?"

"Oh no. He's out working. I think work is the best thing for him. He and some friends bought an old bottomland farm nearby and they're working it. He usually comes home for dinner, which is in about three hours. But I don't know if it would be good for him to see you or not. You know, the memories of what all happened to him might come a-stormin' back in his mind, you see."

"I understand. And I wouldn't want that either. What exactly did happen to him anyway? Did he ever tell you?"

"Oh Lord yes. He talks to me about it, but only me. His daddy lives down in Georgia now, hasn't been home in fourteen years. So there's only the two of us. He sees his cousin Eddie — that's the house you was just at up the cove — and his other friends, is about all. But anyway, what happened to Billy that made him so sick was later on, just before we pulled down the flag and got out of there. When the Communists moved in on Saigon. All those people and children murdered . . . and all the things that he'd worked so hard for and risked his life for . . . it was just too much for Billy for a while. So he spent some time in a special hospital in the Philippines and got home last July — like a gift from God. And I thank the Lord ever day for it. No more fightin' for Billy. He still hunts a lot. We all do here in the mountains. But no more killin'."

138

"Amen," I said.

"Amen."

"Listen, why don't you let me write down some names on a slip of paper. When Bill comes home for lunch, show him the names, and if he'll talk with me, fine. If not, I'll go back where I came from."

She said that sounded fair. I remembered what Pete and Jimmy had told me about being too pushy with these people. I told her I would phone her shortly after noon, to see what Bill wanted to do. I thanked her for the hospitality and left. I wondered how I was going to kill the three hours until lunchtime — called dinnertime in the South — as I left Royce Cove Road for the highway. When I got back into town, I realized it would be handy to know where the farm was that Royce had bought. Of course, if I'd asked his mother it would have set her on edge. I needed to fade back into the bush and observe unseen. The more I thought of this approach the better it sounded . . . and the more I realized my bike was very conspicuous. A bright metallic-red German motorcycle with a Massachusetts plate does tend to stand out a bit in the Smoky Mountains off season. I took my steel thermos bottle into the diner I'd visited earlier and had the waitress drop two teabags into it, some milk and sugar, and top it off with hot water. It was now ten. With nothing else to do, I headed back to where Royce Cove Road left the twisty highway and turned off the road into a copse of thick trees opposite the mouth of the cove. There was no sun in there, and the morning was chilly anyway. I took a space blanket from my saddlecase, folded it twice, and used it for a seat. The tea would also help keep me warm. I had my binoculars out, too. I sat and waited. In the two hours I sat there, four cars came and went. Two pickups, a station wagon, and a sedan. One of the pickups, a tan Ford with a long antenna, swept up the cove road just before twelve. I couldn't see who was at the wheel. Ten minutes later I left my observation post and stopped at a gas station to call Sairy. She answered, saying Bill would see me, but only briefly.

I returned to the house. The first thing that caught my eye was the tan pickup in the driveway. Sairy came to let me in. She said that Billy was in the back room, listening to records.

"He tuckers easy, Mr. Adams. Please don't stay too long."

Bill Royce rose from the couch to greet me as I walked into the sunporch. He was taller than I, but not as tall as his air force comrade, Fred Kaunitz. His hair was light brown and very thin, long and brushed back, which accentuated his near-baldness. He wore aviator glasses with steel frames. The first thing I noticed about Bill Royce was his eyes. All the other Ducks I had met had flat eyes. Dead eyes. Eyes that revealed the total lack of emotion and tenderness in the mind and soul behind them. Eyes that could watch a man die on the stake without flinching. But this pair of gray-green eyes that looked into mine were sensitive and — in the words of Mike Summers — idealistic. He looked studious, thoughtful, and caring. And that, I decided, is why he couldn't take it. That's why his soul had cracked under the horror of Southeast Asia.

"I can still remember most of it, Mr. Adams," he said as we sat down. "They gave me ECT treatments at first, but your memory comes back."

He took the last sip from a can of root beer and tossed it into the wastebasket. Royce had barely a trace of Southern accent.

"Just call me Doc, Bill. Most people do."

The record was playing a Chopin piano piece. "I can remember almost all of it. I just don't like to think about it. Have you seen any of the other guys on the patrol?"

"Yes, three of them, including your leader, Roantis. By the way, about eight weeks ago, he was shot while leaving my house. He almost died. We're still trying to figure out who did it. Do you have any ideas?"

"No. Absolutely not. I haven't been around soldiering now in years. I've lost touch. Is he going to recover fully?"

"Probably. He's especially anxious to find Ken Vilarde. He wants to make contact with him."

Royce looked down and shook his head sadly.

"And while I was sick in Manila, and being put back together again, piece by piece, cell by cell, he didn't make contact with me. None of them did."

Offhand, I couldn't think of an appropriate response, so I looked down at the brown shag carpet and listened to Chopin.

"Ken Vilarde . . . Who knows? I thought he had decided to be a career man. On my last patrol through Cambodia with the Daisy Ducks, that's when I knew I never wanted to be a career man."

"What happened on that last run?"

"Well, we helped destroy a village."

"You mean old Siu Lok's village?"

He looked at me quickly, sharply.

"Who told you? Roantis?"

"Yes. He said the village was about to be overrun by Khmer Rouge guerrillas. You arrived in time to save it, at least temporarily."

"That part is true. But I think ultimately we were as much responsible as the Khmers. That's what makes the whole thing so sad."

"I've heard that war generally is."

"You've never been in war? In action?" he asked me.

"No."

A thin film of sweat had formed on Bill Royce's upper lip. He wiped it off with the back of his hand and sniffed, then scratched his nose nervously. He excused himself and headed for the john, returning a few minutes later with another can of root beer, which he sipped in small doses. He kept sniffing and sipping for a while. I sensed that the fatigue and strain of the interview was beginning to take a toll. What the hell, I thought, I may as well ask the question.

"Bill, do you recollect taking anything from that village after your first visit? That is, before the Khmer Rouge came back and tortured old Siu Lok to death?"

He looked up in surprise.

"He told you the Khmer Rouge tortured Siu Lok? Hmmm . . . That's interesting, Doc, because I'm not sure it happened that way at all. I'm not saying it didn't, or couldn't have . . . I'm just saying it's a little strange. You see, when we went back the second time, Roantis and Vilarde went on ahead. They told the rest of us to wait and they'd signal if they needed help. We were bushed anyway, so we went to earth and crashed for a couple hours. Before long, here comes Ken and Liatis back, saying that

141

the Communists had apparently killed the old chief. But they never saw it happen. And the funny thing was, when we all went walking through the village again, everybody there was terribly afraid of us. They gave us everything we asked for immediately — not making excuses or stalling like villagers usually did. They wouldn't look us in the eye. I just had a strange feeling."

"Are you saying it's possible that Roantis and Vilarde killed the old man?"

Royce paused and sniffed, scratched his nose again, and wiped his face. He tapped his feet on the shag rug. He ran his hand through his hair in agitation.

"No. I'm not saying it. I'm saying this, Doc: in that jungle there, a million miles from home or friendlies, anything could happen. Those villagers looked very scared our second pass through. Very scared. We all commented on it. I don't know. I just got thinking afterward, why did those two go on alone? Why weren't we all together, like the first time?"

"Okay, and you took nothing from the villagers on the first pass-through?"

"Certainly. We always did if they were willing. We needed food."

"Anything else? Any valuables?"

"No. There was nothing in the village of any value I could see."

"That's funny, Bill, because Roantis said you all split up a potload of community relics on the first visit there. Kaunitz and Summers say the same thing. Now you say there were none."

"If the others took anything, they sure didn't tell me."

"Did you ever see anything strange in Roantis's pack?"

"No. I didn't go looking in his pack."

"Uh, how soon after the second visit to Siu Lok's village were you lifted out?"

"The next night, I think. Or maybe the night after. We were heading west that trip, and the chopper came and got us."

I sat there in the sunporch staring at the shag carpet for about a minute. What the hell was going on anyway? All the versions of the story were different, which was understandable, considering the lapse of time. Yet Royce's version differed markedly from the others. Considering his recent ill health and the other men's stories, I shouldn't believe him. But I did. At least, I was convinced he was telling the truth as he was able to reconstruct it. I decided to take a big chance. I excused myself and went outside to the bike, then returned with the photograph in my hand. I showed it to Royce, whose upper lip was weeping again.

"What's that supposed to be?" he asked.

"It's a religious idol, a statue of Siva, which Roantis took from the village, a gift from grateful Siu Lok."

"And you believe it?"

"Why wouldn't I?" I answered. But the answer didn't satisfy me. I had had vague doubts about the statue before, and now they seemed stronger and more focused.

"Well, for one thing, a statue this big and heavy would be noticeable in a rucksack. The Ducks traveled light, as the others must have told you. Secondly, you don't see Hindu deities in Cambodia or Vietnam; they're Buddhist countries. It would be like finding a Lutheran in Mexico. Know what I mean?"

"I know what you mean. Listening to you, I sense a college education. Right?"

"Oh yeah. I had a full academic scholarship to UNC. Did some post-grad work too. Then along came Vietnam and I wanted to be a hero. I always wanted to fly, so I joined the air force, then volunteered for all the special training available. Except for jump school, which was hell, the rest was interesting, almost fun. I shouldn't have done it, Doc. Should *not*. It's wrecked my life."

He paused to wipe his lip and sniff.

"Assuming this statue thing is bogus — why, I wouldn't know — can you think of any object that could have been taken from the village that would be worth a lot of money?"

He thought for a long time before answering.

"I can't think of any object, Doc. But I can think of a substance, especially when I think of Cambodia."

"And?"

"Pure opium, in brick form. It's been cultivated for centuries in Cambodia. They dry the resin into bricks, like hash, and sell to smugglers who sneak it into Marseilles, where they turn it into heroin."

"How much would a couple of bricks be worth?" I asked.

"A lot." He sighed. "I couldn't name a figure. But let me tell you: we saw a few poppy fields in Cambodia. Those peasants need the bread — they still grow the stuff."

"From what you've said, I could believe that Roantis is not an honest man. But having known him for about six years, I have no reason to think this. Though I'm not about to let him slide, if you know what I mean. Why do you think Liatis is lying?"

"I'm not saying he is. Roantis was a good soldier — that's why he was picked for team leader. We weren't paid well for risking our necks, either. Therefore, he's got to be a little honest. No crook would have taken it on. But I will say this: special operations is hairy stuff. You've got to think on your feet. Truth becomes a relative thing. The rule book goes out the window. Follow? A lifetime of doing that stuff can make you say and do all sorts of things most people wouldn't do. That's all I'm going to say about it."

He stood up and offered his hand. Civil enough, but the message was clear: the interview was ended. We shook hands. On the way out, I made what must have appeared to be a strange request.

"Did you wear braces growing up?" I asked.

"You mean on my teeth? No."

"That's interesting. Your bite is perfect. May I look at your teeth a second? Do you mind? It helps me in my profession."

He complied. I had him bite down three times. Amazing fit.

"Good-bye, Bill. Thanks a lot for your time. I apologize if I put you through any trauma. And listen: if you hear of the whereabouts of Vilarde or Jusuelo, would you call me collect at the number on this card? Thanks."

"Sure. What are you going to do now?"

"I guess I'll turn around and do a little sightseeing on my way home to Boston. Might as well. I'll say hello to Roantis for you."

I said good-bye to Sairy, who was knitting in the living room, and left. It was not even one o'clock. I went back into Robbinsville and ate at a fast-food joint. Over the coffee I had myself a longish think. Royce's version of the village massacre was interesting, and credible too. Royce seemed intelligent, sensitive, and sincere. I should probably call up Roantis and give him hell for sending me on a wild goose chase, even though I'd come down on my own.

But I didn't. Because two things about Mr. Royce had me thinking. One was the condition of his hands. I felt the right hand as we shook good-bye. He had that horny ridge of callus running along the side of it. Roantis still had his, but he was a martial arts instructor. Even Kaunitz and Summers had lost theirs. Not Bill Royce.

The second thing was a vague suspicion that began gnawing at me as soon as the interview began. The sweat on Bill's lip. The runny, itchy nose, and most especially the craving for sweet soft drinks. The glance I got inside his mouth, and the damage to the teeth and gums, confirmed my hunch. You can tell an awful lot about a person by looking in his mouth. More than once, after doing minor surgery on a high school student, I found myself having to make a painful, but vital, phone call to the parents. But when you see those symptoms, and the condition of the teeth, you know.

Bill Royce was a heroin addict.

15

I KNEW how I could find out where Bill Royce's farm was without alerting him or anyone else. The Graham County Courthouse was easy to find. It was just down the street from the Robbinsville Police Department. The police department was simply a blue door on the street. It appeared to be a one-room department. I suppose the total police force was about three men. I went to the front desk of the courthouse and asked where I could find the real estate transactions for the past year. Since all real estate transactions are a matter of public record, it is the duty of any county clerk's office to show them to interested parties. In twenty minutes I was sitting down in front of voluminous records detailing every sale and title transfer in the county. It didn't take long. One William R. Royce had purchased forty acres of bottomland from one Randall J. Plemmons on September 22. Six months previous. The farm property, complete with dwelling and two outbuildings ("herein described") was in a valley seven miles northwest of town. I rode out there and had a peek. I saw the place briefly from the highway. Most of the farm was the wide valley, with a bottom that was ironing board flat. That was extremely rare in these mountains. A stream zigzagged lazily through the valley. That meant nice topsoil. All in all, a prize bit of farmland. I didn't park the bike. I knew that Royce or his buddies would spot it immediately, and I wanted him to think I really was returning to Boston. I headed back to Asheville to trade in the bike, if only temporarily.

I arrived in midafternoon, grabbed a phone book, and located a big dealer at the edge of town specializing in recreational vehicles. After an hour and a half of looking and haggling, I rented a chassis-mounted camper on a GMC truck. It slept four and had a big double bunk extending out in front, over the cab of the truck. It was roomy but not too big. The dealer assured me it could go off the road for short distances and was powerful enough to handle the mountain grades. I gave him a week's rent, stowed the BMW in the back of his garage, and repacked my gear in the camper. I kept the keys to the bike. I stopped at a supermarket and stocked the camper with enough food for four days.

I bought rib-eye steaks, chicken, game hens, and lamb chops, plus a few sackfuls of produce, spices, sauces, and other things I knew would make my chow at least bearable during my short recon visit. The grocery store was interesting. In place of the kosher deli section, which was all but absent, there was a huge counter display of tobacco in all its various guises — the most popular, it seemed, being chewing tobacco and snuff. They had leaf and they had plug. They had cable twist, too. They had wet and dry snuff. The products had names like Days O Work, Cannon Ball, Red Coon, Hound Dog, Brown's Mule, Taylor's Pride, Levi Garrett, Beechnut, Big Duke, Workhorse, and so on. Just for the hell of it, I bought a little can of dry snuff — the kind you sniff up your nose, as they all did in Concord in the days of the Revolutionary War. I took the five sacks of food and supplies out to the camper and stowed them all neatly in the paneled cupboards and little racks. The camper reminded me of my sloop, the *Ella Hatton.* The dealer had given me a little directory of nearby campgrounds. I found one right by Robbinsville that was open year round for RVs, called the owner, and reserved a spot.

So back out I went, this time lacking all the speed and maneuverability I'd had on the previous trip, but taking my house on my back. Best of all, with the camper rig I had a Carolina plate on the back, so I fit right in with all the other campers, hunters, and sightseers. My first stop was at the campground, where Mr. Hardesty, the owner, showed me my site. I backed into it, made sure the proper cords and connections fit, paid Mr. Hardesty for two nights, and was told that the gate to the grounds was never locked. I liked that. There were only two other rigs in the entire campground that I could see. One of them, a big motor home, was occupied by a retired couple. The other camper was scarcely visible from my site. The campground was surrounded by hills and thick woods. I told Mr. Hardesty that I was enjoying a three-day vacation from the wife and kids. He nodded in sympathy.

I disconnected my power cords and water hose and rolled out of the campground. Soon I was again on the tiny highway that bordered the Royce farm. I passed it twice, deliberately not slowing down. There seemed to be no convenient, inconspicuous place to park the rig, so I went farther up the highway opposite the next farm. There I found a wide, flat space off the road where I could leave it when I returned. It wasn't perfect, but it would have to do.

I returned to the campground, hooked up my rig again, and went outside to start a campfire. When it was going, I went inside, popped two small potatoes into the oven, and made a drink. I sat watching my small fire and thought. I realized that I was at the turning point. I could still pack it in and go home. I could then tell Roantis all I had learned from my little trip and my debt to him would be retired, at least to my own satisfaction.

On the other hand, I was here now. I had arrived at my destination, discovered enough about Bill Royce to sense that something wasn't right, and was now in a position to perhaps find out something more specific and concrete. Wouldn't I be a fool to quit now?

Yes.

But wouldn't I be a fool to continue, especially alone and so far from friends?

Also, yes.

What conclusion can thus be drawn from these two inferences, Dr. Adams?

"I'm a fool," I said out loud to myself.

Well, that was hardly news.

But one thing I should definitely do: call Roantis, now.

I secured the fire by putting big rocks around it and walked back to the campground office, where the pay phone was. I found him at home, of all places. Surprise, surprise. Roantis had definitely turned over a new leaf.

"And you're already in Robbinsville? How'd you do that?"

"Just kept pushing on."

"You move real fast. What's the name of the campground again?"

I told him. Then I told him about my interview with Bill Royce. I didn't mention that I'd showed Bill the photo of the statue, but Royce's comments had me going. I had to ask Roantis a question.

"Liatis, is there really a Siva, or is it a cock-and-bull story you made up so I'd help you find Vilarde?"

"Why don't you believe me?"

"A lot of reasons. One: nobody else saw it, and it was supposedly big and heavy. Two: a poor village wouldn't have a gold statue, especially one depicting another religion. Now are you going to level with me?"

"I have already. Siu Lok was a river pirate, and that loot was his, not the village's. I think he was a selfish old crook who gave us the loot just to spite the Reds. He knew the Khmer Rouge would find his stash and use it to buy more guns. Nobody saw the statue because Ken and I wanted it that way. Now listen Doc: sit tight in that campground. Don't budge. Mike and I are starting down there early tomorrow. We'll be there the next day. And watch out for Royce, too. I don't like what I hear about him so far."

We hung up, and then I called Mary. It wasn't bad at all. She missed me. I missed her. I explained that I was about to head home, but not before Liatis came down to take over.

"Take over? That means he'll be in danger and not you?"

"Absolutely. He's good at it and I'm not."

"*You're* not kidding."

"So when he gets down here to wrap things up, I'll start home."

"Good. Let's do this: you call me tomorrow at dinnertime and tell me when you're starting back and what your plans are. And leave me the number of that campground. And goddamnit, Charlie, don't do anything stupid."

"I'll use my best judgment."

"*Don't.* Your best judgment is inadequate. I said: don't do anything stupid."

We said good-bye, and I left the little office and walked back to my rig. The potatoes were nearly done. The fire was low and beginning to make big coals. I mixed together equal amounts of cottage cheese and sour cream in a small bowl. Then I added a little grated Parmesan cheese, some chives, and crushed garlic. I fried three bacon strips in a pan. Then I took the rib-eye steak from the tiny icebox and put it on the wire grill I'd bought and placed it on the fire. When it was done, I yanked it off fast and stuck it in the oven on a plate. Then I crushed the bacon strips and put the crumbs on a bowl of raw spinach and cut mushrooms. Into the rewarmed bacon grease I mixed in sugar, white vinegar, a raw egg, and a teaspoon of stone ground mustard. I heated and stirred this mixture until it thickened, then poured the hot, German-style sweet-sour dressing over the spinach and tossed it. I cut the potatoes open and put butter and the cheese and sour cream mixture over them, then put them on a warm plate with the steak. I wolfed it all down. It was a sin, a Sodom and Gomorrah of the palate. To help wash it down, I had a split of dry red and a whole bottle of sparkling mineral water. Then I had a cup of strong coffee. To top everything off, I opened the can of dry snuff I had bought at the grocery store. It was a small cylindrical tin with a blue label on it showing a steam engine. It read: "Railroad Mills Mild Scotch Snuff." Mild, huh? I sniffed in a couple of doses and could feel my pulse go up. Talk about substance abuse. I thought of all the old geezers, male and female, up in the hills, who dipped snuff continually. The junkies in the South Bronx had nothing on them.

After the initial rush wore off, I felt sleepy. I opened the camper windows to let the cool air in, turned down the bunk bed, and went outside to sit over the fire while it died. From far off down the hillside, I heard the faint sound of spring peepers, those tiny tree frogs with the ultra-shrill voices. They seemed to be out early. But then, I was hundreds and hundreds of miles south of Boston. The fire died. It was not even ten, but I went inside the camper, doused the lights, and crawled into bed. I decided to leave it to fate. If I awoke early, I'd go have a look at Royce's farm. If I slept through, then I'd stay put and spend the day reading. So be it.

16

AT TWO-THIRTY, I found myself pulling on my thermal under-wear. I had gotten out of the bunk, found the clothing in a drawer, and was putting it on even before I was fully conscious. Half asleep, I sat at the dinette table and placed my Browning Hi-Power on it. I slid out the magazine, which was filled with thirteen nine-millimeter Luger rounds, hollow point. I squirted some WD-40 on the magazine and the rounds. I wanted them to snake out of there lickity-split if need be. They would. I put on a thick sweater over a quilted thermal liner, then the leather motorcycle jacket. Its side zip pockets were large enough for the pistol, but just barely. I wouldn't be able to get it out fast, but that was okay. I knew I could use the piece if I really had to, but it would take a bad situation for me to consider it. The second item was a flashlight. I put this in the left pocket along with the two spare magazines for the Browning. I made coffee and filled the metal thermos bottle. I poured the rest of the coffee into a mug and downed it along with a Snickers bar.

Then I almost tried pulling out of the campsite without discon-necting the hoses and cords, but I remembered at the last sec-ond. In less than thirty minutes, I was pulling onto the level space off the shoulder of the highway that fronted the Royce farm. I carried my thermos of coffee and my binoculars out and locked the camper. I looked up; there was a sliver of moon up there, with silvery-gray clouds ghosting across it. The night was cold; I could see my breath. I walked along the road. It was dead quiet. The one thing that had me worried was the possibility of dogs. Even if not mean, they would raise a ruckus if they detected me. Everything was still when I came up alongside the farm. The camper was parked a quarter of a mile away, which I liked. If anyone happened to pass it, I hoped they would assume it had broken down and I had abandoned it, or else that I was a hunter and had left it to roam in the woods. I didn't know what, if anything, was legal in North Carolina this time of year. Turkeys? Raccoon?

From a knoll not far from the highway, and hidden from it by thick brush, I could get a good view of the valley and the farm. The binoculars helped gather enough light for me to see the buildings clearly. The house had no lights on, no vehicles parked nearby. From the looks of it, it had been abandoned some time ago. There were two barns. The big one was diagonally planked on the sides, with cracks in between to let air in. I knew what that was: a tobacco barn. And its wide doors were open. The smaller outbuilding looked as if it might have been a chicken house or swine shed at one time, but it too seemed deserted. I sat on the little hill and stared at the place for a long time. Something was missing. What? The machinery. Where were the tractors and cultivators? Then I spotted them. There was a big tractor in the tobacco barn that had been invisible earlier because my eyes were still getting used to the darkness. Behind the barn, drawn up near the edge of the forest, was a smaller tractor with a scoop on the front, turning it into a skip loader.

I glassed the place a while longer to make sure nothing was up. Then, just before three-thirty, I stowed the thermos bottle and the binoculars under a bush on top of the knoll and walked down into the valley. It would have been easier to walk right up the road, but I stayed at the edge of the trees as I walked toward the buildings. I came up to the old swine shed, or whatever it was. The roof peak was only about eight feet tall, and its sides, of corrugated steel, sloped gently down. I crept around the side and peeked into one of the low windows. Nothing. I took out the flashlight and shined it in. Dirt floor, old animal stalls for pigs or calves, some old hand tools such as spades, scythes, and rakes. That was it.

Over to the big barn. I examined the diagonal planking. Nice work. Fieldstone foundation also. Sixty or eighty years old at least and not even cracked. Some Scots-Irish or Moravian ancestor had done an excellent job of barn raising. And since I'd heard that most of the mountain folk had come down here from the Pennsylvania Dutch farm country, this wasn't surprising. I walked into the big barn and scouted it. There were no stalls or partitions. Elaborate drying racks still hung from the rafters overhead, but there was no tobacco on them. Old fuel and oil cans stood against the walls. Mostly, this barn was the home of the big Ford tractor and its various attachments. The one affixed to the tractor now was one I had never seen before on a farm tractor, a disk harrow with remarkably small disks and a series of heavy chain links that dragged behind. It was probably a planting or sowing rig of some kind, and I remember that planting time was several months earlier in the South. But I didn't see any drills or seed holders, so it remained a mystery to me.

Another mystery in the barn was the bottom half of an old tractor. The big wheels and the undercarriage were there, all right. But where were the engine and the drive shaft? Why half a tractor? Strange.

Then I went to the edge of the clearing and examined the smaller tractor with the skip loader blade in front. There was a big pile of gravel next to it, which meant that they were using the rig to fill in low spots on the land. The house was next, and I wasn't anxious to go inside. I circled it once before drawing near, then went up the three steps to the old verandah that went around two sides of it. As I got close to the first window, I realized I had taken out the Browning and was holding it in my right hand, the flashlight in my left. The beam of my light played through the old window glass, sweeping through dark and dusty rooms. No carpeting or furniture. Old ripped windowshades. Vacant. I continued my tour around the house, shining the flashlight inside every available window. I tried the front door. Unlocked. I went in, leaving the door open. It took me less than a minute to scan the downstairs because there was nothing there. I stood and stared at the old stairway. Dark wood, with thin turned spindles in the railing. Forget it, Adams, and the cellar too. No. I walked up the stairs and checked all the bedrooms. There was an old bed in one; the rest were empty. The john was ancient, with a toilet tank high on the wall and a pull chain to flush. Old torn shades and boards on the floor. That was it. Quickly, before I had time to change my mind, I went halfway down the cellar stairs and shone my light around. Nothing but an old furnace and some cardboard boxes that looked stuffed with pieces of rug. Enough of that. I padded out of the house quickly, on cat feet, shutting the door silently behind me. I wasn't sorry to leave; I'd had some bad luck in similar old buildings.

I shone the light on the footpath that led to the steps and the porch. Grass grew there plentifully. I walked around the house and checked the ground behind the back door and found it was the same. The grass showed me nobody was using the house. I returned to the old porch and sat down with my feet on the stoop steps, watching my breath in the faint moonlight. I rummaged in my pockets and took out the can of snuff. Nasty habit, snuff. I did a couple of sniffs. My eyes watered and I felt a ring of fire around the edge of my scalp. But it gave me a lift. Yes indeed, it did do that.

Well, I thought, there's nothing here. Whatever personal problems Bill Royce has with substance abuse, it doesn't affect his farm. And maybe he sees this place as a kind of therapy — working with his hands on the land of his youth. What's that his aunt had told me? "Being home is the best thing for a body." Yes, she was right.

I replaced the flashlight and the automatic in my jacket and began the walk back to the edge of the woods. I went along the road first, then began to cut across the field. I tripped hard on a small tree stump and fell on the cold ground. I spent the first few seconds cussing and grabbing my knee, which felt as if it were broken. In a few minutes the pain eased up a bit, and I could walk. I shone my light down to look at the stump. I found it, sticking up out of the ground about half a foot, hidden from casual view by the tall pasture grass.

But it was the strangest stump I'd ever seen.

My flashlight beam reflected back at me from a big glass eye. The eye, a dome of glass about four inches across, sat on the end of an aluminum cylinder, which appeared to be a hollow tube. I squatted down and grabbed the metal base and tried to wiggle it. Wiggle it did, and I pulled it up a few inches, revealing a thick metal spike. An electrical cord led from each side of the contraption. The cable, thick and black, dove into the earth only a few inches from each side of the object. I peered in through the glass eye. The top end of a two-hundred-watt lightbulb stared back: lightbulb pointing skyward with a weatherproof cover. Keeping the flashlight on, I hobbled in pain along the road. Fifteen paces farther, I found another glass eye, again with a subterranean cable leading in one side and out the other. Another fifteen steps and another glass eye, and so on, right up to a few hundred feet from where the farm road ended.

Farm road, my fanny. I was looking at an airstrip. The road was straight, wide, and very smooth. The tractors, with their special blades and drags, made certain of that. I crossed the road and walked back on the other side. Lights on that side too. I followed the trail of glass eyes maybe two hundred feet beyond the buildings. At that point, the road took a right turn and crossed the creek, then disappeared into an adjoining field. I wasn't interested in that; I was following the cable from the last set of lights. I didn't want to rip it out of the ground, but I did want to see which way it was headed. I walked not more than forty feet before I saw a small, very low structure with a slanted tarpaper roof about four feet high. It looked like a pump house for a well. I shone my flashlight all around it. Sure enough, the black cable snaked into it under the tall grass and weeds. I tried the low door. *Locked.* Ha! The whole place open to the wind except this one, and it's nailed up tighter than a drum. There was a small vent window in back. I peeked through with the light. I saw eight auto batteries, connected all in a row. There was also a portable Honda generator that appeared to be hooked up to the batteries. As I stood up to leave, I noticed the cable snaking out the back of the structure and into the grass. Now where did *that* lead? I yanked up on it. Two feet of the cord flew up out of the ground. It was headed right toward the woods at the foot of the mountain. I walked slowly in that direction, sweeping the flashlight beam ahead of me the way a blind man sweeps his cane.

I walked into the trees. The ground began to rise. I looked for perhaps half an hour, afraid my batteries were going to give out, before I saw the cord again. This time the little devil was sneaking up a tree trunk. It went up the side of a straight pine, through a gray metal electrical box, and then joined a metal mast that appeared to be bolted to the tree. I don't know much about electronics, but it didn't take a genius to figure out that this end of the cord terminated in some kind of antenna. And the metal box? It looked like a fuse or switch box, the kind you see everywhere. It was chest high. I pulled the lever on the side of it and opened the door. I saw the end of the cable at the bottom and three wires coming from it — not the usual two, but three. One could have been a ground wire, but it didn't appear to be. Each wire end was connected to a different brass screw. There were some other gizmos in there too, and a "B-X" cable running out the top of the box to the whatever-it-was up in the tree. The inside of the box was dominated by a black plastic switch knob that was pointing to the right. I stared at it for about a minute until I couldn't stand it any longer. I turned the knob to the left to see what would happen.

It was one of the two or three dumbest things I've ever done in my life.

The whole valley lit up. Looking down the hill through the pines, I saw the two rows of bright lights. I turned the switch back immediately. Nothing happened. The lights continued to illuminate a big portion of Graham County. It looked like there were twenty squad cars down there.

I flipped the switch back and forth repeatedly, but it was no use; the landing lights kept shining away like there was no tomorrow. And if the farm crew saw those lights and caught me on their property in the dead of night, for Charles Adams there would probably *be* no tomorrow. Nothing I could do would turn them off. There had to be some kind of automatic timing device that kept them on for a certain length of time no matter what happened to the switch. In a near-panic, I slipped my fingers beneath the ends of the cable and yanked. One of the wires came off its brass screw, and the lights finally went out.

156

I could have monkeyed around with the cables and the box for quite a while trying to figure it out. *Could* have. I slammed the box shut and skedaddled.

I mean, there are limits to stupidity — even mine.

I walked briskly back toward the buildings. As I approached them, I thought again about all those lights. They had been on for half a minute or more. I was in trouble. That's when I realized that "walking briskly" probably wasn't going to do it. I went into a jog, then a trot. I kept the trot up all the way to the highway, where I saw two pairs of headlights streaking my way.

Apparently even the trot wasn't fast enough.

17

I GOT almost to the highway before the lead car swept into the farm. A sedan. Dark green. Fairly recent model. Two drivers. The second auto went on up the road. It seemed older and mostly yellow. I looked at my watch. Quarter to five. What were they doing on the road at this hour? Did the lights draw them? Not from bed; the cars had appeared too fast. Maybe they were hunters or moonshiners. Were they Bill's friends, arriving at the farm early for an extra-full day's work? I doubted it. I stayed in the trees and watched the green car. I saw the headlights wink out and heard a door slam. I headed out to the main road and began a steady jog back to the camper. Whoever they were or whatever brought them, I didn't care to find out.

Up ahead I saw my camper. I went up to it fast and was just lucky I heard something from the other side of it that made me stop. I sidestepped off the shoulder and went into the trees, creeping ahead. A car with its lights off was parked just ahead of my vehicle. Two men were leaning against the car and talking. A big dog stuck its head out of the driver's window and whined. One of the men went over to the window and petted the dog. Oh Jesus, don't let it out!

I stayed in the trees and watched and waited. It was beginning to get light out, and I could see that the car was an old Ford, yellow and white. The men got inside and drove off down the road. I wanted to move fast now. Once inside the camper I started it, turned around, and headed back past the farm at a pretty good clip. Looked like nothing was happening there. Then, as I swept past the place and looked back at the valley, I remembered.

My binoculars and thermos bottle were still under a bush on the little knoll.

Would they find them? Who knew? But if they did, would they figure out who'd left them there? The answer to this was easy: yes, they would. Because yours truly, in the cautious and compulsive tradition of American property owners, had carefully inscribed the binoculars with name, address, phone, zip code — the *works*. Everything but my blood type was on those expensive German binoculars.

Genius, Adams. Sheer genius.

Just as I reached the outskirts of Robbinsville, a car caught up with me and passed at high speed. Was it one of the two that had pulled into the farm property? It didn't look like it. A sour face stared at me from the shotgun seat. In most of rural America, that's just a slang expression. Not so here.

Having coffee at an all-night joint in town, I considered how to get my things back before it was too late. My watch said five-fifteen. There was still time. I could sneak back in there, retrieve the items, and leave before anyone was the wiser. I decided to try it. But back on the farm road, another vehicle appeared in my side mirrors. Tan pickup truck. Moving very fast. Bill Royce himself shot past me on the narrow road. As he went by, I leaned far back in the seat so that my head was behind the window, out of sight. And with the overhang of the camper above me, I doubted if he could see me in his rearview mirror. He passed the farm road without turning in. Strange. There was nothing to do but follow him, which I did. About three miles farther up the road he made a left turn onto a narrow, rutted road with no sign. There was a mailbox there, painted white. Nothing else. I went on, turned around, and drove back to the faded white mailbox and took a picture of it. The mailbox had a name printed on it: Spivey. That was all. The road — if it could be called that — ran uphill fairly steeply. I returned to the farm again, but decided not to risk it. It would be impossible to hide the camper, and with the way my luck was running, Royce would return just as I reached the spot. "Use some sense for once," said a voice in my head. For once, I listened. I doubted very much if the cache would be discovered in a day; the little rise on which it was hidden was untouched by the plow, and from what I'd discovered, Royce and Company weren't that interested in plowing anyway. Would they discover the disconnected wire in the box? Maybe. So what if they did? It would look as if it had broken loose. I knew one thing for sure: I wasn't going near that box again.

Well, I pulled into my little space at six-thirty, dog tired. I hooked up the required hoses and plugs, drank a big mug of coffee into which I'd poured two ounces of Scotch, climbed into the bunk above the cab, and dozed off.

I woke up at two in the afternoon. I hate that time of day anyway, and the situation I found myself in didn't make it any better. I decided to see if the shower in my rig really worked. It did not; I hadn't switched on the water heater. I used the campground shower — not an enjoyable experience in March — and changed clothes. I was starved. I built a small campfire and sat watching it while the potatoes baked. I had chicken breasts marinating in a mixture of olive oil, Italian dressing, crushed garlic, lemon, and Parmesan cheese. When the fire was down to a cheery glow, I would broil them over it, basting them heavily. But for now I thought about what might happen and what I should do.

One of the first puzzles concerned the two cars that had come streaking down the road just after the lights of the runway went on. Who were those guys? Friends of Royce and Company? If they were, Bill would find out about the lights. Knowing him and his background, he would follow up, and thoroughly. He would examine all the parts of his electrical system and find the disconnection in the box. What would he think? Would he assume it had just worked loose? No. Would he, could he, assume a raccoon had done the damage? Those critters are clever, and good with their mitts. But what coon would disconnect a wire, then close the door on the box again and fasten it? Naw, nix on the coon theory. Gee, if only I'd left the box *open* . . . And that, I realized, is why criminals always return to the scene of the crime. They've screwed up some detail and are trying to erase it.

Or Royce might become suspicious immediately, especially in light of my visit earlier the same day. This wasn't far out at all. It was, sad to say, highly probable. Then he would search the farm grounds from end to end and find my cache.

If that happened, I somehow didn't think he'd snap his fingers, say "Aw shucks!" and go listen to Chopin.

No. He would explode and come a-hunting me.

This scenario was unpleasant, so I switched to another.

Okay: the two cars at dawn don't know Royce. They were merely out for some nighttime frolic and saw the lights. Therefore Royce wouldn't find out about the malfunction and would continue business as usual. Therefore he wouldn't check the box, search the farm, or find the stuff I'd left behind. So I could mosey on back there in the wee hours of tomorrow morning and retrieve it. This I liked better. I opened a beer, lighted a pipe, and was feeling almost jovial.

But then why was Royce on the road so early this morning? And what was that back road he turned in to? And also, even if the two jokers in their cars didn't know Bill Royce, what if they reported the strange lights to the sheriff? What then? And finally, all three vehicles got a damn good look at your movable digs, old buddy. They would recognize the camper if they saw it again. And one of those cars sure thought it was suspicious, the way you'd parked on the shoulder in the middle of the night and —

"Oh shut up!" I shouted at the voice in my head, throwing another log on the fire. It popped and shot sparks and cheered me up. But one thing was for certain: I'd blown the expedition completely. As a nighttime recon man, I was a total washout. Roantis had been right. He'd warned me not to make contact, to leave that job to him.

When the fire was ready, I put the chicken on. When it was done, I took it inside and sat at the little Formica dinette table and ate. There was a knock at the door, and I was on my feet and

161

fishing for the Browning with a speed and determination that surprised me. Whatever illusions my conscious mind had managed to construct for me, the deeper centers of my brain weren't fooled one bit. I was in potential trouble, and I had reacted accordingly.

"Dr. Adams, you got a phone call in the office," said Mr. Hardesty through the door. Relieved, I shelved the automatic and followed him there. I noticed it was colder outside and getting more so every minute.

"Is it a woman?"

"Naw suh. A man, talkin' funny, like he was born somewheres else."

It was Roantis. Damn. I was hoping it'd be Mary. Why? Because I missed her. And she sounded too damn happy in Schenectady. I was hoping she missed me too, and —

"Hey Doc. Mike and I are in Virginia. So far, the old wreck's holding up real nice."

What had happened? I had picked up the phone without realizing it. I had Mary on my mind.

"We'll be out your way by tomorrow night or sooner. Hey Doc, you there?"

"Uh-huh," I said, and I told him about my nighttime misadventure. He listened awhile before he spoke.

"You dint blow it, Doc. You did a good job. There's always a risk of something happening you don't expect, but you did fine. Just don't go back there. I think Jusuelo must be in this somehow. I been thinking. Vilarde dint talk much with Royce. But he and Jusuelo were close."

"I know. That's what Kaunitz told me. Said they used to speak Spanish all the time."

"Right. So I'll bet Jusuelo's in the picture somewhere. Anyway, just sit tight. When we get to Robbinsville, we'll call you again."

"Maybe. But I may not be here by then. If I'm not, I'll either be at the Holiday Inn in Asheville or else at the number I'm about to give you. Got a pencil?"

I gave him Pete and Liz Sluder's phone number. Who could tell? It just might be an ideal place to lie low for a while if things

got hot. No doubt Roantis thought all this precaution unneces-
sary. And well he might: I hadn't told him about leaving my
binoculars at the Royce farm. I mean, he might have thought I
was a bungling novice.

I hung up and called the Brindelli residence in Schenectady.
My mother-in-law, Anna Brindelli, answered. We chatted pleas-
antly for a few minutes. I noticed that Anna lapsed into Italian
phrases a bit more often than she used to. The pleasantries over,
I asked her to put Mary on the line. Anna told me Mary was out.
Out where? She didn't know. Mary said she'd be home late.

Out? Home late? What the hell was this?

When I got back to the dinette table, the remains of my dinner
were cold. It didn't matter; I seemed to have lost my appetite.

I poured three fingers of Scotch into a tumbler to which I
added some soda, no ice. I went outside to look at my dying fire.
It was downright cold now. I saw little snowflakes blowing
around the trees. Well, it figured. The campground was at thirty-
five hundred feet. I'd been told that the high southern mountains
routinely get snow in April. I went back inside, turned up the
wall-mounted gas heater, and settled down for a long winter's
evening. I sat smoking a pipe and reading and wondering about
Mary. Then I wondered about the snow. When I went back to
the farm later, I would leave tracks to and from the little knoll.
And what if the snowfall was heavy and I got stuck on some back
road? I tossed these and countless other thoughts around in my
head until I grew tired of it. Then I wondered if I should call
Mary. It was ten o'clock. What if I called and she still wasn't
home? What then? Well, I wasn't going to call her.

I stripped to my underwear and went up into the bunk. There
were windows in front, and I had a good view of the campground. The older couple in the big motor home had departed.
Now I was the only vehicle left. It was very cozy in that wide bunk.
I had left a tiny light on in the camper, a little bulb near the sink.
The heater was off, and I could hear the faint patting of snowflakes against the metal roof over me. The snowflakes were hard
and small, almost like sleet. I propped my head up high on the
pillow and gazed out the window at the snow falling on the
campground.

Out?
Home late?

Waking up shortly after two, I found it hard indeed to get out of bed. The long bike ride and the midnight expedition were beginning to tell on me. I looked out the window: the campground was covered with white, and the snow was still falling. The flakes were bigger now and soft. There would be a sizable accumulation then, and that meant I was going to leave footprints on Bill's property. But better that than his finding my stuff.

I made coffee and drank it along with a big Snickers bar. Then I lighted a pipeful of flake-cut Virginia tobacco. If these didn't get the bloodstream moving, nothing would. When I was almost fully conscious, I went outside to unhook the camper from its life support system. I paused as soon as I stepped down out of the vehicle. It was darker than the previous night; the cloud cover blocked most of the moonlight. But the fallen snow reflected and magnified what little light there was. I tried to remember when I'd last been outside. Had there been any snow on the ground when I went out to check the fire for the last time? No. The snow was beginning to fall, but the ground had been bare. I looked at the ground again. There was no mistaking the vague depressions in the snow. They weren't fresh tracks; the edges of the depressions were gently curved and smooth. But tracks they were. Human footprints. I followed them. How old were they? Making a rough estimate from the falling snow, I guessed less than an hour. The tracks led around the camper toward the far end of the campground.

I went back inside, got the Browning and a battery lantern, and followed the tracks, holding the automatic down at my side as I walked. The tracks disappeared down the mountain. I didn't follow them, mostly because they weren't clearly visible in the undergrowth and dead leaves of the wooded mountainside. An expert could have followed them, but not me. So that's where the visitor had headed. Where had he come from? I went back to the camper and looked around. He had come from out of the woods behind the campsite, walked around the camper and stood awhile, and then walked over to the far end of the campground and gone down the mountainside where there was no trail. Why? Why go where there was no trail? Of course, I knew about the old trick of walking backward in the snow. The visitor could have sneaked around the campground in the deep woods, then walked backward to the camper from the far end, giving the appearance that he'd gone that way. But whatever his true direction or motive, it seemed as if he were just passing by and looked at the camper out of curiosity more than anything else.

I heard the baying of a hound in the cold air. Then another, and another. A pack of hunting hounds on the run. What were they after? Bear? Coon? Boar? Or didn't they know? Were they just out enjoying the air and the new snow? Their voices became higher pitched, punctuated with sharp cries and yelps. They had something treed over in the next valley. Was anyone with them?

There were a lot of questions I didn't have time to answer. I unhooked the rig and pulled out of the campground. If Mr. Hardesty saw the tire tracks, he might be curious about where I went in the dead of night. But if the snow kept falling, I knew that by the time I got back with my forgotten gear, it would cover them. And if by some chance my nighttime visitor hadn't wanted to be discovered, he would have reasoned likewise: that the falling snow would obliterate his tracks too. But I had arisen at two-thirty and seen them.

Handling the camper rig on those slick mountain roads was no picnic. I was used to driving in snow and ice. But I wasn't used to a four-ton truck, and I certainly wasn't accustomed to the steep grades and hairpin turns as well. I eased down out of the campground in first gear. When I reached the highway, I kept my speed under twenty-five. I had the roads all to myself and turned off on the little highway leading to the Royce place. Almost immediately, a patrol car with its blue light winking was behind me. Although I had no official reason for alarm, a cold sweat formed on my head and neck. Like most Northerners, I'd heard stories about the law in small southern towns arresting passers-through on trumped-up charges and holding them for a few days in intolerable conditions. But the police car swept right around me and barreled down the road. At the rate he was going, I hoped he had studded tires on his cruiser. Two more bends and

I saw a solid line of winking blue lights. A state highway patrolman with a lighted red wand waved me over.

"Been a wreck up yonder," he said. "Where you headed this time of night?"

I answered that I thought I was lost. I was trying to get up to Knoxville, Tennessee. The trooper squinted at me and asked for identification. He wasn't buying. I showed him the papers, including the rental agreement. I was perfectly willing to play the dumb, lost Yankee. And of course I pointed out that I was a physician. Americans trust doctors. The trust is often not deserved, but it's there. Still, the state trooper with the weather-wizened face and the hillbilly twang was not impressed. He stared at me keenly, then looked at the papers, then back at me, then the papers.

Finally he wrote my name and tag number in a notebook, then gave me directions on how to proceed to Knoxville the sensible way. I managed to back up to a wide spot on the shoulder and turn around. As I slipped the rig into first gear, he came up to my window again.

"I just wanted to ask you what you's a-doin' out on these mountain roads in the middle of the night in a snowstorm," he said.

Now that was a good question, a damn good one. I don't know why rural Southerners are so often portrayed in the media as stupid and comical. Tain't so, friends, at least with the mountain people. What they may lack in formal education is more than made up for in cleverness, sagacity, and dogged determination. I had to think of an answer that would satisfy him or there was no telling what would happen next. I started to explain, and as I did so he reached into his jacket pocket and drew out a gold foil pouch with the name R. J. Gold on it. He opened the pouch, took out a dark plug of tobacco, bit off a big hunk, and settled it snugly into the pouch of his left cheek. His eyes softened, glazed over, in the ecstasy of it.

My explanation went like this: I was staying in a nearby campground and could not sleep, so I had decided to make an early start over the mountains to see Knoxville and Gatlinburg, which I had planned earlier. I had apparently taken a wrong turn,

166

because this road looked too small to be Highway 129. I sure was thankful he had set me straight on how to get there. Yes sir!

He thought awhile and took out the notebook again. Uh-oh.

"Now, lessee. What's the name of the campground?"

I told him, and he wrote it down. And then it was impressed upon me, if it hadn't been already, that I must play it as straight as possible with this man or I would find myself up to my neck in quicksand.

"Now I know John Hardesty, and believe me, I'll check on this. Thank you for answering my questions. You can see why I was curious. It don't make a lot of sense for you to be traipsing over the mountains in this weather. It's bad here, but it's pure hell further west. My advice is that you head back to Hardesty's and stay put till she clears. But then you can do what you want — "

I eased away from the roadblock and headed for the campground. If I wanted to retrieve my items, now was *not* the time. But retrieve them I would, if only for the pair of four-hundred-dollar Steiner binoculars. Maybe that could be the first item of business when Roantis and Summers showed up.

I was back in the bunk just before five, so tired I couldn't stay awake.

I awoke at one in the afternoon, very hungry. The camper lockers were stocked, but I had my mind set on a New England boiled dinner, just the thing for a snowy day. I headed down to the supermarket in town. The snow was still falling, but not as heavily. All the footprints from my nighttime visitor had vanished. I bought the ingredients for the boiled dinner and an afternoon paper and headed back to my site. I filled a big aluminum pot with water and set it on the stove. When it was boiling, I put in the corned beef, turned down the heat, and covered it. In a short time the camper smelled terrific. I made a cup of coffee and sat at the dinette table with the paper. It was the *Asheville Times,* the afternoon paper. Page 1 wasn't that exciting.

But page 2 was dynamite.

A big picture, a photograph of a small plane crashed in the woods with its tail up in the air. It reminded me of a feeding mallard. Next the headline:

And then the copy:

Robbinsville — A light, single-engine aircraft loaded with cocaine and heroin crashed in a wooded area near here early this morning. The pilot, who is in critical condition, was not carrying any identification. He remains unconscious at Vance Memorial Hospital. Local police and state troopers suspect that the pilot ran into trouble trying to negotiate the mountains in the sudden storm and attempted an emergency landing in a pasture on the edge of town.

Since the plane was being used for smuggling, police speculate that the aircraft was flying without lights or radio contact with an authorized tower, thus increasing the hazard.

Authorities have not yet determined the plane's origin, except to say that it does not bear the standard "N" prefix that identifies aircraft registered in the United States. The pilot, who appears to be of Hispanic origin, will be questioned as soon as possible, according to Sheriff Roger Penland, assuming he does regain consciousness.

Concerning the destination of the aircraft, Penland speculates it was probably Charlotte or perhaps Atlanta, since "there would be no market for a haul that big up here in the mountains." A preliminary estimate of the street value of the illicit drugs was put at $1–$1.5 million, but Penland said, "It could be two or three times that. I just don't have the experience with this kind of thing to make a good estimate. I'm better at judging the value of moonshine."

The plane came to rest in deep woods bordering the farm property of William Royce. The plane's landing gear and both wings were sheared off at impact. There was no fire and no other injuries.

I looked at the photo again. It had obviously been taken early in the morning, after the sun was fully up. The plane had come to rest not far from a road, part of which was clearly visible in the lower left corner of the picture. I recognized the place exactly. When I was talking to the patrolman who mentioned a "wreck," the aircraft was less than a hundred yards away from us, in the trees opposite the Royce farm. Of course I had assumed he meant car wreck. Not so. And something else was bothering me even more. It bothered me so much I found myself pacing up and down the tiny camper, my booted feet stomping on the tiny linoleum floor of the camper.

"Damn!" I shouted.

I swore and paced for a good reason. Without knowing it, I had caused the plane to crash. When I'd pulled that wire in the switchbox, I had screwed up the runway lights. And if the pilot died, drugrunner or no, I would be his killer.

That's a nice thought indeed for someone whose career is supposed to deal with the alleviation of human suffering. I sat down again, put my chin in my hands, and thought. Outside, the snow was coming down again. Within five minutes, I was in the phone booth at the campground office, placing a call to my friend at Hanscom Field, James McGrevan. He remembered me and said he'd answer all the questions he could.

"I'm going to describe what I saw on a field down here," I began, "and see if you can tell me what it is and how it works, okay?"

So I explained everything that had happened at the Royce farm: my discovering the hidden runway lights, the power source in the old pump house, and the electrical box and antenna. Before I could even finish, he interrupted me.

"Okay, Dr. Adams, I know what you found. What you ran into is a unicom, a remote-activated radio tower. This system allows a pilot to turn on runway lights from his plane without anyone on the ground to help him. It's for seldom-used runways or ones in remote locations."

"That sounds exactly right. This place is certainly remote and seldom used."

"Okay, the system is run by a radio, or at least a receiver, which can pick up certain frequencies from an overhead plane. The frequencies most often used in unicoms are 122.7 and 122.8. The plane, when approaching the field, switches to this frequency. Then, when the pilot presses the push-to-talk button on his microphone, the system on the ground activates a switch that turns on the lights."

"I see. And once they're on, do they stay on?"

"Yes, for a certain length of time, usually eight minutes. Then they turn off automatically. If the pilot needs or wants more illumination — say he's forced to circle or make another approach — he simply pumps the microphone switch again. Presto, another eight minutes of lights."

"And the lights can also be switched on manually from the ground?"

"Sure, by turning a selector switch."

"Well thanks." I sighed. "You've certainly been a big help."

I trudged back to the camper with my worst fears realized. I sat at the little dinette table and worked it out. When I'd turned that knob in the control box, I'd switched the system on manually. But as McGrevan had pointed out, once on, the lights were designed to remain on for some time. The only way I could shut them off was to unhook one of the power wires. There was probably a master power switch for the system, but it wasn't in the box. No doubt it was in the locked pump house.

I could imagine, in my mind's eye, the pilot coming in low over the mountains. Probably he was running silent and dark, using Robbinsville as his last landmark. From the lights of the town, he would use his gyrocompass to set a course toward Royce's place. At the same time, he'd pump his microphone button to switch on the lights down below. But there were no lights because I had disconnected them. Add to this the confusion and danger of the snowstorm. The pilot had obviously overshot the field and crashed in the woods. He was coming down low, looking for the lights that weren't there, thinking he'd spot them any second. And then he went into the trees before he knew what hit him.

"God, please don't let him die," I whispered aloud.

Of course, there would be those upright citizens who would praise me, saying that I had nipped evil in the bud. And speaking of human suffering, how much had I prevented by keeping that planeload of hard drugs off the street? But I didn't buy that. Drugrunner or not, he was in the hospital, in critical condition, and I had put him there.

To clear my mind of guilt temporarily, I placed this new information into the chain of events to see how it altered them. For one thing, it was now clear that the men in the two cars that had happened by the Royce farm in the dead of night weren't friends or acquaintances of Bill's. If they had been, they would have told him about the lights, and he would have then inspected the system and replaced the disconnected wire. He did not make such a repair because he assumed the unicom was working.

That left two possible scenarios. Unfortunately, neither of them was cheery.

Scenario one: The men driving the two cars, hearing about the plane crash, go to the law and report the strange lights they saw on the farm the previous night. The police get a warrant, search the farm, and find the lights, which are enough to incriminate Royce. They also find binoculars belonging to one C. Adams, of Concord, Mass. Who's he? they wonder. Then one of them, the trooper who directed traffic at the crash site, whips out his notebook with my name and plate number in it. Hearing the description of the camper, the drivers of the two cars chime in that, yes, they *too* remember the camper: it was at the farm the night *before* the crash. So Adams was at the farm two nights in a row, just before and after the plane — carrying illegal drugs — was due to land there. Fade-out. Curtain.

That chain of events, perhaps beginning to unravel at this very moment, was bleak indeed. However, the second scenario was surely no improvement.

Scenario two: The drivers of the midnight cars do not go to the law. Perhaps their innate distrust of the police, or some shady nighttime activity of their own, rules this out. So the law assumes the crash was simple pilot error or equipment failure. But at least one person knows better: Bill Royce, ex–air force commando. At his first chance, he examines the signal box on the tree. A wire pulled out. Who did it? He searches the farm, finds binoculars belonging to one C. Adams, of Concord, Mass. Dr. Adams, the well-mannered guy who's a friend of Roantis. The guy who said he was returning to New England. The guy who lied, sabotaged his unicom, ruined his million-dollar drug deal, and will probably get him arrested and thrown in the pen . . . Oh yeah, *that* Dr. Adams . . . What are Royce and his friends going to do about him? What do they have in mind for this Yankee sneak and traitor?

I had no idea, except that it would *not* be Dinner at the Ritz. Fade-out. Curtain.

I sat for a while inhaling the fragrance of the boiled corned beef. It didn't help. I could, no doubt, put forth several more scenarios, each a variation on a theme. I had a feeling none of them would conclude with C. Adams remaining a free and/or healthy human being.

I ducked into the tiny bathroom and lathered my face. I wanted to look as nice as possible. I didn't want an open-casket funeral, but one never knows.

Assuming the law found my equipment and came knocking on my door, what would happen? Jail as a suspect. Phone calls home. A hearing. Perhaps a trial. The odds were good I would eventually walk.

What would happen if Royce got on my trail? How could I hide or escape from him, a man who could jump from an airplane at twenty thousand feet? Rig explosives anywhere. Kill with his hands. Who knew these mountains like the back of his hand. A master at espionage, terror, and mayhem; a man at home with things like machine guns, garrotes, C-4 plastique, claymore mines, tripwires, and torture.

I picked up the razor and started to shave.

"Well, hot shot," I said to the clown who stared back from the mirror, "looks like you've really done it this time."

Fade-out. Curtain.

18

STRATEGIC WITHDRAWAL. That's what they called it in the Daisy Ducks' war in Vietnam. As I finished shaving, that phrase was echoing in my head. I thought it might be a good idea under the circumstances. The law knew where I was. Royce could, and would, find out in short order. I was therefore a sitting duck. It was true that Roantis and Summers were on their way. If Roantis's old crate was still in forward motion, they were certainly in North Carolina by this time, probably almost to Asheville. I'd feel a bit safer in Asheville. For one thing, they had lawyers there. I had a hunch I'd be needing one.

But first things first. I had to call Mary.

"It was *not* a date, Charlie. Your saying that makes you insecure. There were other people there, too."

"Couples?"

"Yeah, some of them."

"And so old Leon Kondracki — recently divorced — just happened to know you'd be in town, and so he called you to reminisce?"

"Uh-huh. Something like that."

"What do you mean, 'something like that'?"

"Charlie, c'mon! Give me a break. How can you mash with

Janice DeGroot in the phone booth, for Chrissakes, and then get pissed off at me when I go out for a pizza with my old high school boyfriend — and *nine other people?*"

"How can I get pissed off? *Easy,* that's how!"

Well, you get the general drift of the conversation. It was not pleasant. And I'd be the first to admit that I was being overly possessive. But dammit, I couldn't help it. I couldn't shake the feeling that Mary was trying to get revenge. And doing, I had to admit, a thoroughly good job of it.

We called a truce to bury our dead, and we agreed I'd phone her again in Concord after her flight back home. I went back to the rig, unhooked it, and rolled out of the campground in a sour mood. I made it a point to tell Mr. Hardesty that I was going over the mountains to Tennessee. I wanted to lay a little false trail for my acquaintances on both sides of the law who might be interested in following me. I felt a sense of relief being on the road again. My aborted New England boiled dinner could wait a few hours. As a matter of fact, after the phone call to Mary, it could wait till hell froze over. And it's not every day that Charles Adams would say that about food, either.

But before I left Robbinsville, there was one thing I had to do.

Vance Memorial Hospital was not large. I stopped at the reception desk to ask about the injured pilot and was directed into the next room to wait "with all the others." There were five other people in that room, sitting around smoking and drinking coffee. If one of them hadn't been a woman, I would've sworn it was a maternity waiting room. Who were they? Reporters, I figured.

Before long, a white-gowned attendant told us to follow him. We walked down a corridor, up a flight of stairs, and approached a section of hallway that was being guarded by a police officer sitting in a straight-back chair. I didn't like this. What would I show for credentials? But the officer scarcely gave us a glance as we all walked past. At the far end of this corridor there were more chairs set up outside the last room. We sat down while doctors and nurses came and went. We were told to wait a few minutes until the attending physician could give us a full report on the patient's progress. Meanwhile, a Catholic priest had shown up, and he sat solemnly with his little black case on his lap. I knew what was in that case; I had seen hundreds just like it in all the hospitals where I've performed surgery. It held silver vials with screw tops, and inside the vials were rare oils in solid form, rather like petroleum jelly. Except they came from whales and other exotic creatures and had a lovely musky scent. These were anointing oils and were rubbed on the foreheads of parishioners at the time of various sacraments, such as baptism, confirmation, and so on. There was a different oil for each sacrament. One of them was for extreme unction. In the old days this was known as the last rites. The problem with this nomenclature was that it understandably scared the hell out of hospital patients. So now the Catholic church refers to it as "prayer for the sick." Better. The priest, a swarthy fellow who looked rather Hispanic himself, would perhaps speak to the injured man in his native tongue and give him comfort.

"Father, you can come in now," said a tired physician in a disheveled smock. He beckoned to the priest, who entered the room and sat down by the bed near the window. I looked in and could see the pilot, his head bandaged, lying motionless. But he turned his head when he saw the priest. He appeared to be just regaining consciousness. The priest rose from the chair and drew the screens around the bed. The doctor closed the door and faced us. When all the reporters had their notepads ready, he began to speak.

"The patient, identity as yet unknown, has suffered multiple injuries as a result of the plane crash early this morning. In addition to many lacerations and fractures, there are two serious injuries: a skull fracture and a punctured lung. The lung was filling with fluid until midmorning, then it stopped. We are getting it under control now and are optimistic. Skull fractures, as you may imagine, are always serious, as there is the possibility of brain damage. However, at this time, intercranial pressure is normal, which indicates no inflammation of tissue or infection as a result of the injury. The preliminary EEGs we've done indicate no brain damage, at least at a substantial level, although we'll need several days to a week to get the entire story. Tomorrow, we plan to transfer the patient to St. Joseph's Hospital in Asheville to undergo a CAT scan. He will probably remain there for the duration of his hospital stay."

"So you expect full recovery?" I couldn't help asking.

"Frankly, I can't see any reason why he shouldn't recover fully within a few months, barring complications, of course."

Well, I felt like a million bucks on hearing that news. With a private sigh of relief, I sat down on one of the chairs. I stared at the floor awhile and breathed deeply. One of my big problems appeared to be gone. I saw the door open and the priest walk down the corridor. The press followed the attending physician partway down the hall and formed a circle around him. I saw him talking to the reporters, gesturing with his hands and pointing to his head and neck and his chest.

I looked into the room again. Mr. Fly-by-night seemed to be resting comfortably. I went in for a closer look. Hispanic, yes. The man was sleeping with a pleasant look on his face. A beatific look. Prayer works wonders. But he was going to be disappointed indeed when he awoke to find local, state, and federal law enforcement officers waiting to question him. I looked at the big bandage on his head. Nasty. I could also see some of the strips of adhesive tape on the upper part of his chest. They'd wrapped him up tight as a mummy. There were other smaller bandages all over his arms and one on his neck. No doubt a lot of the cuts had required sutures. And yet his face wore a rapt smile. Yes, prayer works wonders.

"May I help you, sir?"

I turned to see a nurse standing in the doorway. As usual, this question did not mean that she wanted to help me. It meant, What the hell do you think you're doing?

"Ah, yes. I am Charles Adams, a physician who happened to be at the crash site early this morning. I stopped by to find out how the patient is doing."

"He's fine. Now I got to ask you to leave. How'd you get in here anyway?"

I explained I had straggled in with the press.

"You ain't supposed to be here then. I think you better — "

"I understand. Thank you. By the way, what analgesic are you administering, may I ask?" I said, pointing to the I.V. bottle.

"We're not giving any analgesic. Not until he wakes up."

"Right, that's the usual procedure. But he was regaining consciousness a few minutes ago and now look. He's in a deep sleep. And look at his face. Certainly, even in semiconsciousness, he would be in some discomfort."

The nurse looked down at the sleeping man. Without a word, she drew the screens around the bed.

"Look Dr. Whatever-your-name-is, he's sleeping nice. Let's let him sleep, okay?"

I followed her out of the room and we shut the door. I walked down the corridor, past the police guard, down the steps, and toward the reception hall. As I approached the front desk, the phone on it rang. The receptionist nodded and covered the phone with her hand, looking at me.

"Are you the gentleman who was just upstairs with the crash victim?"

I nodded.

"The doctor would like to speak with you for a minute. Would you mind waiting here?"

I sat down in the little room again. The door opened and the doctor came in. He was staring at me intently. Behind him was the police officer who had been sitting in the corridor. He was standing in the doorway, filling it.

"I am Dr. Gayle," he said. "And your name is?"

I told him.

"And you are a bona fide physician?"

I nodded.

"The problem is, Dr. Adams, that the patient is dead. He died less than ten minutes ago. And you were the only one with him at the time."

"Sir," said the officer, stepping forward, "I'm afraid I'll have to ask you to come along with me. Now lessee here . . ." He fished out a plastic card and began to read it aloud: "You have the right to remain silent. If you do not remain silent, anything you say can and will be used against you in a court of law. You have the right to an attorney. If you are unable to — "

"Dr. Gayle, would it be possible to go back upstairs for a minute or so? With the officer, of course?"

He said he didn't see why not. The officer followed, completing his spiel from the *Miranda* decision. Back in the dead pilot's room, I explained my earlier curiosity to Dr. Gayle, who confirmed that no painkillers whatsoever had been administered.

"Before you shut the door on the patient and the priest," I said, "he was regaining consciousness. I saw him move his head. Shortly afterward he was in a deep sleep and obviously in no discomfort. Considering the extent of his injuries, I suspected a strong analgesic. Since you did not give any, I now suspect something else."

"Such as?"

"Such as heroin. A massive dose. And we both know how it could have easily been given."

Dr. Gayle examined the top of the latex I.V. tube just beneath the bottle. Squeezing the rubber between his fingertips, he found the tiny hole where the syringe had been inserted. This is standard procedure for additional medication, as it does away with the need for additional injections in the patient's arm.

"The priest?"

"Yep. Only he wasn't, of course. Have you ever seen that priest before?"

"No. I assumed he came from out of town because he spoke Spanish."

"Well, he came here to kill the pilot, and he succeeded. He injected the tube with a lethal dose, knowing it would take a minute or two to reach the pilot's vein. The killer knew he had enough time to disappear."

"Let me ask you a question," said the officer. "How do we know you didn't kill him?"

"What reason would I have to kill him? The man who did killed him because the pilot would eventually talk, revealing him and his partners."

"Uh-huh. And how do we know you're not one of the partners?"

Good question. I thought for maybe twenty seconds, then decided to go out on a limb. After all, it appeared that I was going "downtown" whether I liked it or not. Undoubtedly the state trooper with the notebook would appear on the scene sooner or later. I had to cooperate now, and spill the beans totally.

I sat at the table in the Robbinsville police station. It was only a few minutes before the sheriff, Roger Penland, came over from his office behind the courthouse down the street to look in on me. Right neighborly of him. Then, after we'd been there forty minutes, my old friend came sashaying in: the state trooper with the R. J. Gold chaw in his cheek. Gee, the place was friendly. Southern hospitality is real.

"Well, lookey here," he said. "If it idn't the doctor who's always trying to git over to Gatlinburg. Well, they told me on the radio you wanted to see me."

He introduced himself as James Hunnicutt, and I shook his hand.

He sat down at the table with the local police. All of them stared at me.

"I'd rather you not tape this conversation," I said, "but I suppose I don't have the final say on that. But I am waiving the right to a lawyer. I am trusting you, and I hope you trust me likewise. Mr. Hunnicutt, I'll tell you straight off I was not trying to get to Gatlinburg last night — "

"Early this morning," he corrected me, looking at the notebook. "Three forty-seven A.M. And I didn't think you's a-goin' to Gatlinburg . . . or Knoxville neither."

"No. I was going to visit the Royce farm property to retrieve some personal items I had left there the previous night."

The men around the table looked at each other. Two of them took out notebooks.

"You're admitting to trespassing?" asked Hunnicutt.

"Yes. Trespassing only, not breaking and entering. I stole nothing. But I did come across some interesting equipment there which you ought to take a look at. That plane was not there by coincidence."

Then I proceeded to tell Sheriff Penland, Sergeant Hunnicutt, and the local officer what I had found while another patrolman placed two phone calls, one to Brian Hannon and another to Joe's office. By the time he returned, the station had received a preliminary report from the county morgue that the blood-stream of the dead pilot had contained enough heroin "to fell a timber-haulin' mule."

The men then turned to the junior officer, who had just returned to the table.

"You git through?" asked Hunnicutt.

"Yes sir. I caught 'em both in, too. The police chief, Hannon, told me he could vouch for his character, but not for his intelligence or common sense."

The men around the table stared at me.

"Umm. And what did the other man say? The state trooper?"

"Same thing, sir. Said that Dr. Adams was not a killer. But he said that any other damn fool thing he might have done, well, he could believe it."

They stared at me again. I shrugged and swiveled in the chair. When I got back to Concord, I would get them. *If* I got back. Who could tell? Maybe I'd be doing two-to-five on a chain gang. Oh well, at least I'd stay in shape and learn some good songs . . .

"All right, doctor. Let's go over to the Royce place. I can have a warrant real fast. But there better be something there, hear? Bill Royce and his family are friends of ours. And he's a veteran of VYETnam. I mean, I like to tell you, there better be a *reason.*"

I assured them there would be, but I was careful to mention Royce's positive qualities as we got into the patrol cruiser and headed for the farm. On the way, I filled them in on the exploits of the Daisy Ducks, the shooting of Roantis, and my involvement in the affair, which had taken me to Texas and Carolina. We went to the farm first. I led them over to the farm road and began pacing the edge of it. Any second now I would see one of those glass eyes of the runway lights . . . any second . . .

But after ten minutes it was clear they weren't there. I remembered that they had been stuck into the ground on metal spikes. All Royce and his men had to do was yank them out. And the cable connecting them to the power source? Yanked out too. I pointed out the shallow furrows in the soil that marked the cable's eruption and disappearance. The officers were curiously unimpressed. Strange, I thought, for men who were supposedly well trained.

Next, I led them over to the old pump house. Empty. Finally, the tree with the antenna and the control box. Gone. I searched the pine tree carefully and found the faint marks in the rough, resinous bark where nails and staples had been driven into it. But they cared not a fig. I ask you, is this law enforcement?

"I know this doesn't look good," I said to the four stone faces giving me the once-over, "but believe me — "

"*We don't,*" growled Hunnicutt.

And it didn't get any better when we went into the old tobacco barn, either. Fastened to the tractor was an honest-to-God drill planter, complete with seed cans. And there were sacks of seed around the walls, too. Damn!

"Well, let's go back to the cruiser, boys," said Hunnicutt. "Hell, at least Bill didn't know we was here. It'd be right embarrassin' if he'da known."

"Can you wait a second? There's one more thing I'd like to check," I said, heading over to the brush-covered knoll at a fast walk. But I knew the answer before I even got there. The binoculars and thermos bottle were gone. I wasn't surprised.

Back at the station, they had me wait in a cell while they all sat around the front table and had a powwow. The cell was unlocked and the door slid open. I'll give them credit for that. But it wasn't a nice place.

I had myself a little think while I sat on the prisoner's cot. Life is funny. You never know what curves it's going to throw you. I mean, take my situation: three months ago I was getting fresh with lovely Janice DeGroot in the phone closet of my elegant house in New England. I was a hot shot. Now I'm sitting in a jail cell in North Carolina while my wife is going out with her high school sweetheart. Yep, life is really funny. Life is a regular riot, is what it is.

I had stamped three cockroaches to death before the door opened and Sheriff Penland walked in. He returned with the announcement that while they weren't going to detain me, I had certainly better stay put in North Carolina — in either Asheville or Graham County. And I had better let the authorities know where I could be reached at all times.

"We'll be a-watchin' you, Doc," said Sheriff Penland. "Don't do nothin' silly."

I answered indignantly, saying I was not in the habit of doing silly things.

So I went back to the campground and told the perplexed Mr. Hardesty that I'd be staying another night. I hooked the rig up again and sat and thought, then called Mary. She was home by now. Or supposed to be. Who knew? Maybe she and Leon Kondracki were on the interstate this very minute, heading for Niagara Falls. . . .

"Hello?"

"Mary! Thank God, you're home!"

"Hi honey. Of course I'm home. Where else would I be?"

"Oh, anywhere. Niagara Falls maybe . . ."

"Charlie, are you okay?"

"No, and I'll tell you why."

I told her exactly what had happened.

"Charlie, I warned you not to use your best judgment. But you went and did it anyway. Now let me ask you this: what's going to happen when Bill Royce comes looking for you?"

"He wouldn't dare. He's in too much trouble already. And he knows that the law is watching me too. I'll just sit tight until Roantis and Summers show up, then let them take over."

"What makes you so sure Royce was involved with shooting Roantis?"

"One: he was in the outfit. Two: he appeared stateside at the right time. Three: he's a crook and a drugrunner. Four: he's an addict now and desperate. Desperate for drugs and money to get them, both for himself and his pipeline. Five: hell, I don't need five. Four's good enough."

"Charlie? Promise you won't do anything until they show up?"

"Yes."

"Good. And when they show, you head for New England."

Then I had to give her the bad news about my having to stay in North Carolina until various matters, like murder, were resolved. Needless to say, she wasn't pleased. She said she was going to have a talk with her brother Joe, then she was going to call me back.

"Mary, do you love me?"

"I guess." She sighed. "But it's getting hard, pal. Real hard."

Back in my RV, I realized how hungry I was; it was almost six, and I hadn't eaten all day. I set the fire going again under the big pot that held my half-completed New England dinner. When it was boiling, I added the vegetables to the meat and let it cook. I lighted a pipe and put coffee on. Things weren't so bad after all. While my dinner finished cooking, I read the new *Sports Afield* and looked outside in the dying light to watch the snow melt. More and more patches of ground were visible, and the trickle and wash of runoff grew louder and louder. It was what was going to happen back home in six or seven weeks. I wished I had some company. I missed Mary. And her absence was more painful not only because of recent events but because of the great distance. Being thirty miles away from a loved one is much easier than nine hundred. I missed Jack and Tony. I missed my dogs too. I would have felt a lot better with a couple of them lounging around the campsite. I took the coffee mug and my pipe outside and sat on a picnic bench. The earth was soft and aromatic. But I still had the feeling that somebody had painted a set of giant concentric rings on the earth around my camper: it was a huge target, and I was sitting right in the center of it.

I sat outside and ate two big bowls of the New England boiled dinner, spreading fresh horseradish all over the chunks of corned beef. By then it was dark and getting colder by the second. I quickly built a small campfire, then walked down to the office and asked Mr. Hardesty if anyone had called. He said no, which seemed a little strange. Where was Roantis?

"Mr. Hardesty, has anyone called making a reservation for a hook-up site?"

"Nope. Not a one. I guess if you hadn't come back, I'd of closed up."

"Would you mind if I closed your gate and locked it until tomorrow morning? I got hassled by a biker gang on the road earlier today, and I think they might come here looking for me."

He went outside, shut and locked the gate, and returned without uttering a word. I returned to the rig feeling a little relieved. Only a little because I knew in my heart of hearts that if Bill Royce and Company wanted to pay me a visit, they probably wouldn't come stomping in through the gate. Oh no. They would drop out of the sky, or come shooting down long ropes from the mountain peaks, or sneak in, snake-crawling on their bellies through the undergrowth, K-bar knives in teeth.

Aw c'mon Adams . . . That stuff only happens in movies.

I sat outside by the campfire and listened to the silence. The snow was mostly melted, but now the splash and tinkle of snow-melt had stopped too, and what snow there was left would remain through the night. The temperature dropped still more, and I went inside. It would have been enjoyable if Mary or the boys were with me. Or even Moe, and we could play chess and talk. I drew the curtains all around and read *Scientific American* for two hours. I drank a mug of hot water and bourbon to which I'd added lemon and honey. The hot toddy made me warm all over, and sleepy too. I realized as I crawled into the bunk that I'd had a rough day and it had left me exhausted.

There is what I call a *presence*. When I use the term with patients, I am referring to a faint, gnawing discomfort that is not yet pain. When you are aware of your molar, or your elbow joint, or your big toe, but it doesn't hurt yet, it is a presence. The same is true of vague and indefinable noises or that intuitive sense of the proximity of another person, that violation of your space that signals presence, welcome or *un*. I was sitting upright in the bunk, my head bumping the cabin roof. I had awakened without knowing why. I looked at my watch: quarter to two. What was the presence I felt but did not see or hear?

I slipped out of the bunk and stood in the camper. I had left no light burning; the interior was completely dark. I walked to a window, lifted the curtain slightly, and peered outside. I could see nobody, but I had heard the chassis springs creak a bit as I moved. That was because I had simply parked the vehicle and not set up the leveling jacks that take the weight off the suspension system and anchor the truck firmly. So if somebody were outside watching, they would hear the springs, too, and know I was awake.

I sat down at the table and looked across the clearing into the trees. Nothing moved. Everything was quiet. I got dressed, picked up the automatic, and opened the camper's door. A cold wind hit me; I returned and put on the motorcycle jacket and my watch cap, then stepped outside into the darkness, shutting the camper door behind me. The easy thing would have been to stay inside. But then I would've been up all night worrying and wondering. The best way to set your mind at ease, over any problem, is to face it head-on, even if there is a risk. Standing there outside in the cold and darkness, I savored the risk and the aloneness. Did I like it or fear it? Both, I decided. Did I hear anything? No. I realized, dressed in dark clothing, that I stood out against the white camper rig, so I sat down on the ground and waited.

Before long I felt the presence again, a sound that shouldn't have been there. I wasn't sure what it was, but it was coming from behind me, from the far side of the truck. I have very keen long-range hearing, especially for faint sounds. Instinctively, I flattened myself on the ground and rolled underneath the truck, holding the pistol out in front of my head. I saw two dark lines advancing toward the camper. Legs. I slipped the safety off and drew back the hammer. The legs kept winking in dark lines toward me. They stopped not a yard from my face. The hiking boots went up on tiptoe. The prowler was trying to see in the windows. No such luck; I'd left the curtains closed, and he obviously hadn't seen me leave. The legs walked around the rear of the vehicle, and I turned silently on the earth, following him. If he ducked down for a look under the truck, I would shoot him, because I was sure he had a gun too.

The hiking boots and jeans now stood at the door I had just left. Again they went up on tiptoe. I was belly down behind the rear tires, which were double tires on each side. I had the feeling that even if he looked underneath, he wouldn't see me right away. I wasn't resting on my stomach. I was in a low, wide crouch on my knees and elbows, my head up, gun held out in front.

And then I got mad. Who the hell was this guy, anyway? What gave him the right to sneak up on my camper rig in the dead of night and lay for me? I was more than a little sick of being pushed around and questioned. Now I'd finally had it. When the feet came back toward the rear tires — about two feet from my face and only inches from my hands — I put the automatic down on the grass and sucked in a deep breath. My heart was going like a steamhammer. I knew it had to go just right or I was in trouble, maybe even dead. Thank God for the truck's high clearance. I could never have attempted this from beneath a car. In fact, I thought, if I had any sense, I wouldn't be attempting it now. And that revealed the fundamental problem: I had no sense. Mary, God bless her heart, was right. Brains, yes; sense, no. No, wait: brains *maybe* . . .

The boots paused right near the tires, toes pointed toward me. He was trying to look in the wide galley window. I reached around slowly so that my hands were directly behind his ankles, and I braced my right knee up against the tire for more leverage. I had to remember to pull straight back, not back and up, which was the natural inclination. Then, having mentally rehearsed my moves, I grabbed the ankles and pulled with all my might. There was a cry of agony as the man's shins hit the bottom of the truck frame and he went down hard on his back. I heard the air *whoosh* out of his lungs. Grabbing the pistol, I rolled out from underneath the truck and found myself on top of him, staring into shiny jet black eyes that squinted in pain beneath a ski cap. The priest. I began to raise the pistol to clip him on the side of the head, when he grabbed my shoulders. But before I could bring the gun barrel down, I felt a knee under my chest that heaved up just as the hands on my shoulders pulled down. The world did a flip-flop all around me, and I landed on my back.

Keep moving, Roantis had told me time and again in class. Roll, jump, run, spin, but keep moving as long and as fast as you can. If you don't, you're dead. I rolled over three times as fast as I could and at the end of the third roll came up on the balls of my feet, my legs bent and the left foot forward. Where the hell was the gun? The man came at me, waving his arms. I shot mine up to block and was caught dead center by a sweeping side kick I hadn't seen coming. The arms were only a diversion, and he caught me a good one. I rolled with the kick, spun again, and came up as before. He tried another kick, but I jumped back. As long as he kept this up, I couldn't get close enough to touch him. And I still hadn't seen the gun. There was another sweeping kick from Father What's-his-name, but as the foot flew past me sideways I pushed it along hard and fast, throwing him off balance and leaving his back exposed to me. I waded in and threw a punch with all my strength into his right kidney. I can't throw a punch worth a damn, but any hit to the kidneys hurts like crazy. He grunted and spun an elbow around which clipped me in the jaw. The world went fuzzy, and I was in slow motion. I saw the low kick coming but could not move. It caught me in the groin, and the pain was so bad my knees buckled. Then he moved in close, ready to chop away at my head and throat. I was about to say the Hail Mary when I heard a voice.

"My God, it's you!"

He leaned over and peered at me. It wasn't the priest I had seen in the hospital. But I knew the face. How could any man forget it. And then the ski cap came off and I saw that jet black hair all around her face. I could even smell the sandalwood.

"It *is* you, isn't it, Doc?"

"Think so," I said, holding my crotch. "And who are you?"

"I'm Daisy."

19

I LET OUT a slow sigh that was half relief, half agony. I hobbled around and leaned over to ease the pain. It didn't work.

"So you're Daisy," I moaned. "Figures. I knew there was a Daisy somewhere in this surrealistic mess. And lady, you're not easy to forget. So you *were* on your way to see Roantis when you passed me on the hospital stairs."

"Yes."

I began to stagger over to the camper, and she put her arm around my waist and helped me along. It made me feel really macho, having a woman help me inside after she had beat the snot out of me.

"Uh, this may be a silly question, Daisy, but why hasn't Roantis mentioned you?"

"Good reasons. For one thing, the work I'm doing now is, shall we say, sensitive. I work for the government. I'm out of the country a lot. I came back when he was shot. That time you and I passed each other on the stairway was the first time I'd seen Papa in three years."

"*Papa?* Jeez, no wonder he's kept you under wraps."

"It's not what you think. He's my stepfather. I've heard a lot about you, you know. I knew who you were when I saw you the first time. Papa's spoken a lot about you."

"That's nice. But why are you down here? Did Liatis send you down here secretly to babysit me?"

"He suspected there might be danger here. From what I've seen on my own so far, he's right. He wanted me to keep an eye on you, just in case."

"Well, you're doing a great job looking out for me, Daisy. You do your job any better and I'll be dead. Gee, it's a good thing I've had all my children."

"I am sorry, Doc," she said as she tightened her grip around me. I grabbed her upper arm. It was thin, but hard as cable. Once inside the camper, I sat down and stretched out my legs. Daisy locked the door, removed her cap, unzipped her parka, and sat down next to me. Her English had a French accent. This, coupled with her lovely Eurasian features, made my ticker skip a few beats. She looked down at my groin.

"How's the pain?" she asked.

"Bad. But it's happened before. It'll go away with time. Where did you learn all the deadly stuff, anyway?"

"From Papa, same as you. And some of it I learned on Okinawa as a kid. It's a long story. Anyway, when I knew he was going to be all right, I volunteered to come down here. It's a good thing you called Papa the night before you left, Doc. I barely had time to catch a plane the next morning."

"So you beat me down here? Were you walking around my camper rig last night? I found tracks."

"Yes. I thought the falling snow would hide them. I was just checking up. I was doing the same thing just now, when you grabbed me. I didn't know it was you; I was positive you'd be inside asleep."

She winced quickly and swayed on her feet. Her eyes closed.

"Hey, you all right?"

She was holding her stomach and her mouth twitched.

"I don't know. I don't think so. I feel sick. I feel like I want to throw up, and it hurts in front and back."

I turned her around and pulled up her sweater in back. Just over her right kidney was an ugly bluish bruise. It seemed to grow darker and bigger even as I looked at it. I pressed it softly and she flinched.

"How did that happen? You fall down?" I asked.

189

"You hit me there, Doc. Don't you remember?"

"Uh-huh. But I can't throw a punch. I couldn't have done that."

"Well, you did it. You're tougher than you think. I think I have to go to the bathroom now."

"Has it been a while since you urinated last?"

"No. I went in the bushes just before I came up to the trailer to look inside. The cold weather makes me go a lot. I'm not used to it."

"But now you feel some urgency?" I asked her.

"Yes."

I didn't like the sound of it. I told her to sit on the toilet and urinate, but not to flush it. She was in there a long time, which I also didn't like. When she came out, I looked in the toilet bowl. The urine was tinted a faint pink. I didn't like it at all. I looked at her buttoning up her jeans. Her shiny black hair cascaded all down the front of her sweater. She looked like a coed. God, she was gorgeous. And I had hurt her. A bruised kidney is serious, and can be critical. Daisy asked for some tea, and I brewed it. I poured us each a dollop of whiskey. It might not be the best thing for her, but it would take the chill off and ease the pain a little. After she drank the whiskey and the tea she took off her shoes, climbed into the bunk over the cab, and slipped under the covers. She rustled around underneath them, and then the jeans slid out from under the blankets and fell to the floor. I picked them up and folded them. She lay there on her back, staring up at the cabin roof. Her eyes and mouth were tight with pain.

"I'm sorry, Daisy. I thought you were Jesus Jusuelo trying to kill me."

Her eyes widened.

"You know a lot about this then, don't you?"

"Sure do. Enough to get me killed, maybe. I think I've seen Jusuelo, disguised as a priest, at the hospital. The more I picture the priest's face in my mind, the more it looks like the one in Liatis's old snapshot of the Daisy Ducks."

"It's him. I tailed you to the hospital, Doc. I saw him leave. I tried to hide my face, but I think maybe he saw me."

"And he knows you?"

190

"Sure. All the Ducks know me. Papa named them after me."

I stared at the lovely young thing in the bunk. She sure was full of surprises.

"I can't wait till Roantis gets here. By the way, can you tell me what your connection is with him?"

"As I said, he's my stepfather. My father was René Cournot, a foreign legionnaire. I never knew him. He was killed at Dien Bien Phu fighting alongside Roantis. I was in Hanoi at the time, just a year old. After Papa survived the forced march and imprisonment, he came back and got me. My real name is Danielle Cournot. Roantis always called me Daisy. I can't tell you more right now. I already told more than I promised — "

She grunted and turned over on her side, facing away from me on the bunk. Then she spoke again.

"I think I really trust you, Doc. It's a feeling I have. I know now why Papa trusts you too. Also, you're the first man ever to injure me in unarmed combat. I don't know what that means . . ."

"I don't know what it means, either. I'm certainly not proud of it. You won the round — it was just a lucky punch. Er, unlucky punch. Now listen: I'm going down to the pay phone and call an ambulance. You've got a distressed kidney, and it could get worse before it gets better."

She sat up and pulled off her sweater, then lay down on her stomach.

"It doesn't feel so bad anymore. I'll just lie still. Will you rub my back so I can go to sleep?"

I reached up and stroked the smooth tan skin that was tight and wrinkle-free over the firm muscle. She turned her face to me and smiled. A knockout. I felt very young and very old at the same time. Daisy made little sighs and cooing noises. She raised herself up on her elbows and shook her hair around. Then she had turned her face around and it was close to mine. She leaned back on her far elbow and reached around behind my head with her hand. Then we were kissing. She didn't rush it.

"Daisy, I don't think — "

She held her finger up to her pursed mouth, then drew back the blanket. There she was, stretched out in the bunk in her undies. I tried to move my eyes, but they wouldn't budge.

191

"Daisy, I, uh, don't think — "

"I like the way you look, Doc. That's one reason I wanted to come down here. Want to come on in?"

"No. I can't."

She said nothing. She turned over on her stomach again, and the sight of her panties stretched tight across her rump—shiny and satiny with the little pull wrinkles in just the right places — and her long black hair down her back — well, it made me think. It made me realize that I was a strange mixture of wanton desires and ironbound restraints. But one thing I knew, and I knew it even when Janice DeGroot and I were in the phone closet: I loved Mary. And only Mary. And that I would not jeopardize.

I leaned down and kissed Daisy on her back, watching the deepening bruise over the small of her back where I had smacked her. Her dark skin smelled like sandalwood.

"I'll be right back," I said, and put on my jacket.

She pulled the covers back up and closed her eyes. I shut the door and began walking toward the pay phone next to the office, about a hundred yards away. Not far from the door I kicked a heavy object ahead of me. My Browning. I put it in my jacket. The phone call was brief: Vance Memorial had only one ambulance and it was engaged on an out-of-town run. Could I bring the patient in myself? Certainly. I gave Daisy's name, not mine. In fact, I speculated about their reaction when they saw me again. The more I speculated, the more I realized I didn't want to think about it.

I hung up and headed back. Thirty yards from the camper, I knew something wasn't right. The door was open.

I took out the Browning and slipped off the safety. I walked around the rig twice. Then I took a deep breath and jumped inside, landing in a combat crouch and spinning around fast. Nobody home. I opened the toilet door. Vacant. I called Daisy's name twice. No answer. Where were her jeans, sweater, and shoes? Gone. Had she left voluntarily or been taken? She would be hard to take, I thought, if my experience had been any indication. And then, looking at the little dinette table, I had my answer.

Sitting there were my binoculars and thermos bottle.

20

I WAS STILL SITTING at the dinette table, staring at the two
objects on it, when John Hardesty roused me from my stupor to
say I had a phone call.

I followed him to the office in the early light and picked up the
phone. I was shaking a little; I was expecting it to be the kidnap-
pers, perhaps giving me secret instructions and a ransom de-
mand. No such luck. It was Roantis, telling me they'd been
delayed because his car had blown up.

"We're here at an Exxon station in Asheville. It's on Patton
Avenue — you know where that is?"

"No, but I'll find it. Listen, Liatis: they got Daisy."

There was silence at the other end. Then I explained exactly
what had happened.

"You mean you caught Daisy sneaking around the camper in
the night?"

"Yes."

"And you two fought, and you injured her?"

"Yes."

"Now Doc, tell the truth."

"It's all true. Then, when I went to call the hospital, they went
inside and grabbed her while she was in the bunk."

More silence.

"Get here as fast as you can. We'll decide how to do this."

"Will they hurt her?"

"No. They're buying some time. Dat's what I think. But hurry."

The ride back to Asheville wasn't pleasant. I couldn't stop thinking about Daisy and what was happening to her. What about her injury? If she got plenty of rest and enough fluids to keep her kidney clear, she would probably be fine. Still, an antibiotic would be wise. And if she was mistreated or forced to travel any distance, the results could be disastrous. I could not stop blaming myself, even for a second.

On the outskirts of the city, I asked directions for Patton Avenue and discovered I was on it. I headed in until I saw the Exxon sign and Roantis's old crate. I swung into the station and saw Roantis inside with his wallet out. I went in and shook hands with him. Though he was not a person to show emotion, his eyes were crinkled up in the corners with tension. Mike Summers was sitting in a chrome and vinyl chair reading an old copy of *Outdoor Life*. He looked up and nodded, smiling. But there was reservation in the smile too. He stood up and talked softly to me.

"Shame about Daisy, Doc. But don't worry, we'll get her back. She means a lot to all of us. Only thing worries me is Royce. If he crazy, he might hurt her. But I don't think so. Daisy's special. Fact is, that's how we got our name."

"She told me. I think Jusuelo's the one who nabbed her though, not Royce."

"Jusuelo's here?" said Roantis, turning to face me.

"Looks that way. I thought I recognized him, and Daisy confirmed it just before she vanished."

"Shit! Worse than I thought."

I felt a big slap on my shoulder and heard a booming voice to go with it.

"Oh my Jesus! How ah yah, Dawk?"

"What the hell are you doing here?" I asked Tommy Desmond, who towered even over Summers.

"Figured I got nothing better to do. Between jobs again."

Tommy Desmond, the laughing, lovable Irishman from D Street in South Boston, was another friend from the BYMCU

194

club. He spent most of his time fighting off women, or failing to. In and out of work, on and off the bottle, he sailed through life like the briny wind off Galway Bay. He could brighten up hell. And it was damn good to look up into his smiling face. I needed it.

Roantis finished his business and joined us.

"The car will be laid up a few days. Doc, we've got some stuff to unload. Can you pull your rig closer to the car?"

I helped them transfer their gear. There were duffel bags, a small grip for Tommy, and two backpacks. Then Roantis and Summers swung out the rear seat and began handing Tommy and me long bundles wrapped in brown rust-inhibiting paper. The bundles were heavy, and it didn't take a genius to figure out what they were. We loaded all of them as quickly and discreetly as possible. Then we boarded the camper rig and rolled out of the station. At the first shopping center, I pulled into an isolated parking spot. We all gathered around the dinette table. I put on coffee and spread out the road map of North Carolina. Roantis said he was familiar with the western part of the state.

"They used to airlift us out here from Bragg for survival training in the Pisgah Wilderness," he said. "It was a long time ago, though." He sat with his chin on his thumbs, staring at the road map. "Speaking of Bragg," he continued, "I've got an old friend on Smoke Bomb Hill. Maybe I'll give him a call."

I then explained everything that had happened during the previous four days: every detail concerning the plane crash, the murder of the pilot, and our visit back to the Royce farm. Roantis took notes on a napkin; I'd never seen him so serious. Summers and Desmond listened intently, too, giving low whistles of amazement several times. The conference lasted forty minutes, at the end of which Roantis lighted a cigarette and let the smoke dribble out of his nostrils, like a dragon.

"Here's the way I read it," he said softly. "I say there's at least six of them, judging by what Doc has told us. And that includes Jusuelo, who's fierce as hell and smart. I don't know how many of the rest are trained military men and how many are punks. But I think, considering Royce knows the country like he does, that we need more help."

Summers nodded. Tommy and I stared at our coffee mugs, not knowing what to say.

"I say this cause Doc's had no combat experience. You, Tommy, it's been since Korea for you, right?"

"Yeah, but I've had some street combat."

"Don't I know it."

"Also," I chimed in, "I thought I'd let you all know that while I'll do everything to help, I am not planning on getting any combat experience in the near future. I say that just so you'll all know."

But Roantis proceeded as if he hadn't heard me. This was disquieting.

"Now," he continued, "I think one of two things has happened. One: they've taken her with them on the highway and are using her as a hostage to protect them while they get away. I don't think they've done this. It's dangerous and amateur. And Royce and Jusuelo woun't run like that. Whatever else they are, they're not cowards."

Summers nodded.

"The other thing is maybe that they're holed up in some canyon or mountaintop hideout. They discovered both Doc and Daisy on their tail — fucking things up — and they dint like it. So they've taken one out — a real pro — and they'll hold her to buy time. We don't have anything they want. So no ransom money. See? They want time. Time to get whatever incriminating stuff they've got out of the way. They know I'm their greatest danger, and they know how I feel about Daisy. If anything would make me back off, it's her life in danger. They figure with Daisy they've got that protection, at least for maybe a week. Thing is, they don't know I'm down here *now,* ready to go. They won't expect anyone nudging their perimeter wire right away."

He snubbed out his Camel and hissed out the bluish smoke.

"But . . . if they have taken off, then we've got to tell the police. If they're on the road, we can't trail them without police help. So, first thing is, we go to the police."

"And . . . ?" I asked.

"And while they're watching the roads, we'll be tracking 'em in the bush."

"We will?" I asked.

"Yep, and that includes you, Doc. We need every man we can get."

I found myself nodding in agreement. I hunched over the table, feeling a flush of excitement sweep over me.

"Now, here's what we'll do. We'll go first to the highway patrol. Then I'm going to make a few phone calls. After that, we'll head out there. Doc, you still have Freddie's phone number?"

"Who? Kaunitz? You're calling him? Listen, Liatis, we'd better have a talk. I think he might be involved with Royce."

He stopped and thought for a few seconds, then shook his head.

"Naw," he said, half under his breath. "Okay then, let's get moving."

By nightfall, a lot had happened. First, I rented a motel room on Patton Avenue. We stowed some of the conspicuous hardware under one of the beds there. The room would hold two men while the other two shared the camper. Next, Roantis and I went to the Buncombe County courthouse and found the sheriff's office, where we explained Daisy's abduction and Roantis gave them a snapshot of her. I also explained, as diplomatically as I could, my connection with the various recent events in Graham County. The desk officer was courteous and cooperative, but told us to stay where we could be reached. He promised to get in touch with the proper officials in Graham County. I could just imagine their reaction.

Then we all went to a sporting goods store that sold rock climbing gear and hiking equipment and bought maps. We also bought gear from big bins of army surplus clothing. Roantis was all set, but the three of us needed bush pants, jackets, field boots, floppy bush hats, and backpacks. All the clothing was soft, comfortable, and cheap. Roantis seemed to spend every spare second on the telephone. He told us that the next afternoon Fred Kaunitz was going to arrive at the Asheville airport. Roantis's old buddy from Fayetteville, a certain Sparkles MacAllister, was due shortly thereafter.

"Why's he called Sparkles?" Summers asked.

"You'll see."

So that evening the four of us were sitting around a table in the motel room. Spread out on the table and beds were eight USGS topographic maps of the region around Robbinsville. These maps, used by experienced hunters and hikers, are very detailed, with all the elevation contour marks and landmarks that would enable a skilled woodsman with a good compass to penetrate the thickest mountain forest or most remote cove or valley and find his way out again. From even my brief encounter with the area, I realized we would need all the help we could get.

Speaking of needing help, I knew that sooner or later Mary and the Concord contingent would have to be notified of my upcoming trek through the mountain wilderness. This call to her was going to be dicey, to say the least. It seemed that each time we talked, I had worse news.

When I finally called, Roantis, as promised, helped me out by positively assuring Mary I would be in no danger.

"Listen, Liatis," I heard her say as he held the phone slightly away from his ear, "if anything goes wrong — if Charlie gets even a skinned knee — I don't care how many people you've killed with your bare hands, you're going to wish you were dead."

"Uh, sure Mary, I understand. Do you want to speak to him again?" He handed me the phone.

"Listen Charlie: I don't know exactly what's going on down there, but I don't like it. This is sounding more and more like a bad dream. When he was driving me home from the airport, Joe said he was taking some time off. He asked if I wanted to drive down to the Carolinas and make sure you don't get your ass in a sling. I told him no. But now that the cops are making you stay put there and you're planning some hare-brained rescue mission, I'm calling him back. You can expect us tomorrow."

"But honey, it's a two-day drive."

"Then we'll fly down and rent a car at the airport. We'll arrive by tomorrow afternoon. You'd better be there, buddy. I mean it."

I returned to the men at the table. Roantis and Summers were going over the maps inch by inch.

The next afternoon, we watched a light plane circle and approach the Asheville Regional Airport. The Flying K Ranch's Mooney touched down on the tarmac and taxied over to the tie-down area. Fred opened the cabin door and motioned all of us over with his arm.

"Lend a hand, guys — I can't carry all this stuff," he said, removing his mirrored aviator glasses. We leaned into the cabin. Piled lengthwise along the tiny cabin aisle were four gun cases. These we put into the camper. Then there were several heavy canvas rucksacks and a long package wrapped in cloth. Fred grinned as he peeled the top of the package off. I saw a long, pointed cone of metal peeking out at me. It looked like a steel ice cream cone. It looked nasty.

"What the hell's that?" I asked him.

"Soviet rocket launcher. RPG-Seven."

"Where'd you get it? *How'd* you get it?"

"A friend."

"That's nice."

We all went back to the motel so Kaunitz could settle in. He rented the room next to ours. An hour later Roantis, Tommy Desmond, and I went back to the airport to pick up Mary and Joe. I was glad Tommy was coming along; he could charm a cobra out of its skin.

Mary came down the boarding stairs quickly, as if she couldn't wait to look around and see what I was up to. Her wide, Italian cheeks shook a little with each step. She pranced along on the blacktop with a no-nonsense look in her eye. Joe followed his older sister in that shambling, shoulder-swinging walk that moved his 220 pounds along faster than it seemed to the casual eye. Mary spotted the three of us and put her hand up to her forehead. She trotted over and planted a kiss on me. I hugged her.

"Pretty down here, isn't it hon?"

"Uh-huh. I can't wait to leave. Now what's going on? Liatis, what the hell's going on?"

199

He told her as we all walked back into the terminal.

"Daughter? I never knew you had a daughter."

"Stepdaughter. They took her. We're going to get her back."

"Not Charlie. He's not going."

"Yeah Mary. We need him. We need Joe, too. And maybe you."

Mary glared at him. But he just stood there with that pit bulldog look in his eyes. It wasn't a mean look. It was a look devoid of any emotion. It was all business.

Mary put her hands on her hips and thrust her chin forward. I knew what that look meant.

"Then what the hell am *I* supposed to do?"

"Help us out. Two, maybe three days. Doc won't be in on any rough stuff. Okay?"

She didn't say anything, just strutted away. Joe came forward and shook all our hands. Good old Joe. Roantis buttonholed him and told him about our predicament with the state police. Joe shifted his feet and looked at the ground, then asked for a cup of coffee. We all went back to the motel.

It was when Joe was calling Trooper Hunnicutt out in Robbinsville that I saw the egg truck pull into the motel parking lot. The name on the side of the truck was IDLENOT FARMS — POULTRY AND EGGS. I wasn't paying close attention, and only the appearance of the driver jerked me out of a daydream.

The man was short, stocky, and rust-colored, both hair and skin. His eyes were a piercing blue and seemed to reflect light back out of them, like airport beacons. He came down out of the cab, walked quickly around to the side of the truck, and leaned back against it, his legs crossed at the ankles. He stared up at our room. I walked out onto the balcony. The sky was turning a fiery reddish gold out over the distant peaks to the west. The man nodded ever so slightly at me, his hands shoved deep into his pants pockets. He had a special aura about him, quick and intense.

"Hi ya, feller," he said in a scarcely audible voice. "Ya doin' all rhat?"

"Liatis," I said over my shoulder, "I think your old buddy Sparkles MacAllister has arrived. But did you know he's driving an egg truck?"

"Huh? Oh yeah. I ordered some eggs. Half a dozen. Doc, come with me while I get 'em."

We walked down the motel's outdoor metal staircase and strolled over toward the truck. As we drew closer, I could hear the purring and grinding of the cooling unit over the cab. MacAllister snapped his Zippo and lighted a cigarette; the smoke floated around his ruddy face. The eyes flashed at Roantis.

"Hey sport. How's tricks?" he said, shifting his feet and re-crossing his ankles.

"Okay. How's stuff with you? Got any eggs?"

Sparkles's face lit up. "Oh yeah. Definitely hard-boiled. You wanted six?"

"Yep. And the other?"

"Uh-huh."

"How much?"

"The eggs are thirty apiece. The other . . . cost you eighty bucks."

"Doc, this here is Randall MacAllister. We call him Sparkles because he's into pyrotechnics. You know, fireworks."

Sparkles shook my hand and walked around to the back of the truck, exchanging news and pleasantries with Roantis. The men mentioned several names I hadn't heard before. Then Royce's name came up.

"He was over to see me couple of months ago."

"What did he want?"

"I'll show you," said MacAllister as he opened the back of the truck. It was filled with egg cartons and was cool inside. Sparkles jumped up and searched among the cardboard cartons. He drew out three metal rods. One of them he held like a soda straw and tapped it against the metal floorplate so that it pinged like a tuning fork.

"Thermal lance," said MacAllister. "Hollow magnesium rod. Attach it to the end of an oxyacetylene cutting torch and it catches fire. It can melt concrete."

"What the hell did he want that for?"

"Didn't say. But he bought a hundred of 'em. Want to see the eggs?"

He rummaged deep down and brought up an egg carton cut in half. Roantis hefted it, then opened it for a quick peek. Inside

201

were nestled six shiny brass spheres with ring handles. He shut the carton fast, keeping it out of sight.

"Hey, those are cute," said Roantis. "From Holland?"

"Uh-huh. Just like I promised. Return 'em if you don't use 'em. I'll charge you just for what you use. Now be careful with this . . ."

He was holding a long cylinder in his hands, an inch and a half in diameter and maybe ten inches long. It was a rolled newspaper tube covered with some kind of grease and shone gold in the setting sun. The newspaper covering oozed oil with a faint and strange odor. MacAllister produced a red cardboard object in his other hand that resembled a truncated railroad flare.

"This is the fuse. Heat-sensitive. Affix it to the wand when you're ready, not before. I'll also give you an electrical cap. You can take your choice, depending — "

"Yeah, okay," said Roantis absently. "What about this oil?"

"Put talcum powder on it until it dries out. Should be all dry and ready to go by late tomorrow. You wanna pay me now?"

"Doc, will you help pay?"

"Pay for what? For those metal eggs? Are they what I think they are?"

Roantis nodded slowly.

"I'm not paying for hand grenades, Liatis. I'm a doctor, for Chrissake. You know what will happen if you're caught with those?"

He nodded again. "But I won't," he said.

I turned and walked back up to the room. Mary asked me who the fellow with the truck was. I said that he was an old friend of Liatis's, then flumped down on the bed without saying anything else. Roantis came up the stairs, passed our room, and went next door where Kaunitz was staying; I heard his loud knock on the metal door. Soon afterward, the two of them walked back down the staircase. Curious, I rose and went over to the window, looking down into the parking lot. Kaunitz was carrying the long wrapped bundle with the steel cone at the end. This they gave to MacAllister, who accepted it eagerly. After the goods had all been safely stowed, the three men stood talking and laughing softly around the truck. Glancing down at them, I had a hard time believing my eyes. Was this really happening in America? Yes it was. Sparkles MacAllister had carved himself a lucrative niche in the underground economy by dealing military weaponry to whoever wanted it. Now, it seemed, he'd taken the rocket launcher in trade for the items Roantis needed, or thought he needed. What else did he have in that egg truck? Spare parts for a trident sub?

"Well hon," I volunteered to Mary, who was lying on the bed reading a paperback book, "it looks like an interesting few days coming up."

She turned her head in my direction. Before she could say anything, Joe and Mike Summers knocked and entered, carrying huge paper cups of coffee. Mike gave one to Mary.

Joe said, "I talked to Hunnicutt and other officers in Graham County. They told me they got a call today from the Buncombe County sheriff's office. Oh, they remember you, Doc. Seems like you're already famous here in North Carolina."

They all stared at me. I pretended I didn't notice.

"They'll help search for Daisy. But Doc, they feel there are so many loose ends and unanswered questions, they want to interview you and Roantis tomorrow. They said 'in depth.'"

"Why sure," I said, turning my head and watching the egg truck swing out of the motel parking lot. "I mean, what have we got to hide?"

21

IN THE REGION of the Great Smoky Mountains National Park, there are many mountain ranges with distinctive names. Besides the Smokies, there are the Balsams and the Plotts, the Elks, the Swannanoas, the New Founds, the Nantahalas, the Tusquitees, the Cheoahs and the Snowbirds. The last two ranges, the Snowbirds and the Cheoahs, lie in the westernmost part of North Carolina, along the Tennessee border just south of the Smokies.

The day after everyone showed up, I was standing at the railing of a forest service lookout tower in the Snowbirds. The tower was ninety-two feet tall, on a mountain that was five thousand feet high. It was quite a view: I could see Tennessee and Georgia. With me at the rail were Roantis, Summers, and Desmond. From this height, the mountains looked less like a frozen sea of giant waves than a massive green velvet carpet that lay around us in monstrous folds and wrinkles. Mountain lakes, cobalt blue and silver, glinted in the clear air. The big impoundment of Lake Santeetlah lay in the broad valley below us. Scars of white against the green were waterfalls and fast rivers. Far out on the horizons, the mountains had a lazy, hazy, smoke blue look. The only sounds to reach us were the distant caws of crows on the wing and the wind-hum sound that you hear in high, remote places.

"That's him now," said Roantis, squinting at the clear sky through his binoculars.

A tiny white plane droned closer. As it neared the tower, it rolled over and flew upside down. Then it rolled over twice more and banked into a tight turn. I recognized the Mooney by the tail; it still looked like it had been put on backward. Kaunitz was up there doing "reconnaissance." Mainly, though, he was just strutting his stuff. He was to land the plane at a small field in Robbinsville, and we were to pick him up.

Then I heard a squeak, and the door to the tower cabin swung open. Trooper James Hunnicutt and Sheriff Roger Penland came out and joined us at the rail. Hunnicutt sighed, leaned over the rail, and spat a stream of brown juice from his plug. It took a long time to fall.

"Now jest don't forget, fellers. You are not the law. We are the law. You uncover anything on your own, we want to hear about it. Don't y'all go messin' where you shouldn't be messin'. Now Mr. Roantis, Lieutenant Brindelli tells me you've had quite a background in the rough stuff, including a lot of time in the bush over in VYETnam. Just remember, you're in the U S of A now."

"I won't forget," said Roantis with tight lips.

The discussion with the Robbinsville law earlier in the day had not only been "in depth" but intense. Joe and Mary had come with us, which no doubt had made all the difference. The mountain men seemed to mistrust and fear Summers, since, as a rule, black people aren't seen west of Asheville. His fullback size and facial glower didn't help, either. Gradually, however, as the talk progressed, they seemed to grow more at ease with his presence. They liked Tommy Desmond immediately, as anyone would. And it was soon clear that they almost worshiped Fred Kaunitz. With his soft Texas drawl, huge physique, and legendary marksmanship, he epitomized the mountain man of old. They took to Fred in a hurry. And so the deal was struck: we were free to roam about in the woods, like any citizen. Yes, they admitted reluctantly, we could carry firearms, like any nonfelon, provided we did it within the law. They couldn't stop us.

"But I better not hear about any shootouts, trespassing, or terrorizing," warned Sheriff Penland, "because let me tell you, nevermine you guys been in VYETnam, you rile these folks out here, you in a heap of shit."

I assured him we understood perfectly.

"And also," continued Hunnicutt, "Mr. Brindelli let it slide that you, Mr. Roantis, have been in a few scrapes with the law yourself up north. Fact is, you been on probation several times."

Roantis said nothing; he continued to sweep the vast wilderness beneath him with crinkly eyes and a tight mouth. It was as if he wasn't even listening to the lawmen and couldn't wait for them to leave. When Penland and Hunnicutt finished their lecture and we could hear their feet clattering down the long wooden staircase, Roantis took out the maps and his binoculars. We moved inside the tower and spread the maps out on the ranger table mosaic fashion, so that each section interfaced with its neighbors. From our vantage point, and with the help of Jack Gentry, the ranger, it was amazingly easy to match up the peaks and land forms on the map with the actual ones outside the windows. Our binoculars and the ranger's transit sight made the job easy, and we spent two hours examining the terrain and the maps. Ranger Gentry gladly explained the gorges, coves, and peaks to us, for he had been in almost all parts of Graham County at one time or another. Roantis pointed to a symbol on the map, a crossed pick and shovel.

"This mean what I think it does?" he asked Gentry.

"Mine. Gems though, not coal. Mostly sapphires and rubies. Some gold. Most of 'em are abandoned now. See, lookit all of 'em here — "

"Anything else we should know about?"

"Watch the laurel hells. They'll kill you."

He explained that the mountain laurel, which is really a rhododendron, could grow in vast jungles, with plants so tall and thick that they were impenetrable. To get lost and entangled in a laurel hell was serious indeed.

"And also watch out for cliffs, sinkholes, quicksand, pison ivy, oak, and sumac, copperheads, mountain rattlers, bears, wild boar, river currents, hornet's nests, wild dawgs, pison berries, cold snaps, and — "

"Yeah, okay," growled Roantis, "I seen all those. Listen, if you were on the run and wanted to stay hidden, where out there would you go so nobody could find you?"

"Hell mister, anywhere out there would do."

Roantis returned his steely gaze to the vast mountain wilderness that lay spread out below us.

"Yeah." He sighed. "I think you're right."

"Course, like the other fellers said, maybe they took off to Tennessee."

"No," said Roantis, shaking his head slowly, "Bill Royce was born and raised in these mountains. He knows them and feels safe here. He's somewhere out there, gone to earth. I know it."

We trudged down the stairs, got into the camper, and drove back to Robbinsville. On the way, I remembered making love with Mary and kissing her good-bye before I slipped out of the motel bed at six-thirty. She had been sweet, but as I put on the brush pants and shirt and hefted my bulky pack, she started to cry and call me names. She'd said I had four days. That was it. If I wasn't back then, whole and in reasonably good health, she was going to do the following: (1) put a contract out on Roantis, or kill him herself; (2) forget I ever lived; (3) go back to Concord and sell the house; (4) move to Phoenix or Vegas and start over with a man who was sensible and rich.

I was running through this itinerary as the truck swung into Robbinsville. We went to the tiny airfield, where Kaunitz had already tied down the plane. We all thought it might come in handy. He jumped in, and we headed on. Okay, four days. That was all the time I was going to give it. We went through town and headed toward the old logging road near Hanging Dog Creek. It was far enough from the Royce residence and farm so they wouldn't be watching it. Roantis was all business, grim-faced and quiet. In the three days I had been with him, I noticed that he had not taken a drink. He smoked less, and only tobacco. He was noticeably thinner, his leanness showing the muscles and blood vessels under the skin. His eyes had grown brighter, his whole being more alert, as each hour passed. Roantis was back in his element; he didn't need booze or drugs. He was on a constant high: he was going hunting.

He spread the maps out on the table again to show us the lines he had drawn on them. He lighted a fresh Camel and outlined the rough plan.

"I'm going on a hunch, based on what Doc's told me so far, that they're within this radius. So we'll confine the tracking to this area. We'll split into three teams at first to try and pick up their trail. This way, we cover a lot of ground at the start. When we find it or make contact, we'll regroup and go in together. Mike, you and Tommy will take this ridge and cove here, to the south, along Sweetwater Creek. Freddie, you take Doc and go up the li'l road Doc found that Royce drove his truck up. Beech Creek will be just north of you. I'll go alone, working fast along the north ridge and this creek, here. We'll have two camps. One will be this rig, the base camp. I think we should leave the rig here in this cove. It's practically deserted and it's on public land in the national forest, so the law can't say we're trespassing. Does this sound okay? Remember, I'm not the CO this time; you guys speak up if you want to change anything."

They all nodded. I guess I did too, but I was a little uneasy. I especially did not relish the idea of being alone in the bush with Kaunitz.

"Liatis, what if a team gets lost?" I asked.

"Nobody will get lost. You and Tommy are each with an experienced man. That's how I split up the teams. Now, we've only got two field radios. Both belong to Freddie. There's one in his plane too. And it's powerful. I thought we might stick Freddie up there in the air later on if we don't make contact. But we know from Nam that it's impossible to see much from the air, 'specially a li'l group like the one we're after, right Freddie? Now I say you two teams take the radios. When we decide where we think they are, we'll set up a forward camp nearer the action. I'm sure it'll be in a place where the camper couldn't go anyway, like up on a cliff with a good view."

He paused to look at his new plastic digital watch. We'd bought them the previous day, all the same model, and had synchronized them to the second. They also had light-up dials that Roantis said could be used for close-range signaling in the dark.

208

"Now, it's almost two. I say we try the teams out for a short hitch today. We'll be going out in midday, which is bad, so we'll have to move slow and keep to high ground. You can bet Royce has his back trail covered. We'll go light. Your prime weapon and ninety rounds. One back-up sidearm. One canteen: we can fill them almost anywhere. Thank God for that! Remember Nam? Each of us has a pair of good glasses. We've got freeze-dried chow . . . That's it. Let's do it."

He sat down on his ancient army duffel just outside the camper's door and began feeding his Streetcleaner. Poor li'l baby was hungry. He had taken out the old Remington Wingmaster scattergun from its hiding place in the rust-resistant paper and laid it across his knees. It was about as attractive as Lubyanka Prison. With its shortened barrel, extended magazine, worn bluing, and battered stock wound with electrician's tape, it wasn't exactly a dove gun. He opened a box of double-O buckshot and began feeding the red plastic cartridges with "high brass" bases into the pump gun's belly.

"I wish you wouldn't do that," I said.

"Why not?"

"I mean, do we need the artillery? I don't think I want a rifle, Liatis. I couldn't shoot anyone."

"Oh yes you could. You *did* two months ago. Remember?"

"But that was in defense. To protect you."

"That's all I'm talking about. Take it in case, Doc."

I edged close to him and spoke in a low voice.

"I don't want to go with Kaunitz."

"Why not?"

"Because there's a chance he's in this thing with Royce and Jusuelo, that's why. Because there's more than a middling chance that he's the one who shot you. And therefore I have shot him. Notice the limp? He still has it. And how about his prime weapon? You get a look at it?"

"Yep. FAL assault rifle. So? I told you, Doc, all the old-timers carry those. Best damn rifle ever made."

"Is that all you're going to say?"

"What else you want to hear? Listen, you're nervous about going out. But don't worry. If things get hot, you won't be anywhere around. I guarantee it. All we're going to do for the next coupla days is look and hope to find. No fighting."

"You don't think there's even a chance Kaunitz is involved with them?"

"Naw. No more than any of the others. Suppose he did shoot me? Would he parade around here with the gun he used? Nah."

"Then how come he came so willingly? You didn't offer to pay him, I hope. So he gives up a week to come help you. For what?"

"For what? For the rush, Doc. For the *rush.* Look over there. What do you see?"

"I see three middle-aged lunatics playing with guns."

"Ha. You see three guys who are bored with civilian life. Guys who don't fit into suburbia, corporate allegiance, buying on time, and retirement planning. Guys who can't do a nine-to-five job and who probably don't even belong in this century. And you know what? You're one of them too."

"Oh bullshit."

"Oh yes you are, Doc. You just don't know it yet. You wait."

He stood up, checked his sidearm, and walked over to the other three. Kaunitz had a radio strapped to his back and the FAL slung on his shoulder. He wore jungle boots with cleated Vibram soles and a loose-fitting bush outfit of dark brown canvas. On his head was a wide, floppy bush hat. We all wore rough variations on this same outfit. I had my Browning on my belt, which I hoped I would never need. Roantis pressed a rifle on me, a civilian-version Colt with two spare magazines. I didn't take it eagerly, but if somebody started shooting at us, I wanted more protection than a pistol. Roantis, still not totally recovered from his wound, carried only the shotgun and a canteen. The last thing he donned was a reed crow call, which he wore around his neck. Kaunitz had given it to him. He gave another one to Summers and kept one for himself. We stood around the camper and ate candy bars and drank coffee. Roantis smoked a cigarette, and I took a hit of snuff and passed the can around. It was popular. We had parked the rig two miles up the old logging road, which hadn't been used in years. Our base camp was secluded and hidden.

"Okay, you Ducks," growled Summers, "let's get ourselves in a line and strut on outa here."

He swung off down the overgrown road. The field radio rode high on the center of his wide back, and when he was two hundred yards ahead of the rest of us, he and Kaunitz tested both of them. We followed him down the winding road, cutting through a stand of pine trees that were a hundred feet tall and straight as organ pipes. We walked in silence, not saying a word. It was a habit the Ducks had, and a good one. Birds sang, and the sun-dappled shade swept over us in a pleasant fashion, with the shadows leaping up and down our clothes as we passed beneath the boughs. The air was cool and dry, and I felt as if I could walk a million miles.

This initial euphoria wore off soon, however, and then it disappeared with a vengeance, you might say. By the time Roantis peeled off on his own at Frank's Creek, my legs were singing the blues. Now I run about thirty miles a week, but it's on level land. Mountain walking with a load on your back will take the tar out of you in a hurry. Still, Roantis showed no pain or strain, despite his recent convalescence. He didn't seem to pant or puff either, even though he smokes like a chimney. He simply waved at us, wished us good hunting in a loud whisper, and walked right up the mountainside. He amazes me.

After we crossed Beech Creek, which was the next one over, Kaunitz and I peeled off and began to work our way up the ridge. Summers and Desmond were to head south to the valley of Sweetwater Creek, which would eventually lead to the little town of Sweetgum. We set up a call time, a frequency, and some elementary code words to keep in touch, then split.

Kaunitz and I went uphill for forty minutes. We didn't walk; we climbed. It was so steep we had to hunch over low to keep the weight of our packs over us and not fall backward, and we grabbed saplings and branches to pull ourselves up. We slipped a lot on the damp clay and loose stones. It was very hard work. Once atop the ridge, however, the vegetation thinned out. There were more large trees spaced wide apart, with fewer thickets and less brush. Kaunitz soon found a game trail that made easy walking. I couldn't see the trail; it was invisible from above, since it was mostly used by small, four-legged creatures. But the ground beneath the vegetation had been worked clear of undergrowth and snaggly vines by hundreds of tiny feet and teeth, so walking was easy. Most people think a game trail is used only by deer and bear, and resembles a path in a forest preserve. Not so. It's so small you can hardly see it, but your feet know the difference. The fact that Kaunitz could find these trails almost every step of the way revealed his long experience in the wilderness. He paused often to drop silently to a squat, and he would remain motionless for half a minute, looking and listening. Then, without speaking, he would rise and resume walking. We made absolutely no sound except for the inevitable *swish-swish* of our legs parting leaves and small branches. But the racket kicked up by the birds and falling water drowned out this noise. After an hour we stopped to rest, our backs against a gigantic tulip poplar tree with lichens on it the size of dinner plates. He held a finger up to his lips and spoke so softly I had to cock my ear to hear him. And I was less than two feet away.

"A bass voice can carry three hundred yards," he said, taking a tiny sip from his canteen, "or at least a hundred in vegetation like this. Did you see anything of interest?"

"No."

He shrugged his huge shoulders. "Same here. Now the road that runs past the farm is down the other side of this mountain. The small road you saw Royce drive up, the one with the old mailbox, should join it just about where we come out."

"Why didn't we take the road around instead of climbing over?" I asked. I wished I could take off my boots and fan my feet, but I had a hunch I wouldn't be able to get the boots back on.

"They're watching the road, that's why. From a place we can't see. This way, we've got a guaranteed blind insertion. Ready?"

I took to my feet, and they wished I hadn't. We moved on, walking silently through the woods, then began to go down the far side of the mountain. A creek roared and sang on our right. The cool mist that blew from it felt good. We walked faster alongside the creek; Kaunitz had told me that running water masks noise. Still, we were careful, because it can work against you too. We made good progress walking twenty feet parallel to the creek. Moss and lichens covered all the ground and rocks. Big swatches of ferns brushed us. We worked our way down the far side of the mountain in the cool, damp air. At its base was a road, the same one that ran by the Royce farm a couple of miles to the south. But sure enough, as I peered across it I saw again the old white mailbox marked Spivey and the tiny road that snaked up and away from it. Kaunitz had set us down right on the money, just as he'd done in the Mooney in Texas. We squatted, resting our rifle butts on the clay between our feet, and watched the road for a long time. Kaunitz swept the opposite bank and forest with his glasses, and I kept a sharp eye all around us at closer range. It seemed there was nobody else but the birds and squirrels. We waited almost twenty minutes, my legs killing me, before we broke out of the forest, took a final peek up and down the road, and dashed across, hiding ourselves on the opposite side in a kudzu thicket. Kudzu! The most unpopular Asian import since the flu. In a patch of that snarly tropical vine you could hide a football stadium and nobody would know. Kaunitz kept looking at his watch. We were supposed to contact Summers and Desmond at four, and it was ten till.

At four exactly they contacted us, saying they'd found nothing. They were turning north, heading back up toward where we were. Kaunitz answered that we were going to work our way up the road, and we'd let them know if we saw anything. Otherwise, we'd be in touch again at five, which would be an hour from sunset and time to start back. We left that kudzu thicket on all fours, crawling on hands and knees for forty yards through the green tangles. It wasn't fun, but it was the only way out.

22

FRED KAUNITZ and I started making our way up the little winding road. We proceeded parallel to it, walking silently and slowly ten yards to the left of the shoulder. On this leg of our trek he instructed me to fall back and follow him at five yards. I noticed that he now held his rifle at port arms rather than slung across his back. Trusting his alertness and marksmanship, I kept mine slung. Twenty minutes later Kaunitz froze, then motioned me up with slow waves of his arm. He was looking at something just ahead of him on the path. A snake? He didn't move his head. I crept up behind and looked over his shoulder. He pointed his finger at something I couldn't see.

"What?" I asked.

He pointed closer and almost touched a pale filament that stretched across our path.

"Monofilament fishing line," he whispered, "about eight-pound test. Damn near invisible, especially in the afternoon light. Shit. It's a good thing I know the guy we're stalking. Don't forget: Royce and I've been through exactly the same training. Let's see what it's connected to . . ."

He followed the line to the left, where it was anchored to a locust tree. To the right, it terminated at a clip-style clothespin.

Here was the setup: the clothespin was fastened securely to a tree by a tenpenny nail driven through the bore of the pin's coil spring. The jaws of the clothespin were facing toward the path. Two wires were fastened to the wooden pin: one along the top jaw, the other underneath. The exposed ends of these wires were crimped around the jaws but weren't touching because a wooden golf tee had been inserted in the spring jaws, holding them apart. The monofilament line was tied around the fat end of the golf tee. The two wires met at a coffee can wired to a tree. One of the wires ran through a dry cell battery.

"Ha! What do you think, Doc? We pass through these woods at dusk and the point man walks into the line. The line pulls out the golf tee, the clothespin snaps shut, the two wires meet. Current goes through the wire and into the can. Let's look at the can."

The back of the coffee can was stuffed with a puttylike substance that Kaunitz identified as C-4, a military issue plastique explosive. Stuck into the center of it was a detonator with both the wires attached to it. The can was originally blue, but now was mostly covered with swirls of brown spray paint.

"In the bottom of the can, which is now the front end, are probably nuts, bolts, nails, or whatever. You can see it's aimed right at the trail. And from this distance, about twelve feet, I would guess it'd kill the point man and severely injure those following closely. Man oh man — that coffee is definitely what I'd call bad to the last drop. Okay Doc, from now on we increase our distance from each other. You've been following at five yards. We'll increase it to ten. That way, if I walk into one of these, at least you won't get greased along with me. And we'd better not try to come back this way in the dark. No telling how many of these nasty things they've laid out for us."

Kaunitz considered the situation and decided to disconnect the wires from the dry cell battery, which disabled the device without destroying it. We walked on, even more alert than we'd been previously. No doubt Royce was confident that the booby traps would slow us down. And while it seemed rather odd that a man would try to kill his old war buddies, I considered what had happened to Bill Royce, especially his feelings of betrayal

215

and abandonment and the fact that we were messing on his turf, and it became a little more understandable. But I followed Kaunitz with a growing lump in my throat. What would Mary think of that little booby trap? Roantis had promised both of us I wouldn't be involved when things "got hot." Maybe so, but I was apparently in some danger already, and things hadn't even begun to simmer yet.

We wound our way up and up, and the tiny road thirty feet off to our right was made almost invisible by the undergrowth and thick stands of timber. Kaunitz kept his rifle ready and seemed constantly to scan the hillside above us with his glasses. Finally, at the foot of a particularly steep incline, he paused and turned to face me, placing his open left hand over his face, clutching at it with a claw grip. He had taught me earlier what the sign meant: ambush ahead. I felt my skin crawl, my knees start to tremble slightly. He motioned me forward with very slow waves, and I proceeded accordingly. When I finally got up to him, he leaned right into my ear and whispered very low.

"See that bright slab of granite up there? Now look through your glasses directly below it."

I did and saw a strange motion in the trees: a brown circle that came and went, came and went, seeming to wave back and forth. I kept studying it until I suddenly realized it was a bush hat, just like the kind we were wearing. Next to the hat appeared a face, a young man's face, which had strawberry blond hair and small eyes. He looked young — too young, in fact, to be toting the bolt-action sniper rifle with long scope that he cradled in his lap. He sat under a pine tree, fanning himself with the hat. Kaunitz settled back against a tree and squinted his eyes.

"Question is," he whispered, "do we go around him or take him out?"

"What do you mean, 'take him out'? Remember, we're only here to watch."

"I won't hurt him. I'll just take him out," he said, laying his FAL on the ground carefully and loosening the big bandanna from around his neck. He removed his radio and backpack too. He stripped down to his clothes and knife. "Now don't you go anywhere, Doc. Stay low and quiet. I'll be back."

He slipped away into the bush in a low crouch. I sat back

against the same tree he had used, drew up my knees, and held my Colt across them. I pulled my hat down low, raised my binoculars, and watched the young sniper on the mountainside above me. I watched him for maybe fifteen minutes before a pair of hands flashed down over his head from behind and snapped backward with blinding speed. The sniper grabbed for his throat, which had the bandanna stretched across it. I heard the clatter as the rifle fell from his grip. In a second he had disappeared. Had Kaunitz killed him? No, because five minutes later he was back. He gathered his equipment and motioned me forward.

"What happened to the kid?"

"You'll see. I've got him right up here. Come on."

We made our way up the mountain to where he'd left the kid. He was sitting on the ground, his arms thrust backward around a beech tree. Kaunitz had tied his hands, and the boy's mouth was gagged with the bandanna. Kaunitz put his hand on the boy's shoulder — the boy was plenty scared — and told him not to worry, that we'd be back to pick him up in a little while and we weren't going to hurt him.

"That is, unless you don't answer the questions we're going to ask you when we get back, son. Then I'm going to hurt you real bad. You hear? I want you to think about this while we're gone."

So we left, and kept climbing. I couldn't help feeling sorry for the kid, who looked as if he were about to cry. It was twenty to five and growing dark when we reached the top of the mountain, which was actually not a peak but the beginning of a long, flat plateau. The vegetation had thinned a bit toward the summit, as it tends to do, and the road off to our right was much easier to see. We crept along the fringes of the bush, keeping a sharp lookout. It wasn't long before we came up to an ancient railroad spur, which swung in from the right. We followed this along the flat ridge, keeping to either side in the thinning cover. I noticed that the very tops of the rails had a faint shine to them, a narrow band of fresh metal. That meant they'd been used recently, but apparently for light loads. But without a heavy locomotive, how did the wheels move?

Just coming up to five o'clock, we spotted some ruined

wooden structures up ahead. One was quite tall. We slipped up closer to the place and glassed it from the bush. Kaunitz worked the place over well, skipping nothing. We waited and watched, watched and waited, in silence.

Finally he whispered, "Old log depot and sawmill. Spur goes down to town, I bet. Hasn't been used, but did you notice the rails?"

"Yeah. Been used for something. Not trains."

"Uh-huh. Let's go up softly. Keep your safety off, but don't shoot at birds. Make sure first."

We got up to the place with no disturbance. I noticed two tall towers with big cables and drum winches fastened to them. At their base were the old gasoline donkey engines to work the winches. They winched the logs up and over to the mill, then loaded them onto flatcars or sawed them up. But all that had been a long time ago, according to the ranger, Jack Gentry. It was back in the twenties and thirties, before the logging gave out and all the toppers, buckers, and choker setters packed up their cork boots and peaveys and headed out to Puget Sound. Now all that was left were old forgotten railroad spurs and ruined sawmills, like the one we were looking at. Kaunitz raised Summers and Desmond on his field radio. They said they weren't very far from us, and moving closer. Kaunitz mentioned our sniper friend and the can of bad coffee.

"Be careful as you approach," he said into the microphone, "especially in this falling light. Doc and I will be inside the buildings or off to the side in the bush."

We had a look at the old buildings. There was nothing unusual about them. The only thing we noticed was against the outside wall of the largest structure: a big horizontal tank on a metal rack with a lever spigot. Kaunitz rapped the tank up and down and pronounced it half full. Of what? He opened the spigot for a split second and let the gold liquid gush onto his hand, which he sniffed. Diesel fuel, he reported.

"Diesel? For what? The old engines are gas powered. And I'm sure the locomotives they used to have out here were steam."

"I know," he said. "That's why it's interesting."

"Where do you think the tracks lead in this direction?" I asked.

Kaunitz gazed at the old right of way that disappeared into the pines, heading west.

"Who can say? They might go all the way to Tennessee." He had put his boot on the rail and stood there, his foot cocked up, looking at the old rails as they converged far away in the trees. Then he looked down at his boot.

"I think I feel something," he said. I knelt down on the ties and put my ear to the rail. A faint thrumming and clicking came through, and we jumped for the trees, went to earth, and waited. A few minutes later we both heard the growl of an engine, then saw motion through the trees. A strange vehicle ghosted into view. It was a small wooden flatcar, like the kind used by railroad work crews, that appeared to be homemade. The platform was mounted on a pair of standard boxcar trucks, but the engine was the interesting part. It was an old Minneapolis-Moline farm tractor. The cowling was still in place over the engine, but its wheels and undercarriage had been removed, and the spinning drive shaft connected to a drive wheel and chain drive that ran down through the platform to the truck wheels. The exhaust stack stuck up through the tractor's cowling. It was sooty black at the tip, and dark smoke chuffed out the top. And that, I realized, solved the puzzle of the half tractor I had spotted in Royce's barn. They'd pirated its engine and drive mechanism to power their little train. The wooden platform clickity-clacked by us, going about ten miles an hour. On the platform were two men in fatigues, each holding a rifle. They didn't stop at the mill, but rolled right by and disappeared around the bend, headed in the direction we'd just come from.

"Don't like that," said Kaunitz. "One: they're probably going to relieve that sniper. And they'll find him trussed up, which will blow our insertion we worked so hard for. Two: that contraption with two more men, plus our sniper friend, means that Royce has a bigger operation than we thought. This isn't going to be a cake walk."

"I've had that feeling for some time."

We lay low until we heard a crow cawing nearby. Kaunitz waited, then blew into the crow call he had hung around his neck. The crow cawed back. Soon Summers and Desmond were with us. It was past five-thirty, which meant less than an hour of daylight left. I said we should head back. Night comes fast in the mountains; once the sun goes down, the valleys fill up with darkness quickly. We all agreed and had stood up for the trek back when the sound came through the trees again. We hit the dirt.

There was that little trolley once more, huffing and chuffing back the way it had come. But this time there were three men on the little wooden platform. The third man's face was almost hidden by his bush hat, but the setting sun caught his face for an instant as the car rolled past, and I recognized the priest.

"Jusuelo," said Summers under his breath as the iron wheels clicked and chuckled past our heads. I noticed that in addition to the extra man, the platform was also loaded with gear: olive drab ammo boxes and several wooden and cardboard cartons. Then it was gone, and only the dark wisps of oily smoke and the distant *click-clack* of the rolling trucks were evidence of its passing. We stayed put until Kaunitz got to his feet, looking warily around him.

"C'mon," he said. "Let's get back to our gagged sentry and march him back to camp."

We retraced our earlier route. There was the kid all right, just where we'd left him. Kaunitz unfastened him from the tree and let him take a leak. Then he retied his hands behind his back and took off the gag.

"What's your name, boy?" he asked.

The kid didn't answer. Kaunitz made a half turn away from the boy, as if he had given up and would continue walking. But then, quick as lightning, he spun around and swung with an open hand that was a blur, catching the kid's jaw with the heel of his palm. The boy, not expecting the blow, was knocked spinning into the bush.

Summers reached down and picked him up by the collar. He shook him twice, the way a terrier shakes a rat, and set him on his wobbly legs.

"Man ax you a question. What's your name?"

"Why do you want to know?" the kid managed.

Whap! Summers popped him hard on the face with the back of his big hand.

220

"Don't gimme no mess-around," he said.

"I . . . I—"

Whap!

"Don't gimme no jiveass," growled Summers, popping the kid again.

There were two bright red streaks coming from his mouth and nose now, mixed with snot and tears. I felt sorry for the boy, who probably wasn't older than twenty. I stepped between Summers and the kid, wiping his mouth with my handkerchief.

"Listen kiddo, you can go either way with these guys. You can play it tough, like they do in the movies, and get the shit beat out of you. Or you can tell us what we want to know and save your skin. Believe me kid, they mean business. I want you to think about this on the walk back."

He looked into my face and the tears came hard. He bit his lip to keep them back, but it didn't work.

"My name's Darryl Royce," he said. "Please mister, don't let them kill me!"

He was crying in earnest now and could barely stand. I was about to cry too, dammit. I couldn't help it; I saw Jack and Tony in the kid. Nothing like being a dad to make you soft. I turned the kid around and pointed him in the right direction.

"We're not here to kill you, son," I said. "I think you've got a good idea why we're here, don't you? Now these gentlemen are going to ask you questions. For your sake, and for the sake of your friends, you'd better not hold back. As soon as we get what's ours, we'll leave these mountains. If you help us, we'll leave quickly and without hurting anyone, including Bill Royce. Is he a brother or a cousin?"

"Cousin. How I know you're not lyin'?"

"Unfortunately you don't. You'll have to take my word. Now march, and don't you forget what I said."

So we walked on until we hit the highway. It was almost dark now, and we weren't worried about blowing our cover, since no doubt they would miss the kid anyway. We decided the best thing to do was to get back to camp fast. We marched the kid along the shoulder of the road, leaving it and going to ground when we heard vehicles. Just before eight, we caught sight of the camper through the trees. As we approached it, Kaunitz blew on his crow call. We got an answer from the trees, and Roantis appeared. As soon as he saw the kid, he went right by us, walking intently toward him. The kid stood on the old logging road with his hands tied. Then we were all standing in a circle around him, asking questions. Was Daisy all right? How many men were with Royce? Where were they? What were they doing? What did they want? The kid began slowly, but once started, droned on and on. He puked twice; he was literally scared sick. We left him there with Desmond, who was soon sitting with him under a pine tree, talking like an old friend.

We went inside the camper and sat around the dinette table drinking coffee. There were several avenues we could take. Summers and Kaunitz wanted to repay in kind, holding young Darryl Royce until we got Daisy back. I knew it was time to speak up.

"We could hold the kid, sure," I said. "But it's dumb. One: we'll need at least one man to watch him, and we need all of us. Two: up till now, they haven't hurt her, or me. And they've had reason to and plenty of chances to do it. I don't think they want any bloodshed, and I'm telling all you guys, I don't either. I say we march the kid into town and hand him over to Roger Penland. The law can question him and get some answers. That makes us the good guys, Royce and Jusuelo the bad guys. The law can get special teams to go after them. Helicopters, dogs, the works."

There was silence. The men looked at each other, then at me. Summers sighed and shrugged his shoulders, glowering in my direction.

"Doc's right," he said simply. From the guy I least expected. But Roantis shook his head.

"Okay," said Roantis, "except for one thing. Bringing in the heat like that. If they crowd Royce, he might kill her. I'm pretty sure Jusuelo would. Also, how much of a chance will the deputies have against that bunch? Huh? You tell me, Doc. Freddie says you just missed getting blown away by a booby trap, right? Ha! They go after Royce and Jusuelo, they'll get chewed up. I don't care how many choppers and dogs they got. And a lot of people are going to die."

"Then what do we do?" asked Kaunitz.

Roantis lighted a Camel and thought for a few seconds.

"First, we bring the kid in here and find out all we can. Exact numbers and locations. We'll use the maps and decide how to go after them. We can go in quicker and softer than any police team, Doc. Believe me. We know how to do it."

Kaunitz and Summers nodded.

"Okay," he continued. "Then we take the kid to town and leave him somewhere where he'll be found in twelve hours or so, to give us a head start — "

"Yeah, and then he'll tell the heat where to find us," said Summers. "Ain't no good."

"No," said Kaunitz, "I'm not so sure he will. He'll spill to us because he's afraid we'll kill him. But why tell the law?"

"Don't kid yourself. They could make him spill," said Summers, whose experience with the police on Chicago's South Side I could very well imagine.

"How about this?" I said. "We take the kid into the police and tell them just what happened. Then we go back to Asheville and wait till they release Daisy. When she's back safe, let the law go after them."

"Nah," said Freddie. "The law will start after them right away, and Royce will get wind of it. Then they won't release Daisy, or they might even hurt her. You're right about one thing, Doc: so far they haven't hurt anyone. But the law goes after them, that will change."

"We'll tell Penland to wait until we get her back."

"He won't do it," said Roantis. "The law's not trained to wait. They'll rush into the bush, get chewed up, and a lot of people will get hurt. Guarantee it. Now here's the drill: we truss the kid up somewhere so he'll be found the next day, and then we move in on them fast, before Royce even knows what's up."

All the Ducks thought this was the best plan. I thought it stunk. Problem was, so did every other plan we could think of.

So we got the kid inside in front of the maps and pumped him good. Twice he hesitated. The first time, Summers popped him in the face again. The second time, Kaunitz took him out into the woods. He brought the kid back shortly; the boy was shaking and ashen-faced. I don't know what Kaunitz said or did to him out there, and I still don't want to know, but the poor boy would've turned in his own mother.

We learned that Jusuelo was the drugrunner, not Royce, although Bill was going along with it to supply his own voracious habit and to finance a community of survivalists in the mountains along the North Carolina–Tennessee border. Though fed up with the military, Royce was, according to his young cousin, set on establishing his own little wilderness outpost. In a cave and two abandoned mines, he'd set up living quarters, tool sheds, a field hospital, a training camp, and vast storage facilities for food, arms and ammunition, crude agricultural equipment, and off-road vehicles and fuel. He had done this in less than a year with the help of soldier friends, relatives like young Darryl, and mostly young drifters from the small mountain towns who didn't want to spend the rest of their lives pumping out children and debts, working at gas stations and hardscrabble clay farms, or moving down off the mountain to work in the mill. About ten or twelve men were actually out there now, at least half of whom were also hiding from the law. The kid pointed out their location on the map. Daisy was in the mine, but they moved her often. She wasn't hurt or sick, not that he could tell.

"Now why?" asked Roantis as he helped the kid to his feet. "Why's he doing all this? What does he want?"

The kid wasn't sure. He suspected that Royce wanted to set up an armed and fortified haven to survive the nuclear war he was certain was coming and to hold sway over his little kingdom, where nobody would ever abandon or betray him again. Ever.

"It sounds to me as if Bill still isn't out of the woods," I said.

"What do you mean?" asked Desmond.

"I mean he's still feeling persecuted. I suppose he was stable enough to be released . . . but I'd say he's far from well. And the drugs — I'm guessing he's on heroin, or maybe coke and speed — aren't helping either. Maybe if we could convince him that we're really his friends . . ."

"I don't know, Doc," said Roantis. "I'm thinking it's too late for that. And if it's true he's still a little nuts, I sure want to get Daisy out of there. Quick."

We packed up the rig and headed out. It was three hours into night now; time to set the kid free, the way we'd planned. Roantis had a couple of pairs of thumbcuffs with him. These are miniature handcuffs that fit over the thumbs. They're so small you can fit several of them in your pocket. We rolled into town and cruised around, looking for a likely spot to leave Royce's cousin. Finally Kaunitz spotted a big playground with a jungle gym in the center. Nobody was there, and the field was dark. We pulled over and doused the lights.

"I'll take him over," said Kaunitz. "After all, I caught him in the first place."

"Don't you want any help?" I asked.

"No. Besides, the more of us that go, the greater the chance we'll be seen. Lieutenant, you got the note?"

Roantis handed Kaunitz the scrap of paper with his message on it, which said:

To Mssrs. Penland and Hunnicutt:
This man was trying to snipe at us in the mountains near Beech Creek. We are returning him to you unharmed, as you requested. As soon as we have more information, we'll let you know.
> Sincerely,
> Liatis Roantis, Professional Soldier

Kaunitz folded the note twice and taped it to the back of the kid's neck, where he couldn't pull it off and where nobody would miss it. Then Kaunitz took the pair of thumbcuffs and hustled the kid out of the car and down to the jungle gym in the center of the dark field. The kid didn't say boo; he was probably glad as hell we'd spared him and were letting him go. We saw the two dim figures down there, but only when they moved. Kaunitz was back in a flash, saying he had fastened the kid's hands around a corner pole and gagged him with the bandanna again so he couldn't yell for help. This meant he wouldn't be found until the next morning, which would give us the head start we needed. On our way to find another base camp, Kaunitz said he wanted us to drop him off at the airfield.

"I'll just be up about forty minutes," he said. "I really want to go over the area in the dark. See if I can see any lights."

"C'mon Freddie," said Roantis. "What are your chances of seeing anything?"

"Almost nil. But we've got to do it. Anything at all that'll help."

"How 'bout a spotter? Mike, you want to go too?"

Summers nodded. But Kaunitz said no, he'd go alone.

"I'm going to be doing some hairy stuff. Treetop-level stuff, maybe, in these mountains. I'll go up alone."

And he did. He zoomed off into the wild black yonder and was gone. While he was up, we decided to move the camper rig to a new location. We also decided to leave it before dawn, carrying gear for two nights in the bush. Thirty-five minutes later, the little Mooney came back down and Kaunitz joined us in the truck, saying he had seen no lights. As we drove up the old logging roads, looking for a nighttime haven for our rig, I wondered if the others were thinking the same thing I was.

23

IN THE DEAD QUIET of the predawn darkness, I rolled out of my blankets onto the pine needle forest floor and listened. Faint snoring came from inside the camper, where Summers, Desmond, and Kaunitz were sleeping. The fire was down to a red glow. Roantis was squatting by the fire, dressed only in bush pants and a gray cutoff T-shirt. The blood vessels in his arms stuck out like spaghetti. He was squinting into the faint red light, his Mongol eyes and droopy mustache making him look like a Vietnamese village chieftain. I crept close and he looked up. I put my finger to my lips and squatted next to him, enjoying the warmth of the tiny fire. The Indians are right: build a small fire and get close.

"What?" he asked in a barely audible whisper.

"What are you thinking?"

"About Daisy. I love her more than any person alive. If I have to die to get her safe, I will."

I nodded and waited.

"Can't sleep? Nervous?" he asked.

"Uh-huh. I'm thinking about Mary. How she'll feel if something happens to me."

"It won't. If things get that hot, we'll hold back and get more help. I've done this stuff all my life. Only reason I'm still here is because I'm not reckless."

"I'm also thinking of something else. I'm thinking about Freddie Kaunitz."

"Yeah?"

"I keep trying to put him out of my mind, Liatis, but he keeps popping back in. Remember how he took the kid out into the woods to question him, away from all of us? Why did he do that?"

"Freddie knows how to make people talk."

"Uh-huh. But I was thinking something else. Just suppose for a second, suppose he knew the kid. Suppose he's in on this thing with Royce and knew the kid beforehand. So we capture him, without hurting him, and take him back to camp. Kaunitz takes the kid out alone and says, answer my questions like you're scared shitless and we'll set you free. Okay, the kid answers the questions. But maybe he gives us the wrong answers."

"Hell Doc, you could suppose anything. Suppose Summers is in with Royce? So what?"

"We both know Mike never had the time, mobility, or motive to be in it. Kaunitz has all three — and an airplane he can land anywhere. And believe me, Liatis, he does need the money. I visited his ranch and overheard some private conversation. I know. Okay, next point: Kaunitz insisted on taking the kid down to the playground alone. Who was there to see him cuff the kid around the jungle gym pole? Nobody. What if he didn't cuff the kid and told him to scoot after waiting ten minutes? Then the kid could make his way back to Royce's camp and tell him we're on our way."

"You're driving yourself nuts, Doc. Sure, a lot of things could happen, but usually they don't. Besides, Royce already knows we're on our way — he just doesn't know how fast. He took Daisy for a bargaining chip, thinking it would give him power to keep us away for a while. I bet he's already sorry he did it. Listen Doc, what I'm counting on is this: we get out there twelve hours before he thinks we can, slip under his guard half a day early."

"Okay, the final thing: Kaunitz's solo night flight over Royce's position. He refused to have anyone go with him. Know why?"

He thought for only a second before answering.

"Radio. You're thinking he radioed Royce from the plane."

"How powerful is the Mooney's radio?"

"Very. Much more reach than those backpackers we got. Yeah, he could've done that. What would he say?"

"What do you think? Tell Royce about the kid, about us. Our strengths and weaknesses. What to expect. The works. I'm thinking there's a king-size surprise waiting for us out there. And it'll be no fun."

Roantis thought hard, smoked half a cigarette, before answering.

"Nah. I just don't think Freddie's a traitor, Doc. The Ducks were close. We hadda be. Freddie's solid. I can't say that for Jesus Jusuelo, though. He always had a mean streak, and some hatred for Anglos, too. He's fierce, yeah, but not solid. Royce . . . Well, he's had his problems. But I'd say Fred's as solid as they come. As solid as you."

Somehow, his opinion of me did not cheer me up. Yeah, Doc, admit it: you're scared. You bet I am. That wired coffee can and the kid's sniper rifle had me going. Jesus Jusuelo, blood in his dark eyes, riding that little flatcar on the mountaintop spur — he had me going too. I would have about as much chance against a guy like that as that poor pilot lying in intensive care at Vance Memorial. To top it off, I still had grave doubts about Kaunitz.

I crawled back into the bedroll and stared up at the dark shadows of the big tree limbs overhead. Then I looked at Roantis again, squatting in the red glow of the fire like a Stone Age hunter or shaman priest. What crude gods were being summoned, what atavistic powers invoked?

A little after five, Tommy Desmond poked me awake. It was pitch black out under the trees; two hours until sunrise. We had coffee and sweet rolls, locked the rig, slung on our packs, and walked out. By the time we left the rig, there was barely enough light to see where you were going if you looked at the ground directly ahead of you. It was cold; our breath came in great clouds. Roantis led the way, heading for the railroad spur he wanted to follow. He reasoned that if they used the track, they wouldn't wire it. We headed up a different way from our initial approach, having guessed that we could make contact with the spur much sooner than previously. We did, but it was a hell of a climb, and it was sunup when we finally came to the old logging spur.

Walking on that level right of way, with no undergrowth or dense cover to hide booby traps, made me feel much better. We walked 60 feet apart, which meant that with five of us, we were strung out over 240 feet. We walked at a good clip, making no noise, for miles and miles. Men walking with rifles, I thought. Some things remain unchanged through history. From Ethan Allen and his Green Mountain Boys, to the Swamp Fox, the Gray Ghost, to Darby's Rangers, the Chindits, the SAS in Africa, to the Vietcong and the LRRP teams like the Daisy Ducks: you cannot stop men walking with rifles, no matter how many men, ships, guns, and jets you have.

I hoped Royce and his mountain men wouldn't stop us. We had a good field of vision off to our sides and some tree cover overhead because the tall poplars and pines had grown back, leaning in like a canopy. We walked with Roantis leading, followed by Summers, Desmond, me, and Kaunitz bringing up the rear. We changed now and then, but always with an experienced man at each end and Desmond and Adams in the middle. It was Roantis's plan to move ahead quickly, making more headway than Royce would expect and placing us inside his defensive perimeter. This sounded like a great idea as long as it hadn't occurred to Royce as well.

At eleven o'clock, the woods thinned out and we had a better view of the high, narrow plateau we were walking on. Below us, the ground fell away a great depth to a broad river valley to the south. To the north, it descended in a series of rolling hills.

The railroad spur turned softly to the right, continuing westward across the spine of the plateau. Then it crossed the deep river valley in a descending swoop of track that went over the water on an ancient metal trestle bridge and disappeared into the woods again in a lazy curve of track on the other side of the valley.

The terrain here was rugged and steep, with many outcrops of bare rock, sheer vertical cliffs, and castle-like promontories overlooking wide vistas. It reminded me of the rugged country of Auvergne, in central France. It was the perfect place for a wilderness stronghold.

Creeping up to the edge of the woods, we lay on our stomachs, holding binoculars braced by our elbows on the ground, glassing the valley below us. It was the valley of Yellow Creek, and from our spot on the mountaintop to the opposite summit was a distance of a mile, maybe more. And a few miles beyond that was the Tennessee state line. If what the kid, Darryl Royce, had told us was true, Royce's wilderness retreat was on the mountaintop across the river. We glassed the entire area, looking for any movement, reflection, or signs of human presence. We saw none.

"Well lieutenant?" said Kaunitz, who was now sitting upright, his back against a tree. "I think I see something below that bare rock just below the ridge over there. What do you say?"

We directed our search to a shiny white patch of bare marble that protruded through the trees near the opposite summit. For half a minute, I couldn't see anything. Then I noticed faint movement on the hillside below it, a black upright line that moved. From a mile away, a man walking against the rock. When viewing distant people through lenses, it's hard to see them actually move. What you notice, as in watching the sun set or a flower open, are distinct stages of the occurrence but not the actual process. I saw the tiny dark streak change position from one end of the white patch of rock to the other. Then it was gone, obscured by the trees.

"Hey," whispered Desmond, "look above that rock. Oh my Jesus!"

Right away, I saw four men up there on the ledge. Two had glasses and were using them. Roantis had all of us go to earth a little deeper. He also said we would do no glassing of the far mountain after noon, when the sun's rays would be pointed toward us. As it was, there was no chance of a reflection giving us away. Not yet. I switched back to the base of the white patch of rock, looking for the lone walker again. I finally spotted him making his way much farther to the right, which was in the general direction of the track. I figured they must have some sort of supply depot there. But where was the mine tunnel the kid had mentioned? So far, the kid's description of the place fit. And I could guess there were plenty of men up on that cliffside and summit. So how were the five of us going to unseat them?

I crawled back into the bush, wiped off my brow, and replaced my wide hat. All my muscles ached. Not just my legs, but my back, my arms, even my neck. I took a pinch of snuff and it gave me a lift. I was getting hooked on the stuff. Maybe I should try leaf or plug next. Roantis and Kaunitz were poring over the map, running fingers down slopes and up ridges, murmuring.

"Who's tired?" asked Kaunitz.

"I am," I said. "And I ache all over too."

"Then unroll your pack and sleep. We're not going to move until after dark."

I did, and Desmond joined me. Summers opened ration cans, and Kaunitz pumped up the little primus stove and boiled water for coffee. It was just like the boy scouts, and I was getting a warm, homey feeling until Roantis dug into his pack and pulled out that paper wand dripping talcum powder. He laid the cylinder on the ground, took a tiny plastic bag, and shook more powder on it, then rubbed it carefully over the paper.

"She's drying out real nice," he said to Kaunitz. "Now I just got to decide where to use her."

"What is that? Plastique?" I asked.

"Same family. A li'l different and better. It was developed in Yugoslavia a coupla years ago."

"What would happen if that thing went off?" I asked. Funny, but I couldn't help being a little curious.

"Ha! Blow us all to jelly. Nothing left."

"Well, uh, isn't it a little dangerous? What if a spark hits it?"

"Nothing. You can light this with a match and it'll burn, just like Sterno."

"Then how does it work?"

"Detonator. Either electric or heat-sensitive. Like this." He fished into the pack again and drew out a red cap that fit over the end. Then he put it back. "May not even use this thing. Or these . . ."

He brought out those little pocket-sized brass grenades, made in Holland, and gave Kaunitz and Summers two apiece. Desmond felt left out, so Kaunitz gave him one of his. Summers offered me one, but I declined. I was starting to feel a little queasy. I rubbed my stomach and tried to sleep. Finally, I fell into a doze.

I woke up at twilight. Desmond was asleep next to me, giving off a soft snore. The sun was behind the far mountain now, and Summers and Roantis were glassing the rock wall across the valley. I yawned and stretched. The aches were worse; I had stiffened up in my sleep. Still, I felt rested. I scooted up to the other two and had a look through my glasses. I saw two bright yellow specks near the white rock. Campfires. Royce's men were apparently not bothering to stay out of sight.

"Where's Freddie?" I asked.

"Down at the river looking for a place to cross. How are you?"

"I've been better. Why are they showing lights?"

"Because they don't think we're here. They probably think I'm still in Boston. Thanks to Freddie's snagging that kid, we're way ahead of them."

"I'm glad you're so optimistic, Liatis. How do you know they're not just being bait? Acting unprepared so we'll walk right into a trap?"

"Nah."

He answered a lot of questions with that monosyllable. It was simple, definitive, and probably dumb. I let out a slow sigh and felt my stomach churn. My mouth and throat had a sour taste. I had enough acid in there for a truck battery. I wished I were home pulling teeth. Boy, did I wish it. Roantis stifled a yawn. Typical. The sonofabitch was bored. Kaunitz came creeping back up the hillside, breathing heavily. His pants and the bottom half of his shirt were soaked. He stripped off his wet clothes and put on dry bush pants, hanging the wet pair in a tree to dry. Then he and Roantis went back to the maps. If Kaunitz felt the cold, he sure didn't show it. I was chilly. I wasn't made for this stuff. If I learned nothing else on this fool's errand, I would learn that.

And then I thought of it: Freddie's leg injury. I should have looked at his leg when he changed clothes, but it had slipped my mind.

"I'd be willing to bet they've got the trestle bridge wired," Kaunitz said. "If we use it, they could blow it when half of us have crossed it, cutting us in two and maybe killing a couple of us. Crossing the creek is the only way to go, but it's a long hike."

"Okay, you Ducks, get some sleep," said Roantis. "We'll get moving just after two. That'll give us a couple hours of moonlight for the hike and climb before it dips behind the mountain wall."

My aching body didn't want to hear that. For that matter, neither did my tormented mind. I glassed the cliffside across the valley again. The sides of that hill looked awfully steep, and the ridge on top was dotted with towering hunks of rock. It looked like a huge, dark castle. And just as forbidding.

24

THE MOON was silver white. Smoke-colored puffs of cloud drifted in front of it. The mountainside across the valley was all dark. The river washed far below us in little beads of white reflection. You could hear it now, a faint rushing sound that on an ordinary night could sing you to sleep. You couldn't hear it in the daytime. Why was that? The air too damp and hot? Too many other noises? Why?

I crept out of the bedroll and stretched. I hurt. But soon I knew the fear would take over and the adrenaline would hide the pain. Hell, I'd rather have the pain. I crept away from the others, found a spot where nobody could hear or see me, and threw up.

I felt much better after that. It had been building all afternoon and night. And now, like a nervous runner entering the blocks on the cinder track, I was ready to run the race.

The others were stirring when I got back. The air was dark blue, and there was an electric current passing all around us. You could feel it, see it in everyone's face. The Ducks' eyes were bright. Oh, they were glad; they liked this stuff. They were happy as pigs in poop.

"I want to take plenty of rope," said Roantis in a low voice. "Also some gaffer tape. And Mike, be sure to take your wire cutters."

Then we crept down off our mountain, heading for the valley six hundred feet below. Thanks to Kaunitz having scouted the way, we made it in under an hour. But it was tough going, and one slip in the dark meant falling down a long, steep grade that was studded with rocks. We went light. Roantis carried a small assault pack, and Summers had a big coil of rope slung over his shoulder. Otherwise, all we carried were weapons and flashlights.

We reached the river, and after twenty more minutes of hiking along the gravelly bank, we were at the fording place. The water, largely snowmelt, was ice cold. We could not wade through it with our pants on; we would be chilled to the bone afterward and stiffen up. So we crossed it by stripping from the waist down, tying our pants and boots over our shoulders and holding the rifles high over our heads, not making a sound. Kaunitz was leading the way, and I strained to see any mark on his bum leg, any sign of a healed gunshot wound. But it was too dark out, and then we were waist deep in the icy water. I was freezing, but feeling better and better. Nothing like actually doing something to take the edge off fear. It's the waiting that's a killer. We came up the other side on another gravelly bank. Kaunitz was out of the water first, and I noticed some discoloration on his right calf. A gunshot wound? Couldn't tell, but it didn't look like it. We dressed again and walked briskly along the far bank to get warm. Then Kaunitz showed us a niche below the overhanging rock where we could remain invisible. We crawled underneath and hunkered down over the flashlight while Roantis spread out the rough map he'd drawn of the immediate area. He had put it together from the kid's interrogation, Freddie's reconnaissance, and watching the mountain for hours on end. But at best it was an educated guess. We all knew there could be big surprises ahead.

"First, Doc and Tommy," Roantis said. "You guys will be in observatory positions. You shoot only to signal an alarm. Four quick shots in the air, like we said. Tommy, you'll be here once we get up to the ridge." He tapped the map and Desmond nodded. "Doc, if it's okay with you, we're putting you here, right below Tommy. It's more in the middle of things, so stay low and out of sight. Mike, you'll come with Freddie and me along this ridge trail we've been watching. There shouldn't be anyone around this time of night. As soon as we find her, I'll get her out. When she's safe, I'm going back with anyone who wants to come with me. I'm going to get what's mine. Then we'll split. Finally, if there's big trouble, everybody get out fast. Look out for number one and meet here."

Then, before we moved out, Roantis surprised us by slipping off his bush pants and shirt. From his pack, he took out a dark bundle. He put on a close-fitting suit of black with faint purple swirls and a pair of strange-looking slipper socks that had a gap in the sole between the big toe and the foot. He strapped a black dagger to his right calf, and exchanged his floppy hat for a dark wool watch cap that could be pulled down into a hood. He left his bush clothes in a heap under the rock. The only things he carried were the shotgun and the assault bag with spare ammo and the fireworks. Both he could ditch instantly, leaving him unencumbered, agile, and invisible.

We crawled out from under and walked along the riverwash for a quarter of a mile. The rushing water sang a song to me, but it didn't help. Up ahead loomed the trestle bridge. It looked very high up, and that was how far we had to climb in the dark. I tried not to look at it.

"I'm looking for a big spruce that's leaning out from the cliff," whispered Roantis. "I spotted a nice crevice underneath it from the hill. That's where we'll go up."

When we found the spruce, I could see a dark, tall depression in the cliff face right beneath it. Here Roantis did another strange thing: he dropped all his gear, took the nylon climber's rope, slung it over his neck and shoulder like a bulky Sam Browne belt, and backed up to the cliff face. He stood there, back against the rock, and did some strange mumbo jumbo with his hands and fingers. It looked in the darkness as if he had twisted his fingers into painful configurations and was contemplating them. Next, he extended his arms out in a grotesque ballet stance. It looked as if he were performing tai chi. Then he snapped his toes together, heels splayed outward, knock-kneed.

"What the — " I said.

237

"*Shhhh,*" said Kaunitz. "You watch him. This is Ninjitsu's Seventh Step, and it's extremely difficult. It's called *ch'iang pi kung,* or wall climbing. It takes years to master. Roantis is the best I've ever seen."

Well, I thought it was horseshit. But, lo and behold, before our very eyes Roantis began to ascend that vertical cliff face. Without the rope fastened, without pitons, crampons, or any of that other stuff. It was levitation. It was a miracle like the loaves and fishes. It gave me the creeps.

He climbed backward, his back pressed tight to the wall of rock, his weight directly over his heels. He used only his fingertips and the backs of his heels for purchase. It must have required awesome finger and hand strength. But through it all there was no panting or puffing, no evidence of exertion. He made absolutely no noise. Liatis Roantis was languidly statue-dancing his way up, defying gravity. He had conquered that cliff wall before he'd even started, conquered it in his mind. It did not exist. It was level greensward in an English country garden. And viewed from any distance, what was most spectacular — due to his strange clothing, slow movements, and grotesque positions — was his invisibility.

This first part of the cliff face was about twenty-five feet high and absolutely vertical. Roantis, with all his smoothness and grace, made it to the top in less than five minutes. Once up there, he tied the rope to the spruce and lowered it so we could follow. Getting up there was a big chore, and I was tuckered at the top. Summers and Desmond had the most trouble because, despite their great strength, they were just plain big and heavy. So was Kaunitz, but he had awesome upper-body strength from wrestling steers day after day. After we collected ourselves up there at the first level, it was obvious to all that Royce knew what he was doing; the place was a natural castle, with the spur and its trestle the drawbridge over the moat. And we'd only gone a fraction of the way; the rest of the mountain still loomed over us.

All the days of my life, I will never forget that climb. It was terrifying and exalting. The darkness made it very tough, but I was thankful for it too, because I couldn't see how high we were. Roantis climbed ahead, feeling for the easiest route and making

238

fast the rope when necessary. We stopped in tiny level spots when we could, and caught our breath. The river sang its rushing song below us. The mountain breeze washed over us. I felt a strange and tremendous gladness and camaraderie going up that cliff in the nighttime wilderness. Although I knew I was not cut out for this kind of adventure, I then knew, and would forever know, why some men like to do it.

We made it up the mountain to just below the bare patch of rock by four forty-seven. The climb had taken almost two hours. I was exhausted and knew the others had to feel it too. After ten minutes' rest, we began to work our way slowly upward to the rock lip above our heads. Summers went over it first. Then I saw the light of his watch wink once, the signal for danger. We all froze and waited. After several minutes, I heard what sounded like an earthy thump. Summers came to the lip and asked for rope. Soon afterward we saw his watch wink twice at us from over the lip, and we followed him up. We found ourselves on a flat, narrow ridge, and we walked along it until we saw Summers kneeling over a man stretched out on the ground, his arms tied.

"Daisy's in front, in the old mine," he said in a barely audible whisper. "She all right, this dude says." He pointed at the prostrate man. "He goin' off watch at five-thirty — that's about a half a hour."

We left the sentry well trussed in the bush, with two layers of gaffer tape over his mouth. We started along the ridge, one man moving at a time. The last man in line would work his way up to the front, passing all the others and tapping each man lightly on the shoulder as he went up the line. The rest remained frozen, heads searching in all directions for sound and motion. When he was in place ahead of the first man, we'd pass a signal down the line; then the new last man would turn and move up, leaving the man directly ahead of him to turn around and watch our rear — and so on, over and over. Then Roantis motioned for Tommy to peel off and go to ground on the rock summit just above us. He settled down there like a mother hen, his rifle across his lap and binoculars up. Those big lenses would gather weak light and enable him to keep an eye on most of us. He winked his watch three times as we left him, saying everything was okay. Farther along, it was my turn. I went to earth just off the rocky ridge, in a patch of brush between two boulders. I sat down, holding the rifle upright between my knees, and flashed the others good-bye.

Good-bye and good luck. I sat looking into the dark all around me. Half an hour. Could they sneak in, find her, and get her out in that time? Yeah. Roantis was good. We'd pull it off without any violence. We'd get Daisy out and go back to Asheville. I still had doubts about Fred Kaunitz, but I hoped that if he were going to pull anything, he would have done it by this time. I sat watching the dark, keeping my ears alert.

It happened before I knew it. A man walked past me down the ridge, going in the direction we'd come from. I saw only his shadowy outline. Was it one of us? No. He wore no hat and carried no weapon.

Wait a minute, Adams. This guy's walking down the ridge from the direction that the Ducks are headed. *How come they didn't meet on the trail?* Good question. Then my ears picked up an unmistakable nighttime sound that every wilderness camper knows: the brassy, patting stream in the brush that means some-body's taking a leak. No doubt that's why the midnight walker was up and around. Wait and see if he returns. Sure enough, within seconds he was back on the trail and passed inches from me in the predawn darkness, headed back to . . . where?

My mind returned to our crude plan. I was posted as a lookout. I was supposed to give warning. Should I let off four shots? In short order, things were coming unraveled. What the hell to do?

The best answer was not to shoot but to follow him. We were just too close now to abort the plan. Also, the guy wasn't armed. Best to follow him and perhaps even get the drop on him.

I swam out of the brush and headed down the rocky ledge in a low crouch. When I caught up with him, I decided, I'd smack him on the noggin with the pistol barrel and go ahead to tell the others what had happened. It was by no means perfect, but it was all I had.

Except the guy had disappeared. I moved faster, making as much noise as I dared, but I still couldn't see him. Then brush parted lightly to my left, and I froze in a full crouch. The brush continued to snap and hiss softly, but the sound grew fainter and fainter. The man had left the trail and was moving away from it through the growth. But where was he going? I had to find out, so I followed the noise.

I kept a safe distance behind, which meant I couldn't keep close track of him. After a couple of minutes, I found myself staring up at the pale rocky face that rose vertically only a few feet in front of me. A cliff wall. Now where was he? He didn't disappear into thin air, like Judge Crater. Where was —

Then I felt it: a cool draft of damp air that smelled like old cellars and new sidewalks. It was blowing all over my face. Coming right out of the mountain.

25

HELL, it was better to be in the tunnel than silhouetted in the opening. I ducked inside. The passageway was very narrow and twisting, which meant it had been a natural seep. The floor was irregular and sloped, which made normal walking impossible. I crept along, feeling the way with my hands on the narrow walls. Sometimes the passage closed up tight and got scary. I can't stand closed, dark places at all. But I kept at it, knowing that the other guy had done likewise and that he sure hadn't come from just a broom closet in the rock — there had to be some sort of room in there.

But three or four times I had to fight back panic. It would be scary enough in the daytime on a friendly spelunking expedition. But in the dead of night, in the house of the enemy, it was a bit too much. Having finally stopped again to catch my breath — the fast breathing of fear, not exertion — I decided to creep forward another twenty feet. If the passage didn't open up, screw it. I mean, there are limits to my foolishness. I think. I still had not turned on my flashlight for fear it would be seen. But I knew my nerves wouldn't allow my going much farther without a light. Two more bends in the passage was all I was giving it. One bend. The passage was still dark and damp and so tight it kissed my stomach and back. Not the kind of kiss I like. The kind of kiss I like is with Mary in the sack. Or Janice DeGroot in the phone closet. Good. Think about Janice in the phone closet, not the cave. Dammit. That's what started this whole mess: Janice De-Groot in the goddamn phone closet. Oh well, live and learn. Of course, my problem is that I do the former, but the latter does not follow. One thing I was *not* going to do was belly-crawl through a low passage. If it couldn't be walked, the hell with it. If I got stuck on my tummy in a cave passage in the dark . . . Well, I'd be a screaming meemy in two seconds. And then I would spend the remainder of my life in a rubber room, drooling and singing Gregorian chants. Just to hell with it.

Why are you talking to yourself in your mind again, Adams? — I asked myself. Because I'm scared, that's why.

And also, I thought, if this passage does lead somewhere — and I was beginning to doubt it — why didn't the kid, Darryl Royce, tell us about it? Simple: he was smarter than he looked and didn't want to give us any extra help. That's why.

Second bend now . . . around it. Glory be: a light. The light was not close and it was a small bulb, almost around a rock corner from my line of sight. It was obviously placed there so people could find their way in the perpetual darkness. It wasn't there for direct illumination. I went for it, looking around me as I walked. I glanced at my watch. Almost ten minutes had elapsed of the half-hour deadline. We had twenty minutes left until the fresh crew woke up. I walked past the light with my rifle held at the hip. I prayed more than anything that there would be no shooting. I passed the light, turned to my right, and saw the cave open up. Was it a cave or a mine? Who knew? Who cared? In back of the room were stacks and stacks of cardboard boxes. As I sneaked past them I looked closely. Most had the three-diamonds trademark of Mitsubishi or whatever it is, that huge Japanese conglomerate that makes everything from autos to transistors. What was in the cartons? Auto parts? No. Tunafish. *Tunafish?* That's what it said: chunk light tuna, in water and oil. Looked like five thousand cans of it. Looked like restaurant grade, wholesale. Why all the tunafish? Was Royce smuggling something other than dope?

Then I remembered: young Darryl had said that Royce was a survivalist, a man waiting for nuclear war to destroy civilization. And I had read somewhere that currency in the postnuclear age would consist mainly of two items: 22-caliber cartridges and cans of tunafish. So I was looking at his nest egg, his private hoard of survivalist currency. Like as not, the ammunition was in some other passageway. In a cave, no less. So we'd be back in caves for a few thousand years after the fireballs died out. And then we'd learn to hunt wild game and wear their skins and fur when it got cold. Generations later, we might scratch the soil with the sharpened femurs of elk and bison (or perhaps the tusks of woolly mammoths, if they decided to come back too) and put seeds in. We'd start training dogs again, if any were left.

One day a young woman might have the temerity to mix sacrificial blood with soot and ocher in her tough palm, sneak into the farthest corner of the clan cave where she would not be seen, and by the faint light of a tallow lamp begin with trembling hands to draw a crude wall painting of the beasts of the fields . . .

Oh, it was a cheery thought.

I went on, making a gradual turn to my right. Ahead, I could see what appeared to be a second room, bigger than the first, barely lighted with several of the tiny bulbs. The light shone against the rock walls so faintly that the shape and size of the place were not clear. But it was big — much larger than the small seepway I had crept through. A dark circle at its far end was the main entrance. The place smelled of damp rock and wood smoke. I saw a fire-blackened section of wall on the far side and the remains of a fire below.

Men were sleeping on the floor of the cavern on army cots. I stayed in the near-darkness of the rear of the cave and swept the prone figures with my binoculars. They gathered enough of the feeble light and magnified the images enough for me to see them. One man stirred in his cot. Probably the guy who'd just returned from his call of nature. Then I saw Daisy. What was holding her? Some kind of shackle. Could we cut it off? Pick the lock? Blast it apart without maiming her? Roantis would know.

It was dark in there; the lights were barely strong enough to allow people to see where they were going. The one in the passage was probably burning all the time, and no doubt they all were powered by a generator like the one Royce had hidden in the old pump house back at the farm. If I could get to that generator and kill the lights, perhaps I could sneak up to Daisy and free her to run out the front entrance.

No, I'd better wait for Roantis.

But where was he? And Kaunitz and Summers? They were supposed to have worked their way around to the front by now. Time was getting short. I decided to go back, find Roantis, and tell him about the passageway; it might change our plans and make things easier. But I had to hurry.

I crept back into that cramped passageway, which smelled like a new sidewalk, and wriggled and squirmed my way through it. If it was so hard to get through, why had the man decided to use it rather than the main entrance? But I didn't have time to consider this fully because then I was fighting my way through the tangles of brush and creepers again back to the narrow ridge.

I looked up; the cloud cover was thinning and the stars shone brightly. It was lighter out; it would be dawn pretty soon. I walked as fast as I dared, half bent over and holding the Colt at my hip. I was shivering. I didn't think it was from the cold. The path on the ridge wound down and to the left. After I'd gone about forty yards, I saw a pale yellow opening in the cliff ahead of me, some twelve feet above the path I was on. That was the entrance I had just seen from the inside. I went on, and soon more of the place was visible. Below the entrance and to the side stood the flatcar we'd seen on the spur earlier. In the dark, I could see it only through my glasses. The spur ran on past the cliff and continued westward. Near the flatcar was a clearing. I could barely see the cartons and other supplies stacked on pallets. The clearing was ringed with woods. Roantis, Summers, and Kaunitz would be in there; all I had to do was find them.

I left the path twenty yards from the clearing and took cover in the trees. It was a good thing too, because after creeping forward a ways, I went to the edge of the bush and had a peek. I looked up at the entrance and saw what I had suspected: a sentry on watch just below the lip of the hole. He had a good view of the clearing and would have seen me approach on the path.

245

Now it was obvious to me why the Ducks had been delayed: the entrance twelve feet up a sheer cliff and a sentry to guard it. There was a crude wooden stairway leading from the clearing up the cliff face to the entrance, and the sentry was at the top of it, looking down. Tricky. Very tricky indeed. It would take even a man as skilled and cold-blooded as Roantis an hour. And that we did not have.

I sank back into cover and kept moving. Before I'd gone six feet, an arm caught me around the face, a huge hand covering my mouth and nose.

I dropped the rifle and knew that in less than a second I would feel the white-hot wall of agony when the dagger plunged into me. Either my right kidney — death in thirty seconds, and the most painful stab wound possible; or my subclavian artery, between neck and shoulder — death in three seconds; or perhaps below my rib cage and up into my heart — death in three seconds, unconsciousness immediately.

Instinctively, I made a hitchhiker's thumb with my right hand and shot it backward. I felt the wet syrup of an eye. The hold on me relaxed, and I heard a deep grunt of pain. Without stopping, I stood up and sent my right elbow back with everything I had, then turned and kicked. The man faded back and sat down, holding his eye with one hand, his groin in the other, and cussing in a hoarse whisper. I heard reference to an intimate relationship between me and my mother.

"Mike?" I whispered.

"Who the fuck you think it is, jiveass?" he growled under his breath.

"Sorry."

"Man! You sposa be up — "

I apologized and explained. Where was Roantis?

Summers swept his arm out toward the clearing on the other side of the brush. "Out there. Freddie's up ahead. Better let 'im know you're comin'."

I left him clutching himself and crawled on. I decided to flash my watch three times instead of waiting to get grabbed again. It worked; I saw an answering flash through the brush, and Freddie Kaunitz scooted over to me.

"Que pasa?" he whispered.

"Where's Liatis?"

He told me, and I took up my glasses and swept the clearing. Kaunitz swore he was out there, but I'd be damned if I could see him. I now noticed a block and tackle rig above the cave entrance, much like a bale lifter on a barn. That's how they got the heavy supplies up there. But they obviously did not use the main entrance at night, which explained why the nighttime leaker had taken the back way out. Were there any other side passages? How could we know? Where *was* Roantis?

The clock was ticking.

Then I saw him. Even through the glasses I had to focus on the distant figure for several seconds before I was convinced it was a human being. Roantis had snaked his way up to the cliff on the far side of the clearing. He was standing against the rock, but was all but invisible because he had distorted his human silhouette by assuming a crooked-leg, splayed-arm stance that resembled a gnarled Monterey cypress. It was weird, but it worked. I found out later that this was inpo, the Ninjitsu art of hiding. More specifically, it was the part of inpo known as *pu neng mu,* "hiding behind nothing." Since the human eye discerns movement first, silhouette second, and color third, Roantis had, in the dim light, negated all of these by his dark, swirled clothes, his deformed silhouette, and his extremely slow motion. He moved but appeared not to; he moved the way a flower petal opens. Soon he was within seven feet of the platform car that sat silent on the old spur, the old tractor cowling and stack jutting up into the purple-blue of the night like a frozen monster. Roantis stand-danced his way over to it, before the very eyes of the sentry above, and soon stood on it, right next to the engine.

Then, with a languid movement, he drew a long, pale object from the front of his shirt. He dropped to a half crouch behind the tractor and affixed something to it. What was he doing? As he rose slightly and peered over the top of the engine cowling, I recognized the paper wand Sparkles MacAllister had given to him. Roantis rose to his full height and for an instant seemed to hover over the machine, then he held the wand over the smokestack, the dark tip of the fuse on its lower end. Then it was gone, and the dark figure pirouetted slowly off the platform and eased his way, crouching, back toward the cliff. He never saw me and wasn't coming back. My watch said we had twelve minutes left. I didn't hang around. On my way back, I told Kaunitz I was going in the back way again.

"We're out of time, Freddie. If he comes back your way, tell him I'll meet you up there. I counted eight men inside. They look like kids."

Then I skedaddled. I didn't see Summers on the way back or any sign of Tommy Desmond, either. I assumed they were somewhere in the brush, ready for whatever came down. I worked my way through the thickets again, then went back inside that narrow seep. I did not want to go back in there. Every cell in my body said no. My common sense — what little there is of it — said no. But something stronger said yes. I didn't know, then, what the voice was.

So I dragged my aching body through that damp crack in the cliff again. I was carrying only my Colt rifle; even that was a chore. I squirmed through and worked my way back to the big, bowl-shaped room again. Was it my imagination, or was it lighter in there? Regardless, predawn light wasn't far off. I knew I couldn't crawl over to Daisy with the rifle, so I leaned it in a crack, took the safety snap off my pistol holster, and got down on the damp rock, belly-crawling toward where Daisy lay on her cot. I was shivering. None of the men was close to Daisy, but I knew that at least two of them — Royce and Jusuelo — were trained to wake instantly at the slightest disturbance. I inched onward, staring out the mouth of the cavern. It looked black out there, just because it was slightly darker there than inside. And just out of sight, over the rock lip of the cave's mouth, was the crude front stairway, guarded by the sentry who was probably less than fifteen feet from me. When I finally reached her, I took a deep breath and slowly placed my hand over her mouth, ready to grip it tight as iron if she began to cry out.

But old Daisy was a pro. She opened those black eyes slowly, as calmly as a typist awakening from a lie-down, and stared at me. Then she gave me a slow wink, removed my hand, and pointed toward the foot of the cot. Her left leg was shackled by a big brass padlock to a length of aircraft cable. That steel cable is light-weight and stronger than chain.

"Who's got the key?" I said in a whisper so low I couldn't even hear it.

"Bill," she answered.

I pointed around us.

"Where?"

"There. Against the wall. Next to Jusuelo." She pointed them out. I saw Jusuelo first, recognized the face of the priest in the hospital. The murderer-priest. Royce's head was covered by his arm, but I saw the familiar big form, and in the faint light I could see that the tufts of hair that were visible were light in color. Jusuelo and Royce. The two remaining Daisy Ducks. Turned bad. Not that the other three were angels. I wanted to walk over there and put bullets in their heads. I felt a tug on my shoulder.

"It's hanging on a ring on his belt, Doc. You'll never get it without waking him."

But I hunkered down and began to ease along the rock toward Royce. I doubted he would wear the keyring while sleeping; it would hurt if he turned on it. Twice I had seen and heard the sleeping men stir. Outdoor people like these rise early. Time was just about up. It was now or never, and all up to me. "Observatory position," my ass.

I crept over the rock floor to Bill Royce's cot. It only took about three hours. Hell, I had loads of time left. A whole minute and a half. *Loads.* And there, thanks be to God, on the ground right next to the cot was the first lucky break I'd had — a ring of keys. Royce flinched, then turned over on the cot. I saw in the rising light a faint sheen of sweat on his upper lip. Oh God. If he got the drug shakes he'd wake any second, and in a foul mood. Also, considering how I'd already managed to muck up his plans, he would waste no time in dealing me out.

I snagged the keys and belly-crawled back to Daisy. I wanted to rush, but I made myself move slowly and in silence. When I got to her, Daisy took the keys. Pulling up softly on the cable, I saw the tether end was made fast to a massive screw eye — the size they used on telephone poles — set into a hole in the rock filled with concrete. No way was it going anywhere. Daisy, whose stepfather had taught her well, had memorized the key and found it fast. When the lock snapped open, I took the keys and stuffed them in my pants. Then I closed the padlock on the cable. I didn't want them to be able to shackle her like that ever again. I leaned over and told her the drill.

"We'll ease out the back way, kid. There's a sentry guarding the front. He's right below us and — "

She didn't wait to hear the rest, just eased to her feet and crept ahead of me toward the back of the cavern. Then she stopped, dropped to a crouch, and motioned me toward the front. I heard it too: somebody scuffling around in the rear passage. Somebody was coming our way, walking in through the narrow seep. Too late. We changed direction and moved fast now, the scuffling behind us growing louder. Was it running? I looked back to see a dark figure enter the room. We had to go out the front way now, and down the stairs. No other choice. What about the sentry? Could I shoot him in the chest with my pistol? Easy answer: not in a million years. But he had a rifle, maybe a submachine gun. I patted myself down, looking for any kind of weapon. I found it.

But the sentry didn't wait; he had stood up, cocking his ear at the noise above him. His head was visible above the lip of the entrance. So was the muzzle of his weapon: a short, stubby grease gun. He hadn't seen us yet. I had the little can in my fist now, the top unscrewed.

"Hey!" shouted a voice behind us. Loud enough to wake the dead. I turned for a millisecond to see the man standing in the rear of the cavern. He held something long and dark. My rifle. He'd found it. No time at all now. I jumped over the lip and down onto the wooden platform that was the start of the stairway down. Daisy followed me, and then we were eye to eye with the sentry, who was bringing up the submachine gun to point at our chests. That slug spitter could cut us both in half with a burst of fire. Oh Christ.

"Halt!" he shouted. Holy Jesus. The voice of a teenager. He was just as scared as I was. And I was scared plenty. I emptied the contents of the can into my left hand, thinking, you don't know just how dangerous this game can get, kid. You've been reading too many comic books.

There was an ear-splitting ripping and tearing of the rock wall behind the boy. I saw dust and rock flying off the cliff face. One of the Ducks below us was giving the place a hosing down with a long automatic burst. The racket was deafening — and scary. So scary the kid turned around for a split second, which was all the time I needed to begin the long, underhand sweep of my left arm, with a whole can of snuff cradled on my cupped palm.

The brown dust cloud flew around the kid's face, with a lot of it going into his eyes. Boy, did he scream. I knew it must have hurt like hell, and the pain would last and last. Would he ever see again? At that instant I didn't care. I saw Daisy grab the grease gun from midair as he dropped it in his agony. Without missing a beat, she raised the muzzle and bopped him a good one on the side of the head. He fell down the stairs, still screaming and trying to take his eyes out with the tips of his fingers. If he kept at it, he would succeed. We stormed right over him and down the stairs.

But we still weren't home free. Not by a long shot. Because waiting for us at the very bottom of the walkway was Fred Kaunitz. He didn't even say hello, just held that black rifle pointed right at us. You know the one: black plastic foregrip with three vent holes, carrying handle over the receiver . . .

And Fred Kaunitz never missed.

26

DAISY LOOKED CONFUSED and didn't raise her gun. I grabbed her shoulders and pushed her down toward the rocky gravel where Kaunitz stood. Not that it would do any good. I heard two quick shots from the FAL and turned to see Daisy's blown-away head.

But she was fine. And so, apparently, was I. There was a thumping and clattering behind us, and a figure in camo continued his slow, spastic somersaulting down the last steps of the walkway. He rolled one last time, tried to stand on his head, and didn't make it. He eased back into death, spread-eagled at our feet, with two neat holes in his chest, dead center. My Colt rifle, which he had picked up just before he yelled at us, was still on the stairs. I leaned to pick it up and heard Kaunitz telling Daisy to get into the trees and go to ground with me.

"Thanks, Freddie," I said as he jumped for the stairs.

"Don't mention it," he hissed through clenched teeth, leaping up the stairs three at a time. We scooted for the woods and almost got knocked flat by the burly form of Summers, who followed Kaunitz up. Then we were in the trees and vines and Daisy was hugging Roantis, calling him Papa. He beamed for maybe half a second, then looked up at the cave, frowning.

"Both Royce and Jusuelo are in there," I told him. "And about eight others. There's a back way — that's how I got in."

"Where's Desmond? He in there too?"

When I shook my head, he drew a brass egg from his assault bag and stepped to the edge of the bush, looking up at the hole in the cliffside. If he was going to throw it, he'd have to do it fast, before Summers and Kaunitz got in the way. He had depressed the side lever and started to pull out the pin when he stopped.

"How old are they?" he asked Daisy.

"Mostly boys, Papa."

"Shit," he said, returning the bomb to the bag, "I'm getting too old for this I think."

Then he bolted across the clearing and leapt onto the steps, his Streetcleaner in his left hand. I knew he could clean out that cavern in three seconds with it. At a demonstration, I'd seen him work that pump like a Vegas crapshooter rolling bones. But I hoped he wouldn't; I knew these rough, tough survivalists were, as Daisy had said, mostly boys. Summers and Kaunitz went over the lip. I expected to hear fireworks, but it was eerily still. I thought I knew why. Daisy knew too, and we both trotted up along the ridge toward the seep.

I forced myself to follow Daisy as she ran and slunk from tree to tree, boulder to ledge, peering cautiously ahead, waiting, then dashing forward. She had that M-3 grease gun up at chest level, sweeping it back and forth in front of her as she went. I knew she wouldn't hesitate to use it. But we saw nobody, friend or foe.

Then two men scampered up the ridge ahead of us. Both were unarmed and looked scared. They headed up the cliff and over the top. Little puffs of rock dust followed in their wake, with the buzzing and whining of careening slugs. Then I saw Tommy from the chest up, peering from behind a fallen tree, using his rifle to keep them moving. A third man came scurrying out. Armed. I knew who he was. I remembered those dark eyes. Jusuelo ran crouched and very fast. He had a canvas satchel slung over his shoulder. He must have seen Desmond, because those dust puffs raked the rock around Tommy and he went down. Daisy had the M-3 up and she got off a short burst, but

253

Jusuelo was already gone, over the mountain to God-knows-where.

Daisy wanted to go after him. Dumb. She started running up the rock and I caught her in back by the top edge of her jeans. Without slowing down, she kicked back and caught my shin with her heel and told me to leave her the fuck alone. I sat down fast, holding my leg. Nice broad. I followed her up, and then we were lying on the top of the rock, looking down the other side of the mountain. It was all rock and brush and a few tall pine trees. No sign of Jusuelo. Then I heard that electric snap above my head that told me a supersonic bullet had passed over us. We hunkered down.

"I don't think he wants us to follow him," I said.

Below us, Tommy Desmond shouted. I asked if he was hurt. He said no. I walked down, leaving Daisy to watch the other side. She wasn't about to move anyway. I had a feeling there was no love lost between her and the man scurrying down the cliff to safety. I took another look at her as she lay on her tummy at the top of the rocky ridge. Lord help me, why do I think about these things at the strangest times? But there was no denying it. No denying it at all: Daisy had a killer ass.

I told Tommy I was going in the back way to see how the others were doing. He would cover that point until I returned.

Well, I went into that seep again. I heard nothing, and it made me uneasy. It meant things were either really good or really bad. I went ahead carefully, my safety off and tense as a coiled rattler. What I saw in the main room I wasn't prepared for. The Ducks had four of the young men face down and spread-eagled on the dirt. Summers stood over them with the shotgun while Roantis helped the sentry off the walkway and sat him down. He was still rubbing his eyes, obviously in great pain. I was sorry I'd thrown the snuff in his face, but it could have been much worse. The most surprising thing of all was the last remaining defender of the fortress, Bill Royce.

Bill was squatting on his heels, rocking back and forth, crying softly. His arms were clasped around his legs, his head resting on the tops of his knees, like a kid in front of a warm fireplace. Fred Kaunitz knelt on one knee beside his old wartime buddy, patting his back and talking softly. I didn't go near them.

"Where's Jusuelo?" asked Roantis, eyeing me sharply.

"He went over the far side of the mountain, toward Tennessee. Daisy's watching for him on the summit."

He swore and said we'd never see him again. I knew that Roantis was now convinced that it had been Jusuelo who'd shot him. It was also clear that given the chance, Roantis would kill *him*. But I was just as glad Jusuelo had split; only one man had been killed: the guy Kaunitz had nailed before he could shoot Daisy and me in the back. Everyone else was fine. Let it end that way. I turned to see Kaunitz comforting Royce. Royce was talking now, intently telling Fred an important story. Roantis yanked one of the guys off the floor of the cave and told him he wanted a tour of the fortress, no doubt to uncover anything of value. The two of them went off. I got a canteen and helped the sentry wash out his eyes. I felt sorry for him, but I didn't apologize. I got him as comfortable as possible, then joined Summers, watching the young prisoners.

"How's the old groin?" I asked.

"Still hurts, James. I won't forget it soon — tell you that. Good thing you helped me out, Doc, or I'd be pissed."

"What happened to Bill?"

"Found him like that. Curled up in the corner of the place, like a baby cryin' hisself to sleep. Poor guy. Bill wadn't never bad. Jusuelo now, that's another story. Mean sombitch. Sorry he got away."

I heard a sound outside and couldn't place it. I watched Kaunitz help Royce to his feet. Royce was talking in a low voice, but I heard the words clearly.

". . . and then we'd go out to the village at night, you remember, Freddie? And the sky was cloudy . . . big silver-gray clouds low over the trees, remember? And the evening light coming through them. The jungle all thick and green. And remember how it smelled? The flowers and the river . . . and the little kids playing on the riverbank. Then the planes would come in. No bombs . . . It was before all that. The planes would come in at dusk with our stuff . . . You remember, Freddie. Say you remember."

"I remember it, Billy. I remember."

"And remember the birds calling in the evening, and how

255

pretty it smelled? And the choppers' propwash in the grass in the highlands. We were all standing around with those kids . . . Remember?"

"Oh, I remember it, Billy. Like it was yesterday."

The two walked slowly out of the cave, with Royce leaning against Kaunitz. Summers and I left them alone. Then I saw the two of them looking down from the top of the walkway, and Kaunitz pointing down and shouting something. I went out and stood with them. We could see the flatcar clearly now in the glow of the first light. The sound I'd heard was now explained: the old tractor engine was running, running hard. Clouds of oily smoke shot up from the black stack. So much for Roantis's magic wand in there. A dud if there ever was one. There was a cracking and popping along the rock and I ducked back in, with Kaunitz half carrying Bill close behind. Royce was shaking again and Freddie sat him down against the wall inside. Summers and I poked our heads around and looked down again. The flatcar was moving back down the spur, gaining speed. Jusuelo crouched under the engine, looking up in our direction with his rifle ready, the canvas haversack in front of him on the platform. He let off a final short burst. The rock wall popped and cracked as we ducked back in. We peered out again in time to see the flatcar crossing the trestle at a good clip. I'd have sworn Jusuelo was laughing at us. And well he might.

Roantis appeared at our side. His face showed no emotion.

"Liatis, I don't think that wand of MacAllister's was any good. In twenty minutes, Jusuelo will be back at the end of the spur. He'll take Royce's pickup truck, and that's the last we'll see of him."

"My money's in that canvas sack, Doc. That's what the kid tells me. The dope, that was Jusuelo's business, not Royce's. He kept the swag in that canvas sack — and that's the last I'll see of *it.* Now that Daisy's safe, I don't care about Jusuelo. But I want my loot!"

He watched the rickety contraption sway out of sight, cursing under his breath.

"Let's go back downriver and crank up those radios," I said, "I'm sure the police will want to talk to Mr. Jusuelo. They can throw a net around him."

256

"Too late," he snapped.

"No it isn't. It'll take him twenty minutes to ride that spur. Then he's got to hotwire Royce's truck — see Liatis, I've still got Bill's keys in my pocket — hotwire the truck and — "

"Too late!"

He stomped down the wooden stairs and out into the clearing, kicking rocks and swearing. I leaned over the railing.

"We can still stop him and maybe recover something. I mean, how far can he go in an hour?"

"Real far, Doc. Like to kingdom come. Hey, were there any kids with him on that car?"

"No. He's alone."

"Well, that's one good thing."

"Liatis, that gimmick Sparkles sold you is a dud. Admit it."

He looked at his watch, shook his head, and resumed kicking stones. Daisy came up to him and they hugged. I heard her call him Papa again, and they talked in French. They hugged for a long, long time. I was thinking about Mary. I sat down on the sentry's ledge and watched the sun ease up over the mountains. The birds were going nuts. Finches, warblers, thrushes, crows, mockingbirds — the whole crew. I've still never seen anything like the Carolina mountains for birds. I wanted to get back. Now. Now that it was over, I wanted to see Mary. I swayed a little on the rock. Watch it, Doc. Then I realized my legs felt numb. They tingled slightly, but the general sensation was of numbness and heaviness, as if my legs were two felled oak limbs. I swayed again and jammed my hands down on the ledge to steady myself.

"Hey Eugene! You all right, my man?" Mike spread his huge hand on the back of my neck and gently rocked me back and forth.

"I'm okay . . . I think . . ." I said in a fuzzy voice.

"Hah! You crashin' now, baby. When you go into action, you all juiced up. Keeps you sharp. That juice wear off — bam! All she wrote."

Daisy came up the walkway and sat down next to me. She leaned over and planted one on my cheek. Dynamite. She rubbed my back, then let her head fall onto my shoulder. All the Ducks were looking at us.

"Scoot," she said, and kept rubbing. My eyes were beginning to close . . .

KHAAAA-WHOOOOOOOMP!

It was like thunder, only all at once, not rolling, and it came from far, far away. We felt the concussion of it in our chests. The fierce wind of it blew our hair up. An angry hiss came through the trees, then died away fast. Summers looked out across the rolling mountains.

"Whoooo-eeeee!" he whistled, "that Russki cyclonite sure pack a wallop."

Roantis trudged up the stairs and joined us. He kicked the rock wall, looking at his watch.

"Nine and a half minutes. Supposed to go in eight."

Daisy led me inside to a cot. I lay down on it. She was rubbing my back, thanking me. It sure felt good, and she was a knockout. But I was thinking of Mary. Then I fell asleep.

27

ROANTIS WOKE ME in an hour. A lot had happened. He had
changed from his black widow stalker outfit back to the old bush
clothes again. Kaunitz and Desmond had defused the trestle
bridge and hauled our gear from the dry camp over the bridge
and up to the clearing. The Ducks were ready to walk out of
there. They'd even let the remaining kids take off. There wasn't
any fight left in them, anyway. Desmond and Kaunitz would stay
behind with Royce and watch the place. There had been no sign
of the other ragtag survivalists or of the law. But a man was shot
and another presumably blown to kingdom come. We had to let
people know. Kaunitz would try the airwaves while we walked
back along the track. I didn't relish the idea; I had grotesque and
horrid visions of what we might see. But morbid curiosity kept
me going. That and my tummy. I was hungry. I wanted a down-
home meal in town. And I wanted Mary. I wanted her more than
anything. So Roantis, Daisy, Summers, and I took off along the
spur through the deep woods. The only things missing were
Daisy's pigtails and gingham dress and her dog, Toto.

After an hour's trek, Summers found the first of the bills. A
hundred with the upper right-hand corner charred away. He
folded and stuffed it away quick as a flash, saying finders-keepers.

Then Daisy found two of them. One was half charred and probably couldn't be redeemed, but the other one was whole. Finders-
keepers, she said. Then Daisy found another. Then I found three
stuck together. No burn marks. Finders-keepers. Roantis found
a couple. Then Mike found a bunch stuck in a tree branch, torn
up but cashable. And so it went.

The farther we went, the more bills we found. The forest was
lousy with them. Money grew on trees. Before long, we realized
we just couldn't stuff our own pockets; we had to put it together
in a lump sum and divvy it up fair and square. No more finders-
keepers. Then we got to the site. There was no crater, as I had
imagined, but the ground was burnt, the railroad ties charred,
for forty feet. There was also a strange odor that I'll never forget.
The trees all around were blown over, nude and black. Great
pieces of twisted metal had been driven into the tree trunks. It
would take a crow-bar to get them out. It was scary. And there
was no flatcar. And no Jesus Jusuelo, either. If there was, I sure
didn't want to be the one to find him.

We gathered money from the site like peasants harvesting
crops. I was thinking that one of those sticks with a nail on the
end — the kind used to clean up litter — would be just the ticket.
We stuffed all our pockets. Almost all the bills were hundreds,
but there were a lot of fifties and twenties too — nothing lower.
Should we even bother with the twenties? They took up so much
room . . .

"Hi, Mare. I love you."

"Oh Jesus! Where the hell have you been? You jerk! Don't you
know that we've been — "

"Do you love me?"

"Sure, Charlie. Now where — "

"Well I love you, Mary. And guess what? It's only the third
day. You won't have to move to Vegas after all."

"Wanna bet?"

I told her we still had some loose ends to straighten up, but
we'd be back in Asheville as soon as we could. She wanted to
know all about it, but I wasn't telling. I simply told her we'd
retrieved Daisy and none of us was hurt. We left the café and

drove back out to the boonies. Twice, choppers whined and popped overhead.

"Think Freddie got through?" I asked.

"Yeah. We'll have a reception committee. What should we do with the loot?" asked Roantis.

"I told you to stop using that word," I said.

"Well, what happens now?" asked Daisy.

"Hmph! We better get our story straight," growled Summers.

He was right. What to do about the money? How to explain Jusuelo's demise? What about the dead man at Royce's mountaintop hideaway? What about the lads there who took off into the wilderness? Roger Penland, James Hunnicutt, and Company would want answers. If they weren't forthcoming, or satisfactory, we could be doing time in the slammer or on a road gang.

When the phrase "road gang" came up, Summers informed all of us that he was not — repeat *not* — doing time on some jiveass, motherfuckin', nastyass, honky road gang. Period.

We parked the camper rig in our hidden spot, stashed the money in a plastic garbage bag in a rocky crevice twenty yards away, and hightailed it back to the mountaintop. We didn't arrive till midafternoon, and I was finally, totally, fagged out. So, I noticed, was everybody else. Daisy felt no discomfort or urgency from that phantom kidney punch I'd dealt her, but she did tire easily. Even Mike admitted he was pooped. We crossed back over the trestle and saw Tommy waving his arms over his head like a flagman, smiling at us. Just wait till they heard about the loot.

Uh, I mean *find* . . .

Then we saw Kaunitz and Royce below us, sitting on the riverbank. Royce was still talking, throwing pebbles into the water.

The law got there shortly afterward. They had to land their chopper on a wide stretch of gravel riverbank half a mile downstream and walk up. Hunnicutt and Penland were leading the way. First order of business was the dead guy at the base of the cliff. Kaunitz stepped forward and explained accurately what had happened. Daisy backed him up and told of her ordeal. The lawmen made the guy right away: a notorious thief and troublemaker who had been charged a year previous with killing a deputy sheriff. Couldn't make it stick. After all this went down, none of us was very worried about what might happen to Freddie.

Where were the others? One man, we said, attempted to escape on a homemade flatcar and was apparently blown up by a faulty bomb. I told Hunnicutt he was the same man who'd killed the pilot in the hospital, but positive identification of the body would prove difficult, to say the least.

The officers were still skeptical until two things happened. The first was Royce's voluntary private session with them, in which — we found out later — he told them in detail about his founding of the survivalist community. The drug operation was Jusuelo's thing, although Royce knew he was an accomplice. The second thing was the inspection of the mountaintop fortress. There we all saw big stockpiles of small arms, most illegally converted to full automatic fire. We found explosives, rations, two mortars, stockpiles of seeds, huge piles of ammunition, several medium-weight machine guns, reloading equipment, and a generator-powered workshop with a lathe and metalworking equipment used in the firearms conversions. Who knew how many state and federal violations were laid open in that little walking tour?

Then the officers took Royce aside again and pumped him for names, dates, locations, home addresses, and so on. Finally, they found a partial list of Jusuelo's contacts. That put the lid on it.

They took Bill Royce away in the chopper with them, leaving two men to watch over the state's evidence. The officers were pleasant, but made it clear we were not to leave the scene.

That was when Fred Kaunitz approached me and held out his hand.

"You were great, Doc."

"Thanks, Freddie. And thanks for saving my skin. Hope you get off okay. I don't see a problem, do you?"

"No. There shouldn't be any hassle. Listen, seeing you in action, I'm sorry I didn't take you with me that night in Texas."

"What?"

"The night you stayed at Flying K with us, I woke up in the dead of night and couldn't get back to sleep. I kept thinking of those dry-gulchers on my land. So I got dressed and decided to

262

hike down to that arroyo in the dark to see what I could see. I stopped by your room to see if you wanted to come along, but your door was locked. When I peeked in the window, I saw you were asleep. You'd had a tough day, so I went alone."

"Ah! And did you see anything?"

"Not the men, but their dry camp. A week later, I took three of my men out there and set up an ambush. We grabbed two of them and turned them in."

"That'll teach 'em," I said.

"Now, Doc, I got to do something I don't want to do. I've been talking with Bill for two hours, and he's filled me in on a lot. Let's go get Roantis. I want both of you to follow me to the top of the mountain for a few minutes," he said quietly. "The others can wait here."

So, with weary feet, we went to the summit. There, we left the rock face and entered scrubby woods. We walked for twenty or thirty yards through bushy tangles and creeper vines, then descended into a little hollow of bigger trees. There were ferns on the floor of it and softly sighing pine boughs overhead. We all stopped. Roantis and I looked at Kaunitz. What pronouncement was he going to make?

"How's Bill?" asked Roantis.

"So-so, but better than I thought he'd be. We had a long talk while you were gone. He told me everything. Actually, he hasn't been as bad a boy as we all think. Lieutenant, I asked you up here for an important reason. Straight ahead, about ten paces, is the man who tried to kill you."

We both stared at him for a second, waiting for the grin, the punch line, the wry gag. None came. We went forward and saw an upright stone set in a small clearing. There were two little American flags, one on each side of the stone. And carved on its face was a single word:

VILARDE.

28

ROANTIS WALKED UP to the stone and touched it, placed both hands on it, perhaps to see if it was real.

"It's a lie," he said in a whisper. "The one man I trusted and liked above all others was Ken."

He dropped to one knee and stared at the name on the granite. It was a professionally carved gravestone. Somebody had trucked it all the way out there and set it on the grave. He grabbed at the ground, then let the pine needles and sand dribble from his hand slowly.

"Where did you hear this? It's a lie."

Kaunitz sat down cross-legged next to him.

"Royce told me."

"Royce is nuts. This proves it. Either he shot me or Jusuelo. Not Ken."

"Maybe. Maybe not. You remember 1978? Ken was just back from a tour in Syria. He had a month's leave before he went back. This time to Afghanistan. Remember?"

Roantis nodded, wrinkling his brow. But beneath the frown of disbelief a vague realization was coming to him. He nodded again.

"Ken wanted to fly to Kowloon then, but you said wait. Wait till the tour in Afghanistan is over, then you'll be out for good."

264

Roantis flung down the handful of dirt.

"Yeah I remember. But Ken agreed. Listen: I'd had that scrape with the law then. I couldn't even leave the state." Fred said nothing. Roantis stared at the stone. "I mean, at least he dint fight it. He went along with it."

"Uh-huh. Because since you got the Siva in the first place, and you were his CO, he figured it was your place to call the shots. He told Royce about your probation, too. But I guess he figured if you really wanted to go, you could have. So no, the two of you didn't fly to Kowloon. Ken went to the heartland of Asia for a boonie stint and special ops. On one of them he caught shrapnel. Damn near died before they could get him out."

Roantis kept picking up the dirt, grinding it in his palm, and flinging it down. He stared at the carved name inches from his face. Kaunitz continued.

"So, as he recovered he began to think. He thought how close he'd come to dying, how close you'd come to getting it all for yourself. And that maybe you'd half planned it that way. Meanwhile his wife, Rosie, who's sick and tired of living in trailers and government billets, meets this rich real estate developer out in California . . ."

I squatted down on my heels and stared at the ground. The rest of the picture was easy to fill in.

". . . so, when Ken finally comes stateside, he finds his wife and daughter gone. Gone with the rich guy. The rich guy that he could have been."

"So he blamed me!" Roantis blurted out.

Kaunitz drew lines in the dirt with a stick, played with it, the way people do when they're saying something difficult.

"Something like that. He figured maybe it was your long-range plan to take it all. Not that Royce, or any of us, believe it. But something had happened to Ken. The defeat in Nam, the near-miss in the Afghan mountains, and Rosie's desertion . . . These things can change a guy."

A long silence followed. Kaunitz played with his digging stick. I squatted, looking at the dirt. I watched a black ant struggling headlong over twigs and pebbles, as if on a great mission. Did he know where he was going? Did any of us?

"So by last fall, Ken had it in his mind — had convinced himself, you know — that all his troubles could be placed on you. He needed somewhere to put all his misery and — "

"I know, I know!" shouted Roantis, getting to his feet. He paced back and forth in front of his comrade's grave. "I get the picture, Freddie. When he called me about getting the Siva in October, he was setting me up. Tracking me. For weeks I knew something was up. I been doing this stuff long enough to tell when somebody's on my backtrail. But I never thought it would be him."

"Royce told me that when he first saw Vilarde a few months ago, Ken felt betrayed all around. He hated the army. He hated America. He hated Rosie. He hated you. All he wanted was enough loot to take off and forget it."

There was that word again. And I thought back to my little visit to Moe's trailer, when he'd warned me of the Siva, saying it would taint everything it touched. As usual, he was right.

"Just about then, he ran into Jusuelo. The two fit together like meshed gears. Both Hispanics felt used and betrayed by the Anglos. They thought it was time they worked for themselves. Jusuelo was making some big drug hauls out of the Caribbean, where he grew up. Now he needed a big chunk of cash to make the biggest buy ever. And, of course, Vilarde knew just where to get it . . . and get even with you at the same time, lieutenant."

Roantis began walking back. We stood up and followed him through the brush, talking as we went.

"Ken followed me to Doc's house and ambushed me there, out in the country. Makes sense. He wouldn't do it in the city. He takes the key, and then he and Jusuelo fly to Kowloon with both keys, retrieve the Siva, and peddle it."

"Yeah. Royce thinks it was somewhere in the islands, like maybe Grand Cayman, where they sold it. They took the cash from that, made the big buy south of the border somewhere, and arranged for a series of drops by air. The first two drops went okay. The third one, Doc, is the one you jinxed."

"I didn't mean to — it was an accident."

"Yeah, like everything else you managed to do," growled Roantis.

"How did Royce and his little rascals get involved in it?" I asked. "Was he in from the beginning?"

"Naw. Jusuelo was looking for an FOB — that's forward operations base to you, Doc — and South Florida was getting hot as hell. Jusuelo tracked Royce down out here when he heard he was back in country. It didn't take him long to realize that Royce, with his survivalist thing, had the perfect hideout and cover for his operations, including a farm in the wilderness that could be used for the drops. Royce resisted at first, but Jusuelo offered him money, arms, supplies, and help. Finally — and this shows what a bad egg he'd become — he found a way to take advantage of Royce's instability and enslave him."

"Yeah. He got him doing the hard stuff," I said. "I could tell that when I first met him."

"Yep. What he did to Bill, all right. So enter Vilarde, and there you have it."

"And then Jusuelo killed Ken for his cut," said Roantis.

"Oh no. I mean, Jusuelo turned bad, but not totally rotten. He was true to Vilarde till the end. What happened was, after they unloaded the Siva and went south to make the buy, they flew back to Miami. From there they headed back this way, the two of them driving a brand-new Caddy Eldo with a satchel full of leftover cash. That, plus the cash they'd gotten from the first two drops, was what Jusuelo carried away on the flatcar this morning, by the way."

Kaunitz threw his digging stick away. He held it by one end and flung it sidearm, and it made a whirring noise as it sailed out over the valley.

"So anyway, somewhere in Georgia they stop for supper and then go to a road joint for a couple of beers. I guess they were celebrating pretty good. Maybe doing some coke too. Who knows? Anyway, they were flying high and feeling no pain. They're on top of the world. Just when they're about to leave, a bunch of locals come in and start in on them, giving them shit, like why don't they go back to Mexico with the other bean bandits — shit like that, you know. Well, you can imagine they weren't about to put up with it, especially a hothead like Jusuelo. One thing led to another, and the two Ducks were cleaning house on these guys when one of them pulls a blade and sticks Ken a good one, right in the side."

"Oh Christ," grunted Roantis. "What a goddamn waste."

"But see, according to what Jusuelo told Royce, Ken had enough beer in him, and enough God-knows-what too, he didn't feel it hardly. Jusuelo gets the blade from the other dude and sticks him back. Guy passes out on the floor, bleedin' like a stuck pig. So both Jusuelo and Vilarde know it's getting hot. They can't afford to stick around and get pulled in. Both were good enough field medics to stop the bleeding enough to make it back here — maybe go to a clinic or outpatient ward and get Ken sewed up. So they hightail it out of there, Jusuelo driving. Ken says he's tired and he'll get in back and rest. He falls asleep. When Jusuelo tried to wake him an hour later, he was gone."

"Jesus," I said.

"So they brought him out here and buried him. Doc, that was only a week and a half before you showed up here. And let me tell you something: you don't know how close you came to dying. Royce says when that plane crashed, Jusuelo went crazy to kill you. He was going to do nothing until he'd hunted you down. But Royce put the brakes on, saying your death would only draw Roantis and the rest of us. As it was, they didn't know Daisy was out here until they took her from your camper. But Royce described you to Jusuelo, who recognized you at the hospital. After he greased the pilot, he waited outside for you. Then what does he see but you being taken away in a police cruiser! Hell, he thought you were going to take the fall. They all thought that ended their problems. I just say you were damn lucky the police collared you there, Doc."

"And they took Daisy. Were they ever going to kill her?"

"Bill says Jusuelo might have, but he wouldn't let him. No, Bill thought keeping Daisy would make us back off and strike a deal. It didn't work. And we got out here fast, slipped under their wire before they even expected us. If we'd waited another day, they'd have been waiting for us . . . and probably Jusuelo and the rest of the money would have been long gone to Brazil. That's where he and Ken had planned to go: to Rio, and live like kings for the rest of their lives."

"How can we be sure Jusuelo is dead?" I said a little uneasily.

"I think it's a safe bet," said Roantis, taking me aside. "And now, Freddie, if you'll wait a sec for Doc and me, there's something I gotta tell him."

Kaunitz peeled off and went down the rock trail to the cave.

Roantis sat on a boulder, and I leaned against a mountain poplar with lichens and vines all over it. Warblers sang above our heads in endless spontaneous riffs. A buzzard, with wide wings raised in a shallow V, soared in the rising hot air of a thermal. A crow cawed, and the river far below ran gray and white, making a soft whisper like white noise. I should have been relaxed but I wasn't. I did not like the way Roantis was looking at me. His knuckles were caked reddish brown with dried blood. The Colt service pistol, silver gray with the bluing gone, rode in the frayed canvas holster on his hip. The warm wind blew through his thinning hair. He looked old, old and ornery, like an outcast boar grizzly with bad teeth.

"Well," he said, and lighted a Camel.

"Well what?"

"Well Freddie's ruined my day. Now I'm going to ruin yours."

I bristled. "What the hell are you talking about?"

"What I'm talking about is what I said to you earlier. You're one of us, Doc. You may not have realized it yet, but now you're going to."

"I don't know what you're trying to say. I helped you out is all."

"Wait. Wait Doc," he said, holding up his hand like a traffic cop. "Hear me out. You think you're a doctor. You've got the sheepskin, too. But you're not."

"Bullshit. But if it makes you happy to think that, go ahead."

"I've thought it for some time. That's why I singled you out to help me. It worked. Now it turns out I'm not the only one who feels this way. You've spent time with us now. Each one of us. You were at Freddie's ranch. He's the best shot I've seen. He says you're one of the better ones *he's* seen."

"Well, good for him. You know I shoot recreationally. *Recreationally,* Liatis. At targets."

He dragged on the cigarette and nodded slowly.

"Then Summers tells me you did quite a number on him in the bush last night."

"I was scared. I got lucky. I thought he was going to kill me."

Another drag, another nod. I hated him.

"Finally there's Daisy. She told you her story. Her father, René

269

Cournot, was my best friend in the Legion. Her mother was from Vietnamese nobility. After their deaths, I raised her. Still, I was gone a lot, considering my line of work, and she grew up a street kid in Saigon, Paris, and Okinawa. She can take care of herself. You cannot know just how good she is, and how deadly. During the war in Nam, she was a Roadrunner for us. The Roadrunners were indigenous personnel — native Vietnamese — who disguised themselves as VC at night and mingled with them. It was a hairy job. Daisy was great at it."

"Uh-huh. I've had the feeling that old Daisy's been around the block a few times."

"Yeah. You know, Daisy works for the U.S. Government now. That's what sprung Summers so fast when they tagged him at the airport. But anyway, she's good. And here's my li'l girl, who turned tricks with VC commanders before knifing them, who's won every empty-hand combat award there is — even on Okinawa. And who puts her down but good old Doc Adams. What do you say about that?"

"Nothing. She put me down. She could've killed me. I got in a freak kidney shot is all."

Another drag, another nod.

"And then you set her free while the rest of us bozos are fucking around outside the cave."

I slid my back down the raggedy tree trunk and let my butt hit the ground. I rubbed my hand through my hair, suddenly feeling very tired.

"What do you want from me?"

"I want you to admit, Doc, maybe only to yourself, that you don't really fit in your li'l world of suburbia. That's why you're trying to leave it all the time. You're one of us, Doc, whether you like it or not."

"Go fuck yourself."

He laughed at me, the Mongol eyes crinkling up at the corners. He held up his knuckles.

"See? That's what we used on those kids when we got up in the cave. Not the guns. Know why? 'Cause one look and I knew we dint need 'em. Those kids were playing at it. They all had those Airborne T-shirts on. Bullshit. Fakes. Couple good punches and they folded up like day lilies. Not you, Doc. You're the real thing. In another time and place, with the proper training, you could've been one of the best."

Well, I'd heard enough. I got up and stalked off down the trail. Why Roantis was trying to get at me like this was a mystery. I think he was just pissed off that I'd managed to set his girl free. Through a lucky break I'd stolen his show, and he was getting even. I also knew that he had to ask himself some pretty tough questions about his relationship with Ken Vilarde. Real tough questions. And the answers? They'd be even tougher. No matter how much he wanted to put his bad feelings off on me, he'd have to face them sooner or later.

I threw on my rucksack in a foul mood. I was not going to tote the rifle back, either. To hell with it. If the rest of them had to have it, fine. But let them carry it. I stamped around and fumed, getting my stuff together. Why waste time? I wanted to get out of there and back to Mary.

"What's eating you?" asked Summers.

"It's time to split, that's what. Let's walk on out of here."

"Freddie says he can't go: they have to book him. After that he's got to post bond to get out."

"How much will bond be?"

"Maybe five grand. Think we can come up with it, Doc?" He grinned.

"Yeah. Maybe if we dig around hard enough."

I felt a hand on my waist. Daisy. We turned to see Roantis come down the hill to his pack and take something out of it. A pint of booze. Damn. And he'd been clean for a couple of months. He didn't say a thing, just turned right around and headed back up the hill.

"Oh-oh," said Summers. "Think I see a drunk comin' on. He goin' back up to Ken's grave. Bad news."

The chopper came back an hour later to get Kaunitz. Hunnicutt told me they doubted they'd keep him more than a few hours, so we could walk back to the camper again, drive into town to the station, and by that time he'd probably be ready to join us.

That is, if we could get Roantis down off that rock.

We packed all our gear and let them take it in the chopper. When it blasted off the gravel bed and soared out over the river, Daisy and I went up there. Roantis was on his knees in front of the gravestone, hunched over with his head bowed. The tip of his forehead was touching it, his hands clinging to the top of it on each side of his lowered face. He looked like a Moslem praying. The bottle was almost dead. I put my hand on his shoulder and he stood up, reeking. He looked wonderful sad. Daisy hugged him for a long time while I stood by.

Then the three of us went down off the rock together.

29

MARY SHOOK her long black curls around and swept them back over her shoulders. She set her drink on the rock sill of the terrace and looked out over the golf course at the distant mountains. Knockout. Total, absolute knockout. And pissed at yours truly.

As they say in the Dewar's ads, "The good things in life stay that way."

We were sitting on the Sunset Terrace of Asheville's most stately hotel, the Grove Park Inn. It was warm, even for the Carolinas. Below us in the twilight, golfers bounced over fields of green in little carts; tennis players laughed and swore on the clay courts, casting long shadows in the golden light. In the distance were the purplish mountains, with red and gold behind them as the sun went down. A cool breeze fanned us. It wafted up from the valley, smelling of flowering shrubs. Not bad, except my left arm, right below the shoulder, still hurt.

Mary sipped her gin and tonic the way she always sips a mixed drink, a drop at a time. She looked at the players below, folded her hands in her lap, and looked me in the eye. She wasn't smiling.

"Tell me about it," she said.

"Well, we got up to the hideout in early afternoon. Then — "

"You know what I mean. Afterward. After the whole thing was over and you started to drive back here in the camper. And didn't make it."

"Oh that. Well, when we went to spring Fred Kaunitz, Tommy slipped into the booze store. So on the road home, we sat around the little table in back while Daisy drove. We hoisted a few. I guess we were overtired and hadn't eaten much. That didn't help."

"When did you realize they'd passed the Asheville exits?"

"When it was too late. Daisy was in on it, you know."

She drummed her fingers on the table. Gee, I wished Joe were with us. He had gallantly begged off, saying we needed to be together. He was eating his room service dinner four stories above us. I admired his noble gesture, but his presence at that moment would have lent a mollifying influence. I thought I could put my finger on the problem and decided to try a frontal attack.

"Mary, are you worried about Daisy? Do you think I slept with her?"

"Did you?"

"Nah. Not even remotely close. Anyway, we got to Fayetteville even before I knew it, seems like."

"And the others knew?"

"Yeah. See, they all planned it, hon. Behind my back."

"Well, it was a dirty trick. And when I see Roantis next I'm going to — "

"Yeah, well I think he's avoiding you. But as to what happened specifically, it's really nothing much. I think it was a bunch of guys showing their thanks. And that was, uh, how they did it."

In my mind's eye, I could picture the place. The memory was somewhat hazy, due to the late hour and all the celebrating. It was out on Bragg Avenue. I should have known by the elaborate drawings on the walls that the place wasn't a bar. Then we were sitting around a table in there. Daisy was on my lap, doing something pleasant to my face and ear with her tongue. Then the little Chinese man was hovering near my left side, smiling and bowing. He had something in his hand . . . an instrument with a cord. Soldering iron? No . . . I remembered I smelled rubbing alcohol.

274

Then the pain started. Gee it stung. I slept all the way home, as did most of the others, I guess.

I told Mary everything that had happened. I did leave out the part about Daisy, however. I mean, I'm sensible some of the time. She listened, deadpan, to my tale, then glanced at my shoulder. She hadn't seen it, of course, because of the bandage.

"What does it say?" she asked.

"It says, uh, 'Daisy Ducks,' and then a picture of her."

Mary lowered her head into her hands and groaned.

"A *picture?* Good Christ! What's she doing, a parachute jump?"

"No. She's walking with a rifle at port arms, snarling."

"Good Christ."

"Tommy got one, too. It's kinda cute, once you get used to it."

"Well, we're not going to get used to it, Charlie. You're having a skin graft as soon as we get back."

"Hmmmmph! Maybe. Maybe not."

So we went on and on about that for a while, then turned to the matter of the money.

"So how much is there, and what's going to happen to it?"

"We put the bills in stacks of thousands, each with a rubber band around it. There were seventy-one stacks left after the Fayetteville binge. Of this, I get about seventeen. Twelve of that goes to pay for the convalescence of Roantis and Summers. The remaining five you and I are going to use for a nice long vacation — your choice."

She gripped my forearm and smiled.

"The rest of the money will be split up among the other four, with Roantis getting the biggest cut. And we all decided to give Sairy Royce four grand. It's to help Bill. He's had a rough time. None of the guys visited him when he was down. Kaunitz talked us into it, and he's right. Bill's going to need rehab therapy when he gets out, and it costs."

"That's nice, but the original plan called for you and Liatis to split it."

"Well, you know we don't need the money, and — "

"Charlie, we could use — "

"Not what I said. Sure, we could use an extra thirty grand. Buy some more toys for ourselves. But we don't need it. Roantis, he's had a rough time since he found out about Vilarde. Real rough. But I think it's helping him to grow. It'll humanize him. I think it's already started. You know, there's not a thing wrong with that guy except that he's been in the wrong line of work for forty years."

"And you don't think he meant to sell Vilarde out?"

"No. Not consciously, anyway. But, as I said, his profession finally got to him. You can't do that no-holds-barred stuff for years and years and not start thinking like an animal."

"Well, I hope you've had your fill of adventuring, Charlie. I mean for good."

"Don't worry. That part of my life is over, for keeps," I said.

Maybe if I kept saying it, it would be true.

So we finished our drinks and got up to go to dinner. It was getting chilly now. The sun was past down, and there was a lovely afterglow in the west. I put my hand around Mary's waist and led her off the terrace.

"I love you, Mary," I said, "and nobody but."

"Same here, Charlie."

And I was going to be a good boy from now on. You bet. Except that behind me, in my mind's ear, from out of the golden sunset and the swelling folds of the firmament, came the bugles.

276